D0611964

Tak reaches into the case and twists the first knob one click to the right. This causes the green light to brighten and a small humming sound to emanate from somewhere deep inside the device. He twists the second knob three times, the third knob once, and the fourth knob twice. With each click, the humming grows louder and more furious. Each turn produces a slightly different tone, and when Tak finishes, the end result is a chord of almost terrible beauty.

The musical chord rings out with new fury as the device powers up. Just before it reaches fever pitch, Tak wipes his fingers on his pants, places them on either side of the round glass panel, and waits. He's more nervous than he's been in a long time, but also excited. If it works, it's gonna be one hell of a surprise to everyone involved. And if it doesn't . . . Well, at least he'll finally know what it's like to fall to his death.

The light turns blinding. His fingers begin to stretch across the surface of the panel, becoming impossibly long and thin before finally vanishing altogether. Tak's head begins to fog over with a familiar sensation, random thoughts and memories jumbling together into an incoherent blur. He has just enough time to regret not eating his usual prejump meal before the light becomes his entire world. There is a brief flash, a mighty roar from the depths of the briefcase, then nothing.

Seconds later, the bathroom door crashes open, and a large man stumbles through and does a face-plant against the cold steel urinal. One hand, reaching out for support, crashes through the thin metal on the bottom of the toilet and emerges covered in a viscous blue film. The people behind him all take an involuntary step back, then a step forward, as if they can't quite convince themselves of what just happened. Because what they are seeing is, quite frankly, impossible.

Takahiro O'Leary is gone.

# the beautiful land

## alan averill

Elting Memorial Library
93 Main Street
New Paltz, New York 12561-1503

ACE BOOKS, NEW YORK

**THE BERKLEY PUBLISHING GROUP**
**Published by the Penguin Group**
**Penguin Group (USA) Inc.**
**375 Hudson Street, New York, New York 10014, USA**

USA | Canada | UK | Ireland | Australia | New Zealand | India | South Africa | China

Penguin Books Ltd., Registered Offices: 80 Strand, London WC2R 0RL, England
For more information about the Penguin Group, visit penguin.com.

This book is an original publication of The Berkley Publishing Group.

Copyright © 2013 by Alan Averill.
All rights reserved. No part of this book may be reproduced, scanned, or distributed in any printed or
electronic form without permission. Please do not participate in or encourage piracy of copyrighted
materials in violation of the author's rights. Purchase only authorized editions.

Ace Books are published by The Berkley Publishing Group.
ACE and the "A" design are trademarks of Penguin Group (USA) Inc.

Library of Congress Cataloging-in-Publication Data

Averill, Alan.
The Beautiful Land / Alan Averill. — Ace trade paperback edition.
pages cm
ISBN 978-0-425-26527-7
1. Time travel—Fiction.   2. Science fiction.   I. Title.
PS3601.V46B43   2013
813'.6—dc23
2013000225

PUBLISHING HISTORY
Ace trade paperback edition / June 2013

PRINTED IN THE UNITED STATES OF AMERICA

10  9  8  7  6  5  4  3  2  1

Cover photos: feather © Vasilius/Shutterstock; oil drops © Buzz S / Shutterstock;
texture background © Hemera/Thinkstock; bird © VladimirCeresnak/Shutterstock.
Cover design by Judith Lagerman.
Interior text design by Kristin del Rosario.

This is a work of fiction. Names, characters, places, and incidents either are the product
of the author's imagination or are used fictitiously, and any resemblance to actual persons,
living or dead, business establishments, events, or locales is entirely coincidental.
The publisher does not have any control over and does not assume any responsibility for
author or third-party websites or their content.

for sue

# low-rent Suicide

# chapter one

Tak can't answer the phone because the noose is too tight.

Given that he's currently standing on a rickety wooden chair with a length of rope knotted firmly around his neck, the phone should be the least of his concerns. And in truth, he's more worried about the Miles Davis song warbling from a battered tape deck on the floor. Tak had been pondering his suicide for a couple of weeks now, and he eventually concluded that dangling from a rope while *Kind of Blue* played in the background was about the best ending a man could hope for. But the moment he slipped the noose around his neck and tightened the knot, the phone had sprung to life with an incessant clang. And now, after four excruciating minutes, it's all he can hear.

*You should have stuck with the original plan, dude,* he thinks. *Fancy hotels don't have phones like this.*

Said original plan had been to save up money until he could afford a snazzy room somewhere in midtown Manhattan. Then he was going to order a bottle of Scotch, drink it from a fine crystal snifter, and fade to black while Miles played on a million-dollar stereo system with surround sound and a subwoofer. This plan had the added bonus of a Wall Street one-percenter walking into the room and finding a scrawny Japanese guy dangling from the chandelier—a vision that struck Tak as hilarious even though he wouldn't be around to enjoy it. But eleven months of unemployment and serious drinking had all but eliminated that possibility. He'd only been able to afford his current room after selling his shoes for seventeen dollars, which left a pair of jeans, a fifth of cheap whiskey, and a T-shirt with a picture of Donkey Kong smoking a joint as his only worldly possessions.

Ring.

Ring.

"No," mutters Tak. "No, no, no. You're not answering that. You're up here now, and you're going to step off the chair and finish this before your buzz wears off. Ready? Okay! Do it! Do it, do it, do it!"

But Tak doesn't do it. Instead, he stands on his tiptoes, listens to the chair squeak against the top of the old wooden dresser on which it's perched, and thinks about the person on the other end of the phone. And the more he thinks, the more he wonders if it might be a certain young woman with curly black hair. It's a totally impossible idea, but now that it's crawled into his brain, he finds it hard to shake.

*What if it's true? I mean, what if she had a dream or a vision or something, and she knows you're here?*

Ring.

Ring.

*Okay, now you're being a pussy. Just jump off the chair and be done with it already.*

Ring ring ring ring ring ring ring ring ring ring ring . . .

*Fine. Goddammit, just . . . fine. I'll answer the thing.*

But this is going to be difficult. The noose is tied with a complicated knot, and his precarious chair-and-dresser combination won't take kindly to sudden movements. Tak ponders his situation for what seems an eternity as the furniture groans, and the phone continues to scream. Finally, he grabs the rope with both hands and lifts himself up and off the chair. After a few moments of dangling in space like a mobile, he manages to wrap one leg around a rusty overhead pipe and take the strain off his quaking arms. Once the leg is secure, Tak releases one hand from the rope and feels for the knife on his belt. At the same time, he quickly formulates a new plan: pick up the phone, see who it is, then unplug the damn thing and use a bedsheet to finish what he started. Quick, easy, done. Assuming, of course, that he can sever the rope without slipping free and snapping his own neck in the process.

He stops fumbling for the knife long enough to grab the rope again, then throws his other leg around the pipe for added support. After a brief rest and a few deep breaths, he drops his hand, snags the tool on the first try, then brings it to his mouth and opens it with his teeth. Soon Tak is sawing away at the rope, muttering profanities under his breath as he works.

The knife is sharp, and within seconds the rope falls limply to his side and dangles like a macabre necklace. He tosses the knife over to the bed and moves to grab the pipe, but his quaking legs and slippery hands have other plans. At the exact moment when he attempts to transfer his weight from one set of limbs to the other, both finally lose what little strength they have left and send him crashing to the chair below.

The chair shatters into splinters upon impact, causing Tak to slam into the dresser on which it was perched. But where the chair was old and poorly made, the dresser is constructed of good, strong oak; he actually ricochets about a foot into the air when he strikes it. Before he can even come to grips with what the hell is happening, he smashes back down into the corner of the dresser, flies through space for another terrifying second, and finally comes to a halt against the brown shag carpet below.

Brilliant spots of light flash across his vision. His brain senses a chance to slip into unconsciousness and perhaps repair some of the damage, but the carpet, befouled beyond imagining from years of negligent cleaning, is acting as the world's strongest smelling salt. Tak recognizes several unpleasant elements— blood, semen, more blood, bleach, mold, taco meat, even *more* blood—before he finally has enough and pulls himself to a sitting position.

The phone is still ringing. Tak runs his hands across his scrawny frame and through his spiky black hair, realizes that nothing is terribly out of order, and slowly pulls himself to his feet. After sneezing out whatever filth he inhaled from the carpet, he limps over to the ancient phone and picks up the handset.

"Sam?" he says.

"Mr. O'Leary?" replies the voice. It's female, with a slight accent. British, maybe.

Tak stares at the phone. "Is this the front desk?"

"Is this Mr. Takahiro O'Leary?"

"Christ on a crutch. Are you selling something?"

"I need two minutes, Mr. O'Leary. If you are unmoved by what I have to say, you can then go back to killing yourself or whatever you like."

Tak pulls the phone away from his head and stares at it for a good long time. Curling his mouth into a confused grimace, he somehow tears his eyes away from the handset and spares a glance around the room. The windows are shut and covered. The door is locked. "Wait a second," he says. "Wait, how the hell—"

"It's a very long story, Mr. O'Leary, and I am now down to about a minute and a half. May I continue?"

"Uh . . . Yeah, sure. Okay."

"We have a proposition for you."

"Who's we? Who are you?"

"I speak on behalf of a small consortium of international businessmen and scientists. It's not a group you've ever heard of, I assure you."

Tak drops the phone on the bed, wipes the sweat from his eyes, and picks it back up. "Sounds boring."

"Yes, much of it is," says the voice. "For you, however, it represents an extraordinary opportunity to rediscover your greatest passion."

Tak starts to form an image of the woman on the other end of the line. *Red hair. You've got long red hair that cascades down your back in curly waves. Dark librarian glasses, the kind that slip down the bridge of your nose when you're engrossed in something. You like jazz and reading and learning about new things. And you're really into geeky Japanese-American guys who've hit rock bottom.*

A *tap tap tap* sound begins to staccato out from the other end of the line; Tak is pretty sure the voice's owner is clicking a ballpoint pen. He finds this incredibly sexy for reasons he can't begin to explain.

"Mr. O'Leary?" asks the voice.

"I'm here," he says, even though that's only about half-true.

"Mr. O'Leary, our contacts claim that by the age of fourteen you were proficient in cave exploration, deep-sea diving, and wilderness survival. You celebrated your high-school graduation by spending a month alone in the rain forests of New Guinea. You then hosted a Japanese television show where you would travel to the harshest environments on Earth with only a knife and a television camera. Is this correct?"

"Yeah, that's right."

"You are, then, in a word, unique. And our foundation needs

someone with your unique skills and training. Someone who has spent their life exploring the unknown. Someone who has no fear, who can deal with the unexpected, and who can be trusted to keep all that they see in the strictest of confidence. In short, we need you."

Tak's eyes begin to roll. "Okay, I see. Got it. Your rich friends want to see Everest, right? Maybe spend the night in the Amazon? Take some pictures, show 'em at the board meeting, make the other suits jealous? Listen, I don't do guide work anymore. Go find someone else."

"Mr. O'Leary," she says as the pen clicks faster, "there are no guides for where we want to go."

"There's a guide for everywhere."

"We don't need a guide, Mr. O'Leary. We need an *explorer*. Our group has discovered something amazing, an entirely new world never before seen. It is unmapped, uncharted, and very, very dangerous. We need someone to lead a team so we understand what we have on our hands. And we want you to be that man."

Tak laughs, sending the still-attached noose swinging back and forth. "Bullshit. There are no unexplored worlds anymore. I can go on the Internet and see pictures, satellite images, whatever I want. Hell, we mapped the fucking seafloor years ago."

"You haven't seen this."

"I've seen everything. Why do you think I'm checking out? There's nothing left."

"You haven't seen this," insists the voice. "I promise you."

"What are you talking? Ocean?"

"No."

"Space?"

"No."

"Because I'm not getting into some tin can just so you can fire me into orbit for a few days."

"It's not space, Mr. O'Leary."

". . . So what is it?"

"Can I take it from your response that you are interested?"

Tak shifts on his feet and looks around his suicide studio. The sun has gone behind a cloud, leaving everything clothed in a dusty grey film. The shattered chair lies in splinters on the floor, while the dresser leans slightly more to the side than it did when he rented the room less than thirty minutes ago. At that moment, he understands how the furniture feels. Once, he too had been vibrant and new and alive, but he'd slowly spent the previous years stripping the joy from his life; now he was just rolling around like the last drops of beer in the bottle.

"Yeah, okay," he says at last. "I'm interested."

"There is a car outside that will take you to the airport. We have a first-class ticket waiting for you."

"Um, yeah. About that? The cops have my passport. I kinda got arrested a couple of days ago, and I didn't bother—"

"Your paperwork is in the car, along with fifty thousand US dollars. This money is yours to do with as you see fit. Good-bye."

"Wait! Wait!" Tak waves his free hand in front of his face and practically screams into the phone. "Hold on!"

"Yes?" she responds dully.

"What's your name?"

". . . Judith."

"Are you going to be there? I mean, are you going to be wherever I'm going?"

"I will meet you when you land, yes."

"You wanna have dinner?"

"With you?"

"Well . . . yeah. With me."

"We'll see."

The phone goes dead. Tak slowly places it back in the cradle, then reaches up and slips the noose over his head like a necktie at the end of a long day. Tossing the rope into the corner of the room, he pops Miles out of the player, slips him into his pocket, and walks out the door.

**it will be** four years before he sees the real New York again.

clean is better

# chapter two

"You seem distracted today," says the psychiatrist.

Samira doesn't respond, partially because she hasn't spoken to anyone in almost three weeks and feels out of practice, but mostly because she *is* distracted. A bit of black goo is stuck under her middle fingernail, and all of her attention is currently focused on removing it by whatever means necessary. It's probably harmless—a dab of engine oil, or some loose subway grime—but she wants it gone. Ever since she came back from the big desert, Samira had been obsessed with keeping herself clean. Over there, you were never completely clean. Sand. Grease. Small chunks of your friends. Something was always landing on you.

"Samira? Are you all right?"

She glances up nervously. "Yeah! Yeah, I'm fine. I'm just . . . I'm not into this right now. Sorry."

There is another long silence. The doctor—a squishy, serious man named Carrington—jots down a note on his ragged wooden clipboard. Whenever he shifts his not-inconsiderable bulk, the worn office chair on which he rests makes an off-tone squeaking sound. Samira flinches each time this happens. If Carrington notices the flinching, he doesn't say anything. Instead, he continues to make small little notes and stare at his patient, occasionally smiling beneath a bushy grey mustache.

The squeaky chair fits with the rest of the office: a drab, windowless room with off-white tile and walls covered in eggshell sound baffling. Light is provided by a flickering fluorescent tube that gives everything a vaguely washed-out quality. When people heard that Samira was visiting a psychiatrist, they formed images of her lying on a velvet couch in a room filled with important hardback books and a fireplace. Clearly, none of them had spent any time in a VA hospital.

Dr. Carrington clears his throat. Samira jumps, then begins frantically cracking her knuckles, moving from finger to finger with a practiced, unconscious grace. A clock ticks softly from Carrington's desk, muffled under a pile of paperwork like the beating heart of a boarder in a Poe story. Samira briefly considers getting up and walking out of the room but then rejects the thought. Leaving the session will cause more questions to be asked, more tests to be run, more suspicious glances to be thrown her way. And really, Carrington is all right as shrinks go. At least he doesn't make her talk about the war all the time.

She adjusts her bony ass against the hard blue plastic of her chair and tries to think of something to say. "It's . . . It's been a bad week. I'm not sleeping again. One, two hours a night, maybe. The only way I can sleep now is if it's really noisy. I tried turning on the TV, but it's not the right kind of noise. It's too random."

Dr. Carrington leans forward, curious. "What do you mean?"

"Well, you get ten minutes of jangle, like a sitcom, then three minutes of loud ads, then ten more minutes of the jangle. That doesn't work. It reminds me."

"It reminds you of what?"

"Of listening to people die."

That seems to interest Carrington. "I thought you were sleeping well," he says. "The last time we talked—which, granted, was almost three weeks ago—you told me that you'd found a way to sleep."

Samira smiles weakly and runs one hand through her curly black hair. It's been washed twice already today; rays of light practically engage in fistfights to see who gets to shine off it. "I was sleeping on the subway."

"Oh?"

"Yeah. Yeah, the subway is a good noise. It's predicable. Especially at night. You get the clacking, and you get that screech when a train pulls into a station. You ever listen to the way a door opens on a subway? *Whoosh. Whoosh.* It's so calming. I love that noise. I wish I could tape it and run it in a loop."

Samira realizes she's been talking for nearly a minute and stops. She moves back to the knuckles and attempts to crack them again, but she just finished a pass, and nothing will come. That only serves to increase her anxiety. Curling her feet underneath her, she slips off her sneakers and begins popping the knuckles on her toes. Carrington makes a face as she does—something she can't quite read—and scribbles another note on his rapidly filling paper.

"So, yeah," she continues as the knuckles *pop pop pop*. "I'd get on the D line at Kingsbridge and just conk out. Sometimes I'd sleep all the way to Coney Island, then wake up long enough to hop a car back so I could sleep some more." She pauses for a moment, letting her mind drift back to the days where she'd begun to feel something approaching normal. "It was nice."

"But clearly you stopped going," says Carrington. "Can you tell me why?"

He shifts his weight again—*SQUEEEEEK*—and pushes his brown plastic glasses up on his nose. He isn't a bad guy, all things considered, but he has a strange air about him that she can't quite place. Sometimes it feels like he has genuine sympathy for her situation, but other times it seems like he's running out the clock. Right now, Samira is getting the first vibe in waves, which makes her more chatty than usual.

"I had an incident," she says.

"Go on."

"Um, there was . . . There was a guy. He woke me up. Homeless guy, drunk. I was asleep on the A train, and all of a sudden this guy was shaking me and screaming about bugs or aliens or something. I dunno. It's kind of fuzzy. Anyway, I . . . I broke his wrist."

Carrington looks up, a dozen expressions washing over his face at once. He rejects a few—anger, bewilderment, professional calm—and finally settles on concern. "Samira, when did this happen?"

She squirms. "A week ago? Maybe two?"

"Did you tell anyone?"

"No!" she says, loudly enough to make her jump. "God, no. No, I just . . . I got off at the next stop and ran. I ran until I couldn't run anymore, and then curled up in the doorway of a brownstone and cried until I passed out. Some guy with a broom chased me off a few hours later."

The doctor makes a much longer note this time, underlining something a couple of times with a thick, heavy stroke. Samira instantly regrets telling him about the homeless guy. *He won't understand,* she thinks. *He can't. He's never been in the thick. He's just a nice guy who tries to help broken girls like me. People like that can't possibly understand.*

"Samira?" begins Carrington after nearly three minutes of heavy silence. "Samira, I can see you don't want to talk about this, but it may be very important. Can I ask you a few questions?"

"Yeah, okay," she whispers.

"Did you mean to hurt him?"

"No."

"Do you remember hurting him? I mean, do you remember the actual act?"

"No."

"Is that why you stopped riding the subway?"

"Yeah."

"Because you're afraid of hurting someone else?"

Instead of responding, she turns her attention back to the black under her nail. The spot reminds her of a time she pulled on a combat boot with a scorpion in the toe. The ensuing sting had left the digit looking like a rotting piece of fruit straining to burst from the confines of its skin. A week of antibiotics had reduced the swelling and restored her toe to its usual healthy self, but now Samira wonders if the infection has returned in the form of a small black dot. *Is that happening? Am I rotting from the inside? Am I going to split open and pour black ooze all over the floor of this office?*

The thought makes her shudder, so she quickly pulls her hand away and sits on it. To distract her eyes, she stares at her small, thin body, which is clad in a pair of black cargo pants and a grey sweatshirt with the word ARMY stamped across the front. It's almost the only thing she wears anymore, this outfit. She'd been slowly throwing away clothes since she returned to the States six months ago, discarding them as too old, or too big, or—in most cases—too happy. The purging makes her sad in an almost indescribable kind of way, but the more she throws out, the cleaner her apartment becomes, so she keeps at it. Clean is better. Clean is *much* better. Her clothes are from an old life. From an old Samira. She doesn't really understand that person anymore.

"Samira?" asks the doctor.

The one thing she hasn't been able to throw away is a yellow sundress that's hung in one closet or another since high school.

The garment had seen quite a bit of use back then, but in ensuing years it simply became a subtle reminder of better days. Samira never worried about her weight, or her complexion, or the other body issues that plagued modern women, but she also never felt truly beautiful unless she was wearing that dress. She'd put it on a few times in the months since her return, staring at herself in the full-length mirror and wondering what it was about war that made the participants look so sad. Sometimes, she'd stand in the middle of her room, a thin, scared smile on her face, and turn her hips from side to side just to see the dress swish around her legs. The night after the incident on the subway, she'd donned the dress and sobbed herself to sleep. When she woke up thirty minutes later, she was screaming and clawing at the cheerful yellow fabric as if she couldn't wait to get it off. It hadn't left the closet since.

Carrington clears his throat. Samira jumps again. "Um, sorry," she says. "I'm sorry. I was . . . I forgot what you asked."

He nods as if this is the most understandable thing in the world. "I asked if you stopped riding the subway because you were afraid of hurting someone else."

Samira glances at the clock, which is bolted to the wall, sees she has nearly ten minutes left, and licks her lips. The black spot is calling out to her. It takes all of her strength not to put the nail between her front teeth and pull until it comes tearing off.

"I don't remember hurting him," she says. "I just remember staring at him as he rolled around on the floor. He smelled like old egg rolls. I don't know why I remember that, but I do. He smelled like egg rolls, and he had a bushy grey beard, and there was a chunk of white bone sticking out from his wrist. . . . I can still hear the screaming. It was a really familiar noise. Lots of range. I know that sound."

Samira suddenly realizes that she sounds like a psychopath,

so she brings the black fingernail to her mouth and begins biting furiously. Her mind races for something else to talk about and finally lands on a memory of her father drinking tea with a cigarette in his hand.

"When my family fled to this country," she says, her voice muffled by the sound of her chewing, "my father opened an ice-cream parlor. He'd been a highly respected professor in Iran, but then we came here, and he ended up dishing out cones and sundaes to bratty little kids. He *hated* that job. He hated it so much, but he did it, and he never complained. He was always strong like that, and I don't know why I can't be the same way. I'm weak. I'm afraid of everything, I cry all the time for no reason. I just . . . I don't know how much longer I can keep doing this."

Carrington holds his pencil over the paper for a long time, then slowly leans over and sets them both on his desk. He moves forward in his chair and presses his fingertips together, thinking. Samira curls her feet even tighter underneath herself and continues to chew. The room, with its cheap plastic chairs and bookcases full of file folders, seems to shrink in on them. In another room nearby, a man beings to wail. Samira stares at the doctor and gives him a weak smile, which he returns. The action causes his mustache to curl up at the edges.

"Samira, do you have suicidal thoughts?" Carrington asks the question in a normal tone of voice, but she can hear the urgency beneath the surface. "Do you think about harming yourself?"

"No," she says, pulling the finger from her mouth and staring at it. It's bitten down past the quick, but the dot is still out of reach. "Not really. I mean, I think about dying a lot. All the time, actually. I think about it all the time, and there are moments where it might be nice. You know?"

She decides against working on the finger anymore and returns the hand to its hiding place under her thigh. "I don't like my life very much. I feel okay telling you that because it can't be much of a secret. I'm twenty-five years old, and I've spent three tours of duty in strange cities where everyone is trying to kill me. I've made friends and watched them die, made new friends and watched *them* die, then I come back here, and it's like I just don't know how to function anymore."

"You're going to Afghanistan in three weeks," says Carrington. "Is that right?"

Samira nods, a motion so subtle it probably wouldn't dislodge a fly. "Yeah."

"Will that be easier or harder for you than being here?"

"I don't know."

"A fourth tour of duty is unusual. Especially for a reservist."

"Yeah, well, we're low on translators. They keep getting blown up."

She squeezes her eyes tight, trying to hold back the tears that always seem to be there, but it's a losing effort. She's so tired of crying. Every day, something or other causes her to sob uncontrollably for what seems to be forever. Sometimes it's a memory, sometimes a conversation—but more often than not, the tears come from a dark place in her mind that she'd rather not consider. Samira knows how this will play out. Dr. Carrington will reach over to his desk and produce a box of tissues from the stacks of paperwork, her body will take that as a sign to *really* turn on the waterworks, and then all hell will break loose. Determined to avoid such a predictable fate, Samira bites down on her lower lip until she hears a crunch and feels blood pour into her mouth. This stops the tears, at least for a moment.

"Are you all right?" asks Carrington. "Hold on, I think I have—"

"No!" she screams, causing the doctor's eyes to pop open.

"No. Don't. I'm fine. I'm not going to hurt myself. I'm not going to shoot myself in the head or anything. I'm just miserable. That's all. I just . . . I used to be happy. I wish I could be happy again."

Samira is relieved to see Carrington leave the pencil alone, allowing her words to settle and vanish like new-fallen snow. Her hour is up—more than up, actually—but for the first time since the military forced her to start attending counseling, she doesn't feel the need to scurry out of there. She notes absentmindedly that her lip is bleeding badly and hopes it won't require stitches.

"We're almost out of time," says Carrington, "but I want to ask you one more thing. Is that all right?" She nods, and he continues, "Samira, when was the last time you were happy?"

"Graduation," she says without hesitation.

"College?"

"No, high school."

"Tell me about it."

"I went to high school in Seattle. I never really liked it. I spent most of my time trying to be as small as possible so people would just leave me alone. But I had a friend, a really good friend, and after our last day of class, we took off and just . . . hung out. You know, stared at the stars, talked about the future. It was nice."

"Are you still in contact with this friend?"

"He killed himself four years ago." She runs a suddenly shaky hand through her hair and takes a deep breath before continuing. "He used to host this TV show where he'd go into the desert and eat bugs, turn his piss into drinking water. . . . You know? One of those survival shows? He did that for two or three years, then things kinda went bad, and he just couldn't handle it, I guess."

Carrington's eyebrows raise. This is clearly an unexpected bit of news. "Was the show popular? Would I know him?"

Samira shakes her head. "Probably not. It was in Japanese." She sees the doctor's confused look and continues before he can ask the obvious question. "He was Japanese. Well, he was half-Japanese. His mom was from Japan and his dad was Irish. And yeah, I know, it's kinda weird. Anyway, he went to Japan, did that show, took tourists up Mt. Fuji, explored jungles, stuff like that. He was crazy, but . . . God, I miss him. I miss him all the time."

"What was his name?"

"Tak," she whispers. "His name was Tak."

# chapter three

Tak is almost twelve hours into the flight before he notices that something has gone seriously wrong. With only three hours to go on the Sydney to Los Angeles nonstop, the plane is dark, travelers are sleeping, and the attendants should be strapped into their seats with a book or chatting quietly in the galley area. This time, however, things are different. Instead of engaging in mindless chatter, the attendants are buzzing through the aisles with nervous looks on their faces. Occasionally, two or three will duck off behind the bulkhead for a brief, whispered meeting, then emerge from either side and whisk their way up and down the aisles some more.

At first, Tak thinks that there's some kind of low-key mechanical problem—the flaps are a bit sticky, or the hydraulic pressure is off. But after watching the attendants scuttle back and forth for the better part of an hour, he dismisses this option. He's been on planes with problems before, seen that flavor of panic on attendants' faces. This is different. It's almost like they're moving up and down the aisles to avoid attracting attention to something.

*Or someone,* he thinks suddenly. *Could be a problem with a passenger. Medical emergency up in first class, maybe? Some drunk asshat making jokes about lighting his shoes on fire?*

He's on the end of a four-seat aisle in the very last row. This is where Tak prefers to sit. He likes being able to see the entire plane in motion, likes being able to predict and adapt to anything that might come his way. The only things he has to worry about behind him are a pair of lavatories and a small galley, where they store the beverage cart. Some would consider this level of caution to be excessive, but Tak doesn't care. After the last four years of his life, he readily allows himself a healthy dose of paranoia.

As he watches the attendants try not to look as worried as they clearly are, he absentmindedly runs one hand back and forth over the slim silver briefcase in his lap. He thinks about mechanical problems and terrorists and unexplained airline disasters that spontaneously occur at forty thousand feet and gives a small chuckle. *Oh man, if you guys only knew what this was. That would really give you something to worry about.*

The chuckle fades. That thought—*if you only knew what this was*—rolls around and around in his brain, gathering momentum like a snowball down a mountain. As it grows, Tak starts to feel something approaching nervousness for the first time since take-off. He runs his thumbs over the latches of the case and lets the thought fester as he turns one eye toward a group of four attendants standing next to the first-class curtain. They're well trained, but not perfect. Eyes occasionally dart to the rear of the cabin, then down again. Bodies are shifted ever so slightly toward the back, as if ready to spring on a problem. After a few minutes, Tak leans his head into the aisle and tilts it to the side like a dog hearing a quizzical noise. One of the attendants catches his eye and snaps her head around so fast her neck threatens to break. As he stares at the back of her head, he can almost physically feel her trying not to look at him.

The snowball thought is massive now, rolling over trees and skiers and Swiss mountain chalets with impunity. He licks his lips, grabs the briefcase with one hand, and slowly stands up. Not all the way; just enough to keep his knees slightly bent, as if he's going to reach into the overhead compartment and remove a book. As he stands, he keeps his eyes focused on the seat back in front of him. *Wait for it,* he tells himself. *Wait. Wait. Waaaaait . . . Now.*

Tak looks up. Nine wide-eyed flight attendants stare back. As soon as their eyes meet, the attendants see that *he* sees and quickly busy themselves with random tasks that are suddenly very important.

*Oh, fuck me running. They know.*

Tak doesn't know how they know, or even how much they know, but it's clearly enough to assure that a platoon of federal agents will be waiting for him when they land. He drops back down in his seat and allows himself a minute of silent cursing and panicking. *Shit! Aw, shit on a shingle! How the hell did they know? Why'd they let me leave Australia if they knew?*

Tak gets his thoughts under control and quickly considers the question. Either his employers knew his plan and let him go because they want the briefcase to end up in the United States, or they only realized what he had done once the plane was off the ground. Tak thinks that the second option is much more likely. American border security was a mess of gung ho cowboys and angry civil servants; even his employer's impressive political connections wouldn't be able to account for every possible twist. Hell, what if some minimum-wage TSA agent opened the briefcase and started fiddling around? No, they'd clearly discovered that the briefcase was missing, realized who had stolen it, then twisted arms to make sure that it never left the plane.

Tak swears once more and begins drumming his fingers on the

lid of the briefcase. It makes a pleasant, hollow sound that he doesn't have time to appreciate. In less than three hours, they will be on the ground, a gaggle of large men in suits will be waiting for him, and everything will be royally screwed. He runs through various scenarios in his head and quickly dismisses them all. Bailing out over the ocean? Trying to force the back door as soon as they land? Taking a hostage? None of those are even remotely decent options.

*You could use it,* Tak thinks suddenly. *It's just a bunch of flight attendants and maybe an air marshal up here—they wouldn't be able to stop you.*

It's a wild thought, crazy, but now that it's in his head, it pulls up a recliner, cracks a beer, and refuses to leave. He mulls it over for a good fifteen minutes while the attendants continue to ignore him as hard as possible. Using the device on a moving plane would very likely kill him. Or not. It would all depend on where he ended up. Would he reappear at the very spot where he'd activated the device—thousands of feet in the air over the Pacific Ocean? Or would he travel as the plane traveled and pop back into existence once the jet was safely on the ground? And then there's the question of power: did he have enough to make an unplanned jump? *Wish I'd had time to test this thing,* he thinks to himself.

In the end, Tak makes the decision the way he makes all of his important choices: by wrestling with it for a while before kicking down the door and barging through. He suddenly bolts to his feet, secures the briefcase, and slides into the aisle. Before the attendants can do more than begin to point, he slips into the lavatory and locks the door.

There isn't room for the briefcase on the counter, so he sets it on the lid of the toilet and stares at himself in the mirror. He's more haggard than he remembers, with dark circles under his eyes and a kind of maniacal smile permanently plastered to his face. He's wearing a blue T-shirt that reads MARIO IS FULL OF WIN under a black suit coat, and his hair is sticking up even higher than normal. The entire ensemble is a bit unsettling—no wonder the attendants are so damn nervous.

The FASTEN SEAT BELT light dings on. Outside, someone knocks on the door. "Sir," she says. "Sir, we need you to return to your seat." Tak knows this is a lie. The plane is fine; it's him they're worried about.

He ignores the attendant's knocking, sits on the toilet, and pulls the briefcase to his lap. Unlatching either side, he grabs the top with both hands and pulls it open. Instantly, the bathroom is filled with a dim green glow that swirls across the walls like a miniature aurora borealis, shifting and changing by the second. No matter how many times he witnesses it, Tak continues to think it's the most beautiful thing in the world.

The briefcase contains a round glass panel from which the green glow emanates, six metal knobs, and five small lights. Three of these lights are illuminated red, albeit faintly, which is a good sign. If those are the battery indicators—and he's fairly sure that they are—he should have enough juice left for three jumps. Of course, he's not entirely sure that's what the lights mean. He didn't design the device, after all: he just stole it and fled the country.

The attendant knocks again, louder. Tak continues to ignore her and removes a small, leather-bound book from his pants pocket. He puts his tongue between his teeth and starts flipping through it, scanning page after page of seemingly random numbers with scrawled notations next to each one:

1 2 1 0 3 0 — Wasteland
2 7 2 1 8 8 — Wasteland

7 1 3 2 1 0 — False London
9 4 3 4 7 1 — Decent. Not much to eat.
5 4 2 1 1 0 — Wasteland
1 1 1 1 1 1 — Never go here again!
2 1 2 6 7 6 — Wasteland
1 2 1 3 0 0 — ~~Possible winner!~~ Update: Conduit dead.

. . . And so on, through the entire notebook, hundreds upon hundreds of entries crammed onto the front and back of each page. He runs his finger up and down each entry and flips pages at a frantic pace. The gentle knock at the door is suddenly replaced with a loud banging and an angry male voice.

"Hey! Get out of there now!" cries the voice. "Get out before we break it down!"

The voice is from a passenger—loud and slurred with a flight's worth of alcohol—and Tak realizes he doesn't have time for a perfect jump. After a moment, he settles on an entry near the middle of the book:

1 3 1 2 0 0 — Mostly safe. Watch for acid rain.

He wipes sweat from his brow with the sleeve of his jacket and stuffs the notebook back into his pocket. He can hear lots of voices from behind the door—more than a few passengers have clearly joined the mob. The words "briefcase" and "bomb" are being tossed around, and Tak suddenly realizes how his employers must have played this to the flight crew. If they think the device is a bomb, they won't touch it. They'll arrest him and wait for a disposal unit. At which point, it's a simple matter to get your own people onto the plane, secure the briefcase, and whisk it back to Australia.

"Clever bastards," mutters Tak. He reaches into the case and twists the first knob one click to the right. This causes the green light to brighten and a small humming sound to emanate from somewhere deep inside the device. He twists the second knob three times, the third knob once, and the fourth knob twice. With each click, the humming grows louder and more furious. Each turn produces a slightly different tone, and when Tak finishes, the end result is a chord of almost terrible beauty.

The door shudders in its frame: someone, probably the angry drunk, has decided that it's time to stop asking nicely and just kick the damn thing down. The foot strikes the door again, then pauses as the humming grows in intensity. Tak grins slightly as he imagines passengers huddled around a bathroom door with brilliant green light pouring out of it while some wannabe hero starts kicking in the door. *You're probably not their favorite person in the world right now, Drunky.*

The musical chord rings out with new fury as the device powers up. Just before it reaches fever pitch, Tak wipes his fingers on his pants, places them on either side of the round glass panel, and waits. He's more nervous than he's been in a long time, but also excited. If it works, it's gonna be one hell of a surprise to everyone involved. And if it doesn't . . . Well, at least he'll finally know what it's like to fall to his death.

The light turns blinding. His fingers begin to stretch across the surface of the panel, becoming impossibly long and thin before finally vanishing altogether. Tak's head begins to fog over with a familiar sensation, random thoughts and memories jumbling together into an incoherent blur. He has just enough time to regret not eating his usual prejump meal before the light becomes his entire world. There is a brief flash, a mighty roar from the depths of the briefcase, then nothing.

Seconds later, the door crashes open, and a large man stumbles through and does a face-plant against the cold steel urinal.

One hand, reaching out for support, crashes through the thin metal on the bottom of the toilet and emerges covered in a viscous blue film. The people behind him all take an involuntary step back, then a step forward, as if they can't quite convince themselves of what just happened. Because what they are seeing is, quite frankly, impossible.

**takahiro o'leary is** gone.

# chapter four

When Tak's plane touches down, a dozen black SUVs barrel down the runway to meet it. All air traffic into LAX has been diverted for the last fifteen minutes, which means that thousands of people are currently spinning around the airport in a permanent holding pattern so this single plane can take all the time it needs. As the 747 deploys its air brakes, the cars roll in on either side with sirens blaring. Men and women in serious clothing and sunglasses sit behind the wheels and communicate with one another through small earpieces. At one point, a large van with the word SWAT painted on the side takes up a position behind the plane. A square-jawed man with a helmet leans out the window of the van and points a large machine gun at the plane, as if expecting someone to hop out the back door with guns blazing. It's an eye-rolling show of force even for L.A., and if Tak were still on the plane, he'd be laughing his ass off. But Tak is *not* on the plane; indeed, Tak O'Leary is nowhere to be found. And thus all the hullabaloo.

Instead of moving to a gate, the plane rolls over to a small, unused hangar on the edge of the airport. This is where the real party starts, as employees of every government agency imaginable begin lining up like customers at a drab-suit convention: air marshals, TSA agents, LAPD, the FBI, the Port Authority, U.S. Customs and Immigration, even a couple of unidentified large guys from Homeland Security, who just stand to the side and mutter to each other. If you work for an agency with a lot of letters in its name, this is clearly the place to be.

The plane coasts inside the hangar and powers down, engines spinning slower and slower until they finally give up the effort and come to a stop. For nearly forty minutes, nothing much happens, save the agency heads engaging in a spirited discussion as to how to let passengers off and who should be the first to board the plane. At one point, a mobile staircase is rolled up to the front door, only to be removed a few minutes later. The spirited discussion turns heated, cell phones are produced, and various high-ranking people are called. Inside the plane, weary passengers peer out of oval windows with a mixture of frustration and fear. The ones in the back know that something very odd has happened, while the ones closer to the front are running on rumors spread by those in the rear. In the cockpit, the pilot and copilot chat on the radio and endlessly fiddle with buttons.

Finally, the stairway is rolled back into place. The SWAT team moves into position, stationing four men with large guns at the bottom of the plane and four more men on the steps of the staircase. Once they are ready—a state they signify with a needlessly complex series of hand signals—a man from the FBI walks between them and takes up residence next to the door. At this point, the passengers are hopeful that they will finally be let out and arrested or waterboarded or whatever the hell is going to happen, because any of that would be preferable to spending one more minute on the goddamn airplane. But it is not to be. The FBI man is literally reaching for the handle when he suddenly gets interested in his earpiece again and turns his back on the door. The SWAT team hears one guy inside the plane yell "Oh, come on!" in a joyless display of frustration. Thankfully, his anger doesn't have to burn long—after a minute, the FBI man is joined by the large men from Homeland Security, and the door is finally opened.

It takes almost two hours to get the passengers off the plane. As they step out the door, their IDs are perused by the men from Homeland. Once this is done, the travelers walk down the steps, through a gauntlet of heavily armed police, and over to a corner of the hangar. At this point, their IDs are compared against some kind of official list held by a bored-looking man with huge eyeglasses. After this man has confirmed that they are who they claim to be, they are taken to a different corner of the hangar, where a very apologetic and harried member of the airline PR staff offers them coffee or soda, gives them a sandwich, and maintains a tight-lipped smile while the passenger unloads all of his or her frustrations. The passengers are then left to mill around in the small corner, which smells of metal shavings and stale gasoline. A few of the more experienced travelers curl up on the ground and go to sleep, but most of the others either stand around looking dour or sit on the ground looking dour.

As this is occurring, various government officials are pulling luggage from the underside of the plane. In plain view of the passengers, each suitcase, duffel bag, and poorly taped cardboard box is opened and searched—just in case the missing man from Australia happened to crawl into the luggage compartment and fold himself into the size of an egg-salad sandwich. At one point an agent reaches into a hidden side pocket of a black duffel and pulls out a Ziploc bag with four joints inside; much to the relief of a wide-eyed teenager from Brisbane, the man just stuffs them back inside and keeps searching.

While the passengers are being questioned—or yelling at the

poor PR woman—and the agents are searching through their luggage, a small tanker truck arrives. It rolls into position underneath the wing and disgorges a pair of overalls-clad men who unroll a hose from the side of the tank and attach it to the plane's waste-containment system. Ten minutes and a lot of noisy sucking later, the truck is full, the plane is empty, and an unfortunate man from TSA is peering inside the holding tanks with a flashlight in one hand and his tie held over his mouth with the other. After he pronounces the holding tank clean, one of the overall guys sticks a long metal pipe inside and starts moving it around. Everyone watching expects to hear the missing passenger cry out in pain, but the pipe just clangs back and forth against the sides with a dull, hollow sound.

All of the stranded travelers are then loaded into a large bus with a yellow roof. The PR woman, who received two aspirin and a bottle of Jack Daniels from one of the attendants, is saying something to the busload of passengers. When she finishes, there is another round of loud and angry grumbling, but then one of the SWAT guys with a big gun steps up into the front of the bus, and that pretty much ends the conversation.

The bus pulls away in a cloud of exhaust and drops the passengers in the back area of one of the terminals, where they spend the next seven hours answering questions about a man few of them even remember seeing on the flight. A particularly upset fellow—who by now has progressed from roaring drunk to just hungover—tells a harrowing tale about how he tried to save the plane by kicking down the lavatory door, but otherwise offers no useful information. Eventually, someone manages to make a phone call to the local news media, who show up in droves and demand to know why American citizens are being held against their will. Microphones are thrust at spokespeople, tearful children are filmed asking for their parents, and the whole thing dissolves into a large ball of chaos.

At this point, the agencies involved throw up their hands and let the passengers go. None of them are happy about the decision, but there really isn't anything else to be done. The passengers are clean. The plane is clean. The law-enforcement folks have done everything but strip it down to the bolts and sell it off for scrap, and there is simply no Tak to be found. Somehow, a grown man has found a way to vanish from an international flight forty thousand feet over the Pacific Ocean.

The government agents eventually drive away to fill out paperwork and try to explain the mess to their bosses. The plane is rolled out of the hangar and cleaned by a janitorial crew that has no idea what all the excitement is about. Dusk turns to night turns to dawn, and at ten o'clock the next morning, a new and sunny group of passengers files onto the flight and begins cramming their absurdly sized belongings in the overhead bins—none of them suspecting that all the LAX madness they heard about on the news yesterday occurred on *this very plane*. The first-class passengers settle in with their orange juice and vodka; the rest of the plane flips through in-flight magazines and wonder what movies will be shown.

But just as the pilot is getting ready to retract the jetway, a terrible noise roars out from the back of the plane. There is a round of gasps and screams as the noise continues, then another round when a brilliant green flash bursts out from the cracks around the lavatory door. Before anyone has time to start panicking, a man with a silver briefcase suddenly comes crashing out of the bathroom. His shirt is torn across the front, and there are bright red scratches on his face and chest. One of his shoes is melted, filling the air with the scent of burning rubber and plastic.

But most disturbingly, the man's spiky black hair appears to be smoking.

The passengers stare at the man. The man stares back. Then he smiles. His smile gets wider and wider, almost contagiously so, before he finally raises his eyebrows and addresses the stunned travelers.

"Holy shit!" he says cheerfully. "I don't *believe* that worked!"

Then, before anyone can respond, he forces open the rear door of the plane, leaps onto the runway tarmac, and goes running off into the sunshine of another beautiful Los Angeles morning.

# chapter five

The floor won't come clean. Samira's been trying for something like seven hours, but no matter how much she scrubs, there's always one more spot to find. Currently, she's crouched over a piece of darkened tile near the foot of the stove, running a sponge across it with mad abandon. Each time she pushes the sponge forward, the tile is clean. But whenever she pulls it back, a small red streak appears. The rest of her apartment floor—all four hundred square feet of it—shines with almost insane brilliance. An immune-deficient person could perform surgery on this floor while eating a sandwich and come out with fewer germs than when he started. And yet there's the one stupid streak.

It's starting to drive her mad.

She's on a set of bruised hands and knees, wearing nothing but a weathered army-issue T-shirt and a pair of black boxer shorts. The room smells so strongly of bleach that her eyes burn. She's gone through three sponges already, scrubbing and scrubbing until they dissolved into a ragged pile of yellow fibers. But still she keeps at it. It's that damn red streak: it taunts her like something from a Lady Macbeth fever dream.

*Forward, clean. Back, red. Forward, clean. Back, red.*

She's crying again, either from fumes or frustration or a combination of both. Her hands have been gripping sponges for so long that her fingers are stuck in a permanent claw. Her knees are screaming in pain from being pressed against the tile of her cheap Brooklyn walk-up. But she keeps going.

*Gotta get that red streak. Gotta get it. Then you can rest.*

Samira pulls back on the sponge, and the streak returns, larger and more vibrant than ever. She makes a tiny noise of frustration and dips the sponge into her bleach bucket, an action that causes pain to fire up her arm and straight to her head. She cries out and drops the sponge, pulling her left hand back to her chest and holding it with the right as if it might try to break off and run away. Her knuckles on fire, she curls into a small ball on the floor, shuts her eyes as tightly as she can, and waits for the worst of the pain to go away. For a second, she's afraid that she's going to pass out, but eventually the agony begins to diminish. It's not gone by any means, but it's no longer the same stabbing intensity it was a few moments ago.

Samira rolls on her back and opens her eyes, staring up into the dim yellow glow of her kitchen light. As she does, she sees small feathers of dust clinging to the edges of the fixture and makes a mental note to remove them once she can stand. A quick glance at her fridge and stove reveal them to be showroom clean, and for this she's thankful—if she had to clean the appliances, she might just lose it altogether.

Her apartment contains a single window, which she's opened to allow some of the fumes to escape. As she lies on the floor and debates whether or not to look at her hand, she can hear a group of people moving on the street below. They're laughing and screaming and drunk, and for a brief second she feels terribly envious. But then a memory shoves its way into her mind: a severed head, eyes open, rotting in the desert sun. The tongue has been removed and the word TRAITOR carved into the forehead. At this thought, Samira's envy dissolves into grief. She knew the owner of the head once—had even been to his house for tea—but now he was just one more anonymous horror to add to the list.

Samira shakes her head to clear the vision, then turns her attention to the injured hand. Where her knuckles should have contained skin, there were just four red blots. She looks from the knuckles to the floor and back again and suddenly realizes the identity of the mysterious red streak: she's been cleaning her own blood off the floor for the better part of an hour.

"Oh, great," she mutters. "Now I have to throw the sponge away."

A combination of adrenaline and insomnia makes this a funny thought, and she starts giggling madly. She rolls on her side and giggles some more, then uses her good hand to push herself to her feet. Swaying unsteadily, still giggling, she walks out of the kitchen and into the bathroom, where she tosses bottles and ointments to the ground one after another until she finally finds a roll of medical gauze and a tube of Neosporin. Thus armed, Samira sits on the toilet—which could use a good scrubbing, even though she knows she gave it one yesterday—squeezes a copious amount of first-aid gel over her knuckles, and begins to wrap the bandage around her hand. She works quickly and without thought, and soon her hand looks like a lopsided baseball. Satisfied, she seals the ends of the gauze to each other with a bit of medical tape, then stares at her new digit to see if any blood will soak through. The pain is starting to return in full force, and she dimly wonders if she has any more Oxycontin floating around.

Samira is in the process of bending down and looking under her sink for rogue pills when she's interrupted by a bell. She can't figure out where the noise is coming from, so she stands and wanders drunkenly back into the studio portion of her studio apartment. The noise seems familiar in a vague kind of way, but she's having trouble placing it.

"Phone?" Samira asks the empty air in front of her. "Is that my phone?"

It's been weeks since anyone actually called her, long enough that Samira has forgotten the sound of her own cell. But as the ringing continues, a familiar feeling begins to come back. "Yeah," she says again. "That's my phone. Now where did I . . ."

Turning on unsteady feet, she moves in a slow circle until the noise gets louder. After a series of fits and starts, she shuffles over to a gleaming white countertop and peers behind a large teapot, where her phone is sitting in its charger and merrily chirping away. Samira stares at the screen, her vision blurring from the pain of her ravaged hand, until she finally makes out the words UNKNOWN CALLER.

"I don't know who that is," she says to the teapot. When the vessel doesn't respond, she extends her good hand to the phone and slowly picks it up. The device is halfway to her ear before she hears noise coming from the speaker, a kind of whistling, airy sound that reminds her of a convoy driving at speed through a sandstorm.

"Hello?" she croaks, her voice hoarse from the chemical fumes permeating her apartment.

"Sam?" screams a cheerful voice from the other end. "Sam, is that really you?"

Samira blinks a few times, causing her vision to blur even further. *Sam? No one calls me Sam. No one has called me that since . . .*

"Who is this?"

"It's me!"

"Who is this?" she says, more forcefully than before.

"It's me, Sam! It's Tak!"

The phone slips out of Samira's hand and clatters to the floor.

She can hear a voice coming from it, but it sounds very far away. Her blurry vision compresses down even further until all she can see is a colorful flowered teapot floating in an ocean of inky blackness. *I've gone insane,* she thinks, as bright white sparkles begin fluttering in front of the teapot. *This is it. I've finally cracked. So long, reality. I hope the Section 8 ward is clean.*

She feels faint, but somehow manages to pull herself together. The sparkles slowly fade, the blackness retreats, and light returns to her world. Moving like a victim at a bad hypnotism show, she reaches down for the phone and once again puts it to her ear. "You're dead," she whispers at the voice on the other end of the line. "You're dead, you can't call me, you're dead."

"I'm not dead, Sam."

"You hung yourself in a motel room. There was a funeral. You're dead."

"Sam, I swear to God, I'm not dead. I was going to hang myself, but then this company called and I went to work for them and they faked my death."

"I don't believe you," says Samira, as her lower lip trembles. "I'm going to hang up now."

"Wait, wait, wait!" shouts the voice. "Okay, listen, you remember that night where you and me drove to that club to see Kelly's band, and he was so stoned he only played, like, three songs before he knocked over his keyboard and stormed off the stage? And what about when we went down to the beach and I almost drowned and you had to pull me out of the water? Huh? Come on, you *have* to remember that! . . . Oh! Oh, oh! I kissed you! On the mouth! I kissed you in the back of Hilary's car and you said your dad was gonna kill me and I said 'Banzai!' and you thought that was really funny. Come on, Sam! It's me!"

Samira's legs give out at this point, and she slowly slides down the side of her counter and onto the bleach-coated floor. She wants to say something, but she's crying far too hard to make any words come out. Part of Samira's brain is screaming at her to stop with the crying and say something sensible, but all she can concentrate on is the fact that her friend is alive; the emotion of this discovery is overwhelming everything else.

"Sam," says Tak again. "Sam, are you there?"

"Tak. Oh my God, Tak, where have you been?"

The background whistling sound is louder now, and Samira suddenly realizes that Tak is driving a car and talking at the same time. Judging by the howl of the wind, he must be moving incredibly fast. "Jesus, Sam, I'm sorry!" he screams. "I'm so fucking sorry! I couldn't tell you I was okay, I couldn't take the risk. The guys I work for are really terrible people, and I don't know what they would have done."

"Listen," he continues, "I'll explain everything when I see you. But I need you to do something. It's the most important thing you're ever going to do in your life, so you have to do exactly what I say. All right?"

Samira nods, realizes that Tak can't see her, and manages to squeak out a noise of agreement. Her vision blurs again, then alights on the streak of blood next to the bucket. There is a brief, wonderful moment when she realizes that she doesn't give a damn about the unclean patch of tile, then Tak starts speaking again.

"There's a TransAir flight leaving JFK in eleven hours," he says. "It's going to Omaha, Nebraska, and you have to be on it."

"What? Tak, no. I . . . I can't get on a plane."

"You have to."

Samira suddenly feels a very strong urge to put down the phone and find a new sponge. "Tak, I can't even ride a subway. Look, you've been gone a long time, and there's . . . A lot of stuff happened to me, and . . . I can't. I can't do it."

There's a noise on the other end that sounds like a siren. Tak doesn't speak for a few seconds, and Samira can almost feel the fear coming from his side of the call. But then the siren wails past his car and off into the distance, and he's back on the line.

"Christ, that scared the hell out of me!" he says with maniacal good cheer. "Okay, so it's TransAir flight 607. Pack a bag and get on it. And don't check anything—carry-on only, all right?"

"I can't."

"Goddammit, Samira, listen to me! Twenty-two hours from now, something insane is going to happen, and I can't get to you in time. Okay? I'm in the middle of Nevada, and I have to keep stealing cars every few hours, and it's *really* slowing me down! So I can't make it to New York. You're going to have to come to me."

"You're stealing cars?"

"Yeah, there's a bunch of angry guys with guns chasing me, so I can't stay in the same car for more than a few hours at a time. But listen, I don't have time for this. I have to get a new phone before they start tracing me."

"What's in twenty-two hours?" asks Samira. "What happens?"

"You're gonna die," says Tak.

This pulls Samira short. Her friend says it with such finality that she has no fear he might be making it up or exaggerating. He clearly believes this to be true. "Tak, wait. I don't understand—"

"I know. Okay? I know, I know, I know. I can't explain it now, I've only got like twenty seconds left here, and then I gotta go. *Just get on the plane.*"

The thought of getting on a plane, of locking herself in that tiny space with all of those people, makes Samira's stomach clench. She feels the word "no" drift from her lungs and up to her lips, but before she can get it out, her eyes move back to the bucket and the red streak on the floor. *You have to go,* she thinks in a sudden moment of clarity. *If you don't, you'll stay here and clean things until the army bundles you in a plane and sends you off to the mountains to shoot at goat herders and get blown up by an IED. You have to go.*

"Okay," she says finally. "Okay."

"Banzai! That's my Sam! Okay, I've gotta . . . Oh, wait! Wait, wait! Don't eat anything! Not a thing! Empty stomach!"

"I'm not hungry."

"Good! We'll eat when you get here. Super important. Okay, I gotta run. See ya in fifteen hours!"

There is a loud click as the phone goes dead. Samira drops the cell and slowly rises to her feet. Her army-issue duffel bag is in a pile near the front door—she dropped it there when she came home from her last tour of duty and never bothered to move it. Inside are a few shirts, a couple of pairs of pants, some underwear, and a copy of her favorite Murakami book. She looks at the duffel for an eternity, the smell of bleach and blood filling her nostrils, then lets her gaze move to the red streak at the foot of the stove.

*You don't need to pack yet. You don't have to. You can finish cleaning that spot. And there's the dust on the light. Remember that? You need to clean that. You've got time. You can do it before you go. You've got hours before the flight. . . . And maybe you don't need to catch it at all. There's so much to do here. So much to clean.*

Half an hour later, a dazed-looking girl in a yellow sundress hails a cab and promises the driver an extra fifty if he can get to JFK in twenty minutes.

They make it in fifteen.

aMends

# chapter six

Charles Yates stands on the flat white roof of the building he de-signed and watches the fiery corona of Earth's nearest star begin its ascent over the Australian Outback. His right hand holds a yellow pencil worn to a stub, while his left contains a battered black notebook. Inside the notebook is an almost incomprehen-sible series of sketches, equations, and essays written in a never-ending stream of tiny capital letters. A normal person flipping through the notebook would likely dismiss it as the ramblings of a madman, and one look at the owner, with his unkempt grey hair and thick, engineer glasses, would only help to confirm this suspicion.

But if the reader is not a normal person and is instead, say, a Nobel Prize–winning scientist, the notebook would be a different thing altogether. Near the front, for example, written in faded blue ink, is a schematic for a device that can focus light into a narrow, powerful beam. The scientist would instantly recognize this as a laser and probably think little more of the subject. If, however, he happened to glance at the date at the top of the page and see that it read 1954, the sketch would become much more interesting—and the scientist might begin to wonder how this man, this odd little man in a dirty lab coat who looked like some kind of homeless grandfather, had sketched a laser some six years before it was invented by a man named Theodore Maiman.

The scientist would flip through the pages now, eyes growing wide as he read. Here is a device that can capture and store images electronically, put to paper nearly a decade before the first digital camera was constructed. There is a page of notes that seemed to prove Fermat's Last Theorem in a way far more elegant and clever than the solution that would be presented some twenty years later. And look! Scribbled in the margins of a page, a casual after-thought, is a way to double the efficiency of semiconductors.

But as the pages turn, and the years move toward the millennium, the writings start to become incomprehensible. Phrases like "Schwarzschild wormhole" and "cosmic string" begin to pepper the pages, along with cryptic notes such as "Must remember to test this later" and "Find the girl from Shelby." There are designs for batteries and cold-fusion reactors and geothermal-heat transference systems; equations for faster-than-light travel and infinite mass reduction; fantastic rants about nanomachines and red-shift measurements and the capturing of the Higgs boson particle. And as the two numerals at the front of the year shift from 19 to 20, the pages become compressed with notations and concepts so advanced that the clever scientist would simply lower the book with trembling hands and wonder why his lifetime of achievements suddenly felt so meaningless and empty.

But if the scientist ever tried to meet the genius behind these ideas, it would be a most terrible mistake. For when he looked into the eyes of the notebook's author, he would see that the rare and amazing mind which placed these thoughts to paper was, to put it in technical terms, completely batshit insane. And at this point, he would have to smile and nod and back away slowly, fearful to turn around lest the author began to howl crazed laughter before lodging a fire axe between his shoulder blades.

But Charles Yates did not worry about such reactions because he never allowed his notebook to be read. The only person who had so much as glimpsed inside it was a brilliant young grad student named Judith Halford—and that single look had convinced her to abandon a promising scientific career and follow him to the end of the Earth. And now, nearly fifteen years later, their long partnership was about to come to fruition.

Yates considers this as he gazes across the desolate brown surface of the Outback. Thousands of custom-built solar panels, their design lifted straight from his ancient black notebook, stretch toward the horizon in every direction. Each one is covered with a thin film invented by Yates some ten years prior: an improvement that allows them to gather more energy than even the most wild-eyed optimist could dream of.

*All the years of existence compressed to a single point,* he thinks, as the panels go about their work. *And only I can see it coming.*

Though he is exhausted and crying for sleep, Yates will not allow himself that luxury. This is a day over two decades in the making, and he wants to revel in every last moment. Somewhere beneath his feet, a machine hums quietly as it gathers power. And fifteen hours from now, he will descend into the Earth and flip a switch that will change the world forever. No, he will not sleep now. Not when the end is so very close.

He reaches into the pocket of a tattered lab coat and produces a cigarette, placing it absentmindedly in the corner of his mouth. His other hand dives into a different pocket in search of a lighter but emerges with only a single pistachio shell and the rusted blade of a scalpel. Frowning, he moves to the pockets of his old grey slacks, but these hold only lint. He thinks back as to where he might have left the lighter—on his desk, by his bed, perhaps in the cavity of one of the bodies he was working on last night—and is annoyed to discover that he has no idea where it is. Yates is a man used to knowing all things at all times, and he does not handle failure well.

His thoughts are interrupted by the sound of a door opening behind him, followed by the soft shuffle of feet as they cross the roof and take up position somewhere behind him.

"Good morning, Judith," says Yates without turning around.

"Hello, Charles."

"Come to watch the sunrise?"

"Not so much," replies Judith before reaching into her pocket and producing an old silver lighter. She holds it out to Yates, who studies it for a moment before taking it with the fingers of one wrinkled hand.

"Where did you find this?"

"Next to the coffee machine."

"Ah, yes. Of course."

He sparks a flame and lights his cigarette, enjoying the way the smoke burns hot against his lungs. Judith glances at the notebook in his hands and coughs softly. Above them, the sun continues its long march across the sky.

"Is everything ready?" asks Yates after a minute.

"More or less," responds Judith.

The hesitancy of this answer causes Yates to glance over. "You sound troubled."

"We have a problem. . . . Actually, we have two problems."

"Go on."

"Takahiro has fled the country."

"I expected as much."

"He took the briefcase."

The cigarette trembles slightly in Yates's hand, knocking a

small piece of ash into the desert wind. He feels a brief flash of rage rise up in his system. "When was this discovered?"

"Sounds like the board has been onto him for a couple of days. They tried to detain him at LAX, but he got away."

"Do they know what he took?"

"They know he took *something*, but I don't think they understand the importance. They want to talk to you about it."

"When?"

"Now."

Yates nods. Outwardly, he is the picture of calm, but inwardly he is raging. He wishes he were a lesser kind of man who might gain comfort from violence—if so, it might be nice to grab Judith by the nape of the neck and put out his cigarette in her eye.

"You said there were two problems," says Yates, staring at his smoking cigarette. "What is the second?"

"It's Hsu. He wants to turn on the Machine at ten o'clock exactly. I think the others agree with him."

"Round numbers," murmurs Yates.

"Hmm?" asks Judith.

"A round number is a way to assign meaning to otherwise random events. I chose to activate the Machine at ten seventeen because it will increase our battery efficiency by one-tenth of one percent. But, of course, the time ten seventeen holds no meaning. It implies randomness. Chaos. The men who control this company are incapable of grappling with such things."

As he speaks, another image flashes in his mind, this time of grabbing the long red hair that waterfalls down Judith's back and using it to whip her off the roof. The ground below is hard and flat, but not without small imperfections—she would make a terribly interesting pattern when she landed. Of course, at nearly eighty years old, he no longer has the strength to attempt such a maneuver even if he chose to.

"I will talk to Mr. Hsu directly," continues Yates with a blank expression on his face. "Perhaps ten fifteen will be enough to satisfy his needs."

"And if not?"

"If not, then it is no matter. The Machine will have more than enough power to do what we require of it."

They fall to silence again. Judith takes a ballpoint pen from behind her ear and begins to click it slowly. Yates takes a final drag of his cigarette and tosses it off the edge of the roof, watching it spin and tumble through the air before exploding into sparks on the brown desert floor. When the final bit of red flame coughs and dies, he thumbs open the front page of his notebook and stares at one of his early sketches.

"The Machine has taught us many things," he says suddenly, "but its final lesson is this: reality is flexible. Ideas that we accept without thinking, ideas that have *always* been accepted, are just shadows on a wall. We can grant them or take them away as we see fit."

"What are you talking about, Charles?" asks Judith.

"Never mind. It doesn't matter now."

"Do you want me to come with you?"

"To the board?"

"They seem nervous."

"They should be. They've put far too much power into our hands." Yates smiles at this, a horrible thing that appears on his face like a demon in the night. "But there is nothing to be done. I will answer their summons, and they will ask ridiculous questions and take up far too much of my time. But at the end of it all, they will go forward with the plan and hope that everything is going to be fine."

"And is it, Charles? Is it going to be fine?"

Charles pulls the lighter out of his pocket, watching how

the sun glints off its silver surface. "Are you a religious person, Judith?"

"Not really, no."

"I learned long ago that religion is nothing more than an elaborate game of pretend for people who are unable to grasp their own demise. I reject this system. I will not place my future in the hands of chance. This evening is an opportunity for those with cleverness and bravery to find a solution to the puzzle of mortality. You and I, Judith? We will seize this chance."

"And the rest of the world?"

Yates watches a single brown hawk circle over a spot on the distant horizon and smiles to himself. "Life is selfish," he says. "The predator eats the prey, the virus destroys the host. The quest for survival is violent and strange, and only the truly heartless can emerge successful. . . . You ask about the rest of the world? The rest of the world, Judith, can go fuck itself."

The two of them stand in silence, watching the sun move across a harsh and barren landscape. Finally, Judith turns on one heel and slips away, closing the rooftop door behind her. Charles Yates remains where he is, feeling the wind in his hair and enjoying the last full sunrise of a dying world.

# chapter seven

"You look awesome, Sam. Seriously awesome. But you're like Tokyo-skinny now, and that ain't good. You should eat a burger sometime. Oh, wait! Shit! We gotta eat. Hold on a sec."

Tak leans out of the booth and cranes his neck in a futile search for a waitress, while Samira burrows into her red leather bench and smiles. She'd been smiling ever since she emerged from the airport and saw her old friend with a flower in one hand and a small, metal briefcase in the other. He'd given the flower to her—*Because I missed you,* he'd said—and promised to explain the briefcase soon.

*I'll tell you everything,* he'd said, as they hopped into a pickup and screamed off into the orange Nebraska dusk. *Everything. Just lemme get somewhere calm, because it's gonna take a while. We gotta leave major cities, so I'm thinking we find some diner on a rural highway and get ready. Oh, how was the flight? You do okay?*

She'd nodded at this, which was as much of a lie as she could manage. Samira had actually spent the first two hours of the flight scrubbing the mirror of the lavatory with a paper towel and hand soap before the regular drone of the jet engines lulled her to sleep. She'd drifted off in a standing position, face pressed against the gleaming mirror, and dreamed that a cow with no skin was following her down the hallway of her apartment building. Each time she took a step, the cow would scream in pain as a piece of it fell off—by the time she reached her door, the hallway was full of writhing, screaming cow parts, all of them somehow her fault.

But now, holed up in a roadhouse outside Broken Bow, Nebraska, her dreams seem very far away. As truck stops go, this one seems to have joyfully embraced every cliché in the book. The jukebox rests under a picture of a fluttering American flag and belts out Merle Haggard. The smell of potatoes and onions fills the air. And near the front, three large men with even larger asses sit on stools and devour their food in silence. She can feel the men stare at them from beneath the bills of their caps, but it doesn't bother her. *Hell, there's a Japanese dude and an Iranian chick sitting in a truck stop in the middle of Nebraska. That probably doesn't happen very often.*

"Okay, listen, never mind," says Tak, abandoning his quest for food. "It's one thirty in the morning, so there's probably only one waitress. She'll be back. We'll order then. We need food."

He tosses a hand in the center of the table, and Samira takes it without thinking. Although it's only been four years since she saw her friend, Tak looks much older. He doesn't have wrinkles or crow's-feet or greying hair, but there is a depth to his features that wasn't there before. She searches his face for other clues to his recent past and finds indications everywhere of a hard, dangerous life. There is a chunk missing from the top of his left ear, as if an angry squirrel decided to take a bite. His fingers, which had once been long and delicate, are covered with calluses and scars. But mostly it's the heaviness that she sees, the weight of a million deeds haunting him from somewhere behind his eyes. If she didn't know better, she'd swear she was looking at a soldier freshly returned from war.

"Nice dress," he says after a minute. "I missed that dress."

"Thanks," she whispers, turning her gaze to the faded yellow sundress clinging to her thin frame. "I figured . . . I guess I wanted to wear something pretty."

"Hey, what happened?" he asks suddenly, pointing at her bandaged left hand. "Is that a war wound or something?"

"It's nothing. I was cleaning something, and . . . yeah. Don't worry about it."

Tak seems ready to say more but instead pulls his hand away and snatches the briefcase from its hiding spot under the table. Setting it on the bench next to him, he rubs the top for a few seconds, lost in thought. Then he turns back to Samira, opens his mouth, stops, thinks for a few seconds more, and begins to laugh.

"What?" asks Samira.

"Nothing," he says. "It's just . . . This is all so fucking surreal. I don't even know how to tell you. I don't know where to start. I'm afraid you won't believe me."

"I'll believe you."

"I dunno."

"Well, I'll try," she says. "How's that?"

He nods and pulls on the neck of his T-shirt, a blue number with the words I HEART OTAKU scrawled across the front. "All right. I know I told you some crazy shit, like 'you're gonna die in twenty-two hours,' but I can't explain that yet, or it won't make sense. I have to start at the beginning. Cool?"

"Cool."

"Good. Okay. So four years ago, I tried to hang myself."

Samira knows this, but hearing it spoken aloud makes it somehow more real. When she'd received word of Tak's death, she'd been getting ready to deploy on a second tour of duty in Iraq. There had been no time to attend the funeral, no time even to grieve. Seventy-two hours after learning of her friend's supposed

demise, she was interviewing witnesses of a Baghdad car bomb-
ing while men with assault rifles held an angry mob at bay. Tak's
death had become a sad and secret pain that she carried around
like a broken wristwatch. And finally faced with it again, she is
surprised to find that her first reaction is one of anger. *Damn you,
Tak,* she thinks suddenly. *Damn you. You were the last good thing in
my life, and once you were gone, nothing mattered anymore.*

"Anyway, look," he continues, "I can tell you're pissed, and
I'm sorry. But what matters is that I didn't go through with it.
Before I could kick out the chair, I got a phone call from a company called the Axon Corporation. Turns out they wanted to
offer me a job. And so I figured, hey, what the hell, right? Beats
stretching my neck from the chandelier."

"That's not funny," says Samira.

"Sorry. . . . Anyway, after I agreed, they flew me down to
Australia and drove me into the Outback. Like, *way* into the Out-
back, hundreds of miles, until we reached this big white building.
And then took me underground and showed me their invention."

"Which is what?"

"It's called the Machine."

"That's a boring name," says Samira.

"Yeah, well, the guy who built it isn't what you'd call a cre-
ative type. Anyway, this guy, Yates, he invented the Machine, but
he couldn't figure out how to make it work. So that's why they
called me."

"You?" asks Samira, who is getting slightly annoyed at how
long Tak is taking to build up to his obvious dramatic finish.

"Yeah. Me."

"Why you? You don't know about science."

"They didn't need a scientist, Sam. They needed an explorer."

"And why is *that*?"

"Because it's a time machine."

Samira stares at Tak for a long time, then decides to look out the window. A few flakes of snow drift through the light of sodium arc lamps before settling on the asphalt of Highway 2. Tak sits still and silent—both rarities for him—and waits for his friend to turn back. When she finally does, the look on her face is one of bemused confusion.

"You're high," she says. "Or you're crazy. But I'm going to guess that you're high."

"I'm serious."

"Come on. Where have you really been?"

"I'm serious," he repeats. There is a strange expression on his face, as if he both expected her reaction and is somehow disappointed by it. "Sam, I'm dead serious. It's a goddamn time machine."

"There's no such thing as a time machine."

"Yes. Yes, there is. I've seen it. I've *used* it. I've gone in the thing hundreds of times. It's real. It works. I promise."

"I don't know how to believe you right now," says Samira quietly. "I'm sorry, but I just . . . I don't."

Tak shifts in his seat and runs his fingers back and forth through his hair, then checks his watch. "Okay, well, I know it sounds like I'm on crack, but in about six hours, you're gonna *have* to believe me."

"Why?" asks Samira.

"Because. Listen, I'm getting ahead of myself. Can I go back? You need to hear all of this. You don't have to believe it right now, but you need to listen. All right?"

She nods. Tak starts to speak, then notices a waitress appear from somewhere in the back. Waving his hand wildly, he begins to yell at her from across the restaurant. "Pancakes! Hey, wait! We need, like . . ." He glances down at his hand, counts his fingers, then puts his tongue between his teeth and closes his eyes.

"Nine! We need nine orders of pancakes! And three pitchers of water!"

The waitress raises her eyebrows. The three men on stools stop eating with their forks suspended in midair. Tak grins. Eventually, the waitress decides he's serious and wanders back into the kitchen. As the truckers return to their food and commence muttering, Tak spins around and finds Samira staring at him.

"Hungry?" she asks.

"It's for both of us," he says. "We need starches and simple sugars. And lots of water. Pancakes and syrup is the best."

"The best for what?"

"Time travel. Look, I need to just talk for a while. Is that all right?"

Samira nestles herself in the corner of the booth and nods. She should be disappointed that Tak has so clearly gone insane, but in truth, she's secretly pleased that she won't be the only one at the table who's mentally unstable.

"All right, here we go," says Tak. "So! Axon has a time machine, and they want me to change history to make it more beneficial for the company. You know, buy stock at a certain price, patent ideas and products before rival companies can, that kind of thing. Big waste of a time machine if you ask me, but hey, I'm just the explorer. The hell do I know?"

The waitress comes by with three pitchers of water and sets them down. Tak pours two glasses, shoves one in front of Samira, and drains his in a single gulp. He refills the glass and motions for Samira to drink up. "Anyway, so it was my job to travel through time and start mucking around, but I gotta tell ya, Sam, I was worried."

"Oh?" asks Samira, taking a sip of water.

"Well, think about it! Time travel is really messy. What if I screw something up? What if I kill my own grandfather, or step on a butterfly, or whatever? The implications of messing around with a timeline are just fucking terrifying."

"Yeah, I guess I can see that. . . . I mean, if I believed this."

"But that's not how time travel works," says Tak flatly. He tops off Samira's water glass and motions to it again. "Seriously, drink that. You're gonna need it."

"I'm working on it," she growls.

"So the first time I used the Machine, I thought I'd go back a few decades and mess with something small. You know, bury a box in the woods, then dig it up in the present just to make sure everything worked. But when I went back, I found myself in this totally barren wasteland. There were no buildings, no people, no nothing. Just a flat, empty plain filled with red sand."

The waitress comes by with two containers of syrup. Tak downs his water, pours a new glass, downs that, and pours a fourth. Samira, trying to play along, drinks half of her glass before erupting in a coughing fit. Tak leans over the table and pats her on the back before pouring a refill.

"Okay, so I didn't get that *at all*," he says with a wave of the hand. "I expected to be in the 1920s and meet a bunch of guys with awesome mustaches, but I was just . . . nowhere. So I wait around, and after a few hours, the Machine pulls me back and we try again. Same thing. Big wasteland. So we keep trying, and we keep trying, then one day, I finally figure out how to go somewhere else."

"And how's that?" asks Samira, who has decided that playing along is better than trying to convince Tak how nuts he is.

"I don't really know how to explain it. The Machine isn't like a dishwasher or a computer, you know? It's more like a musical instrument. It's like jazz. You just have to get a feel for it."

"Okay. Sure. Why not. So where did you go?"

"I was in Paris, and it was 1954 and everything seems to be

good. But because I'm in a major city, I can't do something small. I can't bury a box because someone will find it before I can get to it in the present. So I decide to do something that no one can possibly overlook and I kinda . . . stole some dynamite and blew up the Eiffel Tower."

"You blew up what?" asks Samira.

"The Eiffel Tower. But just the top. And I didn't kill anybody, so don't go calling me a murderer or anything. I made sure it was empty."

Samira grabs her water glass and drinks deeply. Finishing it off, she utters a tiny belch and pours another. "But, Tak, wait. The Eiffel Tower is still there."

"I know."

"You didn't blow it up," she states. "It's still there."

"Yes, I did."

"Tak! It's *there*!"

"I know!" he says with a grin. "I *know*! That's when I knew we had it all wrong."

"You had what wrong?"

"Time travel! We were wrong, everyone was wrong. You *can't* time travel. Not the way people think. You have to—"

At that moment, the waitress comes over with a tray and begins to set down plate after plate of pancakes. Samira and Tak shove the condiments and napkin dispenser to the far end of the table to make room, but seven plates later it's completely full.

"I've never seen two skinnier kids order more food," says the waitress, who dumps the remaining two plates on a nearby table before disappearing in the back. Samira stares out across the table, buttermilk and syrup overwhelming her nostrils, and suddenly feels a bit ill. For his part, Tak seems delighted. He slides two plates over to himself, slathers them in syrup, and begins to fork huge pieces of pancake into his mouth.

"Eat," he says, spraying bits of breakfast across the table. "Seriously, Sam, you need to eat as much as you can, or the trip's gonna be really gnarly."

She pours a thin stream of syrup over a short stack, cuts off a hunk, and chews slowly. "I'm not really hungry," she says after a minute of chomping. Her eyes are focused on the plate at the far end of the table, where a sideways pat of butter is melting into a sticky yellow film on the table. The dirtiness of it is making her hand itch, but she resists the urge to clean it off.

"Yeah, well, get after it or you're gonna be sick later," says Tak. "So, um, what was I saying?"

"You said you can't time travel. Or something like that," says Samira. She's making a game effort at her stack, but the thought of downing so much food is making her stomach flip. "I don't really remember, Tak. You're not making much sense."

"Yeah, I know," he says. "Okay, here! Here. I've got an idea."

Tak grabs an untouched stack of pancakes, piles it on top of the plate he's already finished, and slides it to the center of the table. Then he takes his knife and lays it across the top cake, creating a depression in the butter. "Look at this," he says. "Now, when you think about time travel, what do you think about?"

"I don't think about time travel," she says between bites.

"Yeah, you're right, that was dumb. So, in general, people who *do* think about time travel think about it like this knife, right?" Tak points at the knife, moving his finger from the end to the tip and back again. "Everyone figured this is how it works. You start here, in your time, and then you jump forward or backward. Everyone assumed time was a straight line, and all a time traveler could do was bounce around on that line. You with me so far?"

"I guess?"

"But we were wrong. It doesn't work that way, because that's not how *time* works. You can't time travel, Sam! You can't. It's impossible. The universe won't let it happen."

Tak flicks the knife off the pancakes, sending it clattering to the side. "It's like I said: what if I kill my grandfather, or step on that butterfly, or do anything at all? Any little thing you do changes *everything*, and that creates these crazy paradoxes that can't possibly happen." He points to the pancakes and moves his finger up and down the pile. "*This* is time travel, Sam! It's not a line. It's a stack."

"You lost me," says Samira. "I mean, you kinda . . . You kinda lost me a while ago, but now you really lost me."

"Think of it like this: our timeline—the one that you and I exist in right now—is a single pancake. It's round and complete and perfect, and everything that happens there stays there. I call it the solid timeline because it's the one that locks everything else down. It's our point of reference. You with me?"

"Yup," says Samira, who tears a piece from her napkin and finally begins to clean the butter off the table.

"But instead of letting me travel forward or backward on the solid timeline, the Machine sends me to a different timeline—a *random* timeline. And once I'm in that random timeline, I can do whatever I want. I can blow up monuments or kill Hitler or whatever, because our pancake, the solid timeline, is still humming right along somewhere else. Got it?"

Samira nods slowly and pulls her hand away from the butter before she starts to wipe down the entire table. Tak, who is so into his story that he doesn't notice her cleaning frenzy, pushes another pile of pancakes toward his friend. "So once I figured this out, once I realized I wasn't affecting the solid timeline, I thought we were done. I mean, Axon is spending *billions* of dollars on this project, but none of it matters. They can't change the past, they can't go back and invent the pet rock, they can't do anything. I figure I'll be fired and they'll shut it down and that'll be the end of it.

"But it's not the end," continues Tak as he rolls two pancakes together and starts eating them like a burrito. "Axon decides to keep going, so I keep exploring timelines, and eventually I get really good at it. I can find timelines that are nearly identical to ours, or I can find ones that are so crazy you wouldn't even recognize them. And this goes on for *years*. Guys come to me with a request—gimme a timeline where bears rule the world, show me a timeline where cavemen never evolved—and then I go search it out. It's kinda . . . fun."

"Why would they do that?" says Samira, who's starting to wonder if Dr. Carrington has room for one more patient. "I mean, if it's all like you say, why would they keep going?"

"They were watching me. Taking notes. Backtracking on all the work I did and reverse-engineering things. They whole time I was fucking around, these guys were using me. They totally used me, and I never caught on."

Tak's smile fades. He reaches out for a another plate, then pulls his fork back and sets it down. For the longest time, he can't seem to meet Samira's eyes. "Six months ago, they came to me with a new request. They wanted to find a timeline where the Axon Corporation controls everything. Governments, banks, people . . . Everything."

"And you did?" says Samira.

"Yeah. Yeah, I did."

"That doesn't strike me as a very good idea."

"I know, but I just . . . I was already into this thing up to my eyeballs, and I figured that even if I found it, it wouldn't matter. I mean, it's a random timeline, right? I thought they were gonna use the Machine to go there and take over. I thought . . . I thought they wanted to *leave*."

Tak stops talking. The waitress comes by and clears the empty plates. Two of the men at the counter pay their bills and leave. Outside, the snow begins to fall with more force. When Tak finally speaks again, it is in a voice deep with regret.

"I fucked up, Sam," he says. "I fucked up *everything*."

"What do you mean?" she asks, as a shiver runs down her spine. "How?"

"They're not leaving the solid timeline. They're bringing the other one here."

# chapter eight

Yates takes the long way to his meeting with the board, stopping first at floor B14 to make a cup of coffee. Though the Axon Corporation exists in a building with the square footage of Central Park, it is staffed by a crew of less than a hundred—most of whom are professional mercenaries used to keep the local population in line. The twelve leaders of the company, who refer to themselves simply as "the board," knew that each extra employee was another security risk, so they made automating the building a top priority. Yates had designed a number of systems along this line over the years, and the end result was a marvel of modern engineering and thought that practically ran itself.

After making his coffee, Yates moves up a couple of floors to check on his latest side project: an ambitious idea that used microscopic robots to repair damaged human tissue. The experiment had been plagued by a steady stream of nagging issues—namely that his machines could not yet distinguish damaged tissue from healthy—and his trials usually ended with test subjects bleeding to death from their pores. This failure bothered Yates, but only in a vague, clinical kind of way. He knew he would eventually succeed, as he had in everything that had come before, so he viewed the deaths as mere bumps along the road of progress. Thankfully, there was no shortage of subjects on which to work; if there was one thing the world did not lack, it was homeless vagrants who would not be missed.

After taking a few notes on his latest trial—and ignoring the man's terribly distracting screaming—Yates finally makes his way to the conference room where the board is waiting. They are seated, as always, behind a massive table carved from endangered Brazilian redwood, a material that seems not to reflect light so much as transform it into a luminous presence. The twelve men behind the table are by any measure the most powerful in the world, used to having whatever they want at a moment's notice. And judging by the scared and angry looks that cross their faces as Yates enters the room, what they want is answers.

Yates sets his notebook down on the small podium and adjusts his glasses. "Gentlemen? I hear you want to speak with me."

"You have heard about Mr. O'Leary?" barks the man on the left, a large Chinese national named Hsu. "You know that he has fled the country?"

"I was just informed."

"And were you informed that he stole something from us?"

"I was told this also, yes."

A man named James Caulfield leans forward and points his index finger at Yates. When he speaks, it is with a soft Southern drawl. "We've heard some disturbing things about this theft, Yates. People tell us he took something quite extraordinary."

"It was a little experiment of mine," says Yates in a soft, controlled voice. "Something I was tinkering with in my off-hours. It is of no consequence."

"Oh, but we heard that it's of great fucking consequence, Yates. We heard the bastard fled the country with a working version of the Machine." Caulfield, an arms dealer who made his

fortune selling yellowcake uranium to various foreign governments, raises his eyebrows slightly, as if waiting for the old man
in front of him to crumble into dust.

"The experiment that Mr. O'Leary stole is useless," replies
Yates. "It does nothing more than weigh him down."

"So you aren't building a portable Machine? Is that what
you're saying?"

"Eventually, yes, I was hoping to create a portable Machine,
but my current efforts have been fruitless. Had I more time, I
might have been successful, but . . . Well, we've all been a little
busy lately."

This elicits a round of chuckling from ten of the men behind
the table although Hsu and Caulfield continue to frown. *They
suspect more than the others,* Charles thinks to himself. *Well, let them.
In a few hours, none of their suspicions will mean a thing.*

"You should not have let him near your experiments," says
Hsu, pressing the attack. "In fact, I thought the plan was to eliminate Mr. O'Leary sometime last week."

"That was your plan, gentlemen. Not mine."

"I think you underestimate your level of involvement here,
Charles," says a fat, bald man named Daniel Peterson. He made
his fortune in the stock market back in the early nineties, then had
the good sense to get out before everything went to hell. He is the
wealthiest man on the entire Axon board, although in Yates's
experience, such wealth did little more than make men soft.
"You're in this just as much as we are. You can't duck responsibility when decisions get messy."

"And you've never struck me as particularly squeamish," adds
Caulfield. "You'd smother a baby with a pillow if it served one of
your damn experiments."

"Do you remember when I joined your company?" asks Yates
in reply. The men in front of him nod slowly, unsure of where this

is going. "I came to you fifteen years ago with the most fantastic idea ever created: a machine that could control time itself."

"We know all this!" exclaims Hsu. "I hardly think—"

"I found a location where we could harness solar and geothermal power at an exaggerated rate," continues Yates. "I designed solar panels, gave you batteries that could store untold amounts of electricity, and created a means to transfer that energy to the Machine. I powered it up, I turned it on, and in the years since, I have solved every technical challenge that you have placed before me. I gave you the world, gentlemen, and all I asked in return was the funding to complete the project. I did not hunger for power, or wealth, or fame. I simply wanted to see if the Machine was possible."

Yates pauses for a moment, then glances from one man to the next. Each one meets his gaze with a look of bemused interest, an emotion that suits Yates. *Very well. Underestimate me yet again. That will work just fine.* "Mr. Hsu, you are one of the highest-ranking officials in the Chinese National Army. Mr. Casipit, you made billions of dollars selling military weapons to various groups across the African continent. Mr. Ritchie, your son currently heads the Central Intelligence Agency."

"What's the point, Chuck?" says David Casipit as he leans back in his chair. He is a thin, wiry man with a vicious temper who once murdered a dry cleaner when he didn't like the starch in his shirts. "Smoke up my ass makes me uncomfortable."

"Gentlemen, I came to you as a physicist and an engineer, and in those capacities I have performed admirably. The killing of Mr. O'Leary, if that was your desire, should have been handled by one of your mercenaries. While my 'damn experiments,' as you so fondly refer to them, sometimes end in failure, I am no murderer."

"Well, we woulda killed the son of a bitch if he hadn't fled the damn country!" says Casipit with a snarl. "Whatcha think about that?"

Yates goes silent as a vision suddenly enters his mind: Casipit trapped inside a large, clear jar, banging on the glass. Green gas flows into the jar from an unseen tube at the bottom, as the man's face begins to bulge and stretch. Such violent thoughts had been coming to him more frequently of late. *This could be related to the grand experiment. Perhaps I have underestimated the effect it would have on my own mind.*

The board mistakes his pause for nervousness and break out into self-knowing grins—they clearly enjoy seeing him out of his element. Yates decides to wait a few more seconds before answering, even going so far as to shuffle his notebook around the podium in a feigned display of nerves.

"I think . . ." begins Yates. "I think that Mr. O'Leary's theft and flight is unfortunate. But I also know it does not matter. Even if he has lost faith in our goals, there is nothing that can be done. What police agency would believe him? What government would think that a private corporation was about to alter reality by way of a fantastic new machine? And even if someone did believe him, they could not possibly act in time. We have only to wait until this evening, and the change will be unstoppable."

"Um, about that," says Daniel, staring into his laptop. "We see here that you want to engage the Machine at ten seventeen p.m."

"Correct. By starting at ten seventeen, the batteries will gain an additional—"

"We will engage the Machine at ten precisely," says Hsu.

"May I ask why?"

"We're, uh . . . we're just not comfortable with the original schedule," stammers Daniel.

"Hell, Chuck," shouts Casipit, "we're already all nervous as a long-tailed cat in a room full of rockin' chairs. Why wait around for an extra seventeen minutes just to get some one billion of one percent's worth of power or whatever it is yer doin'? Let's just turn the fucker on and be done with it."

"Perhaps ten fifteen would be acceptable," begins Yates. "I realize it is only two minutes, but even that extra time would be—"

"The Machine will be turned on at ten o'clock," says Hsu. "Is this going to be a problem?"

Yates takes a moment to stare at the men in front of him as they lean forward in their chairs. He can feel them sizing him up, watching him for any sign of weakness or hesitation. Doubts, any doubts, would be bad right now. If they delayed the transfer, someone might discover his true plan—and that would be a very unfortunate thing.

"No, gentlemen," answers Yates. "Ten o'clock is perfectly acceptable. Gather together at this time, open a bottle of champagne, and celebrate your ascendancy into immortality."

The board leans back as the tension in the room melts away. They *want* to believe him, these men; they *want* to think they will be kings in a brave new world. Daniel motions for Yates to approach the table, then leans his sizeable gut over it and proffers his hand. Charles plasters a false smile on his face and pumps the massive paw a few times, then works his way down the line like a minister at the end of a sermon, shaking hands, exchanging words, telling the men that all will be well. It's long and tiring work, mostly because he has to resist the urge to break into maniacal laughter. Pride has made these men soft, and greed has made them sloppy. Four years ago, they never would have put so much responsibility in the hands of a scientist they did not trust. But the reality of the Machine changed everything, and with ultimate power at their fingertips, they decided it was worth the risk.

The meeting continues with mindless speculation about the

grandeur of their new world, but Yates does not linger. Excus-
ing himself under the pretense of preparation, he returns to the
elevator, inserts a keycard, and rides it as far down as it will go—
farther down, even, than the Machine itself. When the lift finally
grinds to a halt, it spits Yates out onto a hidden floor that he had
constructed in secret. He takes a sip of lukewarm coffee as he
strolls down a long, dark hallway. At the far end, he stops at an
imposing metal door and begins to disengage a complicated system of locks. A soft gurgling sound emits from somewhere behind the door, as well as an unpleasant stench. This continues to
amaze Yates—even with the best air-filtration system he can
build, the smell still manages to escape.

When the door finally swings open, he steps into a large white
room. To his left is a supercomputer of his own design, one far
more advanced than anything else currently in operation. Thick
bundles of wires spill out from this machine and over to a massive
storage tank. The gurgling sound comes from a system of hoses at
the back of the tank. Pure, clean water flows in, but the stuff that
emerges is blackened and foul.

Yates has spared no expense in the construction of the tank; it
is, without a doubt, the most secure prison that the world has ever
seen. The walls are nearly three feet thick and composed of tita-
nium interlaced with lonsdaleite—a material even harder than
diamond. Surrounding the tank is an electrified grid that could
power a small city, as well as vents than can fill the room with
deadly cyanide gas. And just in case something does happen to
climb out of the tank with revenge on its mind, the entire floor is
wired with nearly a thousand pounds of explosives.

He sits down at the desk and flips on a video monitor. This is
connected to a small camera inside the tank, providing Yates a
view of the thing that lurks inside. He longs to get closer to the
creature, to examine it with his own hands, but such a wish is

folly. Inside the tank is the most amazing and most dangerous thing that has ever existed. It is a creature beyond even death. It is the antilife.

The image on the screen is blackness, and for a moment it appears that the camera has stopped working. Then something shifts slightly, creating a dark blur against the brackish water of the tank. For a long time there is only this blurry darkness, but then it shifts again to reveal a bit of pale, translucent skin. One huge black eye rolls around to the camera and stares into it, watching. It understands what is happening. It knows that Yates is there. But then again, it has always known this.

The pipes gurgle again as a thick, black fluid begin to run though them. This ooze moves through a series of smaller and smaller pipes before finally dripping out into a small glass beaker on Yates's desk. He watches it crawl down the side of the glass with a handkerchief over his mouth; the stench of the stuff is beyond overpowering. After a few minutes, the flow slows to a trickle before stopping altogether. A couple ounces of sludge lie in the bottom of the beaker, and as Yates picks it up and looks inside, he wonders if he might be making the most terrible mistake of his—or any—life.

"Nothing is accomplished without risk," he murmurs to himself as he swirls the liquid. "There can be no progress without fear. This is the only way. Others will come. Other men. Other Machines. . . . This is the only way."

He raises the beaker to his lips and drinks. Foul blackness trickles from the side of his mouth, but he continues to force it down. When he is finished, he falls to the ground and waits for the convulsions to pass. They are worse than ever this time, a thought that brings him a small glimmer of joy. His calculations were correct. When the change happens, he will be ready.

Hours tick by. The thing in the tank stirs, occasionally

74 | alan averill

slamming itself against the sides. Finally, Charles Yates manages to pull himself off the ground and back to his chair. His hands are trembling, and his legs are weak, but he is alive. And more than that, he is prepared.

"Men can keep their money and their power," whispers Yates to himself as a small trickle of black seeps from the corner of his eye. "But I lay claim to the Beautiful Land."

# chapter nine

There are three pancakes left. Samira managed to finish off two plates, while Tak bulldozed through a shocking six and a half all by himself. Minutes ago, the waitress came by to pick up the empties, refill the water, and wipe down the table—doing, Samira thinks, a really half-assed job of it—and now all that remains is a single white plate with three cold flapjacks in a little pile. Samira can't imagine trying to eat them. She can't even imagine expending the effort it would take to lift her fork and drag the plate over.

She and Tak have been eating in silence for the last thirty minutes. Tak's statement that he fucked everything up completely shattered his good mood, and Samira decided to wait it out instead of asking questions. She feels this to be a pretty remarkable display of restraint because when it comes to questions, there are hundreds of them flying around her head.

*What do you mean "they're bringing it here"? Why did you make me eat all these pancakes? What's happening six hours from now? Why am I going to die? Who did you work for? What's in the briefcase? Why do you need me? Is this really happening? And I mean* really, *because it all sounds impossible if you ask me.*

But rather than bother her friend, she waited, and now he

finally seems to be coming out of his minidepression. Smiling at her from across the table—the same dopey grin that made her high-school life bearable—he runs a hand across his face and exhales loudly. "I guess I should finish talking, huh?" he says.

"Guess so," she responds.

"Okay," he begins, leaning back in the booth. "You should understand this about the Axon Corporation—it's pretty small. Just a dozen guys, all of whom are incredibly rich and powerful. They handle the funding, talk to government officials, make bribes, stuff like that. All the science, all the technical stuff, is handled by a dude named Charles Yates. He's a physicist, he's nearly eighty years old, and he's fucking brilliant. He's the one who built the Machine in the first place, and he's the one who realized that time travel isn't a one-way street—that if you could send someone to a random timeline, you could also bring a random timeline here and use it to overwrite our own."

"Is that why you're scared?" asks Samira. "Because you think he's going to overwrite the world in six hours?"

"Yeah. It is. Although now we're down to five." Tak checks his watch and opens his eyes wide. "Shit. Four. I better hurry this up. So in the new timeline, the Axon Corporation functions as a one-world government. They have all the money, all the armies, all of it—and these twelve dudes are in charge."

"Hold on," says Samira, holding a hand to her forehead. "I don't . . . This is so weird, Tak. So this is about to happen? You're saying that four hours from now, everyone's going to wake up, and the US government is going to be gone? That we'll all be slaves for some huge corporation?"

"Basically, yeah."

"I don't get how that would work. I mean, people would revolt. They wouldn't just throw up their hands, and say, 'Oh well, I guess I'm a slave now!'"

Tak shakes his head. "When you overwrite a timeline, you change everything. It's like all the previous stuff never existed. People aren't going to remember they used to live in a different world."

"That might be nice," says Samira. "There's a lot of my life I'd like to forget."

"Yeah, well, that's too bad, because you're going to remember everything."

"Why?"

"Because when Yates turns on the Machine, we're not going to be here. You and I are going to a random timeline until all of this is over."

Samira reaches down to crack her knuckles, then realizes they are covered in gauze. Her head begins to ache. As her breathing quickens, she suddenly locks onto a dirty smudge on the window. Grabbing a napkin and dipping it in water, she reaches over and begins scrubbing with short, quick strokes.

"Uh, Sam?" says Tak slowly. "What are you doing?"

"We can't use the Machine, Tak," she says, ignoring his question. "You said it's in Australia. We can't get there in four hours. And besides . . ."

She trails off, her attention now completely gripped by the window. As Tak watches in silence, she scrubs with mad abandon until the napkin dissolves into a tangled mass of thin wet strands that leave the window dirtier than before. Frustrated, Samira grabs a fork off the table and shoves it underneath her bandage. She rips through the first three layers, then quickly unravels it from her hand until she has a makeshift rag. Carefully turning the bloody sections inside out, she folds the bandage into a square, dips it in the pitcher of water, and attacks the window with renewed fury.

Tak slowly reaches across the table and touches her on the

shoulder. She shrugs his hand away and keeps scrubbing, causing the scabs on her knuckles to burst open and begin leaking red. Upon seeing this, Tak grabs her shoulder again and shakes it.

"Sam. . . . Sam! Sam, stop it!

"No! No, I have to—"

"Sam, knock it off. Stop it! Stop it now!"

He reaches over and yanks the bandage from her hand. She screams and tries to grab it back, but he grips her wrists and refuses to let go. She looks at him, panting, eyes wide, and waits for her breathing to slow. Then she wrestles free and collapses as far back into the bench as she can go, cradling her wounded hand in the folds of her dress. The waitress briefly emerges from the back to see what the commotion is, then decides better about interfering and disappears again.

"Sorry," whispers Samira. "I didn't . . . I didn't mean to . . . I'm sorry. Keep going."

"Sam, what the hell just—"

"I'm fine! . . . Fine. Just keep talking. I'll be okay. You finish your story, then maybe I'll tell you mine."

Tak doesn't seem to care for this arrangement, but, rather than push the point, he leans to his side and taps the top of the briefcase. "This is a portable Machine. Yates invented it. It doesn't work quite the same way—you can only use it to visit timelines you know about, not find new ones—but it'll be good enough. We'll use it to leave the solid timeline, then come back once the change is complete."

"What if I don't want to go?" whispers Samira.

"I know it's scary," he begins, "but I promise, it's gonna be—"

"No!" She screams the word, the loudest sound she's made in months. "No, Tak. Look, I think you're crazy, and I'm not convinced any of this is really going to happen. But if it does? I mean, if you're right, and it does? Then I think that's okay."

"Sam, wait. Wait, you don't—"

"I hate it here," she says. She can feel tears yet again, hot and angry, but rather than being ashamed, she welcomes them. "I hate it. I can't talk to people, I can't sleep, I can't . . . I can't do anything anymore."

Tak's mouth is hanging open—this was clearly not a reaction that he had planned on. *And really,* thinks Samira as she reaches for a napkin to wrap around her bleeding hand, *how could he? How could he know what it's like? He's been messing around with time in Australia while I've watched soldiers shoot families at military checkpoints.*

"I have dreams," she continues. "Every time I go to sleep, which isn't often anymore, I have these terrible dreams. There's one where I'm lying on the ground and a tree starts growing out of my mouth, and it kind of . . . It splits the sides of my mouth open and my face just rips off. I have that one a lot.

"And then there's one where these little kids are chasing me around the streets of some desert town, and I think . . . I mean, when the dream starts, it's like we're playing tag or something, but when they get closer I see the kids are actually made of worms. Just these little worms that are wiggling around, and when they catch me, they hold me down and the worms fall off their faces and crawl into me. They leave these perfect little round holes all over my body."

Samira can't look up. She knows that Tak is staring at her, but she doesn't want to meet his gaze. She hasn't told anyone about the extent of her issues—not Dr. Carrington, not her fellow GIs, not anyone—and now they're flooding out of her in a rush she feels incapable of stopping.

"I can't get clean anymore. I see dirt, and I go crazy. I see a smudge on a window, and it starts to hurt unless I wipe it off. Noises keep me awake. Anything but a constant, steady noise prevents me from even thinking about sleep, then I get tired, then

I get angry, and all the pain comes back all at once. I'm broken, Tak, and it's way, way worse than you know. So if we're going to go to a new timeline where I won't remember my old life, then I'm seriously gonna be okay with that."

Tak leans over for her hand, but this time she refuses to give it. Instead, she sniffles and wipes her nose on her arm. "Sorry"— she chuckles—"that's kinda gross."

"I'm sorry," he says softly. "Sam, I'm so sorry. I had no idea."

"Yeah, I know."

"But listen. You have to come with me."

"Tak, I don't think you—"

"You *have* to."

"Why?"

"Because you're not in the other timeline."

"Because . . ." she begins. "Wait, what do you mean?"

"You're dead," he says in a trembling voice. "All right? In the other timeline? The one that's coming here? You're dead. You got blown up by a roadside bomb, and you've been dead for two years. And when the Machine cycles up, it's gonna over-write whatever isn't supposed to be here, and that means you're gonna die."

"I don't care," Samira says, unsure if she believes the words or not. She folds her legs under her, pops off a shoe, and starts crack-ing her toes with her good hand. Once she finishes a pass, she finally manages to look at her friend, only to find him staring back with sunken, haunted eyes.

"You hate this life, Samira?" says Tak. "So do I. You've done things you wish you could take back? So have I. Working for these men, using the Machine like some kind of fucked-up science project, helping them . . ."

Samira starts to speak, but Tak waves her off. "You want to know the worst part about the Machine? When it finds a random timeline, it creates a kind of door we use to move from one reality to the other. But the doors are inherently unstable, and for the first year or so, we weren't able to keep them open. Every time I came back from a timeline, the door would close, and we could never go back. But then Yates figured out a way to store the doors, to hold them open so we could revisit random timelines whenever we wanted. And you know how he does it? He does it with people, Sam. Fucking *people*. So if you go into that building in Australia, there's this room the size of a football field filled with people. They're all on stretchers, and they're fed through tubes, and they just lie there in a coma so we can use their brains to hold the doorways open. Hundreds of people, Sam. They kidnapped and imprisoned hundreds of people, and I knew about it, and I just . . ."

Tak balls his hand into a fist and raises it over his head, as if he wants to slam it into the table. Instead, he just waves it angrily in the air a couple of times before dropping it to his side in a gesture of surrender. "I kept going," he concludes. "I put it out of my mind, and I kept going."

This is almost too much for Samira to take in, so rather than think about it, she lets her mind go blank as Tak picks up a fork and balances it on a single extended finger. "Why are you here?" she finally manages to say. "Why are you telling me this?"

"I can't stop what's coming," he says, as the fork slips off and clatters to the table, "but I think I can make it right."

"How?"

"There's a woman named Judith Halford who works with Yates. Before this whole thing started, she made a secret copy of the solid timeline—a fail-safe in case something went wrong. If I can find the fail-safe and get it to the Machine, I think I can undo all of this."

Samira lowers her hand, picks up a napkin, and begins to tear it into small pieces. She's never felt more overwhelmed in her life. She doesn't know whether to embrace Tak and tell him every-thing is going to be okay or bolt from her seat and run screaming into the night.

"I need you," he continues. "I need you with me. I've probably caused hundreds of people to die and I don't . . . I can't be respon-sible for you. I just can't. So come with me. *Help* me. Right now, we're two people who've done some terrible things, but this is our chance to make it right."

She lets his words hang, then slowly stands and walks out of the diner without a sound. The cold night air hits her in a rush, but she doesn't mind. Pulling her dress tightly around her, she walks past rows of idled semitrucks until she reaches the edge of the highway. Across the road, tall pine trees with snow on their branches sway in the breeze. She listens for the sound of an ap-proaching car, that satisfying, predictable roar, but finds only the random chatter of a cold Nebraska night.

A few minutes later, she hears Tak crunch his way through the snow and take up a position a few steps to her left. "Two years ago, I found a timeline where snow is different colors," he says quietly. "Over there, you can see different spectrums of light, and the snow absorbed it somehow: blue and green and red all spar-kling in the air. The people live in these little huts, and every time it snows, the kids gather it up in glass jars and shake them until the snow starts glowing. Then they run around in big dumb cir-cles, giggling and holding up the jars to create these miniature firework shows. . . . It's the most wonderful thing I've ever seen."

He places a tentative hand on Samira's shoulder. "We can do a good thing here. We can make amends. And when we're done, I'll take you to that timeline, and you can see that brilliant snow and watch those kids, and I swear you'll never have a terrible dream again."

She kicks at a small tuft of white snow and sends it flying into the wind. Her mind is a blur of dreams and guilt and terrible thoughts, but incredibly, there is also a small flicker of hope. She'd almost forgotten what such a thing felt like.

"I still don't believe you," she says quietly.

"That's okay," responds Tak. "You will."

# chapter ten

They drive for nearly an hour; Tak bearing down on the wheel like a man possessed, Samira staring out the window at an empty Nebraska sky. The entire adventure seems unreal, and Samira finds herself wrestling with the notion that the past few hours have been nothing more than a PTSD fever dream. *What if I'm not really here? What if I'm actually in a VA hospital pumped so full of thorazine that I'm imagining my childhood friend is some kind of time-hopping policeman? . . . God, if that's the case, I hope they just let me sleep it off.*

Tak, however, harbors no such illusions. Samira's decision to accompany him has filled him with a clear sense of relief, but she can still feel stress and tension flowing off him in waves. Every few minutes, he reaches under the seat and feels around until his hand lands on the slim, metal briefcase, as if reassuring himself that it hasn't sprouted legs and run away. Each time a car appears on the highway, he tightens his grip on the wheel and stares at the rearview mirror until some unseen sign convinces him that they are not being pursued. Occasional beads of sweat pop up on his forehead and slowly dry into salty crystals, and whenever he reaches up to wipe them off, he runs his hand through his hair for good measure. After the first sixty miles, it's sticking so high up that it scrapes the roof of the pickup.

Eventually, Samira rolls down the window and puts her head out into the cold night air. Nearly twenty hours from its last washing, her hair is beginning to curl into small, tight ringlets that bounce up and down against her back as the truck rockets along. Her father used to tell her that she had her mother's hair; when she was a small girl, he would often sit on the sofa and brush it while she sat cross-legged in front of him and watched documentaries about African wildlife. He couldn't get enough of such shows—he purchased them in bulk from the local public television station—and by the time Samira was in high school, she felt like a zoologist in her own right. As her father brushed, he would nod at the narration, occasionally interrupting his work to say "Did you know a lion could do that, Samira?" or "The world is fantastic, is it not?"

She finds herself tearing up at the thought of her father and quickly pulls her head inside and rolls up the window. If Tak notices her tears, he says nothing, and they spend another hour driving in silence. She doesn't know where they are going, and actually doesn't feel the need to ask; the more she learns, the more likely she is to decide that this whole plan is madness, and that means returning to her previous life. Even if Tak's new reality is a total sham, she wants to hold on to it for as long as possible.

Finally, as if directed by an unseen force, Tak pulls onto a small strip of dirt pointing away from the highway. He follows the trail, the truck bouncing and juking over ruts in the road, until he arrives at a large, metal gate. Without a word, he shuts off the engine, grabs the case, and slips out the door, forcing Samira to bolt from the truck in order to catch up.

The two of them clamber over the gate and toward the west, skirting around the edge of a small, unlit farmhouse. Behind them, the sun is just beginning to rise, casting a thin pale glow on the surrounding nature. After a couple of minutes of walking, they suddenly stumble into a huge field filled with waving stalks of corn.

"This works," mutters Tak. "Yeah, this'll do nicely."

He drops to one knee and sets the briefcase in front of him. Flipping the catches on either side, he grasps the top with both hands and lifts it open. Samira kneels beside him and stares inside with breathless anticipation. She's been forming ideas of what is inside ever since he described its purpose, and her imagination has been demanding lights and wires and indescribable technology, both alien and frightening. But once the lid is pulled back and locked into place, all she can see is a round glass panel, two lights, and a few knobs. A dim green glow emanates from the panel and shines weakly off the nearby snow.

"That's it?" she asks with dismay.

"That's it," responds Tak.

"This looks like a community theatre prop."

"It'll look better once it powers up."

"I knew this wasn't real," she says with disappointment in her voice. "Why would you do this to me?"

"It's gonna work, Sam. I don't know *how* it works, but it does."

"How can you not know?"

"Because I didn't build it, I stole it. What time is it?"

She glances down at her watch. "Ten to seven."

"Okay, good." He reaches into his pocket, removes a small black notebook, and begins to thumb through it as he talks. "So here's the deal. They're going to turn on the Machine, the *real* Machine, at ten seventeen Australian time. That's seven seventeen here, so that means we have about half an hour before we have to make the jump."

"Do we have to cut it that close?"

"Yeah, because this portable guy here doesn't let us control how long we stay in the other timeline. It could be a day or a couple of minutes. And if we go too early and get pulled back, we'll be here when they activate the real Machine and then . . . Well, you're screwed. So we have to wait."

Samira nods, then leans over and stares at the entries in the notebook. Tak glances at her for a moment, then holds it open so she can see. The page before her reads:

1 2 1 4 5 3 — Wasteland
1 3 7 7 7 1 — Portland? Where is this?
2 3 1 3 2 2 — Wasteland
4 2 1 6 4 8 — ~~Holy shit, dude!~~ Conduit dead.
1 3 2 1 3 8 — I think this was nuked.
3 1 5 7 6 9 — Mario Land! Yay!

"These are my notes," he says by way of explanation. "Each number here corresponds to a dial in the portable Machine. So if I set it to 1, 2, 1, 4, 5, 3, then we'll end up in that red sand waste-land I told you about."

"What does 'conduit dead' mean?" asks Samira, as Tak flips another page.

"That's, uh . . . That means that the doorway to that timeline isn't open anymore."

"Why not?"

Tak starts to answer, then turns away. "It's the people I told you about," he says after a moment. "The ones in the basement who hold the timelines open. Sometimes they die, and then I can't go back to that world anymore."

"You call them conduits?"

"Yeah, well, saying that Mary Joe Ellen died is just too damn depressing. Look, can we not talk about that right now? I need to find a safe timeline for us to visit."

"Okay," says Samira. She rocks back on her heels and twists one ring of hair around her finger. "Hey, Tak?"

"Yeah," he says, distracted.

"What's it going to be like? Time travel, I mean?"

"It's not great," he says without looking up. "You're gonna see old memories, but they'll be all mixed up and weird. You'll probably see some of my memories too, because when you go through the Machine with other people, it tends to smoosh 'em all together."

"Is it going to hurt?"

"No, but you're gonna be sick as a dog when we come out the other side because you didn't eat enough pancakes. So just be ready for that."

Samira giggles slightly at this. "I think I would have puked if I ate any more."

"Yeah, well, you're gonna totally paint the walls when we . . ."

Tak trails off. Samira starts to say something, but he holds up one hand to silence her. As she watches, he tilts his head to the side and closes his eyes, seeming for all the world to be listening intently to nothing.

"Oh, fuck," he says suddenly.

"What?" asks Samira. She is about to ask again when Tak's eyes fly open. One look at them tells her all she needs to know—he is absolutely terrified.

"What time is it!?" he asks.

"Uh, it's . . . It's seven."

"Oh, *fuck*! Fuck, fuck, fuck me running! They're early!"

"What?"

"They turned it on early! Goddammit, we have go, we have to go *now*!"

She is about to ask him how he knows, how he can possibly know what people are doing thousands of miles away, when the air suddenly grows cold and thick. The sky above her, which had been glowing faintly orange just a moment before, begins to darken.

"Tak, what's happening?" asks Samira, as her stomach clenches into a knot. "What's going—"

"Put your hands on the plate!" he barks, flipping through the book with renewed speed.

"What plate? Tak, I don't—"

"The plate!" he screams. "The glass thing in the center of the briefcase! Put your fingers on it!"

She does so instantly. Fear, that old, unwelcome friend, climbs from her gut to her head and makes a home there. She feels the way she used to feel before leaving on a patrol, a combination of nervousness, nausea, and shame.

"Okay, here!" Tak cries. He stuffs the notebook back into his coat and begins twisting the dials. As he does, the green light from the plate begins to brighten, becoming more brilliant with each click. By the time he's turning the sixth and final knob, Samira's fear has abated to a dull throb deep in her chest. There's something hypnotic about the green light, something calm and peaceful and totally wonderful.

But as the final knob clicks, the green light begins to wane. The area around them gets darker, like all the light is being sucked from the world. After a moment, she realizes there's something terribly wrong with the sky. And as Tak puts his hands over hers, and a deep musical tone bursts forth from the briefcase, she lifts her eyes and sees a large purple hole in the sky. It begins to slowly spread across the heavens like a tumor, wiping out the orange of the sunrise and replacing it with a sickening dark color. Lightning crackles from somewhere within the hole, then other sights follow: an explosion of light like she has never seen and colors that she has no names for because they shouldn't exist. But these things are there only for a moment; seconds later, a hellish dark mass belches out of the hole and fully consumes the heavens, leaving the small green glow from the glass panel as the only light in the world.

The wind begins to bellow with fury, kicking up a blizzard of snow around Samira. "Tak!" she screams. "Tak, what's happening?!"

"It's the Machine!" he screams back. "It's overwriting the solid timeline!"

She can barely see Tak anymore, so black is the sky. He's become little more than a dark silhouette with spiky hair. Suddenly, she regrets ever doubting her friend. *It's true. Everything he said. Oh my God, it's all true.*

The moment she thinks this, Samira hears a noise from the depths of the briefcase. Seconds later, she feels her hands getting heavy, then her arms, then her chest. Within moments, it's as if someone has wrapped her in a massive lead curtain, crushing her with equal force on every inch of her body. She tries to lift her head and fails, then manages with great effort to lift her eyes. She can see Tak now because he is glowing with streaks of white and blue, almost like she's watching him on a television with bad reception.

She glances down and sees her hands stretch across the bottom of the case, fingers growing impossibly long and thin until they begin to disappear. The noise is terribly loud, drowning out even the howl of the wind, and she feels it reach into her head and push her eyes against their sockets. Her arms begin to stretch, growing thinner and thinner until they, too, begin to vanish from sight. The darkness and noise sear themselves on her brain until all Samira can do is close her eyes, grit her teeth, and, inside her mind, scream the loudest scream of her life.

*Oh God,* she thinks, as green light leaks out of the case and swirls around her vanishing frame. *Oh God, oh God. This is what it's like to die. I've done this to people. I've sent them to this place. Please, please, let this work. Please help me make it right.*

Seconds later, as the world dissolves around them, Tak and Samira wink out into nothing.

# chapter eleven

The first sign that something is happening is the small black dot that appears in front of the sun. It's impossible to gauge the distance of the object; sometimes it seems to be hanging in the atmosphere, but then it will suddenly shift and move away. It looks like a kind of shadow that's projected on the sky as opposed to being part of it. Most people stare at it with their mouths open and wonder what exactly is going on, but, far to the south, a woman with long red hair stands on a roof and begins to wonder what in God's name she has done.

The dot hangs in space for nearly a minute, pulsing around the edges like the cilia of an amoeba. Word of the event spreads, and soon people all across the world are leaving their desks, abandoning their cars, and staring up at the sky in wonder. Neighbors who haven't spoken more than a few words to each other in years clasp trembling hands across property lines. Soldiers drop their rifles and stand side by side with sworn enemies, gazing into a once-predictable sky that they had long since taken for granted. Presidents, CEOs, schoolteachers, homeless veterans, baseball players, cattle-dung sellers, train conductors, prostitutes, and thieves—billions of people of every race, creed, and status all stand in place and stare at the same black dot in the sky. It's a moment of global unity unknown in human history; and for a few fleeting seconds, it is a beautiful thing.

But then, deep in the heart of a barren Australian desert, the Machine cycles up to half power. There is a terrible sound from the depths of the device. An alarm begins to wail. And suddenly everything goes to hell.

Across the world, people hear the terrible sound: a deep-throated bass roar that blasts out windows from New York to Nanking. The noise seems to be coming directly from the dark spot in the sky, as if it were alive and calling to them. Religious people take it as a sign of the end times—the judgment trumpet for which they have been waiting their whole lives—and suddenly find that they are not so sure of their salvation as they had been moments before. The harmony of billions of people staring into the same sky quickly dissolves into a shared panic. People flee into houses and pull the shades; they run into office buildings and huddle under stairways; they mount horses and camels and motorcycles and mopeds and ride as if they can somehow outrun the very universe itself. The sound rings out forever: a clarion call, a warning, a triumphant scream. On and on it goes, until it seems that the noise will tear the entire world apart.

But then, as quickly as it began, the sound stops. Sirens wail out across the civilized world and slowly die as power grids began to fail. The spot begins to eat its way across the sky, bringing with it an unnatural silence that is somehow worse than the noise of a few minutes before.

Time slows. People feel themselves getting heavy. Those who were trying to flee find that they can no longer move, while those who wanted only to sob in the arms of a companion discover their tears are too weighty to fall. Across the planet, the people of the human race can only stand in place, lift their eyes, and beg for whatever is happening to be over quickly.

The dot becomes a yawning purple hole that leaks out of the sky and into the streets, crawling down buildings like a thick syrup, enveloping everything and everyone in its path. *This is the way the world ends,* thinks the planet with a collective moan of terror. *Not with a bang or a whimper. It ends in blackness.*

The Machine cycles to full power.

There is a brilliant white flash, then nothing. The darkness shrinks down to a pinprick and vanishes, leaving a cheery yellow sun to shine on the daylight half of the earth once again. Across the world, electrical grids flicker back to life. People slowly disentangle themselves from each other and wonder why they are crying. And the memory of the past few minutes fades away and is lost. Mere seconds later, people are going back into their offices, picking up their phones, and resuming their business deals. Teachers go back to instructing their classes. Airline pilots return their attention to the controls. Ministers and priests and imams and rabbis once more begin to wait for a sign from their respective gods. It is as if the entire event, the most remarkable event in all of human history, never happened at all. But while most people simply forget everything and move on, there are a few exceptions. There always are.


**in green bay,** Wisconsin, a policeman named Martin Jarock stares at the traffic whistle in his hand and wonders where the hell it came from. He's standing in the middle of an intersection with cars honking at him in every direction, and yet he can't quite figure out how to put the device in his mouth. *I can't direct traffic,* he thinks to himself. *I sell kitchen equipment. I'm not supposed to be here.*

. . .

in british columbia, a boy named Peter MacDonald stares up at his father, who is in the process of purchasing a pair of movie tickets for their spontaneous day off, and finds himself afraid to take his hand. *You're dead, Daddy,* Peter thinks. *You got hit by a car and you died and Mommy married another man. You're not supposed to be here.*

in new york .City, a young woman named Sara Lin watches her three sons run in excited circles on the playground. She is wearing a ragged blue dress with patched holes, and her shoes have a hand-me-down look. *I was an artist,* she thinks to herself. *I designed characters for video games. These kids are not supposed to be here.*

in hong kong, a man named Hsu claws furiously at the lid of a coffin. *I'm not dead!* he screams. *The Machine was going to make me a king! It was going to make us all kings! Oh God, get me out! I'm not supposed to be here!*

and on the roof of a large white building in the Australian Outback, a woman named Judith Halford stands perfectly still and watches a large purple hole pulse in the sky. As she stares, a pale creature with shaggy black feathers slowly emerges from it, shudders once, then flies away over the horizon.

*I have to get the fail-safe,* she thinks wildly. *I have to leave this place and track down Tak and activate it somehow.*

*. . . Because that thing is not supposed to be here.*

bird

# chapter twelve

A young woman with curly black hair crouches under a window in a darkened room. She's wearing a tan camouflage uniform and a dull, metal helmet, and has an assault rifle gripped firmly in one hand. The gun looks ludicrously out of place against her small frame; it doesn't take an expert to see that she's not very comfortable with it.

*That's Samira,* thinks Tak. *This is her memory.*

Next to her is a young man, maybe twenty, smoking a cigarette. His helmet is lying on the ground, revealing a lumpy head shaved military-close. He is also wearing a uniform, but it's not quite the same—the patches are different, the colors slightly more muted. The two of them speak in low tones, and while Tak can't hear what they're saying, he sees Samira smiling in a way he remembers well. She's clearly into this guy, and Tak is surprised to find that this realization makes him jealous.

Other senses start to filter in now: the dull hum of a generator from somewhere outside, the mingled smells of stale water and human shit. He glances around and is surprised to see soldiers everywhere. A few are crouched against the walls like Samira, on edge and jumpy, while others lie down with rags stretched over

Elting Memorial Library
93 Main Street
New Paltz, New York 12561-1503

their eyes, trying to steal a few minutes of sleep. One group in the corner huddles around the light of a dying flashlight and plays cards. A barrel-chested man with a Southern accent wanders slowly from soldier to soldier, sometimes putting a hand on a shoulder, occasionally saying a few words. At one point he reaches into his pocket and hands a man a cigarette.

*That's the leader. The sergeant or lieutenant or whatever the hell he is. They like him a lot. I bet they're used to dying for him.*

The memory shimmers for a second, wobbling in and out of existence. Tak thinks it's going to go away entirely, but then the reality of the thing reasserts itself, and he's back in the darkened room. Under the window, Samira laughs quietly, a beautiful sound in the night. It's hot here, almost unbearably so, but she seems perfectly comfortable. The man next to her is telling a story with a grin on his face, occasionally moving his hands back and forth in the air like he's pulling taffy. Tak sees how Samira is enjoying his tale and feels another pang of jealousy, this one stronger than before.

*Hey, man, tough titty. You had your chance. You coulda stayed with her. But you went to Japan to be a TV star, then vanished off the grid. Got no one to blame but yourself.*

The male soldier leans in close, and for a second Tak thinks he's going to kiss her. But he just cups his hand around her ear and whispers something that causes Samira to collapse in a fit of giggles. She tries to get herself under control, but one laugh sneaks out as a braying bark, incredibly loud in the tension of the desert night. A few soldiers look over at the sound, then shake their heads and return to whatever they were doing. Tak can see that they don't think very highly of Samira, and at first he assumes it's a gender thing. But then he thinks about her long hair and her different uniform and realizes that it's more complicated than that. These people are Marines, all part of the same unit. She's not. She's something else. It's not that they don't like her; they just haven't learned to trust her.

The young man next to Samira leans against the window with his head poking over the bottom of the frame. She notices this and makes a small motion with her hand, but before she can say more than a couple of words, a loud bang rings out, and the top of the soldier's head is torn off. It happens so fast, Tak assumes at first that the memory is skipping around. One moment Samira is young and beautiful and giggling at a bad joke, and the next she's covered in a thick red syrup.

The other soldiers leap up and grab their weapons, moving toward the window as one. Noise and confusion ring out on all sides: men screaming at one another, the metallic click of magazines being slammed home into rifles, someone behind him yelling into a radio. The dead man slumps back against the wall with his mouth open, as if he can't quite believe what just happened to him. Samira doesn't move; she just crouches in place with a blank expression on her face until one of the Marines shoves her roughly to the side.

The leader presses his back against the wall and yells a command. At his voice, the soldiers, almost twenty in all, pop over the sill of the window and begin firing into the darkness. The sound is deafening in that small space, and combined with the rapid blast of muzzle flashes, Tak finds himself growing disoriented. His only thought is to locate Samira, but all he can see are brilliant pops of white and yellow light. He stumbles forward with the sounds of gunfire and screaming overwhelming his ears, but then the memory warbles once more and finally collapses in on itself.

a teenage boy is lying on a battered couch in a wood-paneled basement; leaning her head against his stomach is a girl of the same age. The boy has dark black hair and almond-shaped eyes, and sports a tiny soul patch at the bottom of his chin. The girl is chattering on about something, but there's no sound to be heard. One of the boy's hands dangles off the side of the couch, but the other is held in midair, as if trying to figure out where to go.

*That's me,* thinks Samira suddenly. *What the hell? That's me and Tak. This is my house. . . . Am I time traveling?*

She knows what her basement is supposed to look like, but it's not quite complete. The television should be across from the couch, but instead there's just a dull white blur. The desk where her father kept his PC should be in the corner, but all she sees is a kind of fuzzy light. The only things that are clear are the couch, its occupants, and a series of photographs hung on the wall behind them. Photographs of her mother.

*This is a memory. But it's not . . . It's not mine. It's Tak's. I think that's why things are missing. It's because he's not focused on them right now.*

Sound begins to return to her ears, and Samira can suddenly hear herself talking. At first the words are stretched and distorted, running far slower than her lips are moving. But then there's another little hitch, and time catches up with itself.

". . . was high!" she hears herself say. "He was totally high, and he was just standing there, like, waving his arms around and staring at them. So of course, Hilary thought that was the funniest thing *ever*, and she starts laughing, and then *I* start laughing, and you know how when I laugh I just can't stop? So we're both sitting there laughing, then Kelly is like, 'Dudes, this is not cool!' But it was just, like, holy crap."

*Did I used to talk like that? Really? I had no idea.*

"Ohmigosh, Tak, I totally wish you were there. Things just aren't the same when you're not around. Promise me you'll come next time, okay? Swear it on your dad's immortal Irish soul or something."

Tak makes a noise of assent at this, but nothing more. Samira can see that he's nervous as hell, but can't possibly imagine why. She doesn't even remember this day—it was just one of a thousand different evenings spent in her basement with the two of them talking about nothing. He takes his free hand and slowly moves it to the space just above her mane of curly hair, then withdraws it again. The expression on his face is one of complete disgust at his own cowardice.

*Oh my God. I think he's trying to work up the nerve to touch me.*

The Samira on the couch is totally unaware of the hormonal drama playing out behind her; she continues chattering away about her friend Hilary and the day they spent at the lake and whatever other nonsense pops into her mind. Occasionally, her head shifts against Tak's stomach, and he tenses, once even producing a sharp intake of breath. But, of course, she notices none of this.

There's a sudden noise nearby, a familiar creaking of old wooden stairs. Samira bolts upright and grabs the channel changer, while Tak pulls his hands back into his body as if they were on springs. The white blur where the television should be suddenly becomes an actual television as the power is turned on, and Tak focuses all of his concentration on it.

*Dad. Oh God, Dad. It's you.*

Ahmed Moheb finishes his descent and peers into the room. There is a cup of hot tea in his hand and an unlit cigarette perched between his first and second finger. He glances from his daughter to her friend and back again, saying nothing for the longest time.

"Hey, Dad," says Samira cheerfully. "How was work?"

Ahmed continues to stare at Tak, who responds by curling his lips inside his mouth and waving the tips of his fingers. "Hello, Takahiro," says Ahmed finally. "I did not know you were here."

"Hi, Mr. Moheb!" says Tak quickly. A small bead of sweat pops out from his forehead and shimmers in the television's glow. "Uh, it's . . . It's good to see you. Again. How's the ice-cream business?"

Ahmed makes a face like he smells something sour, a move that causes Tak to shrink even farther back into the couch. "My business is fine, thank you," he says after another lengthy pause. "Are you planning to stay here long, Takahiro?"

"No! I mean, um, well, not, you know . . . I can leave whenever."

"Dad!" yells Samira from the corner of the couch. "Don't be a jerk. And call him Tak. No one calls him Tak-a-hi-ro." She puts air quotes around this word and emphasizes every syllable, creating a hilarious imitation of her father's precise English pronunciation.

"Mmm," says Ahmed by way of response. "Yes, well. I think I will go upstairs and finish my tea."

"Bye, Dad!"

"Good night, Samira. . . . Good-bye, Takahiro."

"Good-bye, Mr. Moheb! It was great to . . . um . . . talk to you?"

Ahmed turns and ascends the stairs again, one slow step at a time. Tak and Samira sit in silence and listen to his footsteps as he crosses the kitchen floor and opens the sliding glass door to the deck. Once they hear him step outside, Tak exhales and slides off the couch, creating a little puddle of himself on the floor.

"You're an idiot." Samira giggles.

"Jesus, your dad scares the fuck out of me. I'm waiting for the day he brains me with a shovel and buries me in the backyard."

"He likes you."

"No, he doesn't. He wants to kill me. He's convinced I'm trying to get into your pants."

"Yeah, well, aren't you?" asks Samira with a sly smile.

She can see Tak working up the nerve to say something further, trying to decide between a witty response and just opening his heart and letting everything pour out, but then the memory warbles with renewed strength. The couch, the people, the pictures on the wall, everything dissolves into a blurry mash of images and sounds, piling one on top of the other until they become a thick white soup of nothing.

*i can't believe* *I said that to him.*

*Neither can I.*

*. . . Tak?*

*Hey, Sam.*

*Where are we?*

*We're in the Machine.*

*What's going on? Why can I see your memories?*

*It's time travel. That's just how it works. Usually, you only see your own memories, but since we used the Machine at the same time, everything is mashing together.*

*How long will this last?*

*Depends. New memories kinda come and go, so it could be any*

*samira lies in* bed and sobs. She hasn't slept for days. The fan in the air conditioner has a slight imperfection, and each time it spins, it scrapes against the side of the housing and makes a small, squeaking sound. But the imperfection is such that the squeak is never the same—sometimes it comes twice in a second, sometimes it waits for a minute or more. She can't sleep with that noise. It isn't regular enough. It isn't consistent. It reminds her of terrible things, and so she lies in her bed and sobs until her throat is raw.

tak grabs a ledge in front of him and heaves himself onto the bank of the river. His body is shaking and blue from cold. Below him, a torrential stream of water flows away and toward the horizon. He lies on his back, shivering uncontrollably, then flips over and begins crawling toward a nearby grove of trees. Upon reaching them, he grabs a patch of thick green moss and turns to face the waterproof video camera he holds in his left hand. "Old M-Man's B-B-Beard," he says through chattering teeth. "B-best firestarter there is."

a man in a New England Patriots T-shirt and dirty grey slacks runs toward the gate, shoving his way through a long line of young men waiting to apply for the new police force. *"Allahu akbar!"* screams the man. *"Allahu akbar!"* A soldier raises his rifle and fires off three rounds, striking the man in the middle of the forehead. As he falls, he releases a button that was held in his left hand. The world explodes. The man's head goes spiraling off in the air as a massive orange cloud transforms the line of stunned applicants into a dirty red mist.

tak stares at a massive set of blueprints mounted on a wall and tries to wrap his mind around what he's seeing. To his right, a woman with long red hair absentmindedly clicks a ballpoint pen. "What is this thing again?" he asks.

"It's a dark-matter accelerator," replies the woman. "With

enough power, we can use it to create a stable Einstein-Rosen bridge."

"Am I supposed to know what any of that means?" asks Tak as he walks up to the blueprints and crinkles his forehead. "Because I don't."

"You don't need to understand how it works. You just need to use it."

tak holds samira's face in his hands and kisses her. Her eyes fly open in surprise, but as the kiss continues, they slowly close. She grabs a tuft of his spiky hair and digs her fingers into it. Her other hand flutters slightly in the air, then finds one of his and entangles itself with it. When they part, she finds her whole body is shaking.

"My dad's gonna kill you," she manages to say.

"Banzai," says Tak.

samira opens her eyes. She is lying on her back on a patch of tall brown grass. Above her, the twisted branches of dead trees interlock in random patterns, preventing all but the smallest rays of sunlight from filtering through. She blinks once. Twice. A third time. Her stomach is a knot, and her head is spinning. Turning to the side, she sees a familiar face staring at her.

"Did we make it?" she asks quietly. "Are we out of the Machine?"

"Yeah," says Tak. "We made it."

"Banzai."

# chapter thirteen

Samira's good cheer at surviving her first time-travel experience lasts right up until the moment she becomes violently ill. She's been sick before—a couple of particularly nasty bouts of flu, a run-in with some parasite-filled water in the big desert—but nothing like this. The contents of her stomach are already long gone, so she's moved on to the occasional dry heave punctuated by fits of wracking coughs. Her sense of balance is so tripped out it might as well not exist at all. Each time she opens her eyes, the world spins, but each time she closes them, flashing white lights appear and dance around her mind. There's even a high-pitched squealing in her ears that sounds like someone's scraping their front teeth across a blackboard.

*At least I didn't piss myself,* she thinks as she lies on the ground in a little ball and waits for death. *I suppose that's something.*

Tak sits next to her with a hand on her back, rubbing it around and around in a small circle. Occasionally, he holds her hair out of the way so she can do her business, but otherwise the hand never leaves her. She's comforted by its weight; right now, it's the only thing grounding her in the world.

As to the identity of that world, she doesn't have a clue. Before the sickness came, she was able to see a grove of dead trees and some spindly wisps of brown grass. She can tell that Tak is concerned by where they ended up even though he's trying not to show it, and that worries her. She pulls her hands tighter against the knot in her stomach and makes a mental note to ask him once she can speak again.

Time passes in a blur. Eventually, her limbs begin to regain their normal gravity although the tips of her fingers still feel as if they're holding heavy lead weights. The spinning slows to a more manageable rocking sensation, and her stomach finally agrees to stop expelling things that haven't been there for quite some time. Slowly, very slowly, she uncurls herself and rolls onto her back in a half-fetal position. She feels Tak reach for her foot and try to pull it away from her body, but she resists.

"Wait, wait," she says. "Oh my God, don't. Don't touch me."

"You need to stretch," he says, continuing to pull the leg. "Trust me. Stretch your limbs as far as you can. Otherwise, they're going to feel heavy and weird."

"They already do."

"Okay, then this'll help."

He pulls her legs out, then takes her hands and does the same with her arms, raising them above her head and slowly tugging on the fingers. It feels good, and not just because the heavy sensation is beginning to dissipate; she's simply happy to have him touch her.

"I told you to eat more pancakes," he says. Samira is still staring up at the trees, but she doesn't need to see her friend's face to know that he's grinning.

"It isn't funny."

"Trust me, I know. The first few times I did this, I was sick as a dog. Way worse than you, actually."

"That's comforting."

"Here, come on. Try to sit up."

He pulls her arms again, and Samira manages to transfer her weight from her back to her ass. The world gives a final spin once she's upright, but then her balance returns for good. She coughs, an action that causes fire to leap up in her throat. "Water," she says. "Do we have any water?"

"No, but we'll find some. Come on, get up. We need to move."

Tak helps Samira to her feet, holding out an arm for support. She accepts it, wobbles for a second, then manages to stand on her own. Glancing around with new eyes, she sees that they're in what looks to be a city park, albeit one in need of major mainte-nance. In addition to the dead trees and dry grass, she can see a few fire-ravaged bushes dotting the ground. To her left, an old water fountain is covered in rust. Beyond that, a child's playset rests against the cold grey sky, swings gently wobbling in the breeze. The park isn't large—maybe the size of a city block—and past the swings she can see a sidewalk and the outline of rooftops.

"Where are we?" asks Samira.

Tak shuffles his feet and looks around. He looks almost guilty. "Um . . . I don't really know."

"What do you mean?"

"Well, we're supposed to be in this place I call Mario Land, but . . . we're not."

"Mario Land?"

"You remember that old video game Super Mario Brothers? It kind of looks like that. There's this really bright blue sky and these perfectly shaped white clouds, and I thought it would be a good place to lie low. But, um . . . yeah. This isn't it. I don't know where this is." He glances down at the briefcase and rubs it with a finger. "I don't know if I set this wrong, or if using it while the solid timeline was being overwritten screwed it up or what. But we're in the wrong place."

Samira nods. Surprisingly, this doesn't bother her as much as she expected it to. Their current location is a dead world—or at least one on life support—but it's quiet and clean enough that she's not feeling the usual pangs of anxiety in her chest. "Should we . . . I don't know? What happens now? Do we wait here or what?"

"We need to get inside," says Tak. "I don't like being exposed like this. We'll head for those houses over there and see if anyone's home."

"What if they are?"

"Then we run."

"Seriously?"

"Oh, yeah. Ninety percent of time travel is running like hell. . . . I probably should have mentioned that."

He moves toward the roofs in the distance, and Samira follows. When she passes the playset, she sees that the slide is covered in a flaky red crust. Her first thought is that it's rust, but as she looks closer, she begins to think it's actually dried blood. She holds this idea for far longer than she would like before realizing that Tak is almost a block ahead, forcing her to abandon the unpleasant thought and scramble to catch up.

The two of them walk in silence down a cracked street with large houses lining either side. This was clearly a high-end neighborhood once, but now it's little more than a graveyard. Tall grass, the same brown color as that of the park, grows with abandon. Windows are shattered and missing. Open doors sag sadly on rusted hinges. Occasionally, they pass a house with boards nailed over the door in random, chaotic patterns. At one point, Samira glances down and sees a brown teddy bear with a single button eye. She finds this creepier than anything she's seen so far and quickly reaches out for Tak's hand. He takes it with a reassuring squeeze, but she can tell that he's equally unnerved.

At the end of the first block, they encounter a burned-out shell of what must have once been a very impressive home. Charred timbers, long since cold, poke out of the ground like weary sentinels. A large wooden sign has been staked into the ground on the side of the torched house, and on this someone has spray painted three words:

## THEY ARE COMING

"Yikes," says Tak. "That ain't good."

Overhead, the sky has turned a foreboding grey. Soon a flash of lightning lights up the sky, followed seconds later by a loud peal of thunder. Tak glances up, tightening his grip on Samira's hand. "Come on," he says. "We need to pick a house."

"I'm sorry, what?" she says, her eyes opening wide. "Tak, I'm not going in any of these houses."

"Sam, we don't know what happens when it rains here. It could be acid rain, the water could be infected, anything. Plus, if we get wet, we have to worry about hypothermia. We need to get inside."

"You've got to be kidding me," she mutters.

"Look, some of these are definitely abandoned, so we can take one of those if you want. But I think something that's boarded up is probably a better bet. I mean, at least it's been sealed from the elements. There could be people inside, but I'm guessing they're probably . . ."

"Dead," finishes Samira. "This whole place is dead. I've seen towns like this in the war. I mean, not exactly like this, but I've felt this kind of stillness. The people here either left, or they're dead."

Tak nods, glances around, and points at a faded blue house a little way down the block. The windows and front door have been boarded over, and unlike many of its neighbors, it appears to be structurally sound. As they hurry toward it, Samira finds herself looking from window to window, waiting for someone to pop out and start firing. The calmness she felt about the place at first glance fades, and she feels a familiar tightness start to well up in her chest.

The blue house is a single-story number, standing in sharp contrast to the massive structures on either side of it. A few ragged pickets of what was once a fence lean drunkenly in front of the driveway. Tak and Samira move past those and up onto the porch, where Tak begins examining the boards nailed over the door. As he does, Samira moves around the side of the house. Most of the windows have been sealed up, but by tromping through a back-yard garden, she finds a small basement window that the owners neglected to cover. As she's inspecting the glass, she hears foot-steps approach. Panic rears its head again before she realizes that it's Tak.

"I dunno," he says, approaching her. "I don't think I can get the boards off without a hammer or dynamite or . . . Oh, hey, look at that. A window."

"Yeah," says Samira. "Look at that."

"Shit, that's tiny," says Tak as he bends down and sticks his face inside the opening. "I don't think I can fit in there, and I'm a skinny-ass Japanese dude."

"I can."

"Yeah, but . . . Come on, Sam. I don't wanna send you into the creepy haunted house all alone."

"It's okay," she says, leaving out the part about her jackham-mering heart. "Really. I'll be fine."

He makes a face at this but eventually shrugs his shoulders and holds out his hands toward the window like a showroom model.

She hesitates for a moment, but not because she's scared of what might be waiting for her inside the house—she hesitates because there is a long, dusty cobweb hanging across the window.

"Hey, listen," begins Tak. "This is dumb. I'll just find a—"

"No," says Samira, shaking her head hard enough to make her curls bounce. "No, I got this." She gets down on her belly, forcing away her disgust at the damp and dirty ground, and peers inside the home. Her nose warns of stale water and mold, but the darkness is complete enough to prevent even a cursory look. She tilts her head and listens for minute or two but hears only the sound of raindrops falling behind her.

Finally, she clamps her mouth and eyes shut and wriggles through the opening. She twists to avoid the cobweb, but feels something brush across her face at the last moment. As Samira clears the window and drops to the concrete floor below, her fingers begin to itch. She starts to brush her hands through her hair, moving them faster and faster until friction makes them burn. She's sure that there are cobwebs in her hair—cobwebs and dirt and all manner of unclean things—so she tilts her head down and begins rubbing furiously, trying to shake out the army of phantom particles that have no doubt taken up residence. She can feel her breath begin to quicken as she tugs at her hair with renewed fury.

"Hey!" says Tak, peering through the window frame. "You okay? What are you doing?"

Samira freezes in place, then slowly stands and drops her arms to her sides. It takes all of her willpower not to start shaking out her hair again. "What do you mean?"

"It sounds like you're . . . I don't know. Scratching yourself."

"I'm . . . Yeah, don't worry. I'm fine. Do you have a flashlight or something? I can't see a thing."

To Samira's extreme relief, Tak says nothing more about her unusual behavior. Instead, he reaches into his pocket and produces a long, thin piece of metal. There's a hole at the top through which a string is threaded, and a hard stone tied to the other end. "Here," he says. "It's my flint. It won't hold a flame, but you can at least make sparks with it."

She takes the proffered tool without another word and scrapes the rock across the steel. As she does so, bright white sparks leap up, briefly illuminating the room around her. She strikes the steel again and again, each time learning a little more about her surroundings. Spark. *That's an old box.* Spark. *Metal pipe.* Spark. *Bicycle without any tires.* Spark. *Lantern.*

"Hey, Tak!" she yells excitedly. "There's a lantern here! Hold on a sec!" Scrambling around in the dark, hands extended, she bumps and stumbles her way over to where she saw the lantern. After a few more sparks to get her bearings, she manages to open the small glass door that protects the wick. Her first few attempts at lighting it do nothing, and for a moment she thinks it's out of fuel, but on the fifth spark it finally catches. She holds it aloft, enjoying the cheerful yellow glow, and takes a moment to make sure there's nothing hanging from her hair.

"Hey, what's up?" yells Tak from the window. "What do you see?"

"It's a basement," she says, holding a curl in front of her face. "It's full of . . . basement stuff."

"Do you see a hammer anywhere? Preferably a big one?"

"Yeah, hold on. I'm looking."

She drops the hair and lets her eyes roam across the room. She spots a set of stairs leading up to a wooden door, a couple of sagging shelves holding old cans of paint, and a battered washing machine covered in mold. Finally, she turns around and finds a

Peg-Board holding a set of old, rusty tools. Uttering a cheerful cry, she shuffles over to the board and removes a hammer and a pry bar, both of which she passes through the window to Tak.

"Dude, Sam, you're a fucking *rock star*!" he cries as he takes the tools. "Okay, I'm gonna go open the front door. Do you need me to help you out?"

"No, I see a door. I'm just going to head upstairs."

"Cool. I'll be there in two shakes."

He scampers away, leaving a pair of footprints in the soft dirt beneath the window. Samira feels her body trying to move to the moldy washing machine and forces it toward the stairs instead. If she spends any more time in this room, she'll likely never leave— there's so much to clean that her head is spinning.

She hears Tak pulling nails as she ascends the stairs and opens the basement door. Holding the lantern in front of her, she finds herself standing in a small kitchen. At first glance, it seems utterly unremarkable, but then she notices the sink. Where there should have been one faucet, there were three. Moving closer, she can see a set of symbols etched on each one:

$$\% \quad Å \quad \Sigma$$

Samira is so engrossed by this discovery that she doesn't hear Tak until he's standing behind her. Wordlessly, she reaches out and points toward the faucets. He moves in for a closer look, then begins nodding as if he expected this all along.

"Kinda weird, huh?" he says. "You see a lot of stuff like this in random timelines, where something's almost normal, but then it's not. This house probably has little stuff like this everywhere."

"What happened to this place?" asks Samira, as Tak takes the lantern from her hand and begins rummaging through cabinets. "I mean, where is everyone? This house seems fine."

"I'm not sure," he says, as a plastic cup falls from a cabinet and goes bouncing across the floor. "Maybe there was a war or a plague or something. Maybe they just all went to the movies."

"Don't make fun of me."

"Well, it could have been a good movie."

"Tak!"

"Sorry! Sorry. Look, I don't know where they went. I haven't ever landed in a place like this before."

He pulls a small, metal box out of the cupboard and pries open the cover. With a grin, he hands the find to Samira, holding the lantern so she can see inside. The container is filled with what appear to be candy bars covered in shiny silver wrappers. The word PANDONKULOUS! is scribbled across each one in a bright red font.

"I don't want to eat something called Pandonkulous," murmurs Samira.

"I bet they're pan-tastic," replies Tak with as much of a straight face as he can muster.

"Never do that again," says Sam, trying and failing to hold a giggle at bay. She stuffs two of the bars in her pocket, then follows Tak as he wanders out of the kitchen and into the front room, where they discover a faded green couch, an old rocking chair, and a fireplace. Crumpled-up newspapers lie everywhere, as if someone had unpacked the furniture, then split before cleaning up. All in all, the house is in better shape than Samira was expecting. It's musty and could use a good dusting, but she thinks she'll be able to handle both of those things for a little while.

She kicks at a piece of paper as Tak picks up the boards he tore off the front door and starts hammering them across the inside frame, knocking over a small umbrella stand in the process. "Just in case," he says between thumps. "I mean, I'm with you. I think this place is deserted. But you never know."

As he works, Samira explores the rest of the house. She finds a bathroom—faucets marked with the same odd symbols as those in the kitchen—two bedrooms, and a small closet. The closet door is open, revealing blankets, pillows, and a box of something called Beam Brite Cleaner. She picks up the box and flips it over; on the other side, a smiling bald man holds a mop in one hand and a sponge in the other.

"My hero," murmurs Samira to herself.

She drops the cleaner somewhat reluctantly and moves back to the bathroom. There's a tub-and-shower combination that's a bit grimy but could probably be made to work with a little help from Mr. Beam Brite. She turns the nozzle, hoping to see a spray of clear blue water, but doesn't get so much as a drop. *Maybe I can go stand in the rain and clean off,* she thinks, listening to the sound of drops pelting the bathroom window. *I mean, as long as it's not poison or whatever the hell Tak was talking about.*

This thought of Tak makes her realize that he hasn't been hammering for a while, so she wanders back down the hall and to the living room. She finds him facing the fireplace and staring at an unfolded piece of newspaper. As she walks up behind him and places a hand on his shoulder, he flinches slightly.

"Hey," she says. "What's up?"

Tak says nothing, so Samira cranes her head around to look at her friend; the expression in his eyes is one of frightened confusion. "Tak?" she asks, suddenly nervous. "Tak, what is it? What's wrong?"

In response, he hands her the front page of the newspaper, something called the *River Rock Gazette*. The headline reads simply ALL IS LOST. The rest of the page is taken up by a blurry black-and-white photograph of something standing in the glow of a streetlight. At first she thinks it's an extremely tall, thin man, but then she notices how it's covered here and there with shaggy black feathers. Looking closer, she sees a pair of twisted talons where its feet should be, as well as what appears to be a beak protruding from its head.

Samira grabs Tak's arm, digging her fingers into his flesh, as they continue to stare at the photo. After a minute, Tak flips the paper over and holds it out toward the warbling yellow light of the lantern. On the back, printed in tiny font, are hundreds and hundreds of names. The list runs raggedly up and down the page before finally careening off the edge halfway through a name, as if the person operating the press had run out of time.

"Tak," asks Samira softly, "what happened here?"

"I don't know," he replies. "But I think we better get the hell out of Dodge."

# chapter fourteen

Samira is curled into a ball in the corner of the couch and enjoying the warmth of a fire. Tak had been hesitant to spark a flame at first, and Samira didn't need to ask why: flames lead to smoke, and one glance at the thing in the newspaper photo was enough to convince her that lying low was a good strategy. But it was cold in the house, and, more important, they needed water. The rain might be clean, and it might not—putting it over flame for a long boil was the only way to be sure. Tak had used a pan from the kitchen to collect the rain, then hung it over the fire with a series of bent coat hangers. Samira was really impressed with his creativity; all that time spent in the wilderness had clearly paid off.

"How long do we stay here?" she asks. "I mean, can't we just use your magic briefcase to hop back?"

"I don't think physicists would appreciate your calling this a magic briefcase," Tak says, chuckling, as he breaks off a thin piece of wood from a cabinet door and pokes at the fire.

"Oh, okay. Your *science* briefcase."

"That's better. And to answer the question: no. You only use the briefcase for the first leg of the trip. The return is automatic."

"So when does it happen?"

"Dunno. Could be an hour, could be a couple of days. It'll just . . . poof. You know? One minute you'll be sitting here, then we'll be back in Nebraska."

"But a different Nebraska," presses Samira. "I mean, when we go back, that timeline shift or whatever will have already happened. . . . Right?"

"Yeah, that's right. When we go back, the solid timeline will already be overwritten."

"So how do you know the briefcase is going to work? How will it even know where to send us?"

"I don't know, Sam. I mean, not for sure. Look, we're way off the sheet music at this point. I'm just kind of making it up as I go along."

Tak peers in at the boiling water, then grabs a towel purloined from the hall closet, wraps it around his hand, and pulls the pan off the fire, setting it on the fireplace mantel to cool. He takes the stick up again and begins stirring the ashes to douse any remaining flame. Samira tears open a Pandonkulous bar and takes a small bite. Her stomach immediately rebels, but she manages to keep it down. "So when we go back, am I gonna get sick again? Do I need to eat a hundred of these candy bars? . . . Because I will. I totally believe you now."

"No, you don't need to eat. I mean, it's not a bad idea, because you lost a hell of a lot of energy during the last trip, but starches and sugars aren't quite as important. Going back is different. You're not going to be sick, or see those memories, or . . ."

He trails off, staring at the steam that slowly rises from the pan. Samira knows exactly what he's thinking about, because she's thinking it as well, but rather than talk, she takes another nibble of candy and kicks off a shoe so she can go to town on her knuckles. She's grateful for the distraction for once; she's afraid of what her eyes might say if she had to stare at Tak.

"Anyway," begins Tak, "I think the best thing is to—"

"I'm sorry," interrupts Samira, wiggling her big toe up and down violently. It's already popped twice, but she's pretty sure a third one is hiding in there somewhere. "I'm sorry, Tak. I didn't . . . I shouldn't have . . . That thing about getting in my pants, that was a really terrible thing to say."

Now it's Tak's turn to focus on something else. He stands and moves to the window, peering out from between two boards at the darkening evening sky. "Hey, don't worry about it," he says with awkward forced cheer. "It was a long time ago."

"I mean, you were *Tak*, you know?" continues Samira. "You were my friend, and I didn't . . . I didn't think you liked me like that. And then the night we graduate you suddenly kiss me, and I don't know what to think, and by the next morning, you're on a plane to some jungle in New Zealand."

"New Guinea."

"Whatever. It was a long way, and I missed you."

Tak turns back from the window and stares at her. She glances up from her knuckles and catches his gaze, offering a small smile in return. He smiles back, much wider than he means to, and quickly turns his attention to the cooling water. With a slightly unsteady hand, he pours it into two plastic glasses, handing one to Samira as he takes a seat on the end of the couch. After a brief hesitation, she slides her feet onto his lap. He puts a hand around one of them and holds it there, enjoying the feel of her toes beneath her socks. They sit on the couch in silence, slowly sipping the lukewarm water and listening to the sound of rain striking the windowpane.

"We should sleep," Tak says after a while, trying to sound like this is the only thing he's thinking about. "Things are going to move really fast once we get back, so this may be our last chance for a while."

"I can't sleep," says Samira flatly. "Not here. The sound isn't right."

"So what happened to you over there? In Iraq, I mean?"

"I don't want to talk about it."

"Because it seems like—"

"Tak!" she says, her voice incredibly loud in the stillness of the house. "Not now. Okay? I can't. I can't talk about it now. You saw some of it in the Machine, and that's all you need to know. Just imagine that, but then imagine it keeps happening. Every day, something new. Every day, something terrible. I thought I was strong enough to handle stuff like that, but I'm not, and that's all there is to it."

"Okay," he says at last. "I won't ask again."

"Thanks," she replies.

As Tak absentmindedly begins to move his thumb across her toes, a memory from the Machine pops into her mind: Tak's hand hovering over her hair as he tries and fails to work up the nerve to touch her. She glances at her friend and knows, instantly, that he is thinking the very same thing. Their eyes meet, then quickly move away to look around the cold and empty living room. The fire smolders and dies in its hearth. Steam stops rising from the pan. Rain hits the window with renewed force. And two lonely people continue to sit on the couch and realize that what they are feeling—the twisting of the stomach, the nervous flutters in the throat—are emotions they have been carrying around for years.

"Um, so, listen. . . ." begins Tak. He seems ready to continue, but before he can do more than inhale, Samira suddenly leaps across the couch and plants her lips on his. He returns the kiss instantly, reaching into her hair and taking hold of whatever purchase he can find. She shifts, twisting slightly, until her legs encircle his body as if by some strange spell. When the two of them finally part, their faces closer than they've been since a night forever ago, they simply stare into each other and let their shallow, surprised breaths mingle together in the cold air. Samira leans toward Tak and places her forehead on his, smelling him, feeling him, totally unsure of what the next moment will hold and finding that oddly compelling. She can feel his heart racing beneath his T-shirt and suit coat, and knows that her own is doing the same.

"Hey, Sam," he says weakly.

"Hey," she replies.

"So, um . . . What now?"

"I don't know. I haven't planned that—"

THUMP.

Two heads suddenly pivot toward the ceiling as one. Samira's grip on Tak tightens to the point of pain, but he either doesn't notice or doesn't care. "Tak," she whispers. "Tak, did you hear that?"

"Yeah," he whispers back.

"What the hell was it?"

"I don't know. Wind?"

". . . I don't think that was wind."

"Yeah, me neither. I'm just trying to be positive."

They stare at the ceiling, waiting. For a moment, there is no sound other than the familiar patter of rain. But as the two of them ponder the notion they might have imagined the thump, a different noise rings out: a kind of slow, scraping sound like branches being dragged across the tiles of the roof.

"Oh, fuck me sideways," says Tak in a furious whisper.

"There's something up there," says Samira, eyes wide. "There's something on the roof. It's that thing from the picture, isn't it?"

Tak nods slightly as Samira uncurls her legs from his body and scrambles to the far side of the couch. "God, this thing's timing could not be worse," he says as his eyes move from the ceiling to the boarded-up door. She smiles weakly at this, but then the scraping sound rings out again, closer. They hear it move across the space over their heads and stop at the chimney. After a moment, a guttural, clacking sound echoes down the flue and out of the fireplace. This noise is followed by a soft, questioning cry:

*Caw?*

Tak and Samira stare at each other. The noise sounds like a crow, but deeper somehow. Deeper and darker and vastly more intelligent. There is silence for a moment, then a heavy thud. A few crumbled pieces of brick come ricocheting down the chimney, bounce onto the living-room floor, and skitter to a stop near the kitchen.

*Caw. Clicka-click caaaaaw.*

Samira feels a new kind of fear rise up in her chest. It's different than the numbing tightness she used to feel before combat, different than the harsh terror of a bomb propelling shrapnel past her head. The object of the fear is totally unknown, and that makes it far worse than anything she's felt before. She glances around for a weapon and quickly snatches up a long, metal poker hanging from a nail next to the fireplace.

"Tak," she whispers, gripping the poker until her knuckles turn white, "I think it knows we're here."

"I know."

"We have to get out of here."

"Gimme a second. I'm thinking."

"Can we use the briefcase?"

"No. Not once you've made the initial jump. You have to wait for it to bring you back."

The thing on the roof caws again. Seconds later, a thin trail of black slime drips down the chimney and onto the ashes below.

A foul smell of rotting eggs and vinegar rises to their nostrils as the slime slowly pools across the floor.

Tak puts his head inside the fireplace and stares into the blackness above. Samira reaches out to grab his shoulder and pull him back, but a crackling sound from overhead causes her arm to freeze in midair.

"Now what?" mutters Tak, as the popping sound echoes down the chimney.

"It sounds like twigs," whispers Samira. "Like when you step on them in a forest? Or when they're burning in a fire?"

"The fuck *is* this thing?"

As if in response, a single black feather drifts down and lands at the base of the fireplace. Samira touches it with one extended finger, then quickly pulls away. "Oh God, it's . . . it's *furry*."

The crackling sound is louder now, small pops interspersed with the occasional teeth-grinding crack. The cawing grows regular and more distinct, as if the creature is growing excited. Or as if it's laughing.

*Caw,* it whispers in the darkness of the chimney. *Caw caw caw caw caw.*

More feathers fall down the chimney, a couple of dozen in all, floating and drifting gently through the air. The realization of what's happening hits Samira first, and it's so horrible that for a moment she can't say anything. The crackling sound isn't coming from the creature's throat—it's the sound of bones snapping as they twist and contort themselves into a very small space.

"T-Tak . . ." she sputters. "Tak . . ."

"Sam?"

"It's coming, Tak. Oh God, it's coming down the chimney."

Without another word, Tak reaches up and into the chimney, feeling around for the flue cover. Samira grabs his free arm to pull him back, but he shakes her off and keeps grasping. Suddenly, he cries out in pain and withdraws the hand; his little finger is burned where some of the black substance dripped onto it. She grabs the pan of water and makes to throw it on the burn, but he shoves his hand back inside the fireplace before she has a chance.

The black feathers have become a steady rain. The creature can't be more than a foot or so away, and Samira knows that when it arrives, popping out of the chimney like some kind of grim Santa Claus, it will open its arms and shriek with delight before it devours them both alive. She feels fear absorb her body as her senses shut down, preparing themselves for the inevitable end that is coming. The crackling sound fades. Her vision dims to a single point just above the mantel. But just when she's ready to close her eyes and surrender entirely, Tak finds the flue cover and slams it shut.

The thing batters against it once, twice, a third time. It utters a terrible, watery cry, then throws itself at the cover yet again, causing the bricks of the chimney to shudder in their housings. As her senses slowly return to life, Samira reaches out and hands Tak the water; he plunges his smoking fingers into it. "We have to get out of here," he says in a trembling voice, as the thing continues to batter against the metal flue covering. "We have to get out of here *now*."

Samira clambers to her feet and runs to the door, adjusting her grip on the poker as she does. She jams the end of the tool against the wood that Tak nailed up not an hour ago, props her foot on the doorframe, and pulls with all her strength. To her surprise, the board gives way and goes flying off into space. Immediately, she begins yanking at the other boards, ripping the nails out as fast as she can move. Her vision is blurred from tears, and she feels like her chest is going to burst, but she keeps going. Out of the corner of her eye, she sees Tak pick up the briefcase with his good hand.

"Samira, come on!" he cries. "Hurry!"

"I AM!" she screams, as another board clatters to the ground.

The creature has stopped slamming against the flue and is now crawling back up the chimney. The cawing has grown lower and more intense; Samira could swear that the thing is royally pissed off. It's about halfway to the roof when the last board gives way and Samira yanks the door open. With Tak on her heels, she stumbles through the doorway, finds her balance, and starts running. There is no discussion about where to go, no thought about finding shelter or taking a stand—the thing behind them is terror personified, and the only option is escape.

Samira drops the poker, tucks her head against her chest, and pushes forward as fast as her legs will move. Tak keeps pace at her side, the briefcase occasionally banging into his legs. They race down the darkened street and past the park where they first arrived in this dead and hellish land, then turn a corner and keep going. Behind them, the creature makes a terrible cry against the moonlit sky.

"I told you . . ." pants Tak as they fly, "told you that . . . most of time travel . . . was running."

The houses are smaller now, more like townhomes than the grand residences of a few blocks previous. Samira can see that many of them have burned to the ground, and once she thinks she spies a skeleton with a hole in its head leaning over a front porch rail. But it's dark, and she's running, and there's no time to make sure. Her breath comes in short, pained gasps. Her legs are on fire. The knuckles that were scraped in her apartment an eternity ago are burning with renewed fury. But she keeps running.

She hears a hissing behind them and knows the creature has broken free of its brick prison. She forces herself to stare forward and keep moving, knowing that to turn around and see it bearing down on them would cause her entire body to seize with fright.

The thing is close, perhaps a block away, and the beating of wings is heavy in the night air.

"We're not . . . gonna make it. . . ." she pants. "Right . . . behind us . . ."

"Keep running," grunts Tak. "Promise me you'll . . . keep running. . . ."

She reaches down for a secret fifth gear, hoping that it's there and yet not knowing if she has such a strength. To her surprise, her body responds, growing lighter and more agile until the pain and fear suddenly dissipate. She's really moving now, seemingly flying over the asphalt roads of a cold, dead world. *We can make it,* she thinks wildly. *We're gonna make it. We're gonna get away.*

Suddenly Tak drops off from her side. It takes her a few seconds to notice this, then another few to get her head turned around. When she does, she sees him standing in the middle of the road, arms outstretched, briefcase by his feet.

"Okay, you ugly motherfucker!" she hears him scream. "Let's do this thing!"

Samira skids to a stop and tries to turn, but momentum and exhaustion collide inside her, and she tumbles to the ground, rolling over and over until she finally crashes to a stop against the side of a parked car. Bright lights flash across her vision as she struggles to stand. "Tak!" she warbles. "Tak, no!"

"Run, Sam!" he screams back. "Fucking *run!*"

She can see him standing in the glow of the moon, and is horrified to see how small and powerless he seems. Approaching him, flying through the air with talons barely touching the ground, is a thing straight out of hell. Its mouth is a thin yellow beak. Its skin is nearly translucent and shot through with red veins. It has a pair of twisted, useless arms that sprout from its chest as if the creator simply ran out of inspiration before finishing. But worst of all are the eyes: huge black things with no white or iris at all. They bulge out from its head like a pair of overfilled balloons, and they hold a cunning beyond imagining.

*It's a bird,* thinks Samira as she watches it soar toward Tak. *Dear God in heaven, it's a gigantic baby bird.*

The bird opens its arms and emits a hoarse shriek that echoes off the abandoned buildings beyond. Samira feels a cry build in her throat as the thing dives at Tak. It's so close now. Just a few more seconds, and it will be on him, then it will turn to her and everything that she has ever been will suddenly be over.

A green flash erupts from the briefcase. She sees the creature dive, sees Tak cover his face with his hands, and then an ocean of stars explodes in her eyes.

samira's ass is cold. She's not sure why at first, and it takes her nearly a minute to realize that she's sitting in the middle of a muddy cornfield. Overhead, a familiar pattern of stars hangs in the night sky. As she climbs to her feet, she sees a shadow moving through the plants. It's familiar, this shape. She knows every inch of it, and it's all she can do not to dissolve as she throws her arms around its neck and holds on for dear life.

"Sam?" says Tak, as she grips him harder and the tears begin to flow. "I'm gonna vote we never do that again."

h0me

# chapter fifteen

When she was a child, Judith Halford wanted to be an astronaut. It was a desire that seemed out of place for a sickly little girl from the Upper East Side of New York City. Her parents used to joke about it between predinner cocktails with their circle of well-heeled friends. *Judith flying the space shuttle. Can you imagine? She'd crash the thing on the launchpad! . . . Another Manhattan? We're in the perfect town for it, you know. Oh ho!*

Her father, a television executive who spent most of his home life screaming at underlings on his cell phone, even took to calling her Buzz, a nickname that followed her like a bad smell for most of her teenage years. The moniker was especially cruel for a shy girl like Judith, whose family mingled in circles where names mattered more than what was between the ears. Being new money, her parents were already at a disadvantage when it came to social climbing, and so they decided the best way to deal with their quiet, nerdy daughter was to approach her as a kind of private joke that everyone was in on.

When she turned twelve, her parents sent her to the Worthington-Kennedy Boarding School, a fortress of rich and powerful children for whom the word "elite" seemed woefully inadequate. Judith would have rather slept on a subway grate than been assigned to such a place, but sending their only daughter to a standard private school—or, God forbid, a public one—had simply been out of the question. Worthington was also located a good three hundred miles away, which had the added advantage of getting their daughter out of the public eye while hormones and time attempted to transform her from a gawky, long-limbed girl into something approaching the commonly accepted idea of beauty. *You'll love it, Buzz,* her father had said as the family driver wheeled her bag down the stairs and into a waiting limousine. *Gonna love it. They've got the best teachers there, and you're gonna make a lot of friends. Now I gotta go, but we'll call ya in a week or two, all right? That's my girl.*

Despite her father's words, she had not loved it. In fact, she hated it so much she often found herself sitting on a toilet with a razor blade in her hand trying to figure out if death would really be so bad. Near the end of her second semester, after seven months of teasing, taunting, and crushing loneliness, she'd actually drawn the blade across her wrist just to see what it felt like. When blood began to pour from the wound and pool on the floor, all she could think of was her parents' anger that she had damaged the family name yet again. She managed to staunch the wound with a roll of wet paper towels before slinking back to the room she shared with the daughter of a national politician, where she crawled into bed and waited for sleep that never came.

That moment, however, proved to be a changing point in her life. She'd redoubled her efforts in class, managed a transfer to a single-occupant dorm room, and altered her schedule so she would be forced to interact with other students as little as possible. Judith became a ghost that moved between classrooms, staying just long enough to absorb knowledge before vanishing once again.

At the end of her freshman year, her mother called to inform her that she would be staying at Worthington over the summer while her parents jetted off to Spain. That gave Judith a chance to wander the empty campus and immerse herself in its massive library—which, her father had informed her at some point, was endowed by none other than the governor himself. Before long, she was practically living in the science stacks, where she quickly became enraptured by the world of theoretical physics. She began researching quantum mechanics, relativity, and every branch of high-level mathematics she could get her hands on, and within weeks found that she had a real knack for it.

By summer's end, she had the undivided attention of the science dean. By the end of her sophomore year, the quiet, skinny girl who had once pulled a razor across her skin sported a shiny 4.0 GPA, an authorship credit on a paper in the *National Journal of Science*, and a full-ride scholarship to MIT. When she'd called her parents to inform them she was leaving Worthington and heading off to college as a fifteen-year-old prodigy, her mother had simply said: *Dear, that's not one of those . . . science schools, is it? We were so hoping you would find a more appropriate career.*

Three years later, she graduated with honors, turned down offers from Oxford and Cambridge and various companies in national defense industries, and instead accepted a position at a tiny start-up called the Axon Corporation. Her friends—real friends this time—reacted with shock when they learned she was abandoning her brightly burning career for some tiny company based out of Australia, but she had smiled and hugged them and told them it was going to be fine. *I want to work there,* she'd said the night before she boarded a jet and left America forever. *They have a machine they need me to build.*

. . .

**judith finds herself** thinking about that decision as she waits for the elevator to bring her to the lower levels of the Axon Corporation. *I should have taken the money and gone to Microsoft. Or maybe gone to CERN and worked on the Large Hadron Collider. . . . Hell, I should have stayed in New York and taught elementary physics to high-school kids. Because this thing has really gone off the goddamn rails.*

The elevator descends for nearly a minute, allowing Judith plenty of time to pace nervously across the slick, steel floor. Something had gone horribly wrong with the timeline swap, and the more she learned about it, the more frightened she became. All of her readings from the Machine came back inconclusive—even the most basic scientific tests were producing unexpected results. On the Internet, people were chattering about what was becoming known as Other Life, an inescapable sense that things were not how they were supposed to be. And, most disturbingly, reports were beginning to filter in about strange, feathered creatures that had been sighted in cities across the world.

Judith's immediate problem, however, was with her new boss. The entire board had vanished during the timeline swap, leaving behind a power vacuum Yates had gladly filled. The Axon Corporation now answered to him, which would make it much more difficult for Judith to push the reset button on his little experiment. The board had been easy to fool, but Yates was a different kind of operator altogether.

Judith adjusts her laptop bag as the elevator doors open on a long white hallway that ends in a steel door. Taking a deep breath, she heads for it and keys in an entry code. She passes through three more doors with various security measures before finally emerging in a windowless changing area with an air lock on the far side. Etched upon the air-lock door, in large block letters, is a single word: CONDUITS.

The room is silent save for the dull hum of machinery, but she knows that a handful of men—Yates's men—will be waiting on the other side. Working quickly, she pulls on a bulky face mask and blue coverall suit over her black skirt and blouse. Snapping gloves over her hands and booties on her feet, she steps into the air lock, closes the door behind her, and waits for the cycle to complete.

She emerges in a circular room of immense size, with a ceiling so high it seems not to exist at all. The chamber is filled with row upon row of beds, over a thousand in all, that stretch away as far as the eye can see. Next to every bed is a dialysis machine, a feeding tube, and an artificial breather connected to a person long since rendered comatose. All the patients have brightly colored wires implanted into their brains, and these stretch away from their heads and into a thick black cable, which connects to the Machine itself.

A young soldier finally notices her arrival and strides over. He's wearing the same blue coverall suit and air-filtration mask that Judith has, but he is also carrying an assault rifle wrapped in plastic. He examines her badge for a moment before taking a step backward. "Miss Halford," he says, the surprise in his voice muffled by the mask. "We didn't receive word you were coming."

Judith nods quickly. "Sorry for the last minute. Yates needs me to examine one of the conduits."

"Examine?"

"Yes. As in, check in on."

Though she can only see the soldier's eyes, Judith can tell that he's not completely sold on her plan. He readjusts his grip on the gun and shuffles his shoulders back and forth. "Uh, Miss Halford, we're under orders from Mr. Yates to shut down all of the conduits."

"I know that," says Judith with more authority than she feels.

"He was very specific."

"You can shut this one down when I'm done."

"I, uh . . . Okay, hold on. I need to check this."

The soldier hustles across the massive room to a small portable office, where he begins a heated conversation with another blue-clad figure. Judith leans back against the air-lock door and tries to look nonchalant, hoping that no one can see her knees knocking together. Additional soldiers, perhaps two dozen in all, are walking up and down the rows and turning off the machinery. Each time they flip a switch, she watches a person's chest rise and fall, rise and fall, then stay still. *They're killing them,* she thinks. *Oh my God, they're going to kill them all.*

She feels a brief, sudden urge to scream but manages to keep it in place. The soldier is running back to her, assault rifle at the ready. He skids into place a foot or so from her. "Miss Halford?" he asks, his voice trembling slightly.

"Are we good here?" asks Judith. Somewhere nearby, one of the conduits makes a sputtering, gasping sound that she tries desperately to ignore.

"We need a reason," says the soldier.

"A *reason?*"

"We're under orders to—"

"I can see what you're doing," snaps Judith. "Look, what's your name?"

"Simmons."

"Simmons. Right. Okay, Simmons. Are you familiar with string theory?"

The soldier raises his eyebrows. "No."

"Quantum mechanics?"

"No."

"The laws of thermodynamics? Any of them?"

"Uh . . . no?"

"Then this is going to be a *really* long conversation. I don't have time to give you an introduction to elementary particle physics, Simmons. The reason I need this man is because Yates needs this man, and that's all you need to know. You want me to go find Yates and have *him* explain it to you? Because I can do that if you'd prefer."

Simmons dithers back and forth for a few seconds, then finally steps out of the way. "Okay, but look, I'm gonna have to get on the radio and—"

"Call whoever you want," says Judith as she brushes past him and walks away. "You know where to find me."

She expects to hear a shout from somewhere behind her, or worse yet, a gunshot, but there is nothing. She refuses to turn around, instead keeping her eyes focused on a single bed three-quarters of the way down the row. Each time she passes a soldier, he looks up from his task, glances sideways at her, then returns to shutting off the life-support systems. *Keep it together, girl. Just a little farther. Just a few minutes, and it's all over.*

After what seems an eternity, she stops next to a bed with the number 342 etched on the railing. The occupant is an older man with a thick grey beard and hair that flows down his shoulders. His face is a mess of scars, his nose bulbous and swollen. Glancing behind her to make sure she isn't attracting more attention than necessary, she sets her laptop on his stomach, then runs her hand down the wires protruding from his skull. Working fast, she locates the point where they join the black cable and pulls them out, then connects the ends to a port on the back of her computer. When that is finished, she plugs a second set of wires into another port, leaving four male ends dangling down to the ground.

The old man in the bed moans. One of the soldiers in the next row looks over, trying to decide if he should check it out. But then the woman he's disconnecting reaches out and grabs his arm, and his attention is diverted once more.

Judith picks up the loose bundle of wires and stares at them. Then, before she can lose her nerve, she pulls her hair aside, feels around at the base of her neck for a set of four small holes, and plugs the wires directly into her brain. A searing pain leaps up her spine and right into her eyes, and for a moment she thinks she's going to pass out. But she manages to fight through it, pushing the pain down until it's a dull roar in the back of her mind. Behind her, the woman who grabbed the soldier is trying to say something, but a year's worth of forced sleep has made her speech incomprehensible. She mumbles a series of nonsense syllables before the soldier grabs a pillow and presses it firmly over her face. In a few moments, the arm drops limply to the side.

Judith begins typing on her laptop, hoping that the soldier either doesn't notice or doesn't understand what she's doing. But he seems more concerned about the woman he just smothered; he's holding her wrist and looking at his watch in a bored, clinical way.

*You know, it's possible that Yates knew about the fail-safe all along,* thinks Judith as she types. *If so, he may have replaced it. Or just deleted the thing . . . In which case, I guess we're all fucked.*

When Judith first came up with the idea of a fail-safe, she chose to store it in the mind of an old homeless man named Vincent. He had always been one of the more frail conduits—a long-term alcoholic in the late stages of cirrhosis—and her hope was that Yates would never look for something so important inside the brain of someone who could die at any moment. It had been a calculated, dangerous risk, but somehow the old-timer had kept chugging along for four long years.

"Thank you, Vincent," whispers Judith in the old man's ear as she finishes typing. "Thank you for everything."

She steps back and takes a deep breath. On her laptop screen, a single red light pulses slowly. Then she leans forward, grips the edge of the bed with her free hand, and presses the ENTER key.

Pain floods her body, much worse than when she first plugged in the wires. She feels a scream leave her mouth but can't figure out how to stop it. She sees a flood of seemingly random numbers and equations begin to stream across her laptop screen before her vision suddenly blacks out. She can hear a soldier yelling something, most likely at her, but she has no idea what he's trying to say. Her entire world is a searing ball of agony, and for the first time since she was a young girl at a boarding school, she begins to wish she was dead.

Her vision comes back suddenly. In front of her, the computer screen is a solid blur of numbers that race by so fast they seem at times not to be moving at all. The soldier has come around the now-dead woman in the bed and is making a beeline for her current position. *This was a terrible idea,* thinks Judith. *He's gonna kill me before I can finish. Ah God, I waited too long.*

Suddenly, the pain vanishes as her laptop makes a small, happy ding. Sitting on the screen, blinking slowly, are six digits:

000001

She slams the laptop closed and yanks the wires out of her head, feeling a small trickle of blood leak down the back of her neck. As she drops the wires to the floor, the soldier steps around the bed and stares at her. "The fuck are you doing?" he asks, his gun pointing somewhere between the floor and Judith's chest.

"Research," she croaks. She stands up and grabs the laptop, and is immediately hit by waves of dizziness.

"Hold on. We were told—"

"Talk to Simmons," replies Judith as she turns around in a

slow circle and tries to remember where the exit is. "He said it was fine."

"Oh he did, did he?"

". . . Yep."

She turns her back to the soldier and begins walking on unsteady feet. Out of the corner of her eye, she can see Simmons speaking to a group of four or five men and gesturing in her direction, but she keeps going. The soldier who killed the woman with the pillow begins walking toward his companions, but there's no real hurry to his step. This is clearly just a job for him, and Judith another crazy scientist working with materials he can't begin to understand.

She reaches the exit, wobbles her way into the air lock, and waits for it to cycle. When the green light clicks on, she moves down the hall as fast as her legs will carry her, the laptop banging against her knees with each halting step. Her mind is a blur of random images and noise. Ghostly people seems to wander up and down the hall before flickering out in a burst of static electricity. She can hear the noise of a billion separate conversations from somewhere deep inside her mind; they mingle and blur together into an unpleasant white noise.

"Damn," says Judith to herself. "This is a lot worse than I imagined."

The elevator looms in front of her, but she ignores it. Instead, she heads for the staircase—which can't be shut down if they figure out what she's up to—and begins to climb. She continues to climb, step after uncountable step, until her feet begin to ache, and her legs cry out for rest. *Not yet,* she tells herself as she climbs. *Not yet. No rest yet. Got to get out of here first.*

Slowly, things begin to improve. The ghostly images of people fade as her brain figures out how to deal with all the new information that's been introduced. The white noise drops to a dull drone. And her legs begin to regain some strength. Soon, she's taking the stairs two at a time, racing higher and higher until finally bursting through a door near the ground floor and into an underground parking garage. Moving quickly past rows of black SUVs, she finally stops in front of a battered four-wheel-drive jeep that appears to have come from the Second World War. She tosses her laptop in the back, then cranes her neck to peer under the driver's seat. To her unending joy, the briefcase she stashed there some twenty hours ago has not been found.

"All right," she says quietly. "Let's get the hell out of here."

The jeep roars to life, and soon Judith is speeding off across the hard-packed desert floor of the Australian Outback. She rolls down the window and enjoys the night air in her hair, feeling more alive than she has in years. And as the headquarters of the Axon Corporation fades into her rearview mirror, she can just hear an alarm begin to wail.

# chapter sixteen

Tak watches the world rush past a smudged and dirty window and tries to think of something to say. He and Samira are curled up in the passenger seat of an eighteen-wheeler, where the constant, steady sound of the highway has lulled her to sleep. Tak is amazed at how quickly it happened: one minute they were scrambling into the cab, and the next she was conked out against the door with her mouth hanging open and a spot of drool forming on her cheek. The sleep seems troubled—she whimpers a lot and occasionally mutters something nonsensical—but Tak isn't going to wake her unless it becomes absolutely necessary. They have a long and dangerous road ahead of them; sleep is likely to be a rare pleasure.

The driver hasn't said anything since he plucked them, wet and shivering, from the side of the road nearly fifty miles ago. It's unfortunate, this silence, because Tak has a thousand questions spinning around in his head. *What day is it? What year? Are we back in the solid timeline? Did the Machine actually work?* So far, he's discovered nothing to convince him that the timeline change even occurred. The driver's hat has a Kansas City Royals logo, the coffee on the dashboard came from a Starbucks, and the radio is

belting out a heartbreaker by Tammy Wynette. If the Axon Corporation actually overwrote the solid timeline, things should be
very different. Granted, all he can see right now is one portly
trucker and a moonless highway night, so it was hardly a reasonable sample size, but still . . .

Samira turns, a scowl coming over her face. "No," she says
quietly, "that's not what he said." There's a pause, then a couple
of sentences in a foreign language. She raises one hand in the air,
then brings it down and starts rubbing at her face. Tak takes the
fingers and wraps them in his own, which seems to calm her
down.

The driver glances over at Samira with an expression that Tak
can't quite read. "What was that?" he says. "Spanish?"

"Farsi," says Tak. "Or standard Arabic. I can't ever tell the
difference."

"She an Arab?" asks the driver. He pronounces it A-rab, putting a pause in the word that causes Tak to cringe.

"No, she's American. Her parents are from Iran, but they left
when she was two."

"They're from where?"

"Iran? . . . It's the country above Iraq?"

"Oh."

They drive in silence for another few miles, Tak using the time
to size up his new friend. He's a heavy man, older, with folds in
his neck and stubble cropping up everywhere. The hands that grip
the wheel are large and callused, the nails stained a permanent
black from oil and grease. His voice is high-pitched and tinged
with a Midwestern accent, which Tak takes as a good sign; folks
from flyover country were usually nicer than most.

Tak turns his attention back to the road just in time to see a
sign that reads OMAHA: 114 MILES. The thought of spending all that
time in silence begins to depress him, so he decides to take the

small-talk plunge. "I'm Tak, by the way," he says, extending a hand. "Tak O'Leary."

"Tak?" asks the driver, leaving Tak's hand hovering in midair.

"Yeah."

"Like a pushpin?"

". . . Like that, yeah."

"Well, all right then, Tak." says the man, who reaches out, grasps Tak's small hand in his own, and pumps it up and down with enough force to sprain the wrist. "I'm Dennis."

"Where you from, Dennis?" asks Tak. "Nebraska?"

"Wisconsin. Little town called Ellsworth. Not much more than a spot on the map, to tell the truth. You?"

"Oh, I'm from all over. Seattle, mostly."

"So, uh, your gal there. What's her name?"

"Samira."

"Samira," says Dennis slowly, rolling the word around in his mouth like a gumball. "Samira. That's a nice name."

"Yeah, well, you know. It beats Tak."

"You kids married?"

"Us? No, no. We're not . . . We're not married."

"Dating?"

Tak's mind goes blank at this question. How does he even begin to explain the situation? *Well, see, I was in love with her back in high school, but then I left to experiment with time travel and she went off to the Iraq War. But now we're back, and I think there's something going on, but our last kiss was interrupted by a giant killer bird, so I'm not completely sure.*

"Er . . . we're friends," he says finally. "Old friends."

Dennis nods at this, downshifting in preparation for a small hill. The truck growls in response, as if it likes the challenge. "Yeah, all right. I'll drop it. Don't mean to pry or nothing."

Tak is ready to tell him that he's not prying, that he's actually asking very reasonable questions under the circumstances, but he just leans back and says nothing. After a few miles, he reaches into his pocket, pulls out his final Pandonkulous bar, and starts munching. Halfway through he remembers his manners and offers a piece to Dennis, but the man waves him off with a shake of the head.

"No thanks," he says. "I can't handle candy no more. Doc says I'm Type B. Didn't used to be like that, but . . ."

As Dennis trails off, an odd look passes over his face, as if he's concerned about something far more complicated than his current poor health. Tak can see that he wants to talk about it, but also that such a conversation won't happen until he's ready. So instead of prying, he finishes off the chocolate bar and wipes his fingers on his jeans. After a few quiet miles, Samira mutters something unintelligible and shifts her weight, pressing one skinny leg against Tak's thigh. The smell of her is everywhere—a pleasant combination of rain, grass, and sweat—and it's starting to drive Tak a little bit crazy. *This could get complicated, Sam,* he thinks as he resists the urge to run his fingers through her hair. *You're making it awfully hard for me to focus.*

He forces his eyes to move up and over her head until they are once again staring out the window. The world passes in a blur, fields and fences and the occasional small farmhouse all rushing together to become a single landscape—America's heartland at seventy miles an hour. Once he sees a pair of green eyes flash out from the darkness up ahead, and he's sure that it's the creature from the random timeline. He has a vision of its leaping onto the top of the truck and tearing open the roof with a long, serrated beak, but then the truck pulls even with the eyes, and he realizes it's only a deer. The animal gets smaller and smaller in the rearview until finally vanishing into the night.

"You mind if I ask something?" says Dennis. He moves one

hand to the radio and starts flipping though channels as he speaks. "Like I said, I'm not the prying sort, but . . ."

"Uh, no," responds Tak, distracted. "No, that's fine."

"What are you doing out here? I drive this part of the country a fair bit, and ain't nothing back where I found you but farmland and dust."

"Our car broke down," says Tak lamely. "We . . . uh . . . we were driving to Wyoming to visit her grandmother, and the radiator died."

"It died?"

"Yeah, well, you know. Maybe not the radiator. It could have been the carburetor or the . . . uh . . . that other thing."

"Don't know much about cars, do ya?"

"Not a damn thing," says Tak, who suddenly realizes that playing the idiot card is probably the way to go here. "It just stopped working. But hey, we're really glad you came along."

"Mmm," says Dennis.

Tak lets the silence hang for a bit as he works on a way to figure out if the timeline swap had been successful. He thinks of a dozen ideas, rejecting them all out of hand, before finally settling on throwing caution to the wind. "So, say. You mind if I ask you a question now?"

"Sure."

"Who's the president?"

Dennis turns his head to the side and stares. Tak smiles weakly, gripping Samira's hand a little tighter as he does so.

"The president?"

". . . Yeah."

"Of the country?"

"Yeah, you know what? Never mind. Just forget I said anything. I'm tired, it was a stupid question, and I'm just . . . I'm going to stop talking now."

Dennis turns his eyes back to the road, but not before Tak can see that he's seriously troubled. *Nice one, idiot. Now he's gonna dump you off at the next rest stop because he thinks you're a crazy person, and you'll have to start this stupid trip all over again.*

The next rest stop ends up being less than five minutes away, but to Tak's surprise, the truck roars past without a second thought. Dennis fiddles endlessly with the radio knob over the next handful of miles, occasionally opening his mouth as if he wants to say something only to close it a couple of seconds later. As they motor past the outskirts of a one-horse town called Battle Creek, he finally gives up the hunt for music and clicks off the radio, apparently content to let the dull rush of tires on asphalt serve as their sound track. The two men continue in this way for nearly half an hour, not speaking, not looking at each other, the silence broken only by occasional bouts of frightened chatter from a sleeping Samira. Once she even screams, a breathless, terrible sound, but Tak reaches over and places his hand on her shoulder, and the fear dies as quickly as it started.

Eventually they pass a green sign informing them that Omaha is only fifty miles away. This seems to trigger something in Dennis, because he finally stops opening and closing his mouth and moves on to actual speech. "Why did you ask about the president?" he asks with eyes pointed straight ahead.

"Just trying to make conversation," says Tak, acutely aware of how stupid his answer sounds. "You know?"

"You sure that's the reason? You sure you didn't ask because it doesn't feel . . . right?"

Tak perks up at this. Dennis's question could mean a thousand different things—that he doesn't like the president's political party, or that he doesn't think the election was fair, or even that he is just trying to see what the hell would make his passenger ask such a ridiculous thing. But it could also be an indication of something much more important. "I guess that's as good a way to put it as any," says Tak slowly. "What about you?"

Dennis reaches into the overhead visor and produces a toothpick, staring at it for a moment before placing it between his front teeth. "I'm gonna tell you something," he says, the toothpick moving up and down in his mouth like a conductor's baton. "I ain't told no one this yet, but I figure you don't know me and I don't know you and that makes it about as safe as anything. . . . I don't think things are *right*."

"What do you mean?" asks Tak, leaning forward.

"I've been driving this truck damn near my whole life. I remember my daddy teaching me how to run a rig. I remember getting my license. Hell, I can tell stories about trips I took up and down this entire country. I'm near fifty years old, and this is the only thing I've ever known. But then I've got these other memories too, and I know they couldn't possibly have happened, but I remember 'em just the same. It's like I got double memories of my life."

Dennis reaches up and flips the toothpick around so he can worry the clean side a little bit. "I used to work in a big East Coast city. I think it was Boston, but it coulda been Hartford or Bangor or something. I had an office in a skyscraper, and I wore a suit and had a lot of people reporting to me. Had a family, too: wife and three little girls. And I don't mean that I did this before I drove the truck. I mean that I did this *instead* of driving the truck. I remember a whole different life."

Tak sits very still and tries not to freak out. *He remembers the solid timeline. So that means the Machine worked. It worked, and Yates managed to overwrite the solid timeline, but this truck driver can still remember it. And if he can remember it, that means that other people probably remember it. Hell, maybe everyone remembers it. And that's not how it was supposed to be. . . . That's not how it was supposed to be at all.*

"I know I sound crazy," continues Dennis, "but I don't care anymore. I don't know if it's some kinda government mind-control thing or if we've been poisoned by the water or what, but I feel like I'm about to lose my goddamn marbles!"

He emphasizes this point by slamming his hand against the dashboard, an action that causes Samira to bolt upright with a scream in her throat. She looks around the cab wildly for a few seconds before slowly curling into a ball as far back against the door as she can go. "Oh, crap," she whispers. "Freaky."

"Ah, hell," says Dennis. "I'm sorry. I didn't mean to wake you."

"Um, it's okay," says Samira as she rubs the sleep from her eyes before beginning to crack her knuckles. "I'm just a light sleeper." She finishes the pinky knuckle and seems ready to go for the toes, but then a smudge on the window catches her eye, and she starts rubbing it absentmindedly.

"Go on," says Tak, glancing over at Dennis. "What else do you remember?"

Dennis looks from Tak to Samira and back again, then shakes his head. "I dunno," he says. "I probably shouldn't talk about it anymore."

"No, keep talking. I want to hear what you have to say, because . . . because we've been going through the same thing." Tak feels a brief flash of guilt at the lie but quickly pushes it to the back of his mind; there will be plenty of time to feel like an ass after he figures out what the hell is going on.

"You have? I thought . . . I thought I was the only one."

"No, both of us have strange memories, too," says Tak. Samira looks up at this, eyebrows raised in a confused expression, but he holds up a single finger and shakes his head. She shrugs halfheartedly before starting to scrub furiously at the window.

"Well, I've got these other memories," begins Dennis. "You know how sometimes you have a nightmare, and when you first wake up you've got a kind of tightness that eventually goes away? Well, that's what this is like, only it ain't going away. Every time I think about it, I get this terrible pain in my chest like I can't breathe. And if I think about it too long, I start worrying that I'm just gonna . . ."

"That you're going to what?" asks Tak. Keeping his eyes focused on Dennis, he snakes a hand behind him and closes it around Samira's wrist, pulling her away from the window. She makes an exasperated noise and tries to break free, but he smashes it to the seat and holds it firm. "You worry that you're going to what?"

"It's like, if I keep thinking about it, I'm gonna die."

Dennis's lower lip trembles as if he means to cry. Behind him, Samira is breathing heavily and trying to get herself under control, but Tak can tell that it's a losing battle. He finally decides that having her clean the window is better than dealing with a meltdown, so he releases the hand; she immediately attacks the smudge with renewed fury.

"See, in one of my memories, I'm driving this truck through a cold stretch of the Dakotas," continues Dennis, seemingly unconcerned about his passenger's obsession with his window. "And in the other memory, I'm sitting in the office building and staring out over the city. But in both of 'em, I hear this noise. It's kinda like a jet engine, but real low—almost like you feel it in your bones more than hear it with your ears. So I hear this noise, and I look up at the sky, and it's like it's just not there anymore. Instead, there's this big dark hole. It sits there, black as night, until these . . . *things* come rushing out of it. They have big wings and huge, black eyes, and they eat the sky until there's nothing left."

He tosses the toothpick on the floor of the cab and exchanges it for a cigarette, which he lights with a trembling hand. "That sky is the only thing that appears in both my memories, and whenever I think about it, I get a fear that clamps around my heart and won't let go."

"That's rough," says Tak. "I'm sorry."

"Yeah, well, I shouldn't burden you with it, but I dunno who else to tell."

"Does Axon know about this?" asks Tak.

"Who?" replies Dennis.

Tak tilts his head sideways and looks at Dennis quizzically. "The Axon Corporation? They're in control of everything. . . . Right?"

"Sorry, kid. I've never heard of 'em."

"That's not right," says Tak, his mouth working before his brain can tell it to shut up. "They're supposed to run everything."

"Yeah, well, maybe it's your memories that are messed up, because I've never heard of 'em."

Tak slowly sinks into his seat and stares straight ahead. To his left, a large, nervous man pulls on a cigarette, while to his right, a pretty young woman struggles to remove an ancient stain from a window. Tak sees all of this and yet none of it, because his mind is racing with terrible thoughts. *Jesus Christ in a jug band. This is the wrong timeline. Axon is supposed to rule the world, but they aren't in charge of anything. That means either Yates made a mistake, or he never intended to use that timeline in the first place. . . . This is bad. This is really, really bad.*

"You all right?" asks Dennis as he tosses the filter of his cigarette out the window. "You look a little pale."

"No, I'm not all right," replies Tak. "Nothing is all right. I don't think we're supposed to be here."

# chapter seventeen

The Kearney Regional Airfield is hardly what Tak would call a world-class joint, but surprisingly enough, he doesn't mind. In fact, an airport like this, with its small runway, dimly lit parking lot, and limited hours of operation, was exactly what he was hoping to find for the first leg of their journey. He was still a stranger in this timeline, but what little he knew had convinced him that keeping a low profile was a very good idea. Whatever Yates had done, whatever timeline he had substituted during the exchange, there was a good possibility that he was now in charge.

Currently, Tak and Samira are standing outside the airport in ankle-deep snow, waiting for someone to come along and open the doors. Dennis had dropped them off an hour prior with a hearty hug that nearly broke Tak's ribs. More helpfully, he'd also forked over a twenty and told him to buy Samira breakfast. Tak didn't really need the money—he had almost ten thousand dollars stashed in a hidden pocket of his suit coat—but it gave him a chance to examine the bill and make sure his own money would still be good in this strange, new world. If Dennis's gift had contained the scowling visage of President Nixon or the words THERE

IS NO GOD, they could have been in serious trouble—so the face of Andrew Jackson had been a welcome sight indeed.

"So explain this to me again," says Samira, stamping her feet to stay warm. " 'Cause I'm confused."

"Okay," responds Tak. "So when they swapped the timelines, the reality that we know was erased and overwritten by this new reality. You with me?"

"I'm with you."

"But in the timeline I found for them, the one they were supposed to use, Axon was in charge of everything. They were like the US government and Halliburton and the Catholic Church all rolled into one. *Everyone* should know about Axon. Especially an American citizen who spends his time driving and listening to the radio."

"But Dennis didn't know about them."

"Which means we're in the wrong timeline."

"Are you sure?" asks Samira as she blows on her hands. "I mean, what if Dennis was just really stupid? I don't want to sound mean, but—"

"I've been looking for Axon ever since we got back, and I haven't seen a thing. No signs, no newspaper articles, no building names, nothing. But Dennis also said he can remember bits of the solid timeline. He doesn't know that's what he's doing, but it is. He remembers how things used to be, and that's not how this was supposed to work."

Samira leans away from Tak and presses her face against the glass of the airport door. A nearby sign claims the doors open promptly at 5 a.m., which is a little over ten minutes away. "Come on guys, hurry up," she mutters. "I'm freezing."

"You want my coat?" asks Tak, pulling off one sleeve. "Seriously, go ahead. I'm fine."

"No, I'll be okay. Just keep talking because I need to understand this."

"Basically, they brought the wrong timeline here. This isn't
the one I found for them: it's something else."

"So they screwed up?"

Tak shakes his head, then joins Samira at the window. Their
breath makes little round fog marks on the door as they search
the darkened interior of the airport for any signs of life. "Yates
wouldn't screw up something this big. I think he did it on purpose.
I don't know why, but I'm pretty sure it's not out of the goodness
of his heart."

Samira turns away from the door and looks at him. "Who is
this Yates guy? You've mentioned him a couple of times."

"Yates? He's brilliant, but he's also a complete nutbag. And if
he's in charge of this place, we're in a whole lot of trouble."

Samira seems ready to ask more, but then a figure begins
moving toward the doors. Seconds later, they slide open to reveal
an older man in a bright blue vest. "Well, hello," says the man.
"Been waitin' long?"

"Just got here," says Tak smoothly. "You open? We need
tickets."

"Counter's around back," says the man. He reaches for the
door and inserts a small Allen wrench into a slot at the top.
"Christy should be there in a second. I'd help ya m'self, but I have
to finish opening up."

They move past the man and into the airport, stopping for a
second to marvel at its compactness. The terminal, if it could
even be called such a thing, is a single large room with a flickering neon sign for Great Lakes Airlines hung crookedly over a
counter along the far wall. Bright yellow carpeting covers the
floors, while the walls are painted an unpleasant shade of brown.
Another pair of doors along the side wall lead to the outer tar-

mac, where a single-engine plane covered in snow waits to be cleaned off.

"Wow," says Samira. "This place is *tiny.*"

"That's good," says Tak. "That's really good. Tiny is good right now."

There is no sign of Christy anywhere, so the two of them wander up to the counter and wait. Samira yawns and rests her head against Tak's shoulder, pressing her hair against his nose. The smell of her creeps up into his nostrils yet again, causing his mind to temporarily go fuzzy. *Christ, Sam,* he thinks. *You're gonna have to stop doing that.*

Tak sets the briefcase down and begins drumming on the counter, a random pattern of noise against the stillness of the terminal. He can hear someone moving around in the back room, but whether it's Christy or another employee, the person doesn't seem to be in any great hurry.

"So hey," says Samira, her voice muffled by the crook of his shoulder. "What are we doing? I mean, what's the plan?"

Tak pauses. His plan, if you could even call it that, was to fly from Nebraska to Los Angeles to Perth. Once in Perth, they would steal a car, drive into the heart of the Outback, break into the Axon Corporation, and restore the world to normal. Like most of Tak's plans, this one had kind of come together at the last minute. "Well," he begins, "I'm not totally sure."

He expects Samira to be upset by this, but to his surprise, she actually looks up and smiles. "You don't have a clue what we're going to do. . . . Do you?"

"Not really. I mean, I can get us to Australia, but after that, it gets a bit fuzzy."

"Details," shrugs Samira.

Tak stops drumming on the counter as a new, crazy idea suddenly pops into his head. *Or maybe it's actually been there all along.*

*Maybe I knew about this from the moment I stole the briefcase and fled the country, but I just didn't want to admit it.*

He thinks about this new idea for a moment before realizing that he has to act—if he spends much more time pondering the implications, he might realize how little sense it makes. Without another thought, he grabs Samira's head in his hands and leans in close, resting their foreheads together. "God, you smell fantastic," he says quietly.

"Tak?" she asks with a tremor in her voice. "Tak, what are—"

"Listen," he says, "there's another option: Fuck Australia. Fuck reality, fuck the solid timeline, fuck all of it. Let's just run. Find some place to hole up, get work, buy a house, maybe get a dog or something."

Samira smiles at this, but her expression fades as she stares into Tak's eyes. "Wait. You're serious?"

"I'm serious as a heart attack. This whole time, all I've been thinking about is trying to make everything the way it was before, but now I realize that's stupid." Tak pulls his head away from hers and turns to look at the sad little plane on the airport runway. He's shocked by the words that he feels rising in his mind, but has no way to stop their arrival. "I mean, what happens if we do it? I'm back working for a company that I hate, and two weeks from now you get sent back to the desert so people can try to kill you. Here we can start over, you know? We can do whatever we want."

Samira smiles shyly, then reaches down and takes his hand. "Where would we go?"

"I don't know. This place seems nice."

"I don't want to live in Nebraska, Tak. It's too cold."

"Well, California then. I dunno. Look, I'm making this up as I go along."

Samira lets his hand drop and turns her attention to the floor.

*Crap,* thinks Tak, *you shouldn't have said anything. You freaked her out. Now she's gonna wonder if this whole adventure was just one big date or something.*

"Look, Tak," she says. "I don't . . . The nice thing about the past couple of days is that I haven't had to think about certain things. Between the time travel and the freaky creatures chasing us, there hasn't really been the opportunity for quiet introspection."

"I'm sorry, Sam. I shouldn't have—"

"I have problems, Tak," she continues. "Real problems. You've seen a little bit of it, but that's . . . That's just what's on top. There are some terrible things inside my head, and at some point they're going to come out, and it won't be pretty. So if we give this up and just try to live a normal life, I don't think you're going to like what you find."

"Maybe," replies Tak. "But you know what? I'll take the chance. Look, if we decide to drop this and run, and you end up in a nuthouse somewhere, we'll deal with it when it happens. I mean, banzai, right?"

"Yeah," whispers Samira. "Banzai."

The door behind the counter suddenly opens to reveal a young woman. She smiles at the two of them, walks over to the counter, and turns on an ancient PC monitor. A gold name tag, clipped sideways on her blue vest, reads CHRISTY. "Hello there!" she says in an accent that could melt butter. "How are we today?"

"Fine," says Tak. He's only barely aware of her presence—all of his attention is focused on his friend standing next to him.

"And where are y'all traveling to?" asks Christy.

"Australia," says Tak, not looking up from Samira. "Or maybe nowhere. We're trying to decide."

"Oh, wow," says Christy with a smile. "That's quite the choice you've got there."

"We have to keep going," says Samira. "It's like you said: this is how we make things right. I'd love to cut out, Tak, I'd love to hole up somewhere and start a new life, but . . . I don't think it's possible."

A phone on the edge of the counter suddenly springs to life. Christy picks it up with a cheery greeting, then quickly falls silent. As she listens, the smile on her face fades and dies.

"It's gonna be dangerous," says Tak as beads of sweat suddenly pop out on his forehead. "Really dangerous. This is a brand-new timeline, and I don't really have much of a plan."

"You never have a plan. It's one of your quirky charms."

"Um, excuse me," interrupts Christy. "Are you Takahiro O'Leary?"

". . . Yeah? What is it?"

"You have a phone call."

Tak freezes as his mind begins to race. *Wait a minute. She knows my name. How the hell does she know my name? . . . And who the fuck is calling me?*

The woman behind the counter is holding the phone the way one might a poisonous snake. A cold fear slowly creeps in and latches to Tak's spine as he reaches out to take the bright orange receiver. "Hello?" he says slowly.

"Mr. O'Leary," says a voice on the other end. "How very nice to hear you again."

"Who is this?"

"Do me a favor, Mr. O'Leary. Look above you."

"It's a light," says Tak dryly as his eyes raise to the ceiling. "Wow, that is really awesome. I'm so glad you called to tell me about that."

"To the left of the light, if you please."

Tak shifts his gaze from the overhead light to a small black bubble mounted on the ceiling. He feels Samira tighten next to him and reaches out to find her hand. The cold fear on his spine is a raging beast now, and despite his best effort, his voice quakes a little when he responds.

"That's a camera, isn't it?" says Tak.

"Very good. Now let me ask you something, Mr. O'Leary. Are you aware that whenever you use the device at your feet, it leaves behind a large burst of both radiation and tachyon particles? Such things are rarely found in the middle of Nebraskan farmland, and so when we discovered them, it was a fairly simple matter to determine the origin."

". . . Yates?"

"Slower on the uptake than I would have liked from one of Axon's finest, but I suppose we can let it go. All that thievery has probably tired you out."

Tak's eyes grow wide. He takes a step back, then another, his tongue suddenly leaden in his mouth. On his third step, his feet trip on the briefcase and send him stumbling to the ground. The phone flies from his hand and goes crashing against the counter, where it begins to pendulum back and forth on its shiny orange cord.

"Tak?" says Samira. "Tak, what is it? What's going on?"

"Run," he whispers. "Oh God, Sam, we have to run. We have to run right now."

"What's going on? I don't—"

"RUN!" screams Tak, leaping to his feet. He grabs Samira's arm with one hand and the briefcase with the other as he spins in a crazy circle. Through the front doors of the airport, he sees a half dozen black cars crash onto the sidewalk and screech to a halt. Within moments, very large men begin to pour out of them and head for the terminal.

Tak pulls a stunned Samira toward the door that opens onto the tarmac. His only thought is to make it outside, where at least they have some options. He runs full speed at the door and hits the crash bar, but to his horror it doesn't even budge. Momentum carries him face-first into the glass, then sends him stumbling backward, stars flashing before his eyes. Before he can recover, Samira grabs the briefcase from his hand and swings it at the door. Though she puts all of her strength into it, the glass is thick and solid, and the case simply bounces harmlessly off to the side.

Tak hears men approaching behind him but doesn't dare turn around. He lowers his shoulder and runs at the door again, screaming at the top of his lungs. He has a vision of heroics, of fear and panic granting him the superhuman strength required to crash through the barrier and send them spilling out into the world, but it doesn't happen. He simply slams face-first into the door yet again, sending a shiver through the glass as his weakened legs give out and spill him to the ground.

The world fades in and out of darkness for a moment, and though he can hear the faint sounds of a struggle behind him, it's as if his ears are crammed with marshmallows. High-pitched screaming is coming from at least two sources, interspersed with the loud chatter of agitated males. He tries to stand up, but some-one puts a heavy boot down on the back of his neck and pins him to the ground. He hears another loud scream followed by a gun-shot, then silence.

For a brief moment, he's sure they shot Samira. But when the boot is lifted and a pair of strong hands flip him onto his back, he sees her crouched against the counter with a pair of dark-suited men on either side. A small stream of blood flows from behind the counter and toward the front door of the terminal, and he realizes that the men have actually shot Christy, the nice girl who did nothing more than show up for work on the wrong day.

"Assholes!" chokes Tak, knowing that this is probably the worst thing he could say to a group of angry men with guns, but not caring. "You goddamn uncle-fucking assholes!"

Two pairs of hands lift him off his feet and carry him behind the counter. He can see Christy's body now, eyes open in stunned surprise, but then another large man kicks her to the side, and Tak is thrust into a battered office chair.

"Sam!" he yells, as one of the men produces a roll of duct tape and begins securing him to the chair. "Sam, you okay?!"

"Tak!" she yells. She is invisible on the other side of the counter, but he sees the man next to her pull his leg back and give a short kick. Sam cries out at this, a noise that threatens to tear Tak's heart apart.

"Hey, fuckbag!" he screams. "You like kicking girls? How about you come over here and kick me?"

The man turns around to reveal a pair of sunglasses covering a face like a granite carving. Tak is flowing on pure adrenaline now, a dizzy giddiness descending on him like a blanket. "Yeah, that's right!" he continues. "Leave her alone and kick me instead! Come on, you can beat the shit out of me, then we'll go have a drink and I can give you a toothless blowjob. It'll be fun! We'll take pictures for your wife and everything."

Another man hits Tak in the back of the head with something hard. He feels blood rush into his mouth as he bites down on his tongue. The tape seems to be wrapping itself now, a strange silver streak that runs from the top of his shoulders down to his knees. His arms have been allowed to remain free from the elbows down, and as the man with the sunglasses who kicked Samira continues to stare, Tak takes the opportunity to flip him the bird.

"You're starting to piss me off," says Sunglasses.

"I have that effect on people," replies Tak.

The large man hauls Samira to her feet, her head barely rising over the top of the counter. He can see that she's shaking but otherwise showing remarkable calm. "Hey, Sam," he says. "You all right?"

"I'm fine, Tak," she says. "Just stop saying things."

"Listen to the little lady," rumbles Sunglasses. "Stop yelling."

"That's what I told your mom!" cries Tak, unable to help himself.

Samira actually rolls her eyes, a reaction that causes Tak's heart to leap inside his chest. He thinks about telling her this, but then a new thug steps forward and sets the briefcase down on the counter. Popping the latches, he grabs Tak's free hands, slams them onto the glass panel, and holds them in place so someone else can tape them down.

"Oh, hey, wait a second," begins Tak. "I don't . . . Yeah, this is a really bad idea, guys. Can't you just throw me in the back of a van or something?"

Sunglasses reaches forward, keeping one massive paw clamped firmly around Samira's arm, and places the dangling phone back on the receiver. "We're here, Mr. Yates," he says, leaning into the phone.

"Good, good," says Yates, his voice tinny and distant through the cheap phone speaker.

"Hey, Chuck," says Tak, as the men finish taping his hands down and step away. "You might wanna tell your boys here not to play around with gear they don't understand."

"They are men in your mold, Mr. O'Leary: they know enough to cause trouble but not so much that I can't use them."

Tak looks back at Samira and raises his eyebrows hopefully, trying to remain confident despite the presence of a dozen large men and a swiftly cooling body behind him. "So hey, listen," he begins. "I'm sorry I stole the briefcase, but you can totally have it back. I'm done with it. Really."

"Mr. O'Leary, I don't know how much you know about this new timeline of ours, but here, I am a very important, and very *busy*, man. Now, I need you to be quiet and attentive and listen to what I have to say. If you do not, I will have my men do some-thing entirely unpleasant to your curly-haired friend there."

Tak's mouth snaps closed. For a few seconds, the only sound is the whistling of wind through the open front door, then the voice of Yates returns. "I take it you are listening now?"

"Yeah. I'm listening."

Instead of speaking again, Yates begins to cough—a thick, watery sound like a man hacking into a bowl of Jell-O. This goes on for nearly a minute, then finally stops.

"Wow, Yates, you sound like shit," says Tak. "Maybe ease up on the smoking, huh?"

When Yates speaks again, his voice is harsh and low. "I would be much more concerned about your own health, Mr. O'Leary. Rather than mine."

"You switched the timelines, didn't you?" accuses Tak. "I mean, I know chicks dig power and everything, but this seems like a real roundabout way to take over the company."

Yates chuckles. "The material trappings of wealth hold no interest for me, Mr. O'Leary. Yes, it is as you say: I am in charge of the Axon Corporation here, and of course that comes with many advantages. But my ultimate goal is something far more important than a buxom trophy wife."

"So what do you want?"

"What I want is to complete my plan in peace. And that means I cannot afford to have you around."

"So, what then?" asks Tak with as much false bravado as he can muster. "You gonna put a bullet in my head or something?"

Samira's eyes grow wide as he says this, and he finds himself wishing that he'd just kept his mouth shut. Sunglasses smiles as if he finds this idea very appealing, but then Yates speaks once more. "You are not supposed to be here, Mr. O'Leary. You are an outlier, a random *bit* that I had not anticipated. Killing you in this timeline could have far-reaching consequences. Perhaps you will come back in another form. Or perhaps it will throw this timeline into disarray. I am not sure, and because of that, I have decided on a safer course of action. I will send you to one of the random timelines of which you are so fond, then destroy the briefcase. You are a lucky man. As this world's king, I could sentence you to death. Instead, I have chosen banishment."

Tak locks his eyes on Samira. "You mean *us*, right?" he says. "You're gonna send *us* to another timeline?"

"No, Mr. O'Leary. I mean *you*."

Tak feels his mouth dry up. "Wait a second," he croaks. "Yates, wait. Wait, wait. Don't take her, Yates. Send her with me. We'll vanish, we'll go away, you'll never hear from us again."

"Mr. Kazdal?" says Yates.

"Sir?" says the man behind Tak who hit him with the butt of his gun.

"Set the briefcase to 4-5-3-4-2-2."

Tak begins to strain at his bonds as the dials are turned. Green light spills out of the case and washes across the faces of the other men, giving them a dark, unearthly glow. His breath quickens as his fingers begin to stretch across the surface of the glass panel.

"Sam!" he cries. "Sam, I'm sorry! I'm so sorry!"

"Be careful, Tak," she whispers, as her frame begins to warble and disappear from sight. "Please just . . . be careful."

"Safe travels, Mr. O'Leary," says the voice from the phone as Tak's world fades into a dark, starless night. "And don't worry about your friend. I promise to take very special care of her."

# chapter eighteen

Rays of sun filter through a curtain and onto the face of an aged man, his skin a shade paler than the bleached hospital sheets on which he lies. His breath emerges low and rattling—when it comes at all—and his eyes have a sunken, haunted look. Sitting next to him, holding his hand, is an older Japanese woman with silver hair. Everything else in the room is a glowing white blur, as if the two of them exist in a world made of light.

*Oh God. Dad. Oh no. Don't make me see this again.*

A young doctor walks into the room and makes notes on a clipboard. Like all the medical professionals before him, he examines the paperwork, shakes his head, and leaves the room as quickly as he arrived, silently wondering how the man in the bed could possibly be alive at all. Logic and science dictated that he should have simply keeled over in the wilderness when the heart attack struck—a man of his age had no business hiking out of a canyon and driving himself to a hospital with only half a working ventricle. And yet here he is, fighting to the end. He seems the kind of man who has been fighting with something his entire life.

The woman leans forward and says something in Japanese. The man in the bed chuckles a little, his eyes sagging around the corners like an old shirt hung out to dry. She smiles in return and leans back in her seat once more but does not let go of his hand. Soon thereafter, Tak walks into the room and takes up a position at the foot of the bed. He carries himself with arrogance, as if the events happening in front of him could not concern him less.

*Is this the day he dies? Or was it the next day? . . . God, look at me. Look how I'm standing there, like I couldn't give less of a shit. I didn't even tell him good-bye.*

The man lifts his eyes toward Tak, and his expression narrows. Tak returns the glare with defiance, as if the frail figure in the bed somehow presents a challenge. They hold each other's eyes until the woman leans forward and pulls on the sleeve of Tak's shirt. She says a few words in a voice fraught with emotion, but they are blurry and impossible to make out.

*Christ, I don't even remember what she said. What the hell was I thinking about? The show? The next area I was going to explore? The fangirls back in Tokyo with the fake tits and the Hello Kitty skirts? Oh, Dad, I'm sorry. I'm so goddamn sorry about everything.*

A machine behind the man's head springs into view and begins to beep erratically. Tak can see every detail of the machine—every wire, every screw—because all of his attention is drawn to it. A thin green line bounces up and down against a dark black background, spiking and falling with increasing intensity.

*This is it. This is where he goes. Ah, Christ, no.*

The man pulls in a harsh, rattling breath, but his chest refuses to fall again. The pale skin starts to turn blue as a loud alarm suddenly goes off. The woman begins to wail before reaching over the railing and shaking her husband with something approaching fury. Tak stands at the foot of the bed with an expression on his face as if he can't believe this is actually happening.

*I'm dead. I'm not in the Machine, I'm dead and this is hell and I have to live through this for eternity. Please. Please, please, make it stop. Make it fucking*

**people are crowded** into a living room. There are far too many for the small space, and the energy of them is everywhere. Along the wall, next to a large picture window, four old women in traditional garb hug each other and speak comforting words in a language Tak barely comprehends. Men in dull suits stand next to the fireplace with cups of tea in their hands, talking quietly. Smells emanate from a nearby kitchen—coriander and turmeric and cumin and a dozen other spices that seem both exotic and comfortingly familiar. Nearby, a table piled with food groans under the weight of the dishes.

Ahmed Moheb moves slowly through the crowd, people stopping him every few steps to grab his hands, exchange a few words, kiss him on the cheek. An unlit cigarette dangles forgotten from his fingers. Despite the comfort of the family and friends that now fill his small suburban home, there is a profound sadness on his face.

*Oh, wow. I haven't thought about this in forever.*

The crowd parts to allow Ahmed access to the table of food. He clasps his hands behind his back and stands in front of it like a general surveying the troops. Finally, he reaches out, grabs a small piece of dried fruit between his fingers, and brings it toward his mouth. Halfway through the journey he seems to lose interest, and eventually he sets the fruit back among its many brethren.

An older woman comes up behind him and makes a motion with her hands. *Eat, eat,* she is saying. *You must eat something.* Ahmed shakes his head and backs away from the table, making small excuses all the while. Ultimately the crowd becomes too much for him to handle, and he moves through them and out to the back deck, where he lights his cigarette with trembling hands. Rain falls against a dark Seattle night. A cold wind blows. If his plan was to be alone, even for a little while, this certainly seems to be the place for it.

But he is not alone: there is a young man with spiky black hair leaning against the railing of the deck and gazing off into the distance. Ahmed considers his form for a bit as his cigarette slowly burns, then shuffles across the faded wooden boards and joins the other man at the rail.

"Hello, Takahiro," says Ahmed.

"Hey, Mr. Moheb," says Tak. He continues to look out over the rows of suburban houses and their identical peaked rooftops. "How are things in there?"

"Crowded. And noisy. My cousins try to make me eat."

"Which cousins?"

"Pah. All of them." He waves his hand in the air, leaving a smoky trail in the rain. "I tell them not to bring food. I tell them, 'No. We will have a small remembrance. That is how she would have wanted it.' But they bring the food anyway."

"I guess they're trying to help."

"Perhaps they do not know how else to mourn."

Ahmed finishes his cigarette and tosses it into the back lawn. He then reaches into his suit coat, shakes two more free and offers one to Tak, who takes it with a nod. The two men light their smokes and lean against the railing as the noise of the house increases behind them.

"Taslima always disliked this suit," says Ahmed after a pause. He lifts a faded brown tie in his hands and stares at it with a faraway expression. "She told me to throw it out and get a new one, but it was purchased in Iran, and I was . . . fond of it. I have so few things left from that time."

He seems ready to say more, but a hitching sound comes out of his throat instead. The noise seems to surprise him, and he tries furiously to avoid meeting Tak's gaze as he straightens up and runs one sleeve of the old brown suit across his eyes. When the fabric comes away, it is spotted with bits of wet. Tak lifts one arm with hesitation and slowly places it around the shoulders of the older man. "I'm sorry," he says quietly. "I always loved her."

"She was far better than I deserved."

"I don't think that's true."

Ahmed glances over at the young man beside him and almost smiles. "Thank you for being here, Takahiro," he says. "I will always remember it."

They return to silence as the world begins to splinter and dissolve around them, sharp beams of light cutting through the darkness until the memory becomes a shimmering wall of white.

**tak is slumped** in a chair, eyes closed, breathing heavily. To his left, a woman with long red hair scribbles calculations on a whiteboard. From somewhere behind them, a stereo belts out a fierce Thelonious Monk solo.

*Ah, Monk. When you're on, there's no one better.*

"Tak?" asks the woman without turning around. When there is no response, she looks over her shoulder and sees that he is trying to nap. Without skipping a beat, she picks up a dry eraser and hurls it at his head.

"Whuzza!?" cries Tak, bolting out of the chair. "What? What is it?"

"We need to talk."

"Goddammit, Judith, seriously. I'm tired."

"It can wait."

Tak stretches, small pops emerging from the depths of his

spine, and wanders over to the whiteboard. He stares at the mass
of numbers and equations and symbols, trying to find something
recognizable to kick-start the conversation. "Um . . . nice math,"
he says weakly.

"All math is nice," replies Judith as she scribbles a radius in the
one clean corner of the board. "That's why I like it."

"Are you just doing this for fun, or—"

"Have you ever considered what would happen if this project
went wrong?"

Tak yawns, stretches, and wanders away from Judith as a
table warbles into existence on the other side of the room. There's
a bowl of fresh fruit sitting in the middle, and he gladly purloins
an apple from the pile. "Not really," he says through a mouthful
of pith. "I leave thinking to eggheads like you."

"This isn't funny," she says. "We're messing with time here.
We're doing things that no one has ever thought of before. It could
easily have far-reaching consequences."

Tak leans against the board and accidentally rubs a number
out of existence. He sees this and gets a sheepish grin on his face,
then quickly picks up a marker and puts it back. "Sorry," he mutters. "Seriously, though. I'm listening. What do you want?"

"I made a fail-safe."

"You made . . . Sorry, you made what?"

"A fail-safe. It's a copy of our timeline before Yates and Axon
and everyone started tinkering with the Machine. Think of it as
a hard-drive backup, if that's easier for you. I want you to promise me that you'll use it if things go wrong."

Tak raises his hands and backs away. "Whoa, Judith. Come
on, now. I can't promise anything like that. I mean, how will I
even know if things *are* going wrong? I'm just a grunt, you know?"

"You'll know," she replies, staring at the numbers in front of
her. "Trust me. You'll most certainly know."

She pauses for a moment, but before she can say more, the memory shudders violently. Cracks of white move across the surface of Tak's vision and break the world into shards, pieces crumbling off into nothingness before the entire thing finally dissolves into dust.

*well, she was* *right about that. . . . Yeah, well, whatever. I gotta get out of here and go find Sam. Come on, Machine. Let's go. Hurry this up. Let's go, let's go, let's*

**a large fist** is rushing toward Tak's face. It happens so slowly, he has a chance to admire every facet of the hand: the well-manicured fingernails, the slightly scuffed knuckles, the blue class ring with the words MEADOWDALE HIGH etched around the outside. Then the fist smashes into his nose, and the next thing he sees is the ceiling. This view lasts for about three seconds before being replaced by the twisted, angry face of a young man with a bad crew cut.

"Yeah, now what!?" cries the young man.

He sees someone else appear in the corner of his vision: it's Samira, and before he can say anything to the young man, she grabs his arm and helps him to his feet. She might be telling him *let it go, let it go,* but the ringing in his ears makes it hard to hear.

"Yeah, that's right," says Crew Cut as a few of his friends laugh and punch one another in the arms, terribly amused by the entire thing. "You and that camel jockey get the fuck out of here."

Tak stops moving. Samira looks into his eyes, pleading silently for him to do the smart thing, but knowing in her heart he's never been very good at doing the smart thing. He glances over at her and gives a small shrug, to which she shakes her head furiously.

Then, before she can say anything more, he spins around, grabs Crew Cut by the back of the neck, and brings the boy's face down into his knee. The force of the blow actually causes the teen to backpedal a couple of steps, where he wobbles in place like a dying top before reaching to his nose, feeling the first sticky drops of blood, then collapsing backward into a heap.

"You got punked like a low bitch!" cries Tak with a furious grin. He seems ready to say more, but then the other teens rush forward and begin to pound the hell out of him.


**the man stumbles** through the front door of the house with blood smeared in his hair. "Scabs!" he screams, his voice slurred with a night of alcohol. "Fuckin' scabs! Broke the picket lines, crossed over. But we got 'em after the shift. Fucked 'em up good!" A young Takahiro peeks out from between the legs of a chair and watches his father lean against the wall and slowly slide to a sitting position. From somewhere behind them, a woman begins to scream in Japanese.


**two young women** dance clumsily, their forms little more than shadows in the dim lighting of the club. Loud techno music assaults Tak from all sides as he slumps on a velvet couch and watches the women begin to undress. They giggle and raise their eyebrows at him in an attempt to be sexy, but his only response is a slow, blank nod. One of them crawls onto the table where he's amassed an army of beer bottles, takes off her bra, and leans close enough for him to smell the alcohol wafting off her. "I never had sex with TV star," she says in halting English. Tak doesn't reply; he simply stares forward with the same blank expression as the woman begins to nibble on his ear.

• • •

red sand stretches toward the horizon in every direction. There are no mountains, no hills, nothing to break up the immense flatness of the landscape but the fact that it eventually vanishes from sight. Tak lies on his back in the middle of this sand and waits for the Machine to take him home so they can start the process all over again.

he runs from a mob, dodging carts and donkeys and peasants in cloth sack dresses as his sneakers pound on cobblestone streets. *Pitchforks!* he thinks wildly, as a flaming arrow blazes past and takes a notch out of his ear. *They actually have fucking pitchforks!* He turns a corner and sees a man in shining metal armor, then the world spins and heaves and blurs together before finally exploding into stars.

tak opens his eyes and sees a massive building stretching up to the sky. He can hear wind blowing through the city; it echoes and howls as it slinks in and out of a million broken windowpanes. His eyes shift left and find the burned-out remains of a car; they shift right and see a small coffee shop with shattered furniture and a bloodstained floor. He smells the air and discovers rain and smoke, as well as the unmistakable scent of death. The urge to close his eyes and pretend that none of this is happening is overwhelming, but instead he forces himself to his knees and waits for the sickness that he knows will arrive soon. "Hold on, Sam," he mutters, as his stomach begins to clench. "I'm coming. . . . I'm fucking coming."

flicker and die

# chapter nineteen

One of Samira's dreams—perhaps the worst one of all—has nothing to do with Iraq. Although it started sometime between her first and second tour, she's never been convinced that the two things are related, and she hates it more than any of her other dreams for that very reason. At least when she's being chased by children in Fallujah or watching someone be torn apart by an IED, she can match the nightmare to a trauma. The randomness of this one, the way it seemingly comes out of left field, makes it so much more disturbing.

In the dream, she's riding her bike down a suburban street on a gorgeous fall day. She's young, maybe ten, and the wind catches her hair as she races along without a care. Bright orange and brown leaves fall from the trees and land in her path, creating a pleasant crunching sound as her bike rolls over them. When she thinks about this dream during her waking hours, she always wonders why it can't just end here. But of course, it never does.

In the continuing nightmare, she rolls over leaves and smells the scents of autumn and lets the late-afternoon sun warm her face. But, inevitably, a different sound appears—a deep, low growl from somewhere far behind her. Samira always tells herself not to look, but as is the way with dreams, it's impossible not to. And when she turns her head to see what could possibly be creating such a harsh and unpleasant noise, she sees a giant black machine roaring up the street behind her.

It's a street sweeper, the kind with large round bristles mounted on the bottom and a rotating yellow hazard siren bolted to the top. But while most such vehicles top out around fifteen miles an hour, this one moves with the speed of a fine Italian sports car. The bumper is curved like a smile, the headlights are dim little eyes. Behind the windshield, darkened almost to the point of opacity, she can barely make out a shadowy figure with a mad grin; whoever the driver is, there are way too many teeth in his mouth.

At this point, something in Samira's consciousness clicks into action, and the tiny piece of her that understands this is a dream attempts to wake the rest of her up. But the self-aware spark is a powerless thing in the face of the nightmare, and its failure only makes the rest of the event more terrifying. So as the dream continues, and her conscious mind begins to silently scream, she presses against the pedals of her bike and churns her legs up and down as fast as they can go. There are no turnoffs on this illusory street, no driveways in which to seek safety or trees to hide behind; her only option is to press forward and try to outrun the monster coming up behind her. *Faster,* she screams to herself. *Faster faster faster faster faster.*

But she never escapes. Not once, not in all the dozens of times the dream has played itself in her sleeping mind, has she ever broken free of the sweeper. Inevitably, her mad pedaling decelerates until she seems to be moving through a thick syrup. Her vision begins to blur. Her legs churn with agonizing slowness. And when the machine races up behind her and catches her with a triumphant roar, she feels herself being pulled off the bike and into the guts of the thing, wire bristles tearing her apart like so much trash from the gutter, flaying skin from bone while somehow leaving her alive and aware of exactly what is happening to her.

*This* is the point where she wakes up—always with a scream dying in her throat, sometimes with bloody trails in her skin where nails have clawed at flesh. She always cries after this dream—huge, heaving sobs that seem impossible coming from such a small woman. She cries and cries and waits for the dream to fade from her mind. But, of course, it never does. Not completely, anyway.

Samira has never told anyone about this dream—not her psychiatrist, not her military companions, not Tak—but she suddenly feels an urge to speak of it to the man sitting in the seat across from her, the one with his fingertips pressed together and his eye twitching in a distracted kind of way. The reason she wants to tell him is so he knows he can't possibly hurt her any more than her mind has already done, and that whatever plan he's devising will be nothing compared to the knowledge that every night might end with her being pursued by a maintenance vehicle from hell. She thinks it's very, very important that he know this because right now she's as scared as she has ever been in her life.

The man sitting across from her is Charles Yates.

After Tak was strapped to the briefcase and sent to a random timeline somewhere down the stack, the large men in black suits threw Samira in the back of a car and drove like madmen to the Omaha Airport, where she was transferred to a large private jet. The inside of the plane was like nothing she had ever seen: plush carpeting, fine art hanging from the sides of the fuselage, even a crystal chandelier over a dining-room table somewhere in the back. She had been plunked into a cushy leather seat and given an injection in her arm which immediately put her into a deep and dreamless state of unconsciousness. But there had been no time to appreciate the nightmare-free nap because when she finally clawed her way up and out of the blackness, she found Charles Yates sitting across from her. He didn't even need to introduce himself; she knew right away who he was.

He has yet to say anything even though he knows she's fully awake and alert. He's much older than she thought he would be, with grey hair and wrinkles and a pair of thick black glasses that sag on his gaunt face. But the eyes—oh, the eyes. There's something utterly mad lurking behind the surface of his eyes, a look she's only ever seen before in the heat of combat. They contain a dark sparkle that seems to say *I am capable of absolutely anything*, and just looking at them is enough to get Samira's terror juices flowing. The only way her mind can stay connected to reality is if she thinks of Yates as a kindly old grandfather rather than the raving lunatic she suspects him to be.

Yates clears his throat. Samira jumps. He smiles briefly at this, then leans forward in his seat. Through the window next to him, Samira can see their plane racing against the setting sun and wonders anew where these people are taking her. "Who are you?" he asks finally. His voice is surprisingly weak and contains the slight tremble of an old man. "What is your name?"

Samira considers this question for a while. Having spent five years of her life translating between insurgents and military men, she knows all about being a prisoner. And though she doesn't see anything in the fancy airplane that suggests the possibility of torture, the world is full of small brick rooms with drains in the floor. So she decides to respond with truth, and as such, the question-and-answer session moves very quickly.

"I'm Samira," she says. "Samira Moheb."

"Where are you from?"

"Seattle."

"Originally."

"Oh. Iran."

"How do you know Mr. O'Leary?"

"We went to high school together."

"In the singular reality?"

"In the . . . I'm sorry, in the what?"

"I believe your friend calls it the solid timeline."

"Oh, sorry. Yes. In the solid timeline."

Yates leans back in his chair and removes his glasses, then rubs his temples with trembling hands. He's wearing an old cardigan sweater and weathered black slacks underneath a white lab coat. Samira glances at the floor and sees that the hem is darkened with old stains—she doesn't even want to think about what could have made them.

*Coffee. It's just coffee. He made some this morning before taking his grandkids to the park.*

"What is your profession?" asks Yates, still rubbing at his temples. A small drop of black goo leaks out from the corner of his eye, but he quickly wipes it away. It happens so fast, Samira isn't even sure she saw it.

"Your profession," repeats Yates, annoyed.

"I'm military," says Samira quickly.

"Is that why Mr. O'Leary brought you here? As some manner of bodyguard?"

Samira has a sudden image of herself wearing dark glasses with a gun in her hand and begins to giggle. The laughter slips out despite her fear and despite knowing that Yates might take such a reaction very poorly. But she just can't help it. *Go, go, go,* she imagines her bodyguard-self screaming into an earpiece. *Get the president out of there NOW, so I can mop the floor!*

"No, I'm not a bodyguard."

"Is this amusing?" asks Yates in a quiet voice.

"I'm sorry, I just . . . I would be a really bad bodyguard. That's all."

"So what did you do?"

"I was a translator. I grew up speaking Farsi and standard Arabic and a little bit of Pashto, so when I joined the army, they made me a translator."

"You're not a combat soldier?"

Samira shrugs. "I shot a rifle and went through training, but I was never very good at it."

"Then why are you here?"

"Tak came for me. He told me . . . He said some people were going to overwrite the timeline, and I wasn't in it, and that meant I was going to die. So he came and found me, and we used the briefcase and went . . . somewhere. Then we came back, and you found us."

Yates nods and leans forward. His breath smells of onions and stale cheese, but also something else. Something wet and old and terrible. It's a slightly familiar smell, but she can't remember where she's noticed it before. Rather than try, Samira keeps her eyes focused straight ahead and imagines her captor sitting in front of an old-fashioned radio and listening to Lawrence Welk.

"Are you hungry?" asks Yates.

"N-no, thank you," responds Samira.

"Thirsty?"

"A little."

"We have water and tea."

"Tea would be . . . fine. Thank you."

He motions to one of the men sitting behind them, the one who hit Tak in the back of the head with his gun. The man leans down and confers with Yates for a moment, then retreats behind a curtain at the front of the plane. Yates seems to lose interest in their conversation after this, his gaze wandering to a spot somewhere outside his window. For Samira's part, she sits upright in her chair and wonders if suicide is in any way viable. She has a brief flash of leaping up and opening the emergency exit, spinning and falling through twenty-four thousand feet of nothingness before landing in a tiny Samira Splat at the bottom of a strange, new world. It's an option, at least. Not a very good one, but preferable to becoming some kind of subject in this man's experiment.

*No. He's good. He's good and kind and he's going to play checkers with you later. La la la la la.*

The man in the suit returns with two steaming cups of tea, which he deposits on a small table between the seats. Samira picks hers up and blows on it. *What a nice old man. Getting you tea. He didn't have to do that.*

"Did Mr. O'Leary explain the Machine to you?" asks Yates, still staring out the window. "Did he tell you that it was a time machine? Did he use that ridiculous example of the universe as a stack of pancakes?"

Samira nods. It doesn't seem possible that Yates could see this motion, but he clearly does. This only increases her awe of him.

"It is a flawed metaphor," he says, "but I suppose it works well enough for the layperson. Can I also assume he told you we were bringing another timeline here? That we were, in essence, overwriting reality?"

"Yes, he told me that," says Samira. A brief bout of turbulence shakes the plane, but Samira hardly notices. Yates starts to speak again but instead is interrupted by a violent coughing fit that lasts for over a minute. When he pulls his hand away from his mouth, it is flecked with thick black spots.

"This may come as a surprise to you, but I had no interest in such a thing," says Yates as he wipes his hand on a napkin and stuffs it into his pocket. "However, the men who ran the Axon Corporation wanted to live in a timeline where they were kings

186 | alan averill

of the world. It was a predictably absurd request, but once made, I realized it was a fine way to keep them all happy and distracted. So while they worried themselves about stock markets and military forces, I was wrestling with far more important problems. How is the tea?"

Samira blinks. "Um . . . It's fine. Thank you."

"Good." Yates nods. He runs his hand across his mouth and then stares at it, as if expecting to see more black there. "You see, I saw the paradox of the Machine almost immediately. If I could create such a thing, others could do so as well. If I could overwrite reality, men in other timelines could do the same. The very possibility that the Machine could be invented somewhere else threatened our existence. Ergo, the only way to prevent that from happening was to eliminate all of the timelines."

He finally looks away from the window and back to Samira. His eyes flash with the dim light of madness, and any pretense she had of the kindly grandfather is gone. She opens her mouth to tell him about her street-sweeper dream, but he continues speaking. "But, of course, this created a problem for me. I have no desire to die, nor to sacrifice myself for the imagined good of others. I had to find a timeline where I could exist forever, then find a way to avoid being destroyed by the virus."

Samira's hands are shaking like crazy now, drops of tea flying around the cabin like a miniature rainstorm. "The . . . virus?" she manages to say.

Yates leans toward Samira and drops his voice to a harsh whisper. "You see, time—*all* of time—is a living thing. It breathes and moves and changes as events act upon it. And like any living thing, it can be killed."

"You can't kill time," whispers Samira. She knows it's folly to argue with this man, but the words make their way out anyway.

"Ah, but you can," replies Yates. "If you eliminate everything in the universe, if you remove every force which can possibly act, then time itself will simply cease to be. And the virus is the key."

Samira has a vision of the creature she saw in the alternate timeline, the thing that resembled a baby bird, and she suddenly realizes what the virus is. Immediately on the heels of that thought, she remembers why the stink of Yates's breath seems so familiar. *Oh my God,* she thinks wildly. *He smells like that thing. He smells* just *like it.*

"So you see that my problem is twofold," continues Yates. "One: I must eliminate all life in the universe. Two: I must find for myself a perfect timeline where I can spend eternity in peace. I must find the Beautiful Land."

He leans closer and grabs the back of Samira's head. Her heart leaps into her throat and hangs there, as if all the systems in her body are getting ready to simply stop. "I bent all my will to these problems. For the last thirty years of my life, I did nothing but grapple with them until I was sure I had conquered both. And once I was positive that everything was ready, I turned my plan to action. I activated the Machine, unleashed the virus, and initiated the destruction of all existence."

"But you're still here," says Samira, her voice barely audible.

"Yes. I am still here."

"So you . . . changed your mind?"

"I did not," he says, rubbing a thumb against the nape of her neck. "The second part of the plan is already in motion. Timelines are being destroyed as we speak, and the virus will not stop until it has exterminated all life. . . . But that, of course, includes me. So then, how to avoid its gaze? How can I assure myself that the creatures will not follow me to the Beautiful Land?"

Samira shakes her head and tries to swallow, but there's a

huge lump there that prevents it. *Run for the door,* she thinks. *Run for the door and throw yourself out.* But she can't. Her legs simply won't go.

"The only way to avoid them is to *become* them," he whispers. A single trickle of black worms from his gum line and down the front of one chipped tooth. He licks it away absentmindedly as he stares into Samira. "I trapped one. I stole its life. And now that the change is irreversible, I am ready to flee this timeline forever."

"Are you going to kill me?" asks Samira suddenly. She doesn't even feel the question form in her mind: it just pops out and hangs in the air like a sad pinata.

"No," responds Yates, not unkindly. "You are to serve a higher purpose."

"I am?"

"Only someone from the singular reality can interact with the Machine. I will not use Takahiro, because he has proven himself unworthy of this gift. And I cannot use Judith as I planned because she has vanished. So that means you, Samira Moheb from Iran, are the only option left to me."

"I . . . I don't understand."

"You will become a doorway. A conduit. Yours will be the mind that grants me access to the Beautiful Land. And when I take you there and seal the conduit behind me, you and I shall live forever. And it will be *wonderful.*"

He smiles at this, a terrifying thing, and suddenly Samira realizes who has been driving the sweeper all these years. She can feel herself growing faint, feel the familiar terror running inside her, and she knows that this time there will be no controlling it. As her vision begins to fail, she looks longingly at the door of the plane and wishes with all her strength she had the courage to finally set herself free.

# chapter twenty

"That must have been one hell of an important call," says Tak to no one in particular.

He's staring at the bones of a woman lying facedown in the crosswalk. She's draped in the tattered remains of a blue dress and holding a cell phone in one hand. The other hand is splayed across the pavement with most of the fingers gone. There is a large, ragged hole in the top of her empty skull, and the more Tak stares at it, the more it looks like someone jammed a straw in there and sucked out the insides like a milk shake. He can see a handful of such skeletons from his current vantage point, all of which appear to have the same wound. He has an idea what caused the carnage but doesn't want to think about it just yet. There will be plenty of time to freak himself out later.

His pancake-free insides have finally stopped twisting around, a fact for which Tak is eternally grateful. He uses the sleeve of his rapidly disintegrating suit coat to wipe a fleck of puke from the corner of his mouth, then jogs in place to test his legs. When they don't send him crashing to the ground, he takes that as a sign it's time to move. Soon his mind is clicking into survival mode, sorting through his priorities and working on solutions for each. The usual top of the list, water, is shoved to one side and replaced with shelter; Tak is more than willing to die from thirst if it saves him from meeting whatever punched a hole through the brains of an entire population.

*But you can't die,* he thinks. *You can't because Sam is back in the solid timeline with Yates. And you know the kind of man he is. You know what he's capable of.*

The thought of Samira in the company of Charles Yates strikes Tak with physical force, and he finds himself fighting the urge to begin vomiting all over again. Such thoughts are poison if he's to have any hope of surviving this bombed-out shell of a timeline, so he quickly makes a new deal with himself: *Stop thinking about her. Just don't think about Sam until you're out of this place. Then, once you're back in the solid timeline, you can ruminate until your heart explodes. Deal? . . . Yeah, okay. Deal.*

The city in which Tak finds himself is a massive thing that must have once teemed with life. Surely the people who lived here wouldn't recognize the silence of the place now; they probably never knew a time when things weren't loud and bustling and wonderfully *alive.* Judging by the height of the buildings that tower around him—as well as the occasional fine suit he sees shrouding a skeleton—Tak appears to have landed in the financial district. Cars litter the streets and sidewalks, and a few have even slammed into the sides of buildings. These broken wrecks are marked with odd, unrecognizable names: "Solaris," "Technic," "Fananza," "Grin." They look similar to cars from the solid timeline although most have four or five tailpipes where there should be one. When Tak peers into the passenger's-side window of one accordioned Fananza, he sees a joystick instead of a steering wheel.

His legs are coming back to him now, so he picks up the pace. At the next intersection, he finds an overturned tractor trailer with a picture of a young woman on the side. She's holding her hands to the sky as happy-faced pens and pencils dance like maniacs around her head. YOU WON'T BELIEVE THE SAVINGS! claims the tagline at the bottom of the image. The rear of the trailer has been shorn off by the crash, revealing a collection of soggy cardboard boxes scattered around the interior. When Tak clambers inside and tears one open, he's disappointed to find a computer printer staring back. He looks through a few more boxes on the off-chance they contain bottled water, Cheetos, or some other staple of the modern white-collar diet, but all he finds are sodden electronics and a discarded beer can.

Abandoning the truck, he continues down the street, eyes roaming the city as he searches for possible shelter. Some buildings are little more than crumbled heaps of concrete and steel, as if a giant child destroyed them with a tantrum. Others are simply too dark and foreboding, and these he passes on as well. He stumbles upon a small corner deli that looks promising, but when he tries to open the door, a pile of skeletal remains pushes back against him. Rather than try to clear the bones and fight his way inside, he just moves on.

As he travels, Tak picks up anything that could be helpful. His treasures include a can of grape soda from the bottom of a garbage can and a length of chain purloined from the trunk of a smashed car. At one point, a plastic bag emblazoned with the words GAS & MUNCH blows past him. He snatches it out of the air and stuffs his finds inside, then ties the handles around one of his belt loops to create a makeshift purse.

The buildings are getting smaller now, but if anything, the disaster seems more widespread. Most of the dwellings are covered with a thick layer of soot and ash, reminding Tak of the postapocalyptic video games he used to play in high school. The bodies are also more numerous, and some have clearly been felled by their fellow man. He passes one with a power drill sticking out of the rib cage, another with a machete embedded between the eyes. At some point he turns a corner and finds a gigantic pile of bones stacked into a grim pyramid. They are covered with a black substance that looks like motor oil, but when Tak attempts to run a finger over it, the entire stack wobbles precariously. Not wanting to hear the sound of a hundred collapsing bodies—or discover what such a thing might smell like—he quickly skitters around the side of the structure and moves on.

Finally, he comes to a stop in front of a grey building perhaps twenty stories high. The glass front doors are miraculously intact, and he can see faded gold lettering beneath a layer of dark, dusty ash. When he approaches the door and runs a sleeve across the front, five words appear as if by magic: RIVERSIDE STEPS AT THE PEARL.

"The Pearl?" muses Tak. "Am I in Portland? No, wait, this can't be Portland. Portland's full of hippies. They wouldn't kill each other with drills. . . . Right?"

The empty city does not reply, so rather than think about it, he pulls one of the front doors open and steps inside. Once in the lobby, he is immediately greeted by the sight of a skeleton with no head nailed to the far wall. Next to the body, someone has spray painted a rough drawing of what appears to be a vulture, along with the words RUN BITCH RUN.

"Well, hell," says Tak. "I was afraid of that."

He worms his way through a makeshift barrier of moldy, broken furniture—taking special care not to disturb the art-deco wall hanging—and locates the stairs. His goal is to get to the top floor, then take a few hours to rest and figure out his next move. The penthouse will give him a good view of the city, and if there happens to be water or food there, well then, so much the better.

With legs cranky and sore, Tak begins the long trek up. At the landing for floor seven, he finds a dry puddle of blood nearly an inch thick. It trails away up the stairs, occasionally leaping to the handrail, until it finally ends with a single red handprint smeared on the door to floor fourteen. Tak makes a mental note to never go to that floor, no matter how desperate things get. He just doesn't even want to know.

Finally, he reaches the end of the staircase and finds a door marked 22, as well as a ladder that leads up and away into blackness. The ladder is probably roof access, but he has no interest in such things right now; instead, he shoulders through the door and onto the top floor of the condominium.

He emerges in a long hallway with plush brown carpet and tasteful, if somewhat generic, modern art on the walls. To his surprise, there isn't a penthouse suite—instead, he has a choice between about a dozen identical doors. Tak moves down the hall, trying handles until he finds one that turns under his grip. He drops to one knee and puts his eye to the floor, searching for movement. When a minute passes, and nothing happens, he reaches into the plastic bag at his hip, withdraws the chain, and wraps two lengths of it around his hand. Thus armed, he stands up, twists the knob, and goes barging into the condo with his fist raised and ready for trouble.

The front door opens directly into a kitchen/living room combo, the latter of which contains a black leather couch, a decent-looking television, and stacks of unfamiliar gaming consoles. A large set of windows on the far wall look out over the city, its structures tall and grey and utterly deserted. To the left of the windows, a glass door leads to an outside deck maybe ten feet in length. Tak drops his chain and steps outside for a breath of fresh air but quickly finds himself creeped out by the idea of standing watch over a dead city. Retreating inside, he explores the rest of the unit, finding a bedroom with an unmade bed, a closet with a handful of dark T-shirts, and a small, somewhat dirty bathroom. The toilet bowl is completely dry, but Tak is pleased to find a couple of gallons of water in the tank.

He returns to the kitchen and begins opening shelves, shoving aside plates and cups and silverware in a quest for sustenance. After five minutes of rummaging, all he finds is a single box of something called Crisp Rite Crackers. They're old and stale, but he takes out a couple and munches anyway. He's not particularly hungry, but his stomach is still fairly angry with him, so at this point anything is better than nothing.

Tak washes the meal down with the can of soda. Then, uttering a small belch, he wanders back to the living room, flops down on the sofa, and spends a few minutes trying to get his thoughts in order. After a while, the stillness of the place starts to get to him, and he begins talking out loud.

"Jesus, you're really in the weeds on this one," he says with a forced cheerfulness that has never felt so false. "Okay. So. You found another dead timeline. That makes two in two trips, which is pretty damn odd. And it seems like both of them have something to do with big bird. . . . What are the chances, huh?"

Tak figured the chances were pretty damn small. He'd made hundreds of trips during his time with Axon, but never before experienced anything like this. The idea that he'd stumbled into two dead timelines in a row felt far too coincidental. Also, unless the recent shift had changed the way the briefcase behaved, there was no way he could be visiting a new timeline. Which meant that he was in an old timeline. And since this was all new to him, that meant after his last visit, something had come into this world and killed absolutely everyone in it. The idea that this was happening not just here, but in multiple timelines, makes Tak's heart race a little bit faster. Somehow, something was going terribly wrong with reality.

Tak removes his shoes and curls up in the corner of the couch. He thinks about talking again, but the echo of his own voice is more disturbing than the silence of the city, so instead he just stares at the ceiling and wonders about his next move. *How long has it been since I got some shut-eye? Was it the flight to L.A.? Was that really the last time? . . . God, I think it was. No wonder I'm piss-all tired.*

He feels the heavy weight of sleep begin to wrap around him and decides not to resist. He has a brief moment of panic when he wonders if he locked the front door, but then realizes it doesn't matter; if something wants to kill him, it'll just fly up and crash through the window. He has a mental picture of a dark creature hovering outside the condo like some kind of psychotic humming-bird and quickly shoves it to the back of his mind.

But then, just as he is about to drift into darkness, he hears a new sound. At first he thinks he's imagining it, or that days without rest have finally sent him off the deep end, but then he hears it again. It's coming from the street, low and long: the howl of a wolf lost in a forest of endless pines. But then he listens harder and realizes it isn't a howl at all, but a voice, little more than a distant whisper that bounces and echoes off the sides of buildings before vanishing into the dusky grey sky of a dead world. He listens again, eyes closed, until he's sure what he's hearing isn't some kind of mad fever dream. Because what he's hearing should be impossible.

It's a human voice. . . . And it's calling his name.

He springs off the couch, catches his bare toe on a discarded game controller, and goes sprawling down to the carpet. More surprised than hurt, he scrambles back to his feet and throws open the door to the deck. The voice is much louder out here, and he can hear it with greater clarity. It belongs to a woman, and it sounds scared as hell.

"Tak!" cries the voice, closer now. It's coming from somewhere down below, most likely at street level. "Tak, where are you!?"

The smart thing would be to say nothing because it could be a trick, or a trap, or worse. And even if it is an actual person, calling out would reveal his position to any birds that remained, making it likely his life would end with a hole punched in the top of his skull. But, of course, he can't ignore the voice, because he knows who it might be.

"Sam!" he cries, his voice trembling slightly. "Sam, is that you?"

"Tak!?" shrieks the voice. It sounds on the verge of full-blown panic now, as if the owner is barely holding herself together. "Tak, where are you?"

"I'm up here," he yells, cupping his hands around his mouth. "Here! On the balcony!"

Frantic footsteps echo down the street, followed by a metallic crash. The voice cries out in pain, but then the footsteps resume. He hears them approach his position at a furious rate, then a darkened figure with a small backpack rounds the corner and skids to a stop beneath his balcony like a gender-bending Romeo. Tak stares down, mouth wide, and tries to convince himself that he's actually seeing the red-haired woman standing on the side-walk below.

*"Judith?"* he says finally, his voice rising to near-comic heights. "What the crispy fuck are you doing here?"

# chapter twenty-one

When the plane finally touches down, Samira looks out the window and sees a flat, barren landscape covered with sand. She thinks back to what Tak told her in the diner and hazards a guess they've landed in Australia. The runway is little more than packed dirt, and the massive plane bumps and jostles as the air brakes deploy and the plane's momentum gradually slows. She didn't think it was possible to land a plane of this size on an unpaved runway, but clearly she was wrong. Just one more thing to add to the list of surprises.

Once the jet coasts to a stop, things begin to move very quickly. Four large men hustle Samira down a portable staircase and out to a large SUV, which then takes off across a roadless desert. Looking back, she sees the plane get smaller and smaller before becoming just another speck on the horizon. The men to either side of her sit in stoic silence. The one time she tries to ask a question, they both turn and look out the window as if she never spoke at all. A braver or more foolhardy person might have pushed things at this point—yelling at them or demanding answers—but Samira is neither of these. Instead, she shrinks into herself, digs her fingernails into the palms of her hands, and prays for the rest of her life to be over with quickly.

Several hours later, they pull through a pair of gleaming white gates and into a courtyard. Men with rifles lean out of guard towers and train their weapons on the SUV as it trundles into an underground parking garage, where it descends for what feels like forever before finally coming to a stop in front of a large, steel door. The moment the engine clicks off, Samira is lifted off her feet and escorted down a bewildering series of bare white hallways. Eventually, she and her captors come to a round, metal door that resembles the top hatch of a submarine. One of the guards reaches over and presses his thumb to a black pad, while another spins a metal wheel back and forth. After a moment, the hatch opens, and Samira is thrust through the hole and into darkness.

It takes all of her strength not to scream when the hatch slams shut and kills the light completely. Instead, she focuses on some of the relaxation techniques her psychiatrist taught her: standing in place, lowering her chin to her chest, and taking long, deep breaths. "Light as a feather," she says, as the air enters and leaves her body. "Stiff as a board."

She repeats the mantra—some nonsensical rhyme from her childhood—over and over as she tries to slow her racing heart. Her eyes move rapidly around the space in front of her, desperately searching for even the tiniest point of light, but come away empty. For a while, she tries to imagine she's somewhere else. She thinks about lying on a perfect yellow beach or wading through a stream in the middle of the forest, but the illusions eventually dissolve into an image of Yates standing over her with a cleaver in his hand and a mirthless grin on his face.

"I'm going to be okay," she says to the darkness. "It's all going to be fine."

When her heart finally slows from its techno patter to a more rock-and-roll beat, Samira decides to check out her surroundings. Holding one arm in front of her like a sleepwalker, she shuffles forward until her index finger comes into contact with a cold, steel wall. She then puts her back to the wall and starts pacing forward, heel to toe, until she collides with the wall on the other side. By repeating this process on the other two sides of the room, she's able to determine that her cell is perhaps ten feet across. She's in the process of moving her hands across the surface, searching for a window or a door or any kind of a break, when a burst of static fires out from overhead.

"Hello?" asks Samira hesitantly. "Is someone there?"

"Stop moving," says a voice. It's crackly and distorted, as if coming through a cheap set of speakers.

Samira freezes in place. She feels fear begin to rise in her belly and starts whispering her mantra furiously. *Light as a feather, stiff as a board. Light as a feather. Light as a feather light as a feather lightasafeatherlightasafeather . . .*

"Look out," says the voice. "We're going to turn on the lights."

She closes her eyes as tightly as possibly until she hears the familiar hum of overhead fluorescents. She waits a moment, then puts her hand in front of her face and cracks opens her lids. Light pours in and burns her retinas, but she's just happy to see again. Within a few moments, her eyes are fully open, and she's staring at her new surroundings and blinking furiously.

The cell is smaller than she guessed and completely featureless. The walls are painted a pale yellow color, which seems like an odd choice for a jail. At first she can't find the hatch through which she entered, but then she finally notices the barest outline of a circle in the far wall.

"Sit down," says the voice in a bored tone. "Sit with your hands under you and don't move."

Something about the voice makes Samira angry. Rage isn't

an emotion she's used to dealing with, but she finds its sudden appearance on the scene a refreshing change from her usual states of panic or depression. She lets it stew inside her for a bit as she tries to figure out how Tak would respond to such a command.

"I said, sit down and place your hands—"

"No," she says finally. Her voice is weak and noncommittal, but the word feels very good to say.

"This is not negotiable."

"Go fuck yourself!"

Samira has to repress a giggle as the words tumble out. *God, I wish Tak could have heard that,* she thinks. *He would have been shocked.* The voice behind the speaker seems equally shocked because it doesn't say anything more for a time. Samira paces back and forth in the room before finally leaning against the wall and cracking the knuckles on her left hand. She's wiggling the pinky back and forth, trying to get one more pop out of it, when the speaker squawks back to life again.

"This is your last warning. Sit on the ground."

"Suck it, loser!"

This sounds so stupid coming from her that it causes Samira to cringe, but before she can finish her shame spiral, a thick green gas starts filtering into the room. She pulls her shirt over her mouth and nose, but she might as well be trying to catch water with a sieve. A foul smell like warm pickles creeps into her nostrils, then the world turns sideways. Her senses begin to go loopy, but she thinks she hears the sound of the hatch opening. Somewhere behind her, the wall seems to wobble, causing her balance to flee in terror. She stands unsteadily for a moment, then slowly slides down the wall and into a little pile as a pair of men enter the room. She tries to fight them off, but there is no strength left in her body; she's hauled up like a sack of grain, passed through the opening, and strapped to a metal gurney.

The next hours are a blur of jumbled, random images that roll through the confused fugue of her mind. She feels people prodding at the nape of her neck, and at one point notices an odd, stinging sensation from back there. The gurney is wheeled around and around in seemingly random circles. Overhead lights shine in her eyes at regular intervals. A man with a large mustache leans into her face and sticks a tongue depressor into her mouth. Two guards stand in the corner and talk in hushed, worried tones, a pair of shotguns clenched in their gloved hands. She moves past a room stacked floor to ceiling with limp, dead bodies. Someone takes a bite out of a sandwich and drops a piece of lettuce onto her face, then brushes it off with a laugh.

Finally, the gas begins to wear off, allowing Samira to communicate with her brain once again. She finds herself lying on her side and strapped to a gurney in the middle of a sterile operating room. The back of her head is very cold, and for a while she can't figure out why. But as her senses begin to pulse back to life, she realizes a patch of hair is missing from the base of her skull. Nothing that she couldn't comb over given a few minutes and a hairbrush, but enough that she can feel cold metal on the bare nape of her neck.

Her head is firmly tied, but by shifting her eyes left and right, she can make out a few dark shapes rustling around. As she struggles to regain her faculties, snatches of conversation drift through her ears like petals on the wind, leaving her more confused than before.

". . . ready to hook up to . . ."

". . . much time. I'm telling you, something is wrong. We have to . . ."

"Nothing is wrong. It's all going . . ."

". . . strange readings outside Barrow Creek. I think it might be . . ."

202 | alan averill

"... prepared. Just make it happen."

A door slams, followed by the clicking of shoes walking swiftly away. Samira's vision is still blurry, but she can make out a tall dark shape moving into her line of sight. It hovers over her as a shadowy mirage while her eyes try to shake off the gas. Soon the dark blur becomes a light blur, and before long she finds herself staring into the eyes of a nightmare.

"Hello," says Charles Yates.

"Don't . . ." says Samira, her voice thick and slurred. "N-no . . ."

"Your fear is misplaced. Think of what you are about to do, of all that you will bring about. No human in existence has ever had such a chance."

". . . J-just kill me."

Yates leans in close, his face still blurry from the aftereffects of the gas. Samira can feel heat coming off him in waves and wonders briefly if he's contracted some kind of fever, or if that's just what happens when your mind finally snaps. "Kill you?" he asks. "Kill you? Is that what you think of me? That I am a Mengele? That I torture people because I find it enjoyable? I expected more from you."

He reaches into his pocket and withdraws a shiny metal scalpel, which he sets on a table next to the gurney. Samira tries to pull away, but the straps are tight, and all she can do is clench her hands into little fists.

"What are you?" he asks as he removes a half dozen round bits of metal from his other pocket and dumps them onto the table. They shimmer and sparkle in the overhead light as they roll around. "A soldier? A woman? An immigrant? No, you are none of these things. You are a tiny speck on the windshield of the universe; a life-form of such insignificance it is a wonder you exist at all. This is all any of us are."

He leans over and stills the rolling bits before continuing. "You simply do not understand the true scope of my work. I serve a higher purpose, Samira Moheb. I strive to noble ends. What I seek is nothing less than true immortality, a way for my life force to exist for eternity and thereby preserve something of our kind. Only a truly selfish person could object to such an endeavor."

Yates grabs Samira's head in his hands and begins to poke around the bald patch at the base of her skull. Samira feels his fingers pushing at something back there and realizes with growing horror that they aren't just pressing against the back of her head: they're actually pressing *into* it. It's the most unspeakably terrible thing that's ever happened to her, and when Yates shows no signs of stopping, Samira tries to hold her breath and black out—but for some reason, her mind decides to hang on.

"The people I bring here, the conduits, they always say the same things: that I don't understand what I am doing, that I am mad, that they would rather perish. They say these things only because they have not truly considered the alternative. Somewhere deep in their minds, they have been taught to believe in a just and caring God, some mystical force that will grant them eternal life once their physical bodies are no more. *This* is the madness, Samira Moheb. Not me. I have seen the universe, and it is cold and dark and dead."

Yates withdraws his fingers from Samira's skull, shakes them once, then dips them into a nearby jar of clear, viscous jelly. He rubs this on one of the metal pieces from the tray, rolling it around and around in his hand until it glistens. Once it's completely coated, he produces four wires from an unseen source and begins to thread them into the end.

"In five billion years, our sun will collapse upon itself. In another ten billion years, all the suns of all the galaxies will suffer the same fate. The universe is drawn by entropy toward disorder, which leads to a lack of energy, which leads to death. If there is a spark of life that drives us, some kind of divine watchmaker, then it too will eventually flicker and die. This is inevitable. Would you actually stand by and let it happen? Or would you fight with all of your strength?"

Yates finishes threading the wires through the metal bit and holds it up to the light. "This is going to hurt," he says. "Please remind yourself that pain is temporary."

Samira's eyes grow wide as she realizes what's going to happen. She tries to protest, to beg him not to do it, but her tongue has grown heavy and refuses to cooperate. She can only lie there, helpless, as Yates takes the wire and plunges it into the back of her head. The pain is immediate and terrible, unlike anything she's ever felt before. If someone embedded an icicle into the middle of her brain, it might begin to approximate the agony. She feels frost seeping up her neck, through her skull, and right to her eyes, and she screams then—a horrible wail that echoes off the bare walls of the medical room and seems to go on forever.

"The pain will eventually leave you," says Yates, his voice dim and disinterested, "so I need you to focus on me. Will you do this?"

Samira barely hears him. Her mind is a million miles away, dashing off to a better place, where nothing can ever hurt her, and all of this is just another kind of terrible dream. Yates repeats the question with more force, but Samira isn't there to respond. She's somewhere else now, a special place in the back of her mind where deep green grass and the sounds of ocean waves will allow her to sleep forever.

Yates jiggles the wire, and the pain of it snaps Samira back to reality. She moves to scream again, but he claps a hand over her mouth and presses down firmly. Samira tries to bite the fingers, but there's a disconnect between her mind and her body, and nothing seems to be working the way it's supposed to; rather than chomping through flesh and bone, she just opens her mouth and drools.

"I am not able to operate the Machine as your friend Tak does," he says as he inserts another wire, "and so I must build a conduit to reach the Beautiful Land. That is why I do this thing to you, Samira Moheb. You can take some comfort from knowing that I have chosen you, of all people, to continue in perpetuity."

He snorts suddenly, then coughs. A huge chunk of black goo flies out of his mouth and onto the floor. "You see?" he says, turning back around and starting the threading process for a third wire. "I, too, have made a sacrifice. I understand your pain, and I promise that it will end. The best thing you can do now is relax and accept the situation. Resistance will not save your life, but it will make its end terribly unpleasant. Please blink twice if you are understanding any of this."

Samira doesn't have a goddamn clue what the crazy man is talking about, but if it will make the pain go away, she's more than happy to agree. She blinks twice in rapid succession, then adds a couple more for good measure. Somewhere inside her mind, the icicle is starting to melt, spreading its coldness down her spine and out across the rest of her body.

"Will you help me?"

"Y-yes," whispers Samira. She wants to scream again, but the pain is so great, she doesn't think it will be possible.

"Say it."

". . . Yes. Yes, I will help you."

The pain stops instantly. Samira can still feel the metal pushing into the back of her head, but it's a distant feeling, like poking at a foot that has long since fallen asleep. As soon as the last wire clicks into place, Yates leans over and types on a nearby keyboard for a few seconds. Through her daze, Samira can barely make out a long series of numbers flashing across the screen. A weird buzzing begins to emanate from the back of her head as the wires start to tingle. When she looks back at Yates, she is horrified to see a steady stream of black ooze leaking from the corners of his eyes. When he notices the source of her horror, a grin dances across his face.

"The virus will destroy the host," he says, "but not itself. To survive the end of time, you must become that which will bring about its destruction. You must *become* the virus. Do you see now, Samira Moheb? Do you understand the sacrifice I have made?"

The tingling has become unbearable. Samira hears a bright, cheerful ding from the laptop, then the sound of the lid's being slammed down. Her field of vision is nothing but white dots in front of an empty blackness. She tries again to will herself into unconsciousness, and when the white dots begin to fade, she knows the job is almost done.

"We are ready," says Yates in a gleeful whisper. "Download complete." He seems ready to say more, but suddenly the sounds of gunfire ring out from somewhere nearby. Samira barely sees him leap to his feet, knocking over the small table in the process, before hearing the sound of a door opening. Though everything is going black, she perceives a screaming man in a dark uniform as he goes flying overhead, leaving a spray of blood in his wake.

"No!" cries Yates. "No! Not yet! You are not supposed to be here!"

He yells something else, but Samira doesn't care anymore. Just before her mind lets go completely, a massive shape moves across the edge of her vision. She can make out the bloodcurdling caw of a hungry bird, then everything falls into merciful blackness.

# chapter twenty-tWo

"Help me out here, Judith," says Tak, as a pair of candle flames flicker across his face. "There's something really fucked-up happening to the timelines, and I need to know what it is."

Judith nods but says nothing. She's sitting on the living-room floor across from Tak, wrapped in the blanket from the bed. The bags under her eyes are black and miserable, and her teeth have only just stopped chattering. The thin blouse and skirt combination she'd been wearing on her arrival are draped over a chair so they can dry—Tak hasn't yet asked how they got wet—so the blanket serves purposes of both warmth and modesty. Tak had turned away as she stripped her clothes off, but not before he caught a glimpse of the bright red underwear she was wearing. This discovery continues to surprise him.

"Talk to me," says Tak. He shoves the box of Crisp Rite Crackers over to Judith, who takes one and sniffs it hesitantly. "I mean, that's why you came here, right? To find me?"

Judith seems ready to say something, then decides to eat the cracker instead. She takes small, delicate bites, wiping stray crumbs off the blanket after each one. When the snack is gone, she looks over at Tak and shakes her head. "I don't think we have time for the long version. Abridged okay?"

Tak nods. She removes another cracker from its cardboard coffin and stares at it before setting it to the side. A corner of the blanket falls, revealing a brief flash of red, but she quickly pulls it back into place. "First of all, yes: I'm here because I knew they were sending you here. I waited until Yates was finished, then computed your position and went through using the second briefcase."

Tak glances at the small blue briefcase currently resting by Judith's feet. "I didn't know there were two of those."

"I built this one myself. It's special."

"How so?"

"Because it's different. Listen, we don't have a lot of time. Can I talk?"

Tak makes a motion with his hand and settles back into the couch. Judith coughs once and runs her fingers through her hair, taking a moment to work some of the tangles out. Finally, she grows frustrated of the exercise and just lets her hair hang where it likes. "A while back, we told you to find a timeline where Axon effectively controlled the world. Do you remember that?"

"Sure, yeah. We had that big meeting where you and Yates kept drawing graphs on a whiteboard and talking about the gravitational constant or whatever."

"Well, we lied to you, Tak. *I* lied to you. That was never the plan at all."

Tak leans back against the couch and scrunches his eyebrows together. Judith seems uncomfortable with the conversation, almost ashamed, and this is beginning to worry him. "What do you mean, you lied to me? I don't understand."

"Charles was never interested in running the world. He was searching for something else: a very special timeline, one unlike any in existence. So as you were using the Machine, he was following in your footsteps. Taking notes. Making calculations. Watching you. And late last year, he finally found what he was looking for."

"Wait. Judith. Hold on. You knew about this?"

"Yes."

"And you helped him anyway?"

Judith stares at the floor even harder than before. "I'm not you, Tak. I'm a theoretical physicist. I don't know how to steal cars or hack computers or go into hiding. Had I tried to break free, Charles would have tracked me down in a matter of hours. I decided it was better to stay on the inside."

Tak runs his fingers through his hair and wishes that he'd gotten more than a five-minute nap. "Okay, fine. So what was Yates looking for?"

"He calls it the Beautiful Land. It's a kind of flexible reality, a place where laws of physics and motion and everything else we take for granted don't exist. It's a world that builds itself around your wishes and becomes whatever you want it to be. It's the hub of all creation. If I was religious, I'd probably call it heaven."

Tak clicks his tongue on the roof of his mouth and eyes the woman across from him. "You don't have a beer in that backpack, do you?" he asks suddenly. "Because right now, I need a drink like nobody's business."

In response, Judith opens the pack and hands him a bottle of old, cheap whiskey. "I found this in your room after you left," she says. "Figured you'd want it eventually."

Tak moves into the kitchen and returns with a pair of dusty glasses, filling each with a healthy pour. "Drinking is only going to dehydrate us," he says as he downs the shot in a single gulp. "But right now, I don't really care."

He takes his glass back to the couch and collapses on one end as Judith takes a seat next to him. The alcohol bypasses his empty stomach and goes straight for his brain, and he's more than happy to let it. *Whatever. If a bird's gonna eat me, I'd like to be good and sloshed when it happens.*

Judith takes a tiny sip before continuing. "As Charles and I pursued the Beautiful Land, he began to change. He'd always walked a fine line between brilliance and madness, but over the years, he became possessed. He started talking about how the Machine could be anywhere, about how if we could invent it, anyone could. One night, very late, he came to me, with tears in his eyes, and said that he had reached a decision. He said . . ."

She stops talking and takes another sip of whiskey, then reconsiders and downs the entire shot. "He was convinced that someone in another timeline was trying to do the same thing we were, that they would eventually find a way to erase us from existence. He told me we had to prevent it from happening, no matter what."

"So what's his plan?" says Tak. "Wait, no. Let me guess. He's going to try and destroy the solid timeline. Right?"

Judith shakes her head, then turns away. To Tak's amazement, a single tear sneaks out of her eye and down her cheek. He's never seen her cry in all the years he's known her; he actually didn't think it was possible. "Not the solid timeline, Tak," she says, her voice hitching slightly. "*All* of them. All the timelines, all at once. He's going to go to the Beautiful Land and seal the conduit behind him, then he's going to wipe out any reality that has ever existed or will ever exist. He's going to destroy *everything.*"

"Fuck a duck," says Tak softly. "Is that even possible?"

"I didn't think so at first. But then I realized he didn't have to destroy the actual timeline—he just had to eliminate everything inside it."

Tak shakes his head, suddenly annoyed at the way the whiskey is making him slow on the uptake. "Sorry, I don't understand."

"Are you familiar with the observer effect?"

"Wasn't that a prog rock band from the seventies?"

"Stop fucking around. This is important."

Judith reaches out her arm and begins to draw a large, imaginary circle in the air. A corner of the blanket falls down as she does so, exposing part of her torso to Tak's surprised eyes, but because of the alcohol or her focus or possibly both, she pays it no mind. "The observer effect is part of quantum theory. It basically states that reality can only exist as long as there is someone in place to experience it and make it actual. Are you following me so far?"

"I think so," says Tak as he tries desperately to keep his eyes focused squarely on the floor. Even by the dim light of the candles, he can see enough of Judith to know that he should probably stop looking. "Just keep going."

"Charles figured that if he could eliminate every living thing inside a timeline, then it would, in essence, cease to be. To do this, he needed something that could enter a timeline, kill everything inside it, then remain there without disturbing the observer effect. Something smart enough to do the job but not technically alive."

Judith brings her other hand out of the blanket to illustrate this point, causing the entire thing to drop. At this, Tak just turns away and stares out the window, a flush rising in his cheeks. "This is totally crazy, Judith. You're telling me that Yates managed to create some kind of undead killing machine?"

"He didn't create it. He found it."

"How? Where?"

"In another timeline, one you never visited. He found it, and he put it into the Machine and set it loose on all the timelines of the world."

Behind him, Judith finally realizes that she's been lecturing in her underwear and scrambles for the blanket. But she needn't have bothered because Tak's mind is suddenly very, very far away. "You're talking about the creature," he says. "The one that looks like a baby bird."

"Yes."

"What is it? I mean, what the hell *is* it?"

"It's a virus. A virus that strikes at time itself. It moves through the timelines and finds things that aren't supposed to be there and wipes them out. Yates engineered it to think that everything in reality needed to be destroyed, then he set it free. So even as we speak, it's working its way through the timelines and destroying them one by one."

"Why does it look like a bird?" asks Tak.

"I think . . . I think the creature is something so alien and unbelievable our brains aren't able to comprehend it. So they force it into the closest shape they can, which just happens to be a bird."

"A baby bird," repeats Tak, reaching for the bottle. "With huge black eyes and furry feathers."

"Listen, I don't understand all of it either," says Judith. She waits for Tak to finish drinking, then snatches the liquid from his hand and takes a drink of her own. "Maybe it means something to Yates. Maybe he's scared of birds or something, I don't know."

"So what did you do?" asks Tak. "I mean, when you learned all of this, what did you do?"

Judith looks out the window, unable to meet Tak's gaze. " . . . Nothing. I did nothing. By the time I discovered this, he'd already set the plan in motion. Reality was ready to fall; all he had to do was overwrite the solid timeline and get the hell out of there."

Tak stretches out his arm and swings it wildly across the glass window of the condominium, highlighting a darkened, empty city. "Is that what happened here? Mr. Bird came through and ate everybody?"

"Yes. It's happening in nearly all the timelines now, much faster than even he anticipated. The birds are multiplying. There are billions of them now. Maybe more." She stands up, letting the blanket fall to the ground, and walks over to her clothes. Though not quite dry, she picks them up and begins to put them on.

"Samira and I were heading for Australia," says Tak. "We were going to find the fail-safe, but that was before . . . Before I knew any of this. Now that seems like a pretty lame idea."

Judith snaps her blouse with practiced hands, sending a spray of water across the condo entryway. "No," she says as she buttons up the shirt. "That's the only idea. In fact, that's why I'm here."

"So great! Let's go, let's do this thing, and then let's . . ." Tak stops talking as a strange expression comes over Judith's face. "Oh, what? Come on, what is it? What now?"

"How much did I tell you about the fail-safe?"

"Um, I don't know. Nothing? It was years ago. You told me that you made a backup copy of reality and stored it inside a conduit named Vincent, and that if anything ever went wrong, I should go turn it on."

"Did you ever wonder why the fail-safe would work?"

". . . *Should* I have wondered that?"

"When I designed the fail-safe, I knew I couldn't just reset time to the way things were four years ago because the same events would simply happen all over again. I had to make a change; something small enough that it wouldn't upset reality but important enough that it prevented the Machine from ever being used."

"Yeah, okay," says Tak, whose head is beginning to throb. "So what'd you do? What's the change?"

"The change is that I never call you in the hotel room. So you never come work for Axon, and we're never able to make the Machine go anywhere but that red desert wasteland. And because of that, none of this will ever happen."

Tak stares at her for a second, then begins to laugh. It's a loud, hearty laugh, the kind he hasn't made in a very long time. She smiles a little at it, but he doesn't even notice; he just keeps laughing until he's doubled over on the floor.

"Oh God," he says. "Oh God, this is perfect. This is just fucking perfect. So in order to save the entire world, I have to go back in time and *finish* committing suicide?"

"That's what I'm saying."

"Hoooo!" says Tak, as he struggles to a sitting position. "Oh my God, this is a fuckin' riot. I love this town. So where's the fail-safe?"

"I have it."

"You have . . . Oh, come on. *Really?* You mean it's in your brain right now?"

Her only response is to tilt her head back and drain the rest of the bottle. And really, that's all the response Tak needs. He wobbles up on his feet, smooths out the wrinkles in his suit coat, and moves over to the window. "So how do we get back? I mean, if we're really gonna do this, how do I get out of here?"

"The briefcase I used is different than yours," says Judith. "It's not a one-way ticket; I can use it to send us both back."

"Great. So let's make for Australia."

"We're not going to Australia, Tak. We're going to Montana."

"Why?"

"Because there's another Machine there."

A rich combination of alcohol and surprise causes Tak's vision to swim. "Okay, whoa. Hold the phone. There's *another* Machine?"

"Axon constructed a second Machine in case something happened to the first. It's never been tested, but there's no reason we can't use it to activate the fail-safe. And it should be practically unguarded, if that makes you feel better."

"Oh, yeah. That makes everything goddamn peachy." Tak takes a step back from the window and watches the reflected candle flames flicker in the glass. *This is a shit plan,* he thinks. *But then again, most of my plans are shit.*

"Okay," says Tak finally. "I'll do it. But you have to do something for me first."

"What?" asks Judith.

"Send me to Australia."

"Tak, that's crazy. Charles is there. His people are there."

"Yeah, and my friend Sam is there," he says. "So before I do anything else, I'm gonna go save her ass."

Judith mulls this over for a very long time. "No," she says finally. "It's too risky. We don't have the time."

"Then fuck it. I'm not helping."

"Tak!"

"I'm not leaving her, Judith. I don't care if the world ends or whatever. I'm not leaving her again."

Judith sighs and shakes her head, angry. Then she looks up at Tak and sees his stupid grin and something inside her caves. "Okay," she says. "But I can't come with you. I have to get to North America in case you don't make it back. Which I probably don't need to tell you is a pretty distinct possibility."

She reaches down to the briefcase at her feet and opens it. Tak stares, curious, at the insides of the new device. It contains twice the knobs as the one he is familiar with, as well as a small keyboard and what appears to be a thin strand of shiny copper wire. "Come here," she says. "Grab the wire, and I'll get this started."

Tak moves over and does as she asks, kneeling in front of her like a knight waiting for confirmation. She flips the knobs back and forth a few times, then types on the keyboard. "I'll try to get you as close as I can to Axon, but this isn't the most accurate thing in the world. You've probably got a few hours of travel ahead of you."

"That's fine," replies Tak. "What about you? Should I meet you in Montana?"

"I'd rather not go there alone if I don't have to. It's going to be a pain in the ass to download the fail-safe out of my own head." She types a few more times, then turns a knob with force. Green light flashes out of the case and crawls down the walls of the condo. "I'll find a place to hole up and wait for you, then we can go to Montana together."

"What if the birds show up?"

"I think I'll be okay; they seem to have trouble recognizing people who have used the Machine. They'd eventually get around to me, I'm sure, but hopefully they won't be a problem quite yet."

"Let's meet in Seattle," says Tak, as the wire begins to buzz and tingle against his fingers.

"That's a bit far."

"Yeah, but I know that city better than most. If there's trouble, we can get in and out fast."

Judith thinks about it for a moment. "Okay. Seattle. Where do you suggest I wait?"

"How about the downtown police station? You can just hang out in the lobby or something."

"If not, I'll find a way to get arrested. . . . Hurry, Tak. Find her, get out of there, and come back as fast as you can. I can give you a couple of days, but that's it. After that, I'll need to strike out on my own."

"Got it," says Tak with a grin. He looks down at his fingers and sees them starting to stretch across the surface of the wire. "Oh hey, Judith?"

"Yes?"

"Be careful, yeah?"

"You too."

She smiles briefly at him and clicks a final knob. The last thing Tak sees before everything dissolves is a shock of bright red hair and the trembling fingers of its owner. Then his world melts into a brilliant shade of white.

the man with a plan

# chapter twenty-three

Tak's jeep, stolen from a clueless tour group outside the town of Coober Pedy, Australia, chugs along like it's happy to be free. When he appeared next to the tourists in a blinding flash of light nearly an hour ago, they all assumed he was some kind of ancient desert mystic and greeted him with open arms. This hearty welcome lasted long enough for Tak to shake a few hands, pose for a picture, then leap into the driver's seat of their jeep and peel away in a cloud of dust. A hundred yards or so up the road, he stopped to toss the stunned group's backpacks onto the highway before continuing on his way. Tak would have found the whole thing funny if he wasn't convinced the world would end at any moment.

He's currently traveling along the Stuart Highway, or what locals simply call The Track. It's a long, winding ribbon of arguably paved road that cuts through the middle of the continent, beginning at a southern scrap of a town called Port Augusta and ending at the northern paradise of Darwin. Tak had traveled this stretch many times over the last four years, including once a few days prior when he had a special briefcase in the truck and a rough plan in his head. That last journey feels like it took place years ago.

He's heading for a place called Alice Springs, a town located almost in the dead center of the continent. From there, he'll detour onto a poorly maintained strip of dirt called the Haasts Bluff Road, which he will follow for nearly one hundred bone-jarring miles. Eventually, that road will peter out into nothing, which is when he plans to engage the four-wheel drive and head south into the desert, driving another thirty miles over hard-packed red sand until he arrives at a magnificent white building where no such structure should possibly exist.

But that is getting ahead of himself. Right now, he's on The Track, moving at a steady ninety-five and enjoying the ride. He likes driving, especially when it's on a long stretch of lonely road where he can imagine he's the only person left in the world. His only regret is that he doesn't have a bandanna-wearing dingo to curl up on the passenger seat beside him. He knows it's silly, this happiness he feels. A smarter person would be scared out of his mind at the thought of storming the headquarters of the world's most powerful and dangerous man. But Tak is filled with the confidence and fearlessness that comes with an empty stomach, little sleep, and the knowledge he's on a quest to save his childhood love. And so he drives and allows himself to believe that everything's going to be all right.

➤ Trouble comes near a dot on the map called Erldunda, whose biggest claim to fame is the intersection of The Track with the Outback's other major road, the Lasseter Highway. Tak is motoring along, listening to the wind blow through his open window and thinking positive thoughts, when he notices a strange shape in his driver's-side mirror. At first, he dismisses it as another car, or a shadow, or just his own overactive imagination. But the more he stares, the more he starts to worry. Because whatever it is doesn't move like a car—it isn't touching the road so much as gliding over the top of it. Also, there's no dust kicking off the back tires and no sunlight gleaming off the windshield. If it's a car, it's unlike any Tak has ever seen.

The Track is flat and long and completely unbroken, which gives Tak plenty of time to watch the darkened blur. Distance is hard to gauge in this stretch of the world, but if he were to guess, he'd put the thing some fifteen miles behind him. Fifteen miles and closing fast.

"What are you?" he asks himself. "Police? Some of Yates's goons?"

That seems likely—if the shape was an SUV, the lack of glint could come from tinted windows. Tak quickly turns his attention back to the road to make sure there's nothing waiting for him in the distance; his eyes find nothing but a thin strip of pavement moving off into the dusty horizon.

A few seconds later, he glances over his shoulder again, expecting to see the stubby form of a gas-guzzling security vehicle. But what he sees instead makes a spark of horror leap up his spine and right into his brain. The dark blur is closer now, and it's most clearly not one of Yates's men. Nor is it a highway patrolman or an innocent tourist or a bloodthirsty biker gang searching the road for juice.

It's the bird. And it's moving like a motherfucker.

Tak whips his head back around and floors it. The jeep lurches in response, as if unsure that it can even process such a request. Slowly, far too slowly for Tak's liking, the needle on the speedometer climbs until it finally tops out at the disappointing speed of 118 miles an hour. Gripping the steering wheel hard enough to leave small indentations in the plastic, Tak leans forward until his face is just inches from the windshield.

"Come on, you piece-of-shit car! Move! Move, move, move!"

In response, the jeep makes a horrible whining sound and slows by a couple of ticks. Tak screams in frustration and slams his hand on the dashboard, which causes the glove compartment to pop open. Colorful brochures spill out and land in a sad little pile on the passenger's seat, each one extolling the spiritual virtues of a "Real Aboriginal Walkabout!" Such false promises would normally make Tak scoff, but right now he's got bigger fish to fry.

He raises his foot from the gas pedal for just a moment, then slams it down again. The jeep begins to shake like the wheels might fly off but somehow picks up speed. Behind him, the bird is screaming up the road with something like a smile spreading across its beak. A pair of stumpy pale wings, little more than nubs of flesh with a few scraggly feathers, churn through the air with surprising power. Clawed feet float just above the surface of the highway, occasionally dipping down and scraping against the worn asphalt. Each time this happens, a small spray of black ooze flies into the air.

The jeep slows a bit as he crosses a small incline, then picks up a couple of miles an hour down the other side. Once Tak crests the hill, he sees a large semitruck trundling its way across The Track some five miles distant; but aside from this and the winged nightmare fast approaching, the area is completely deserted. There are no roads to turn off on, no places to hide. It's just the semi, a psychotic bird, and about a thousand miles of red sand in every direction.

"Shit!" screams Tak, pounding the dash again. "Not like this! Not here! If I'm gonna kick off in the middle of the goddamn desert, I at least want to be smoking peyote!"

Behind him, the bird crests the hill. A thin watery cry issues forth as it closes the gap between itself and the stolen jeep. The creature weaves across the yellow line like a small-town drunk on a Friday night, useless arms flailing excitedly in the air. Tak knows he doesn't have much time—maybe thirty seconds at the most—before the thing cracks through his skull with a translucent white beak and sucks out everything that makes Tak real. It's a horrible, helpless feeling.

A few seconds later, the bird flaps into the second lane of the highway and closes the gap on the jeep. Tak sees the monster approach in his driver's-side mirror—the words OBJECTS MAY BE CLOSER THAN THEY APPEAR leaping out as an ironic twist he could have done without—moving faster and faster until it finally reaches the rear of the vehicle. When this happens, Tak closes his eyes and waits for the thump that will tell him the creature is on the roof and ready to stab through the thin metal shell so it can enjoy the tasty cream filling within.

But that doesn't happen. Instead, the bird races up to the driver's-side window and begins to keep pace with the car. For nearly a mile, they move as a single unit—the scared time traveler and the virus engineered to destroy time itself. Eventually, the creature turns to stare at Tak with a pair of dead, black eyes before uttering a caw that's somehow audible over the whine of the car and the howl of the wind. Then it looks forward again, lowers its head, and races away up the road.

Tak drives on in stunned silence. He doesn't even think to brake or turn around and try to escape in the other direction; he just keeps pushing the jeep as fast as it can go as the bird soars effortlessly ahead of him. The creature gains ground on the semi-truck in the distance, moving faster and faster until it finally pulls even with the driver-side door. Tak doesn't understand how the trucker could possibly miss the sight of a giant baby bird soaring next to his window, but apparently that's the case. The vehicle doesn't speed up, doesn't waver back and forth across the road like one would expect when faced with something so horrific; it just keeps moving at a steady sixty-five like it doesn't have a care in the world. And then, before Tak even knows what is happening, the bird turns its head to the side and goes crashing through the driver's-side window and into the cab.

The entire truck shimmies like the road is slicked with oil. The back wheels of the trailer begin to slide to the right while the cab slowly drifts left. Though still a quarter mile distant, Tak can clearly see a hairy human arm protrude from the window of the cab and grab the side mirror. It holds on for a moment, then snaps the mirror off, strut and all, before vanishing back inside. The truck makes a high-pitched grinding sound as it skids almost completely sideways, cab in one lane, trailer in the other. Then momentum continues its work and spins the rear of the truck around until the cab is facing Tak. He sees a blur of feathers and pink flesh shaking savagely from side to side before a huge gout of blood flies up and splatters against the windshield.

Black smoke pours from the tires as the entire vehicle begins to tilt precariously toward the driver's side. The first wheels to lift off the pavement are those of the cab, but the trailer quickly follows suit. Soon, the entire truck is skidding on one set of wheels, still spinning slowly around the road like an obese figure skater. For a brief moment, Tak thinks the truck will slow enough for the wheels to right themselves, but then physics asserts itself in the conversation once more, and the entire rig flips up and into the air.

The truck seems to hang in the sky for an eternity; trailer sagging in one direction, cab pulling in the other. Then the front end of the truck strikes the highway with a tremendous bang. The cab crumples into itself like a used paper bag while the trailer swings up and over the top—making it look like the entire vehicle is balancing on its grill. But the trailer has no intentions of stopping there; it keeps falling through space until it finally comes crashing down in front of the cab. The force of the blow shears it off and sends it tumbling off the side of the road, where it rolls over and over, chunks of metal flying, until finally coming to a rest in a massive black cloud of smoke. Near the edge of the highway, a small fire begins to blaze merrily out of control, consuming what little scrub has managed to put down roots in this barren corner of the world.

⁓ The noise of the crash is overwhelming, a kind of grinding, screeching wail punctuated by the heavy sound of metal being torn apart. Ahead, the cab continues to slide, grill-side down, trailing sparks behind like a mad mechanic's fireworks. Oil and gas and various other fluids pour from the broken frame and ignite, leaving a half dozen blazing streaks along the road. After a good hundred feet or so of sliding, the cab finally crunches to a halt, wobbling in place for a moment before crashing back to earth, tire-side down.

Tak is torn between slowing down to avoid the debris and speeding past the wreckage before the creature that caused it decides to do the same thing to him. He's no more than a thousand yards from the crash site now and coming up fast. But before he can weigh his options, the bird bursts from the twisted shell of the cab and goes shooting into the air. It's holding the driver in its twisted lower talons, and Tak is horrified to see that the man is somehow still alive. Alive and screaming, a terrible, high-pitched sound like a little girl with a skinned knee. The creature swirls gracefully in the air, pulls off a perfect loop, then begins soaring down the highway toward Tak.

Tak forms a curse in his mind that his body doesn't have time to pronounce and jerks the wheel to the left. The entire jeep shudders but somehow manages to both obey his command and stay on the road. The bird and its unfortunate victim race overhead, close enough that the trucker's boots knock against the radio antennae. Small drops of blood rain down on the windshield, followed by a single glop of thick black tar. Then the creature is soaring up and into the sky, moving away as fast as it arrived until it's no more than a small blur in the rearview, a blur with kicking arms and legs beneath. The last thing Tak hears is a triumphant caw followed by a heart-wrenching scream, then the moment is over, and he is alone on the road once more.

He drives then. Past the wreckage of the truck, past the smear of red in the middle of the road, past the massive cloud of black smoke and the heat of the fire that is now spreading with fury. He drives with the pedal down and his hair flying and an unfamiliar, desperate feeling burrowing itself into his heart. For the next four hours, he drives and drives and hopes that the horror he feels will eventually go away. But it never does. This time, unlike all the other times in his life, the feeling refuses to leave.

He stops in Alice Springs just long enough to gas up, then makes for the interior as fast as his jeep can take him. Every time he looks in the rearview, he sees a growing column of black smoke and fire. Eventually, he has to force himself to stop looking at it and just drive. Head down, eyes forward, hands trembling, but moving and breathing and somehow alive.

Tak doesn't understand why the bird spared him, or if it is even capable of making such a choice. He plans to ask Yates when he sees him next, preferably with the old man at the business end of a pistol. Where he will get a weapon is a question to be solved when the time comes—like the rest of his plan, this part is somewhat fluid. All he knows now is that he must reach the Machine at all costs. That's the only way everything can be set to rights.

He turns off the road and heads into the desert, teeth clattering together as his jeep bounces and scrapes over a landscape that laughs at the idea of modern, wheeled transportation. He drives by memory, turning at a rock here, going straight at a piece of scrub there, moving through the desert like a dusty metallic nomad searching for the final stop on the trade route. Speed isn't an option on such terrain, and as he slowly crawls his way in and out of canyons and around piles of dirt that threaten to swallow his tires, he can only grip the wheel and pray he isn't too late.

When the pure whiteness of the Axon building finally appears on the horizon, Tak has to resist an urge to scream with delight. Instead, he breaks out into a quick, grim smile and steps on the gas. The last few miles have been smoothed by constant traffic in and out of the building, and he covers the ground quickly. As the structure comes closer, he goes over the current plan in his head one more time.

*Okay. You're gonna ram the gate, drive into that second courtyard, and smash through the guard station. Hopefully, they don't see you coming, and you have a few seconds there. Then you hop out and grab a rifle if there's one nearby. If not, you break for the side maintenance door and run like hell. Once you get inside, find the elevator and slide down to the fifth floor. Lots of storage there, lots of places to hide. Then you can catch your breath and figure out what the hell to do next.*

It's a plan. Not a great plan, or even a very good one, but it's something. Tak doesn't care to admit that the plan will likely end before it even has time to begin—probably with him slumped over the wheel of the jeep with blood pouring from a dozen bullet holes. But at least he will have tried. That's something.

However, once he gets within a hundred yards of the massive white building, he can see that his plan will need massaging from the get-go. Because the part where he rams the jeep through the gate is no longer necessary; the gate is lying on the ground in about a dozen different pieces.

Tak rolls to the edge of the property and drops the car into neutral. He leans his head out the window and listens for a noise of any kind, but all he can hear is the unsteady chug of the engine and a soft, lonely wind. After a moment he honks the horn, an action which should bring about a dozen heavily armed guards running to his position. But nothing happens. It's as if everyone just packed up and left.

*Or was carried off,* thinks Tak. *Carried off screaming into the sky.*

He puts the jeep in gear and moves forward, bumping and jostling over the wreckage of the gate. Guard towers, usually manned with a half dozen mercenaries each, stand silent and empty. The first courtyard is equally deserted. The fountain in the center, which once sprayed water nearly two feet in the air, now gurgles forth a tiny trickle mixed with dusty red mud.

Tak drives through the yard and under an arch, where he suddenly slams on the brakes. In front of him, the second, smaller courtyard is a battle zone. Dark splotches of soot, most likely from grenade fire, cover the previously pristine white walls. Spent shells casings litter the ground, thousands upon thousands of them sparkling in the sun. A couple of dozen bodies lie strewn about, most clad in the black uniforms of Axon's private security force, all with large holes punched in their heads.

Tak turns off the engine and climbs out of the jeep, trying and failing to still his trembling knees. The thought of discovering Samira amidst all this carnage makes him want to throw up and weep at the same time, but he only allows himself to consider this in the very back corner of his mind. All that matters now is getting inside and finding her: dead or alive. And if a certain dark creature happens to be waiting for him? Well, perhaps that will be better in the end.

"Just gonna take a look around," he mutters to himself as he steps over and around the shredded remains of his former coworkers. "Just gonna go inside and see what I can see."

The sun turns red as it begins to dip under the horizon. Tak takes a final glance behind him and considers waiting for it to vanish completely. But instead, he opens the maintenance door with a trembling hand, takes a breath scented with death, and descends into darkness.

# chapter twenty-four

The hallway is dark. Even the emergency lights are out, and those should have enough battery power to last for years. Tak fumbles around in his pocket for his lighter, pulls it out, and strikes flint to steel. He's prepared to see something horrible—bodies or skeletons or blood-painted walls—but when the flame flickers into being, all that stands before him is a long corridor ringed with insulation-wrapped pipes. It's almost as if the devastation in the front courtyard was a dream.

*Maybe they contained it,* he thinks as he moves toward a large, steel door at the end of the hallway. *Or hell, maybe they killed the thing.*

Tak momentarily kicks himself for not examining the bodies in the yard. At the time, he didn't think he could handle seeing people he knew in such a state, but now he finds himself wondering exactly when the massacre took place. *Was it before that bird attacked the truck? Or after? Of course, all of this assumes that it's the same creature. What did Judith say? She thinks they're multiplying? Man, that would be a fucking awesome piece of news right there.*

But despite the courtyard's being a mere hundred feet behind him, he's not about to go back. It's taking all of his not-inconsiderable nerve just to keep pressing forward; if he goes back, he might not convince himself to return. So he stumbles through the door and down a second identical hallway, the flame of the lighter hot against his thumb. The place is almost silent, but not quite—if Tak listens closely, he can just make out the deep, familiar hum of the Machine.

"At least something works around here," says Tak, his voice echoing off pipes and back to his ears in a creepy fashion. Snapping his mouth closed, he exits the second maintenance tunnel and finds himself in the Axon Corporation's main lobby. Tak had never understood why Axon built a visitor's lobby in a top secret building with a security force that shot strangers on sight. Perhaps it was force of habit, or a way to make the employees feel less like they were working in a bunker. At any rate, someone, somewhere had decided that what the building really needed was a fancy front lobby, and on this they had spared no expense.

The front doors of the room are cold steel, but the unnamed architect thoughtfully placed a set of windows above them, allowing a few fading beams from the setting sun to filter in. Tak releases his death grip on the lighter and allows himself a few moments to look around. Imported Italian marble lines the walls and floors. Leather couches that cost more than Tak's life rest against the walls and beg for someone to come along and plop their ass cheeks down. At the far end of the room, a massive wooden desk holds two computer monitors and a sad bowl of candy. A crooked nameplate on the desk reads SANDRA DARCI.

"Sandra Darci?" mutters Tak as he crosses the room and makes for her desk. "I don't remember a Sandra. . . . God, I really should have gone out more."

He pops a piece of candy from the bowl and begins sucking on it, which causes his hunger to roar. The computer seems dead, but he flips the switch a few times just to make sure. When nothing happens, he picks up the phone and is greeted by silence. Putting it back in the receiver, he dumps the rest of the candy into his pocket, straightens Sandra's nameplate, and begins opening drawers.

He finds what he's looking for in the bottom drawer: an emergency flashlight with plenty of juice. Flicking it on, he turns his back to the lobby and makes for a set of massive hydraulic doors to the left of the reception desk. They don't want to open with the power out, but by leaning against them and shoving with all his strength, Tak finally budges one enough to wiggle through and into yet another darkened hall.

When he turns on the flashlight, the shock causes him to briefly inhale his candy. Blood, thick and red, is splattered on the wall and ceiling. Unidentifiable chunks of flesh and bone litter the floor in a random, haphazard way. In the far corner of the hall, a pile of guts lies in a series of ropy coils. There are no bodies, or at least not anything that could be identified as such. Just the remains. It's like he's walked into a blender.

The room reeks with a sweet, almost pleasant smell, and Tak suddenly finds himself wishing for the familiar scent of decay. Pulling his shirt over his face, he steps gingerly around the larger chunks, grimacing once when he crunches down on something hard and brittle. *I think that was a tooth,* he thinks. *Ah, Christ, this is too much. It's all just too much.*

There's no way for Tak to know if Samira is in this hallway: there's simply not enough left to identify a person with. But he doesn't think that's the case. If Yates really brought her here, she would likely be locked in the security hold. . . . Unless he had other plans for her, which is an option Tak doesn't really want to consider right now.

He shines the flashlight forward and stumbles down the hall, focusing all of his attention on the small white dot of light. His plan had been to take the elevator down to the lower floors, but with the power out, that's no longer possible. It would be the stairs or nothing, and this is a depressing thought—the Machine is located almost a mile underground, and that means a *hell* of a lot of stairs.

"Be glad you're not going up," says Tak as he tries to ignore a stray chunk of red in the corner of his vision. "Up would really suck. Hell, maybe you can just slide down the railing the whole way. . . . Whee."

He finds the stairway door and moves through, happier than he thought possible at leaving the blender hallway behind him. The stairwell is dark, but a few passes with the flashlight show it to be untouched by any kind of gore. Tak utters a brief thanks to whatever gods might be listening and begins his long descent.

There are about a hundred stairs between each landing, but as Tak continues down, this number starts to increase. After twenty minutes, he's traversing nearly four hundred stairs between landings, and the doors leading out are becoming much more ominous. Signs with messages like AUTHORIZED PERSONNEL ONLY, RADIATION PROTOCOL IN EFFECT, and DEADLY FORCE ALLOWED start to sprinkle the walls. At one point, he passes a neatly typed sign that reads NO ONE FEARS THE REAPER HERE. Tak would have taken it as a joke if the font wasn't so damn serious.

Finally, the signs disappear altogether, replaced by drawings of stick figures being electrocuted, chopped up by large blades, and dripping some kind of caustic substance onto their exposed digits. A few flights down, the graffiti becomes almost incomprehensible. One figure appears to be dancing on a table filled with wedding cakes while another rides on the back of what looks to be a rabid giraffe. But Tak's winner for the most disturbing image is found on a door marked B-14, where someone has spray painted a huge face that seems to be both laughing and screaming at the same time. The paint has dripped down from the eyes of the face, making it look like the owner reached up and clawed them out of his own skull.

Tak starts down the stairs with new haste. Soon, he's taking them two at a time, racing down and around the darkened stairwell like a man possessed. Something in the back of his mind screams at him to stop, to take his time before he goes tumbling ass over teakettle and lands in a broken heap on one of the steel-grated landings. But fear is driving him now, and the voice of reason is lost in its roar.

Just as he starts to think he might have died and been thrust into a level of hell set on a never-ending staircase, the steps end. Tak is so surprised, he actually turns to continue down and slams his stomach into a metal railing. The force of the blow knocks the flashlight from his hand and sends it tumbling into the darkness below, and for a moment Tak threatens to follow suit. But then balance returns, and he manages to flip his weight back onto his feet. He stares mournfully at the small speck of his flashlight beam as it grows smaller and smaller before finally being swallowed by the black. Then he fumbles the lighter from a pocket yet again and shines it on the nearby door. Though dim, he can barely make out a single marking: B-44.

He pulls away from the door and rubs his eyes, then leans back in to make sure he's seeing it correctly. "B-44?" he says. "Wait, there is no floor B-44. This building ends at B-40. And 38 is security, 39 is the Machine, and 40 is that secret level that Yates thinks I don't know about. . . . So what the hell is this?"

Tak knows that this is a different Axon Corporation in a different timeline, but the discovery still catches him off guard. Both Yates and Judith had talked to him about how the Machine would make the building immune from the change, how it would act as a kind of life raft that allowed everyone inside to surf over to the new timeline instead of being overwritten by it. Clearly, this had been a miscalculation.

"Or a lie," he says to no one in particular. "Could just be another lie."

But, of course, it presents him with a whole new set of problems. The addition of four new floors means that the holding cells are likely not where he expects them to be; if he has to fumble around with only a lighter and his increasingly frayed wits, he might never find them. The Machine, however, is a different story. Even if it's in a different location, he can just follow the sound.

Tak takes another piece of candy from his pocket and sucks on it as he thinks. He was hoping to hit security first, but that's not really an option anymore. Better to find the Machine and see what's going on there, then strike out if the need arises. He crunches down on the butterscotch, enjoying the way it dissolves between his teeth, and opens the door.

The emergency lights are functioning down here, although faintly, and the entire hallway is bathed in a dim red glow. The first thing he sees when his eyes adjust is another body. He moves his gaze away to avoid consuming more nightmare fuel, but then slowly slides them back. There's something different about this corpse. First of all, it isn't shredded into a thousand pieces, nor is there a hole in its head. And more important, it appears to be breathing.

"Hello?" asks Tak quietly. When there is no response, he moves a couple of steps closer and tries again. "Um . . . hey there. You okay?"

The body on the floor, which appears to be an older woman, stirs. One arm flaps out for a second before coming to rest in a pool of blood on the floor. The liquid is most likely coming from her, but Tak doesn't want to get close enough to confirm that suspicion. The way everything had gone so far, she was likely to leap up and plant a pair of sharpened teeth in his neck.

"H-help," gasps the woman. Her voice is rough, barely above a whisper, but it echoes around the empty hallway all the same. "Can't . . . feel myself. P-please . . ."

*Ah, screw it. If she kills me, she kills me.*

Tak moves forward and kneels next to the woman, ready to leap back at the first sign of trouble. But once he gets close, he sees that this won't be necessary; the woman has what appears to be the leg of an office chair sticking from a ragged hole in her chest. Blood drips from an opening in the end and pools on the floor below—by the looks of the crusted bits on the end, this has been going on for some time. It's a wonder she's even alive.

"H-help . . ." says the woman again.

"I will," lies Tak. "I will. Just be calm, okay? Who are you? What happened here?"

"The . . . devil."

"Was it a bird? A big bird with huge black eyes?"

The woman nods, then coughs. A gout of something goes flying across the hall, and Tak is suddenly glad the lights are so dim. "Okay, listen. This is very important. I'm looking for a young woman named Samira Moheb. Have you seen her?"

"S-still here . . . You have to . . . run."

"Okay, I will, but I need to know about Samira."

"It's coming. I hear it coming."

Tak stops talking and listens, then he hears it too—a series of slow, thudding footsteps ringing out from one of the floors above them. "Oh, shit on a sandwich. Okay, so forget the bird for a second. Do you know Samira? Do you know where is she?"

The woman gazes out blankly, eyes roaming back and forth like they're searching for something to grasp on to. "H-hurts. M-make it . . . Make it stop."

"Ah, shit. I'm sorry. I can't. I can't do that."

"P-please," says the woman. This time her eyes stop roaming and lock onto Tak's with blazing ferocity. "Make it stop."

Tak stands up and runs his fingers through his hair. He feels something wet and sticky lodge in there somewhere and forces himself not to think about it. Below him, the woman coughs again, huge, wracking things punctuated with sobs.

"Fuck!" screams Tak, slamming his fist into the wall. "Fuck, fuck, fuck!"

He turns to leave, but the woman snakes her arm out and grabs his foot. It would be the easiest thing in the world to shake her off, to kick the hand away and just continue on, but he knows he isn't going to do that. Instead, he kneels next to the woman and runs a hand through her grey hair, smoothing it down to her forehead.

"What's your name?" he asks as he keeps stroking her hair. His other hand snakes into his jacket and closes around a pocket-knife that suddenly seems to weigh a million pounds. "Tell me your name."

The woman doesn't respond. Her eyes have gone rogue again, and are slowly scanning up and down the hallway. "Petey?" she croaks. "Petey, no. Mom is going to be mad."

Tak pulls out the knife and opens the blade. He reaches one hand around the back of her neck and feels for the base of the skull, searching for the little space between the bone and the first vertebra. Once he finds it, he brings up the weapon with a trembling hand and positions it, point first, at the spot.

"Petey, you're a bad dog," says the woman again, looking directly into Tak's face. "Bad dog."

"Close your eyes," says Tak in a shaking voice. "Oh God, please close your eyes."

To his relief, she does, letting the lids flutter and fall as Tak leans forward and kisses her gently on the forehead. Her breath suddenly hitches as if preparing for another cough, but then Tak brings his arm forward, and the sound falters and dies.

He stands up, leaving the knife behind, and shuffles backward down the hall. Whatever composure he might have had suddenly breaks, and he begins running through the dim red hallway as fast as his legs can take him. He sees things as he runs, horrible things, impossible things, but Tak's brain has decided that he's had enough and mercifully refuses to give them form. He crashes through doors at random, moving through laboratories and barracks and dining halls in a wild frenzy. He's trying to cry, but his body seems to have forgotten how that works as well, so all that comes out is a kind of crazed, hoarse whoop. He doesn't know where he's going, and he doesn't care. He can't take this timeline anymore, and he certainly can't take the pressure of repairing it. All he wants to do is find a dark hole where he can curl up and let the rest of his sanity take a permanent vacation.

Suddenly, his legs stop moving. He doesn't tell them to do so; they just seem to think it's a good idea. Standing in front of him is a familiar white door, made red by the overhead lights. It has the words AIR LOCK stamped across it, and below that a single, perfect set of eight letters: CONDUITS. Dimly, he hears the bird scream out from somewhere high above him. He knows he should be scared of this, but all he can think about right now is the air lock.

Tak extends a hand and pushes hesitantly on the door. To his amazement, it opens, the power outage apparently having killed the air-lock mechanism. He lets his legs carry him past a series of computers and other dead equipment and through another door, where he finds himself in a room the size of an airplane hangar. It's filled with empty metal beds, some of which have been overturned. Sheets and pillows litter the floor, giving the entire room the appearance of a med-school fraternity after an all-night bender. Thousands of feet of wiring snake out of holes in the walls and lead to nowhere. Some of these have chunks and bits attached to their ends, but he doesn't bother to look more closely. He knows where they came from.

He's about to turn around and leave when he notices something: on the side of the room, pressed against the wall, is a bed with a large lump. He shuffles forward, stepping over and around the discarded prisons of the other conduits, until he's close enough to be sure that what he's seeing is real. But even seeing isn't enough—he has to reach out and touch the lump before his mind finally accepts the reality of the situation. At his touch, it stirs. A pair of pale brown eyes flutter open, cross briefly, then lock in on a familiar face floating above them.

"Hey, Sam," says Tak, as the hitch in his throat threatens to turn into a sob. "I told you I'd come back."

# chapter twenty-five

Samira's dream is deep and complete. She's on the back deck of the house, sneaking one of her father's cigarettes. As the first drag travels down her windpipe and into the virgin territory of her clean pink lungs, she begins to cough. She raises a hand to her mouth to still the hacking, but it does no good—and that's when the glee of trying a forbidden thing turns to fear.

"Sam! Oh my God, Sam, it's you. It's you, it's you."

Because her father will hear her, of course. He will hear her hacking up here in the cold night, he will ascend the stairs to see what is going on, and when he finds his little girl with a cigarette in her hand and a face red from coughing, he is going to be *royally* pissed off.

"Christ, Sam, come on. You have to wake up. Please wake up."

It's not a particularly pleasant dream, but the voice that keeps interrupting it is even more annoying: high-pitched, with just the tinge of an accent that you wouldn't notice unless you listened extremely closely. *Go away,* she thinks, as a dim portion of her mind clicks back to life. *Let me dream. Let me go. Anything is better than what's waiting for me back there.*

"Jesus Christ in a sidecar, Sam! Come on! Don't you dare check out on me! Don't you fucking dare!"

*. . . I know that voice.*

Her eyes flutter open. A blurry shape above her turns double for a moment, but then re-forms into an image of a dopey-looking young man with spiky black hair and fear in his eyes.

"T-Tak?" she manages to say.

Beaming is not a strong enough word to describe the smile that breaks out on her friend's face: it's goddamn *luminescent.* Samira blinks a few times and waits for him to say something, but he just stands there like the village idiot, grinning as if his heart is ready to burst.

"Heya, Sam," he finally croaks. "You look all right."

"Wh-where . . . ?"

"You're in the Axon building. Back in the solid timeline. Come on, I'll explain everything, but we have to get out of here. It's not safe."

As if in response, a deep metallic clang rings out somewhere high above them. This is followed by a low groan, as if the foundation of the building were being put under immense pressure. The noise rumbles on for a while before ending in a high-pitched squeal. Tak slips his arms under Samira and tries to lift her off the bed, but the wires in the back of her head hold her fast. It takes him a couple of tries to realize what's going on, and when he turns her head to the side and sees what Yates has done, the happy grin of a moment earlier dissolves into rage.

"No," he says quietly. "No, no, no, no."

"S'okay," whispers Samira. " . . . Doesn't hurt anymore."

"Ah, Christ, Sam. I didn't want this to happen to you."

"I know."

He reaches for the wires and then hesitates, one hand hovering above the back of her head. "I don't know if—"

"Yes. You can. Just do it, and let's go."

She has an image of him worming the wires from her head

244 | alan averill

one at a time, but to her great relief, he grabs them in a single bundle and yanks as hard as he can. A thick, stabbing pain shoots though her head before fading away. *Like a bandage,* she thinks, as Tak slips an arm behind her back and helps her to a sitting position. *Always better to tear it off.*

Once Samira is upright, the nausea starts to fade. She takes a few deep breaths and looks around as her blurred vision tries to normalize. The room is bathed in the dark red light of emergency overheads, which causes the numerous blood spatters on the wall to appear black. There are trays and office furniture and medical supplies scattered everywhere. In the corner, someone has removed the guts from a security guard and strewn them across the floor. She tries to remember if that was the same guard who went flying over her just before she blacked out, but her memories are muddled together and untrustworthy.

"You feel okay?" asks Tak. "Are you gonna hurl?"

She starts to shake her head, but the motion brings the nausea back all over again. "No," she says. "I think I'm going to be all right. I just . . . I just need a minute."

"Yeah, sure. Take all the time you want. We've got—"

Tak is interrupted by another noise from above. It sounds like a set of jagged fingernails scraping back and forth across a piece of sheet metal. This is followed by a ragged, wet scream. Tak and Samira look up at the ceiling for a moment, then back at each other.

"Okay, maybe not all the time you want," says Tak. "Actually, you know what? We should probably get the fuck out of here."

"Where are we going?" asks Samira. Her voice is hoarse and ragged, and sounds to her ears like the voice of her father after forty years of smoking had worked their magic.

"Seattle. There's a timeline there that can undo all of this. I know that sounds crazy, but—"

"Yates put something inside me," says Samira as she swings one leg over the edge of the gurney. When this seems to work, she moves the other leg into position next to it. "He called it the Beautiful Land. He was going to take me there, but then . . . I don't know. I don't know what happened."

"Oh my God," says Tak. "He gave you the Beautiful Land?"

"He said we were going to go there and it would be perfect or something like that. But he said a lot of crazy stuff, so I'm not really . . . Here, look out. I'm going to try and get up."

She drops her feet to the floor and moves to a standing position. Tak reaches out an arm, which she gladly accepts, and helps her to wobble in place. Her legs are jelly, but she thinks they'll work as long as she doesn't have to run.

"You okay?" asks Tak.

"My head's cold," responds Samira. "In the back where he . . . Never mind. I'm okay. We should just—"

A huge bang rings out from somewhere above them. It is followed by a series of shorter, louder bangs that seem to grow closer with each successive one. They have a dull, echoey quality to them, like a child slamming a spoon against the side of a large stewpot.

"Ah shit," mutters Tak. "I think it's in the elevator shaft."

"It's the bird," says Samira. "It was here. I saw it right before . . . I don't know why it didn't kill me."

"I saw it too," says Tak, dropping Samira's arm and moving toward the door. He cracks it open and peers out, then turns his head to continue speaking. "When I was coming here. I saw it on the road. It flew right up to me, but then it killed some other guy instead."

"Weird," croaks Samira.

"Yeah, it's weird. But I figure it's going to get around to us eventually, so we should probably go. Can you walk?"

"I think so."

"Can you climb stairs?"

"If we go really slow."

"Yeah, I don't think we have time to go slow," says Tak, as the banging intensifies. "Okay, new plan. We're getting out of here."

"How?"

"We're going to use the Machine."

He hurries back to her, jumping over a dry bloodstain in the middle of the room, and puts her arm over his shoulder so she can lean on him. Then he slowly steers her through the destruction of the room and out the door. The scene in the hallway is horrifying, but Samira just keeps her focus straight ahead and tries to ignore the scattered bits of what once were living, breathing people.

"Where's Yates?" asks Tak, as they shuffle down the hall. "What happened to him?"

"I don't know," responds Samira. "He was next to me when that thing came in. It might have killed him."

Tak doesn't seem to believe that, but he says nothing. When they reach the end of the hall, he leans Samira against the wall and approaches an imposing metal door. It once boasted a substantial series of locks but now rests on a set of twisted, shattered hinges. He reaches out and pushes it gently, expecting at least some resistance, but the thing simply falls into the next hallway with a dull thud.

"Nice," mutters Tak. "I love it when a plan comes together."

A loud screech suddenly echoes behind them. It is followed by the sound of something large and heavy battering against a door. On the fourth or fifth try, a harsh metallic sound rings out as something goes clattering to the ground. Tak knows that he shouldn't look but can't help himself. Glancing back, he sees that the elevator doors at the far end of the hall are now bending out. Before he can turn away, something throws itself at them yet again, causing the top of the lift to buckle like tinfoil.

"Fuck me gently," he says, throwing his arm under Samira again. "Come on. Don't look! Just move. Move, move, move."

They shuffle down the hall with maddening slowness until they arrive at yet another door. This one seems to be intact, but unlike the other doors, it contains no locks, thumbprint scanners, or optical readers. Clearly, if you made it this far, you were supposed to be here.

Tak kicks the door open with one foot and pulls Samira through and into a room almost as large as the one they just left. There's a new kind of light here, a brilliant blue glow that seems to come from cracks in reality itself, and it takes her eyes a few moments to adjust. But when they finally do, the sight that materializes before her takes her breath away.

Sitting in the middle of the room, as if it has been waiting for them all this time, is the Machine.

The device is a massive cylinder of shimmering silver steel that rises nearly three stories above the floor, surrounded at the top by gossamer-thin planks of transparent scaffolding. Thick, clear wires ring its surface and emit faint pulses of light—blues and whites and greens and a thousand other hues all sparkling in the darkness of the room. The air above twinkles white, as if it were projecting its own little galaxy against a black night sky. It looks nothing like the mental picture Samira had drawn for herself. A lifetime of military service had led her to expect something highly functional and terrifically ugly, a huge conglomeration of steel and sparks and rusted-metal gears. She never dreamed it could be so beautiful.

"My God," says Samira, as the lights dance across her face. "My God, Tak, it's perfect. It's the most perfect thing I've ever seen."

He opens his mouth to respond, but whatever he was going to say is cut off by the sound of the elevator doors collapsing. The thing in the shaft utters an annoyed caw and begins to tear at the remaining metal in an effort to extract itself. Seconds later, the entire works come crashing to the ground, and a new noise rings out: the unmistakable sound of claws scraping across tile.

Samira knows that she should be scared, but she can't tear her eyes away from the Machine. Behind her, Tak sprints across the room and plants himself in front of a long black table, the top of which appears to be an LCD screen. As soon as he touches it, the screen to spring to life, revealing a mind-boggling display of numbers and graphs and mathematical symbols that leaves Samira reeling. He moves his fingers across a nearby keyboard and types furiously as he talks.

"We don't have time," he mutters, as the table projects an equation onto his sweat-covered forehead. "Christ, I don't think we have enough time."

"Time for what?" asks Samira. Her attention is fixed rapt on the Machine, and her question comes out in a voice barely above a whisper.

"It's not like the briefcase. You can't just click in a set of numbers and go. First, you have to actually locate the timeline you want, then you have to set a return point. If we just come back here, we're fucked, so I need it to bring us as close to Seattle as possible. But I have to make sure it's somewhere open so we don't materialize into the side of a building or whatever."

He finishes typing and hits the ENTER key. The numbers on the screen spin around like jackpots, then turn into bright red zeros. "Fuck!" screams Tak. "Fuck, fuck, fuck!"

"What?" asks Samira as the sounds of the creature grow closer. "What's going on?"

"I can't find a timeline! They're all gone!"

"What do you—"

"I mean they're gone! They're all gone! That fucking bird collapsed them all!"

Tak slams his fist down on the screen, an action that causes the Machine to glow a brilliant yellow. He reaches into his hair and pulls with such fury that a handful of strands come out between his fingers. When he turns to look at Samira, the expression on his face is one of utter surrender. "We can't do it," he says. "We're done. We're gonna die here."

"What about the Beautiful Land?"

"What?" says Tak.

"The timeline. The one in my head. Can't we go there?"

Tak stares at her for a moment, then grabs her by the side of the head and plants a kiss on her lips. Before she even has a chance to return it, he lets her go and pops open a small panel on the side of the table. "Of course! Of course, of *course*! I don't need to find a timeline, I can just download it from you! Samira Moheb, you are a motherfucking *genius*."

"I try," she says, as the feeling of Tak on her mouth slowly fades.

"Okay, I'm gonna have to plug some wires into your head, and it's going to hurt. A lot, I think."

"Do it," she says. "If I scream, just keep going."

He pulls a bundle of wires from the panel and unrolls them, then pushes Samira down in a nearby chair. Fear tries to claw its way into her mind, but she pushes it back. *I'm getting better at that,* she thinks, as Tak spins her around and lifts her hair. *I think this whole stupid adventure might make me a better person in the end. . . . I mean, if something doesn't kill me first.*

There is a sudden, terrible pain in the back of her head, then her brain goes cold. She feels a tingling from somewhere deep inside her mind, followed by a horrible sensation of something essential being sucked away. It's an awful feeling—worse even than when Yates put the wires into her skull. All she can think to do is curl up into a ball and sob, but even that simple action is more than she's currently capable of.

Samira's world becomes a confused jangle of images and noise. She hears a dinging from the table next to her, then a terrific roar as the Machine cycles on. It takes her a moment to realize that Tak has picked her up and is half-carrying, half-dragging her over to the Machine, the front of which has opened to reveal an interior shimmering with uncountable lights and colors. She is slowly lowered to the floor, which seems more unsteady than a floor should be, then left alone as Tak runs back to the table and starts punching on the keyboard once again.

Suddenly, she sees a shape materialize out of the darkness behind Tak. *It's the bird,* she screams in the confusion of her mind. *Oh God, Tak, run! Run!*

But it's not the bird—or at least not the bird she was expecting. It's different somehow than the one they found in the abandoned timeline. Where that creature was impossibly tall, this one is little more than six feet high. Oddly enough, it's dressed in the tattered remains of a white lab coat and an argyle sweater. The skin is a soft, milky white—not transparent—and the eyes are small and round and contain a hint of color. Tufts of black feathers jut out in various directions, but far fewer than were on the previous creature. The more she stares at it, the more it doesn't look like a bird at all. It looks like a person and a bird if they had been somehow merged together.

The thing shuffles closer to Tak, who is absorbed in work and doesn't seem to hear. Its mouth—a tiny beak torn through a pair of lips—moves up and down a couple of times as if looking for its voice. After a couple of tries, the thing manages to cough out a single word:

"O'Leary . . ."

Tak spins around and stares at the creature advancing toward him. Its small arms wave at the air as if searching for purchase. One tiny wing flaps and flutters ineffectually. And as Samira watches, she suddenly realizes what she's seeing. It's not a bird— at least, not like the other ones. This is something else. Something much more horrible.

"Oh God," says Tak as he stumbles backward. "It's Yates. It's fucking *YATES*!"

The Yates-bird opens its mouth and screams, the sound all the more terrible for the humanity buried within. It reaches toward Tak and tries to seize him, but its legs are still small and weak, and it goes tumbling to the ground. One clawed hand reaches out and grabs Tak's ankle, but he kicks it away and scampers around to the other side of the table. Rather than try to turn around, Tak just leans over and types backward on the keyboard. As the monstrosity on the floor struggles to rise, Tak punches in his final few commands and slams the ENTER key.

The light of the Machine grows even brighter as Samira's world begins to lose cohesion. She has a brief fear that Tak is doing something incredibly stupid, that he's going to try to sacrifice himself for her, but then she sees him run across the room and leap into the open door of the Machine. The Yates-bird rises to its feet and shuffles toward the Machine, but it's too slow. Before it can even get halfway across the room, the Machine cycles to full power. Samira sees the creature raise one hand above its head and begin to scream, but then the world dissolves to a familiar, welcome wall of white.

# chapter twenty-six

The room smells of rot. It contains a steel table, a wooden chair, and a rusted drain cut into the middle of the floor. A young man with panic in his eyes is tied to the chair with thick coils of rope. Fresh blood leaks from his nose and mouth, shimmering softly in the light of a pale overhead bulb.

*Oh no. Oh no no no no no.*

*Sam?*

*No no no no no. Please no.*

*Sam, what is this?*

A blond man with a shaggy mustache shimmers into existence behind the chair. He has something long and sharp in his hand, which he holds up to the prisoner's eye as he begins to speak.

"Where are the others? Tell me."

Someone to his left repeats the question in Arabic. It's a thin, trembling voice that seems terribly out of place amidst the severity of the room. Though the voice's owner is hidden in the darkness, Tak recognizes it instantly.

*Sam? Jesus, is that you?*

*Tak, no. Don't watch this. Please stop. Oh God. Oh my God.*

The prisoner says nothing. The blond man repeats his question, then motions toward the darkness, where Samira asks it again. When the man in the chair maintains his silence, the mustached man takes his blade and makes a swift motion across the other's cheek. A gout of blood flies from the wound as the prisoner starts to scream.

"You will tell me, or I will kill you. Do you hear me?"

*"Vaallaa bekhodaa nemeedoonam!"* screams the prisoner.

"He says he doesn't know anything," says Samira. Her voice seems on the edge of breaking. "He . . . He means it. He doesn't know."

"Fuck him," says Mustache. "He knows. He knows everything." He leans in to the prisoner and pulls up on the lid of his eye. "I'm going to kill your family," he says with cold clarity. "If you don't tell me what I need to know, I will kill your wife and kill your child and burn your life to the ground."

He pauses for a moment. When nothing happens, he looks over at the darkness with an annoyed expression. "Translate that," he says.

"I . . . I can't. Please, don't ask me to—"

"Translate the fucking message!"

Samira speaks again, her words halting and faint. When he hears them, the man in the chair begins to sob. *"Toro bekhodaa baavar koneed,"* he says through his tears. *"Be hazrat-e Abbas nemeedonam."*

"He doesn't know anything!" screams Samira. "He doesn't know, all right? Now leave him alone!"

The blond man rises from his crouch and looks into the darkness with disgust. Then he takes the blade and drives it violently into the other man's throat, where it penetrates the neck and comes to a halt in the wooden back of the chair. Thick, gurgling sounds come from the prisoner as the man with the mustache turns and walks away. Seconds later, Samira begins to scream.

**oh shit.**

*No no no.*

*Oh shit, they made you do that?*

*No no no no.*

*Sam?*

*No no no no no no no.*

*Whoa. Sam, come on. Stay with me. You need to stay with*

**an older man** with a shaggy grey beard sits at the end of a small kitchen table with his hands balled into fists. Across from him, a teenager rests with arms folded and a sneer on his face. Even through the haze of memory, the tension in the room is palpable.

*Oh, hell. I remember this night.*

"You are going to cancel your flight," says Tak's father in a barely controlled voice. "And tomorrow, you're coming with me to the job site, and we're gonna see about getting you licensed."

"No, I'm not," says Tak. His voice is thick and slurred from alcohol; the scent of it is everywhere. "I'm getting on a plane, and I'm leaving. I'm nineteen years old and I have a passport and I can do what I want."

"We've been a union family since my great-grandfather. We fought the Pinkertons. We fought the scabs. Your grandfather—"

"Yeah, I know. He was killed in a labor riot with the Wobblies."

"He *was* a goddamn Wobbly!" cries the older man as he slams his fist on the table. "Jesus Christ, are you really that thick? Or just that drunk?"

"Fuck you!" screams Tak.

Tak's father leaps up, sending his chair clattering to the floor, and Tak does the same. They stare at each other, neither one willing to break the standoff. Somewhere in the house, an old clock ticks softly, the only noise in an otherwise deathly stillness.

"What am I supposed to tell your mother?" says the older man at last. "That you left? Just hopped a plane and took off for Papua, New Guinea, so you could show the world how big your dick is? That she should get ready for her only child to come home in a box because he got killed by fucking dysentery?"

"Tell her whatever you want."

"You're only doing this to piss me off."

"Yeah," Tak laughs. "You would think that."

"You won't last a week."

"I'll last a month. I'll last longer than you ever could."

His father shifts on his feet and runs a hand through his thinning hair. "If you weren't my son, I'd knock you on your fucking ass."

"Go ahead!" screams Tak, extending his chin toward his father and motioning at it with a single finger. "Come on, old man! Do it! Just hit me and get it over with and then *let me go!*"

Tak's father pulls his fist behind his head, but before he can move it any farther, a thousand tiny cracks appear in the surface of the memory. They run across it like raindrops on a pane of glass before the entire vision explodes into a dazzling white blur.

**. . . *guess you're not*** the only one with a bad past, huh, Sam? *No no no.*

*Sam?*

*No no no no no no no no.*

*Oh shit, Sam, come on. Come on, you can't do this. Don't go crazy on me now. Not when I just got you back.*

samira sits in a chair and cracks the knuckles on both hands. When they no longer make any noise, she takes the ragged ends of her fingernails and begins raking them back and forth across the tops of her arms. One especially jagged piece catches on a flap of skin and tears it open, leaving a trail of nine tiny red dots in its wake. The rest of the memory is a blank wall of nothing; when her psychiatrist begins to speak, the sound comes from a slightly darkened blur somewhere in the distance.

"Samira?" asks the blur. "Do you need me to prescribe you something?"

"No," she whispers. "No, I'm fine."

"You don't appear to be fine."

"Yeah, well, I'm as fine as I'm ever going to be."

The blood turns a deep, rich red against the empty white backdrop of Samira's mind. Soon the rest of her begins to vanish, until all that remains is a pair of disembodied voices and nine small dots that slowly grow as the conversation progresses.

"We need to trust each other if we are going to make progress," says the blur.

"I know," says a small, scared voice.

"Can you trust me?"

"I don't . . . I don't think so. I'm sorry."

"That's all right. Perhaps it will come in time."

". . . Doubt it."

. . .

tak clears a patch of snow from a rotting log and takes a seat. He is cold and shivering and miserable—his seven-year-old body only beginning to learn the wilderness survival techniques that would later become his entire life. To his left, his father cuts into the steaming body of a brown bear not five minutes dead. Tacky blood sticks to the arms of his coat and drips from his gloves, pooling into a puddle at the feet of the animal.

"Takahiro," he says. "Come here, son."

The young boy slides off his perch and shuffles over to his father, who tugs at the insides of the bear. After a moment, he slides his knife over to the younger boy with a piece of something dark and red perched on the edge of the blade. "It's the heart," says his father. "Go on."

Tak shakes his head and backs away, fear blazing a trail across his face. His father smiles a bit beneath his massive winter beard and holds out a hand for his son. He waits like that for a minute or more, patiently, until the boy finds the nerve to scuffle back to him.

"We use every part of the animal, Takahiro," begins his father as he wraps one arm around his son's shoulders. The knife and its contents seem to hang in the air as if by magic. "We use every part, but the heart is special. The heart contains strength. The heart reminds you what it means to be alive. Do you understand?"

Tak nods as a few flakes of snow begin to drift across his long, dark lashes. His father holds the knife out to him yet again, and this time he takes the small piece of meat balanced on the end. As he turns it over and over in his fingers, a wisp of steam rises, then vanishes into the tiny opening of the boy's mouth. The muscle is tough and sour, but he manages to chew until he can force it down.

"That's my son," cries the older man as he enfolds Tak in his wiry arms. "That's my boy."

Tak smiles at the attention as the snow continues to fall. They stay like that for a while, father and son, holding each other in the shivering cold. Soon, the weather begins to blur with the edges of memory, until the entire scene is consumed in a blizzard the color of an old dry bone.

*i killed him.*
*You what?*
*I killed him. I killed him. I could have said something, I could have saved him, but instead I got him killed.*
*Sam, you couldn't have done anything.*
*I want to die.*
*Don't say that!*
*I hurt so much. I hurt everywhere. I want to die.*
*Goddammit, Sam, don't you fucking*

**a blond girl** with short hair pops into view at the foot of Samira's bunk. "Hey," she says. "I hear you've got patrol tonight."

"Huh?" asks Samira. She's busy picking at a small piece of skin on her thumb and didn't hear the question. Her fingers and hands have become more ragged lately, and she's a little bit worried. Two months into your first tour of duty is a little early to start developing nervous tics.

"I said, you've got patrol tonight."

"Oh. Yeah, I . . . I guess."

"Listen, do you want to switch? I've got the morning, but I'm going to try and call my husband before he goes to work."

"Um . . . yeah. Yeah, sure."

"Great! I'll clear it with command, but I'm sure it's fine. They don't care who the hell translates, right?"

"Yeah, no. They don't seem to."

The memory suddenly lurches forward like a broken movie. Samira has a brief glimpse of the girl with a massive hole in her stomach and a terrified expression on her face, but then the image cracks apart and dissolves into a thousand little pieces.

**samira is crying** again. She's so tired of crying. She shuts her eyes as tightly as she can and tries to block out the tears, waiting for another memory to force its way into her mind. For a long while nothing comes, but she keeps her eyes closed and waits. It will be here soon enough. Maybe the small girl in Fallujah, or the old man in the market, or more of her friend Heidi, the one who swapped patrols and came back wrapped in a black plastic tarp.

"Sam?"

Even worse is the face of a scared young man begging her to spare him. She has spent every day trying and failing to bury this memory, and now it's the only thing she can see.

"Oh my God, Sam. We did it. We're here."

The voice belongs to Tak, in a scene eerily reminiscent of the moment forever ago when she found herself strapped to a table with wires streaming from her brain. He's telling her that everything is all right, but it's a lie. It always was.

"Sam, come on. Open your eyes. This is . . . Oh my God, it's *amazing*. You have to see this."

There's another noise behind his voice: the low, steady throb of something large cutting through the air. She focuses on the sound, wondering what it is about it that she finds so oddly comforting, before a slow realization dawns in her mind. The sound is repeating at regular intervals, a low, bass thrum every few seconds.

*Whoosh.*

*Whoosh.*

*Whoosh.*

Samira opens her eyes and finds herself lying in a field of brilliant green grass. Above her, a handful of white clouds drift across
an impossibly blue sky. The sound comes again—*whoosh*—and by
turning her eyes to the left she is able to spot the source. It's a long
row of modern, power-generating windmills, each as high as a
skyscraper, slowly turning their blades against the backdrop of
that flawless sky.

Tak stands a few feet away with his arms in the air and a
stupid grin on his face. And the moment she locks eyes with her
friend and feels a smile begin to come, something breaks inside of
her. All of the heartache and all of the pain and all of the terror
of her previous life just kind of . . . dissolve, as if the massive blades
of the windmills somehow reach inside her mind and carry her
demons away.

"T-Tak?" she asks. "Tak, is this real?"

"Oh yeah. It's real."

"We're not in the Machine?"

"No. We made it. We're done. We're out."

She slowly struggles to her feet and lets the cool breeze play on
her face. She sticks her tongue between her lips and senses the
faintest taste of salt water. Tak crosses over to her and takes her
hands in his. He seems ready to laugh or cry or do both at once,
and Samira can only assume that he is experiencing the same
lightness as she.

"Are we dead?" she asks.

"No." Tak laughs as the grin on his face grows wider. "We are
so fucking alive, you have no idea."

"What do you mean? Where are we?"

"We're in the Beautiful Land."

# the beautiful land

# chapter twenty-seven

The ocean beats against the rocks like it has always done: slow and steady and perfectly predictable. Wave after shimmering blue wave rises and falls against the stones, wearing them down a millimeter at a time, building the sand that will eventually be dragged back to sea to start the process all over again. They come and go like clockwork, and sitting on the edge of the shore watching it happen brings tears to Samira's eyes. She doesn't mind these tears; they are happy ones, and welcome. Right now, everything is as perfect as she can allow herself to hope.

They've been in the Beautiful Land for almost two days. She spent most of that time curled into a tiny ball in the grass, letting the crash of the ocean and rumble of the windmills lull her into a deep and dreamless sleep nearly five years overdue. Tak had dedicated himself to searching for water and food, so their makeshift campsite now contains a large pile of lumpy purple fruit, as well as clean water stored in scavenged clamshells. Only after securing all these essentials did Tak allow himself to rest, and now he was back at the campsite with his mouth hanging open and his lungs snoring away. Samira was prepared to let him snooze until doomsday if it came to that; she'd stolen away an hour previous to sit by the ocean and watch the birds soar overhead and enjoy the feeling of just being alive.

She reaches down for a piece of fruit, brushes away a few stray grains of sand, and takes a bite. It's sweet and delicious, like an especially good pear. Halfway through the meal, a curious black bird hops across the sand and takes up position a couple of steps away. She tears off a small piece and tosses it over; he catches it in the air and flies off to enjoy the snack.

"Never thought I'd want to see a bird again," she says to herself. This makes her think about the thing she saw back in the solid timeline, the twisted and terrible creature that Yates had become, but she quickly shoves the image away. Such dark thoughts seem out of place in this world.

Samira finishes the rest of the fruit and utters a small belch, then stands and brushes off the seat of her dress. She needs a shower and a change of clothes in the worst possible way, but there will be time for that later. Despite the random nature of the Machine, she thinks they have some time left in this place. She doesn't know how she knows that—only that it feels true.

The breeze blows through her hair as she clambers up the rocks and back to the campsite. The vegetation near the beach is little more than wispy strands of dry, dead grass, but as she moves inland, deep green stalks the size of ripe wheat begin to fill in the cracks. Soon she finds herself swimming through a field of the stuff, the smell of rain and chlorophyll rich in her nostrils. It reminds her of childhood—of a time where everything seems bigger and deeper and more alive—but also of how she used to sit on the back porch of her house and watch her father mow the lawn in his dusty brown slacks and a sleeveless white T-shirt. When he was finished, he would look over to Samira and clap his hands together, at which point she would leap off the porch and run squealing onto the lawn, rolling over and over from her back to her belly until she was covered in freshly mown grass. Usually, her father would light a cigarette and lean against the house to watch his daughter giggle while she stained her clothes and skin, but on rare occasions he would dive onto the lawn with a roar, tickling her sides as he called her the Grass Monster.

She glances up at the sun—which is larger than she's used to, and almost red in color—then back to the grass. She doesn't possess Tak's gift for overland navigation, and she's having trouble spotting their campsite amidst the rolling green hills. Finally, she sees a small tendril of smoke drift up toward the horizon and makes for it. Two minutes later, she moves into a small clearing and finds Tak cutting open a piece of fruit. He has a small fire going, and its warmth feels good against the early-evening chill.

"Hey," she says quietly.

"Oh, hey, Sam," he says as he takes a massive bite out of the fruit. "Mmmmrgg."

"What?"

"Mmm . . . Sorry, hold on." He chews for a minute, then swallows with comic abandon. "God, this shit is delicious."

"You're an idiot." Samira giggles. "And you just sprayed juice all over your shirt."

"Yeah, well, it's an old shirt anyway." He finishes the fruit in three bites, then wipes his arm across his face. "Man, that's good. I gotta go find me some more. So how long have I been out?"

Samira shrugs, then holds out her wrists as if to prove that she isn't wearing a watch. "I don't know. Six, seven hours? Maybe more?"

"I should teach you how to read the sun."

"Yeah, let's get right on that."

She sits down next to Tak and presses close, holding her hands toward the fire. After a brief hesitation, he places his arm around her shoulders. She can feel his pulse quicken when she moves against him, and notices the way he keeps glancing at her out of the corner of his eye.

"I still make you nervous, huh?" asks Samira after a pause.

"Muh?" replies Tak. "What do you mean?"

"You know what I mean."

". . . Yeah, I guess I do."

He drops his hand from her shoulder to her hip and begins to move his thumb in a slow, steady circle, an action that makes electricity race inside her. She burrows her head against his thin chest and lets the warmth of the fire play across her face. Eventually, the sun starts its descent toward the horizon, causing the shadows of the windmills to stretch closer and closer to their campsite.

"I don't get the windmills," says Samira as she moves her hand down and meshes her fingers with Tak's. "I mean, there's nothing out here. No roads or power lines or anything, so why build a wind farm in the middle of nowhere? And who put it there?"

"You did," says Tak.

"I did what?"

"You put the windmills there."

Samira looks up at her friend with a quizzical expression. "Tak, what are you talking about?"

"This is you, Sam. The windmills, the ocean, the grass. All of this comes from you. That's how this place works."

"I don't understand a thing you just said."

Tak grins. "The reason Yates was looking for this place is because it's different. Special. There's not another timeline like it in all of reality. Judith says it's 'flexible,' and that's about the best word I can think of. Every other timeline comes with rules attached: atomic particles are always going to interact in the same way, there are a set number of elements that compose all forms of matter, blah blah blah. But that's not how the Beautiful Land works."

"This is a little confusing."

"Okay, remember the pancake stack?"

"Yates said the pancake stack was stupid."

"Yeah, well, he's a big bird now, so fuck him. Anyway, I think it's like this: every other timeline is a pancake—it's a certain shape and a certain size, and it's in the same place every time. But the Beautiful Land is more like the syrup. It *flows*. It can shift in and around other timelines. It can change its location. And because of that, it's constructed from the thoughts of whoever happens to be there at the time. The reason that we're seeing all these things is that you want them to be here. Basically, this is your perfect world."

Samira thinks about this for a while as the sun dips below the horizon and a few crickets begin to chirp. "So that's why I feel so happy here? Why all the sounds are regular and I can sleep and the whole cleaning thing doesn't bother me?"

"There's nothing to clean here, unless you wanna sweep dirt."

"Says the guy with fruit smeared all over his shirt," says Samira, dragging a single finger down his chest. "Normally, this would drive me crazy, but right now, I just . . . I don't know. I don't care at all."

"Yeah, that's probably the reason," says Tak. He licks a finger on his free hand and scrubs at the dirty shirt for a few seconds. "It's funny. When Judith told me about this place, I thought she was totally off her nut. But whadaya know? She was right. She and Yates were both right."

Samira takes her other hand and places it on Tak's knee. "But we have to leave. Don't we? Because even if this place is outside time or whatever, Yates knows about it. And that means he's going to come here."

"I think so," says Tak quietly. Despite the heaviness of their conversation, he seems much more entranced by the small hand currently resting on his knee. "I mean, the Machine is going to pull us back at some point, so it's kind of a moot issue, but yeah. We need to meet Judith. We need to fix this before that bird destroys reality."

"Why do we have to find Judith?" asks Samira.

"She has a timeline in her head. We can hook her up to the Machine and use it to overwrite the solid timeline, the same way Axon did. In theory, it'll prevent all of this from ever happening."

"But what happens then?"

Rather than answer, Tak moves his hand from her hip to her side. She waits to see if he's going to move it any higher, but for the moment, that's as far as it seems ready to go. She can feel nervous energy burning off him in waves, and it makes her smile.

"Look, let's just not talk about that anymore," he says. He tries to say it with nonchalance, but his nerves are working against him, and the final word hits a high note before cracking.

"How's puberty working out for you there?" Samira giggles.

"Great, thanks. Maybe one day I can grow a mustache."

"You'll never grow a mustache. I have more hair than you."

"That's because of your dad. He was like a shag carpet with legs."

He smiles as he says this, but Samira just looks away. She catches a glimpse of his panicked expression and grabs for his hand again. "It's okay," she says. "I've just been thinking about Dad a lot. When I saw him in the Machine, it was like he was still here. I could smell him and feel the hair on his arm and . . . I don't know. It just makes me sad, I guess."

"I know. I'm sorry."

"Do you think . . ." she begins. "Do you think I could bring him back to this place? I mean, if I thought about it really hard, could I bring him back?"

"I'm not sure. I mean, you could probably bring back something that looked and smelled and acted like him, but I don't know if it would really *be* him. It might just be your memories of him given some kind of physical form."

"But that would be enough. Wouldn't it? I mean, aren't people just whatever we remember of them to begin with?"

Tak makes a gun with his thumb and forefinger and presses it against his temple. "Dude, Sam, my head. Look, I don't know. This is way too deep for me. I'm just a guy who jumps through time and knows how to not get killed."

"You're more than that," she says as she finds her hand moving away from his knee and up his leg. "You're funny and you're sweet and you're my best friend in this world or any other. You always have been, ever since the day I met you."

"Um . . ." says Tak.

She moves her head up and presses her forehead to his. "We're in a bad way. I know that. The world is ending and there's a giant bird flying around eating everyone and pretty soon we'll be back in a place where I'm going to start freaking out all over again. And that makes this a terrible time to say the things I want to tell you. . . . So I'm not going to say them. I'm just going to sit here and let you figure it out."

"I . . . I think I know."

"Good," she says as she moves her head down until her lips are just inches from his. "Then you should know what to do."

As it turns out, he does.

# chapter twenty-eight

"Just try it," says Tak. "What can it hurt?"

"I feel dumb," says Samira. She's standing at the base of a windmill and staring at a small circle of earth where Tak has pressed the grass flat. "It's just such a bad cliché, you know? Stare at the empty circle and think really hard about something until it materializes in front of me. It's like a scene from *Star Wars*."

"That never happens in *Star Wars*."

"Nerd."

"Look, Sam. Any minute now, the Machine could decide to pull us back. And when it does, we're gonna be dropped in the middle of the Pacific Northwest with no supplies or weapons of any kind. The only thing I've got is my flint, and even that's a bit sketch."

"What about your knife?"

Tak licks his lips and thinks about his pocketknife—as far as he knows, it's still stuck inside the neck of an old woman somewhere back in the solid timeline. "Uh . . . Yeah, I lost it somewhere between here and there. But if we can use you to conjure up some supplies, we're going to be in a much better position than we are right now."

Samira sighs and turns her head to the sky, watching the massive blades of the mill continue their never-ending journey. It shocks her to think her subconscious mind could be responsible for something so big and real and . . . *there.* The thought of doing it again seems laughably impossible.

"Okay," she says at last. "Fine. I'll try it."

"Great!" says Tak. He scrambles behind her and puts both hands on her hips, pressing himself close. "Okay, so what we need to do—"

"I am *not* going to be able to concentrate if you stand there like that."

"Huh? Oh, shit. Sorry." He takes a couple of steps back, then extends one hand past her head with a finger pointing at the flattened circle of grass. "All right, so you see that spot, right?"

"Yep."

"Okay, so just look at that spot and think about something being there. Start with something small, like . . . uh . . . I don't know. A canteen."

"A canteen?" repeats Samira doubtfully.

"Yeah. You know. Like one of those metal—"

"I carried a canteen for years, Tak. I know what it looks like."

"Right. Yeah. Okay. I'm just gonna . . . stop talking now."

Samira giggles before returning her attention to the patch of grass. At first, all she can think about is Tak, but eventually she gets her mind into gear and the image of her friend begins to slip away. She stares at the grass intently, watching how the shadow of the blades cross it in a steady rhythm. Eventually, individual pieces of grass begin to come into focus and grow clear in her vision. She squints and concentrates more intently, trying to see the grass the way a person might look for a single brushstroke amidst the chaos of a painting. *Canteen,* she thinks to herself. *Small and metal. Small and bright. Desert camo pattern. Canteen. Canteen.*

A canteen is on the grass in front of her. It doesn't materialize like she was expecting, doesn't fade into existence or warble into being amidst a shimmer of sparkling lights. It's just . . . there.

"Christ played the banjo!" screams Tak. He races up behind Samira, wraps his arms around her, and shakes her gently from side to side. "That is the coolest fucking thing I have *ever seen*!"

"I did it," says Sam, as a smile breaks out on her face. "Oh my God, I . . . I did it."

"Yes, you did," says Tak as he bounds off toward the canteen. Picking it up off the ground, he gives it a little shake. "There's even water in there!"

"Are you sure?"

"It's either that or Scotch, in which case I'm totally going to kiss you." Tak unscrews the cap, sniffs the contents, then takes a drink. "No, it's water. Really good water, too. Dude, Sam, this is too much."

"I can't believe I did that."

"Okay, try again! Come on, come on! Try again!"

"What should I make?" asks Samira. "Food? Like, freeze-dried rations or something?"

"No, try something big! Like a car."

"A car? Tak, no. I'm not bringing a car here."

"Why not?"

"Because this place is wonderful, and I'm not going to drop some crappy metal car down in the middle of it!"

"Okay, okay! What about a horse? Or maybe a dog or something."

Samira thinks about this for a bit. "A dog would be fun."

Tak claps his hands together twice, then points at the ground expectantly. Samira rolls her eyes at him, then lowers her shoulders and lets her mind go blank. She's never owned a dog before—her parents weren't much for animals—but she had friends with dogs, and so she tries to concentrate on those. It's harder than the canteen, and she finds herself getting slightly frustrated as the minutes tick by.

"Dammit," she mutters. "I don't think this is working."

"It's gonna work," says Tak. "Come on. Just concentrate."

She closes her eyes and thinks about a scrawny brown dog that used to roam the neighborhood when she was stationed in Tikrit. The other Marines called him Bones because of the way his ribs stuck out, and whenever he came around, they would chuckle and laugh and toss him little bits of food. Once, Samira snuck outside the perimeter and brought him an entire shank of ham that she stole from the commissary storeroom. The dog wolfed it down in an eyeblink, then pattered over to Sam and allowed himself to be scratched.

"Oh, shit," says Tak quietly.

Samira opens her eyes. There's a dog lying on the patch of grass. It looks like a cross between Bones and the dog her friend Kerri used to own back when they were in elementary school. Tak slowly kneels down next to it and places his hand on the dog's side. After a moment, he moves his hand in front of its face, then looks up at Sam and shakes his head.

Samira feels tears coming and quickly turns away. But when she hears Tak struggling to pick the dog up, she starts running in the other direction. She hears him yelling from somewhere behind her, but she doesn't care. The idea that she did this, that she somehow willed an animal into existence and killed him in the same heartbeat, is simply too much for her to bear. She runs without seeing, feeling the grass slap against her hands and the red sunlight beat down on her face, until she finally collapses on the ground in a fit of tears.

When Tak finds her, she's sitting with her knees against her chest by the side of a small stream. Cottonwood trees line the banks, sprinkling small tufts of white fur into the afternoon breeze. He stands behind her for a while, saying nothing, until finally coming over and sitting next to her.

"I killed it," she says.

"You didn't kill it, Sam."

"I did."

"Look, maybe it was already dead to begin with. Maybe you can't bring a living thing into being. Maybe it just doesn't work that way."

"Or maybe I stole someone's dog from another timeline and killed it when I brought it here."

Tak shakes his head. "You remember what we talked about last night? Before we . . . Before? When you were talking about a person being the sum of their memories? Maybe you just didn't remember the dog well enough." He leans over and places a hand on her shoulder. "I don't think you killed it, Sam—it just never really existed in the first place."

"I want to stop making things now."

"Are you sure? Because we could really use more water or a gun or—"

"Tak!"

"Yeah, okay. All right." He grabs a stick from the riverbed and starts drawing small squiggles in the wet earth. "Probably for the best. I don't think we have a lot of time left anyway."

"I know," says Samira as she stares out over the water. "I can feel the Machine pulling on me. I've been feeling it for a while now, but I didn't want to say anything."

Tak sketches out a tall building, follows that with another, then adds a few stick people at the bottom. He keeps glancing over at Sam to see if she's actually angry with him or just frustrated, but can't seem to find the answer he wants. Only after he draws half of a city into existence does he see fit to talk again.

"I'm sorry, Sam," he says suddenly without looking up. "I'm really sorry."

"About what?" asks Samira.

"About this. About bringing you here. I didn't . . . I didn't know that the Beautiful Land was going to be like this. I can see how happy you are here. How peaceful everything is. If I'd known, I wouldn't have told the Machine to pull you back. I would have let you stay here."

Samira turns to him with an expression that he can't quite place. "And what?" she asks. "You'd go back yourself? Find Judith, take out Yates, and save the world while I stay here? I wouldn't want it to be like that, Tak. I couldn't live with myself if I sent you off alone." She seems ready to say more, but instead drops her eyes to the squiggles in the dirt. Tak offers her the stick and she takes it, adding a small smiley face on the outskirts of his city.

"I don't know how much you remember about the war," she says as the stick conjures more smiley faces from the mud. "I mean, you were hopping around other timelines for a lot of it, but even if you were there, it never really got the kind of attention it needed. People knew about it, but they didn't . . . They didn't really think about it. And none of them knew what it was really like. You've seen a couple of my memories—my friend getting shot, the guy in the chair—but those are just images. Actually being there is indescribable."

She drops the stick and reaches out for Tak's hand. When she finds it, she grabs it tightly, as if he might try to flee before she can finish what she is trying to say. As she speaks, Tak watches her move and listens to her voice and wonders how he could have ever left her.

"Most of the soldiers I met joined the military because they wanted to make a difference," begins Samira. "They liked the feeling of being a protector, the thought of keeping an entire country safe. But I didn't join to protect anyone. I joined because I was lonely and sad, and I thought it would harden me."

Tak's eyebrows rise slightly at this news. "I thought it was for the college money."

"That's what I told people, but it wasn't the real reason. I was just tired of being depressed all the time. Mom was always so sick, then you left, and it was like . . . I just didn't want to feel anything anymore." She picks up the stick with her free hand and throws it into the river. It bobs on the surface of the water for a bit before the current slowly takes it away. "But my plan didn't work. I went to war, and I saw terrible things, but instead of numbing me, they turned me into this emotional, quivering mess. Now everything I see makes me scared or upset or sad. Hell, I get sad when I look at signs."

"You what?"

"Remember that sign for the water-heater repair place by my old house? The one where the heater is on a pair of crutches and has a bandage over his eye?"

"Yeah, sure," says Tak. "Ricchardi Plumbing or something like that."

"That's it. Well, a couple of years ago, I was lying on a cot in the middle of Fallujah and trying to sleep and all of the sudden that sign popped into my head. At first it was just another random memory of home, but the more I thought about it, the more I started to feel bad for the water heater. Because he's never going to get better, Tak. He's a *sign*. No one's ever going to come along and paint a new sign where he's jumping around with a big smile on his face, or holding a baby water heater on his shoulders. He's going to be leaning on that crutch with that terrible look in his eyes until the end of the world. And the more I thought about that, the sadder I got, and after a while, I just started bawling." She stops talking for a moment and dabs moisture from the corners of her eyes. "Dammit. I'm getting upset just thinking about it."

Tak chuckles and pulls her close, letting his skinny arms enfold her. "I'm sorry," he says as he tries to stifle the laugh. "I'm not laughing at you."

"You should," she replies, sniffling once. "It's really stupid."

"You must hate those stick figures on warning labels."

"Oh God, you have no idea. Or the one they put on electric fences where the little guy has lightning bolts shooting out from everywhere? That one gets me every time."

A bird drops out of the sky and lands on the bank of the river. It pokes its beak into the water a few times until it emerges up with a long, thin worm. As the two of them watch, it tilts its head back and pulls the morsel down its throat, then flutters its wings before flying off.

"I'm not saying these things so you think I'm crazy," says Samira, as the bird transforms into a tiny speck on the horizon. "I'm telling you because I need to do this. I need to help you save the world. Because if I do something that important, I might finally be okay again."

"It's going to be hard," says Tak. "I mean, I'm not telling you anything you don't know, but it's going to be really hard. I think the timeline is going to be seriously screwed up when we get back. We could find a world overrun with birds. Yates might chase us down. There are a million things that could go wrong, you know? Our chances of actually pulling it off are pretty fucking slim."

"I know."

"But hey, if everything goes off the rails, at least we got each other. Right?"

She smiles and looks around the Beautiful Land for what she

is increasingly sure will be her final time. The river bubbles and gurgles. A warm breeze ruffles the overhead leaves of the cottonwoods. *I wish things didn't have to end this way,* she thinks, as Tak tightens his grip around her. *I wish we could just stay here until the end of time.*

They are still sitting by the river when the Machine calls them home.

# chapter twenty-nine

Samira and Tak stand on the edge of the tree line and watch the city burn. Ahead of them, some twenty miles distant, lies the metropolis of Seattle, Washington. The pair had hoped to catch a glimpse of a few identifiable landmarks as a kind of welcome-home present, but the familiar skyline is currently consumed by a thick pall of smoke. Only the tops of the tallest skyscrapers are visible, and most of those have bright orange flames roaring from the upper rows of windows. As they stare in growing horror, a tiny speck of a man emerges from one of the windows, pauses for a moment, then leaps, plunging straight down before vanishing into the smoky dark below.

Samira is crying. Tak would like to be, but he is so shocked by what he's witnessing that the tears won't come. Instead, he just stands in place with a hand over his mouth and a desperate look in his eyes. He'd expected something like this, but he didn't expect *this*. No amount of worst-case-scenario judgments or hopeless prognosticating could have prepared him for what his home world had become.

Soon a plane flies by—a military transport with four massive engines. It soars off toward the burning cityscape, where it circles twice before dumping a huge load of bright red powder onto the downtown corridor. The stuff drifts down like feathers in the wind before disappearing into the smoke. When things clear again, the flames are diminished. After a few minutes, however, they start licking up all over again.

Moments later, another plane roars overhead. Before this one can reach the flames, it begins to wobble back and forth as the engine chugs and sputters. Suddenly it flips over and goes hurtling down into the waters of Puget Sound, exploding into a huge blue wall of foamy water. The noise of the impact reaches their ears as a sad little thud.

"This is . . ." begins Tak. He wants to say something else, to somehow inject hope into the conversation, but for one of the few times in his life, words fail him. His eternal optimism has never seemed so misplaced or foolish. There isn't hope here. There can't be. The idea of walking into that hell, finding a single woman, and taking her a thousand miles across the country is laughable. Better to stay put and live off the land for as long as they can. Maybe better just to find a weapon and end it all before something terrible ends it for them.

"This is everywhere," whispers Samira. "Isn't it? All the cities of the world are going to be like this."

"I . . . I don't know," responds Tak. "Probably. Oh God, this is . . . This is just so fucked-up."

He expects Samira to start crying anew, but instead her tears dry up and vanish. She reaches out and takes his hand, her skin chilly in the early-morning air. "Well, nothing worthwhile is ever easy, huh?"

Tak glances over at her with brows knitted. It sounded to all the world like she just made a joke, but one look at her face wipes that thought from his mind. Samira isn't joking this time, or trying to deploy sarcasm as an air bag against their current predicament. Her mouth is a thin slit of determination, and her eyes are clear.

"What are you saying?" he asks. "Sam, you can't seriously think that we're going to—"

"Yeah. I do. That's exactly what I think."

"Sam, look at it. *Look* at it! Going down there is suicide."

"Your friend is down there somewhere, right?" says Samira.

"If she's not dead."

"Okay. Then we have to go down there and get her." She turns to Tak and smiles, a reaction so crazy, he can't help but return it. "Tak, we don't have a choice. This is it. Either we go down there and find this fail-safe of yours, or we stay here and everyone dies. Even us. I can't go out like that. I have to try. Even if it's useless, which it probably is, I just can't do it."

Tak exhales and watches his breath fog off and away. *Pay close attention to that breath, buddy. You probably don't have a lot of those left.*

"You're right," he says finally. "I mean, yeah. You're right. We have to try."

Samira wraps her other hand around his and pulls him close. They stand there like that for a little while, two small glimmers of light amidst the raging fires of a world gone wrong. He starts to feel he could wait there forever, but then she plants a quick kiss on his lips, drops his hands, and reaches down to double-knot her sneakers. When this is done, she takes a few steps down the trail, feet crunching across pinecones and dead leaves, before turning back with a sad expression in her eyes.

"Well, come on," she says. "Let's do this thing and get the hell out of here."

Tak looks to the sky as if waiting for a better option to present itself, then gets his legs under him and follows. The two of them scamper down the mountain and away from the cluster of trees, becoming smaller and smaller until they finally disappear into the growing gloom.

the end of all things

# chapter thirty

The first time Samira entered Fallujah was at night. She saw the city through night-vision goggles as a series of glowing green-and-black blurs that occasionally sprang to light when a tracer exploded overhead. That initial look betrayed the actual horror that the area had become, allowing her to believe that perhaps she had been misinformed as to how bad the thick was in this part of the world. But when dawn came, it revealed a twisted, pockmarked city filled with death and decay in equal measure. Between the heat and the stench and the surviving rebels who occasionally sprang out of nowhere to spray fire at her platoon, it seemed she had discovered a literal hell on Earth.

But that city was already dead. Here, in Seattle, the city is just beginning to go. And that made things far worse.

Currently, Tak and Samira are picking their way across the I-90 bridge, a half-mile span of concrete that floats on the surface of a lake. Cars, some burned, some not, lie scattered on the road like small toys. A couple have fresh corpses behind the wheel, but most are empty. Whether the drivers abandoned their vehicles and tried to escape on foot or decided to leap into the icy waters and end it all is unclear, and Samira doesn't really want to think

about it. It's taking all of her willpower just to keep moving toward a skyline that seems almost entirely on fire, a city choked
with the stench of ash and blood and filled with uncountable
screams. She doesn't want to go into that place. She wants to turn
around and flee, and she knows that if she breaks, Tak will be
right behind her. But she keeps walking forward all the same.

Halfway across the bridge, they encounter an overturned
dump truck. The hopper's load, some two tons of dirt, has been
spread across the road, and the steady rain is turning a large
stretch of highway into a soft brown sludge. She and Tak maneuver wordlessly around the twisted shell of the truck and trudge
through the muck. Samira manages to avoid looking inside the
cab, but Tak can't help himself—when he takes a glance, he sees
an overalls-clad man with his mouth hanging open and a giant
hole where his left eye should be.

When Samira breaks free of the mud, she pauses to dangle her
legs off the side of the bridge and into the coldness of the lake,
shaking her feet around until the scum is washed away. Whatever
good vibes she took from the Beautiful Land are long gone, and
her mind is awash with thoughts of cleanliness and cracking
knuckles and self-inflicted wounds. Tak's presence is the only
thing keeping her from going completely mad.

Just before she stands, she glances out at the calm blue surface
of the lake, where an abandoned sailboat is tacking back and
forth on the wind. The vessel's name is the *Anne Marie*, and the
entire stern is splattered with red. She can hear the creaking of
empty sails over the sounds of the city and the misty rain falling
on the water. It is a sound that will stay with her forever.

At the far end of the bridge, they encounter a tunnel. The grey,
overcast sky shines a bit of light into the entrance, but after they
move a hundred yards or so inside, they turn a corner, and the
faint glimmer of early morning is swallowed by the dark. Samira

hears Tak patting around in his pockets before a bright flash briefly illuminates the darkness.

"It's my flint," he says, his voice loud and echoing in the near silence of the tunnel. "I lost my lighter somewhere. I could try and make a torch, I guess. Maybe soak a shirt with some gasoline and—"

"No. Let's just go."

Tak places a hand on her shoulder and squeezes gently; she finds the contact reassuring. Then they're moving again, two small travelers passing through one of the fabled circles of hell, their journey illuminated every few seconds by a bright flash of sparks.

*Flash.* Uncountable cars have slammed into one another, creating a twisted, meaningless tangle of metal and glass. They clamber over and around it, trying to tell themselves the puddles of warm liquid their hands keep finding are nothing more than spilled transmission fluid.

*Flash.* There's a small arm on the ground, its stubby fingers curled as if they were trying to grasp an egg. The owner is nowhere to be found.

*Flash.* A dusty shape runs past them and away from the city. Samira thinks it's a dog, and her mind immediately settles on the poor creature she called into being back in the Beautiful Land. Tak thinks it's more likely that the animal was an abnormally large rat. Neither of them speak their thoughts aloud.

*Flash.* A row of corpses in spandex biking shorts are lined up against the side of the tunnel. Each has been shot once in the forehead. The man on the far right is wearing a pair of old brown glasses, which are somehow undamaged.

*Flash.* A young teenager in a puffy parka lies on the hood of a SWAT van. His mouth and eyes are open, and his legs are gone. One headphone of his MP3 player has fallen from his ear, letting Samira hear the faint bass beats of a Snoop Dogg song.

Eventually, the flashes of Tak's flint are replaced by a dim glow on the horizon. They make for it with purpose, moving around cars and leaping over small piles of people until they are both sprinting as fast as their legs can carry them. When they finally emerge from the tunnel and into the familiar grey light of a typical Seattle day, they turn to each other and embrace fiercely. Samira can feel Tak trembling under her grasp and knows that her own body is doing the same.

Most of the downtown buildings are smoking, and one tall skyscraper on the western edge of the city seems to have partially collapsed. Dirty smoke pours out of the football stadium, where Tak sees what appears to be a giant mound of bodies smoldering at the fifty-yard line. In the middle of Puget Sound, a massive ferryboat is engulfed in flames, making it seem as if the ocean itself has begun to burn. But all of that, all the burning, all the destruction, is not what has Tak and Samira's attention. Instead, they are riveted by the sight of the birds.

. . . Because they are *everywhere*.

Hundreds, maybe thousands of the creatures swoop and caw and soar through the glass canyons of the city. Some huddle on the streets, tearing at bodies with their sharp beaks. Many more cling to the sides of buildings with black goo dripping from their eyes and something like smiles on their otherwise blank faces. As Tak and Samira watch in horror, a young woman appears in the upper window of a nearby skyscraper. She utters a heart-piercing scream and leaps, her dress billowing around her as she tumbles through the air like a wet sack. Before she can hit the ground, a pale creature comes swooping out of the gloom and snatches her in its talons. The woman's scream grows momentarily louder, but then fades as the bird zooms into the dark smoke that now envelops the entire city.

"Christ," whispers Tak. "Ah, Christ."

Samira extends one trembling hand and places it in his. The sight of all these creatures has given the entire scene a vague, almost unreal quality, and she finds this comforting. It's like it's not happening anymore, and the feeling that she has lost all control somehow grants her courage she did not know existed.

"What now?" she asks.

"I don't know."

"You said she was in the police station, right?"

"Yeah."

"Where's that?"

"Downtown. It's right in the middle of . . . everything."

"We're gonna die down there."

Tak squeezes her hand, enjoying for a brief second the warmth of her smooth fingers. "That's not a certainty."

"I don't know," whispers Samira. "It looks pretty damn certain to me."

An idea begins to form in Tak's head, and he pulls on Samira's hand, leading her away from the freeway and back toward the tunnel. She stumbles along behind him, listening as he starts to talk.

"Okay, so bear with me here. Judith said . . . She said that once you use the Machine, the birds have trouble finding you. And that makes sense. I mean, they could have killed me when I was driving in Australia, but they didn't. And they could have killed you on the operating table, but they didn't do that either. They left you alive."

Thinking about the table makes Samira reach up and rub the holes in the back of her head, an action that shoots shivers up and down her spine. "Yeah, okay. I'll buy it."

"Okay. So maybe we can get in, grab Judith, and get out before they really know we're there. I mean, there are still a lot of people in the city, so it's not like they don't have other things to focus on."

Tak enters the dark of the tunnel and sparks his flint anew. Samira follows behind, scratching furiously at the back of her head. After a minute or so, they find themselves back at the SWAT van with the teenager on the hood. Tak grabs him gently around the shoulders, then turns to Samira. "Here, help me."

She slides around a bumper that has been sheared off and finds herself staring at the boy's missing legs. *It's not real,* she thinks to herself as she places her hands under the stumps and helps Tak lift him off the hood and onto a bare patch of asphalt a little ways away. *Not real. None of it is real.* She glances up at Tak, sees the spark of a newly formed plan burning in his eyes, and knows he is telling himself the same thing. It's the only way they can possibly function amidst such horror.

He opens the door of the van and reaches for the ignition. When he doesn't find what he's looking for, he jumps out and sparks the flint a few times until he locates the body of a SWAT member. Patting him down, he comes away with a large flashlight and hands it to Samira. She turns it on, sees much more than she wants to see, and decides to leave the beam focused on Tak.

"Got 'em," says Tak, as he pulls away from the body with a set of keys in his hand. "Okay, let's check the back of this thing."

"What are we looking for?" asks Samira, as they move to the back doors of the van and throw them open.

"Guns," says Tak. "Explosives. Batons. I dunno. Some kind of weapon."

"I don't think we can shoot all those birds."

"I know. They're for us."

Tak clambers into the back of the van, digs around for a moment, and returns with a pair of automatic pistols. Samira puts the flashlight into the crook of her arm and checks the action on the weapon by clicking it back and forth a few times. She then pops the magazine free, finds it full, and slams it back into place. Finally, she clicks the safety off and holds it warily. Tak has done the same, and now the two climb into the van without another word. He takes the driver's side and cranks the ignition, half-expecting to find the battery dead or the engine fried. But the van roars to life with an almost cheerful sound.

Tak turns to Samira and places his hand over hers as the engine chugs and the smell of exhaust drifts into their nostrils. "Okay. So we're gonna drive into the city and find the police station. Then we get Judith, throw her in the back, and get the fuck out of here. If we're quick—"

"And lucky," interrupts Samira.

"Yeah. If we're quick and lucky, the birds won't find us before we're on the road to Montana. There's nothing between here and there but empty space and asphalt. If we stay off the major highways, we might be able to get there in one piece."

"Okay. Let's just do it, then. Let's do it before I lose my nerve."

"Hell, Sam," says Tak as he clicks on the lights and begins to maneuver the van out of the tunnel. "I lost my nerve a long time ago."

The van pulls out of the tunnel and down the cracked surface of the interstate. When it reaches the downtown off-ramp, it hesitates for a moment, as if something inside the metal guts of the machine thinks going down there is a bad idea. But then Tak pushes the gas, and the van heads into the heart of the beast.

# chapter thirty-one

The city streets are slow going. Cars and office furniture and naked mannequins and a thousand other pieces of modern civilization lie in the streets like a bizarre college art project. Much of the material is on fire, creating thick clouds of harsh, toxic smoke. Each time they drive through one of these clouds, Tak and Samira try to breathe as little as possible—the smell is indescribably awful, and the slightest whiff burns in their lungs like hot ash.

There are also bodies—lots and lots of bodies—and that is the most disturbing sight of all. Most have the single-hole entry wound of the birds, but as Sam and Tak slowly roll toward the police station, they find many that have been put down by their fellow man—as if even the end of the world couldn't stop people from trying to settle old scores. A few blocks from the freeway, they come across a bright yellow school bus pockmarked with hundreds of bullet holes. The body of a man is lying on the front of the bus, his throat slit wide. A handmade sign propped in his lap reads simply: MOLESTOR.

Tak and Samira say nothing as the van rumbles down the street. A couple of blocks in, Tak reaches over to the radio and turns it on. He rolls the bar up and down the dial, finds nothing but static, and clicks it off. A moment later, the van lurches to the side as it runs up against a particularly large mass. Tak floors the gas and clears the obstruction after a few seconds. There's an odd smell in the air when he does so—something like burning tires mixed with shampoo—but neither one of them bothers to look back to see what they hit. It seems better not to know.

Eventually, they turn west and drive under the tracks of the city monorail. After a couple of blocks, they come upon the train resting silently above them. Samira cranes her neck, sees a single bloody handprint on the front window, and immediately regrets the decision. She snaps back into the passenger seat and turns her attention to her own hands, watching herself peel the skin from the cuticles around her fingernails and wondering why they don't seem to hurt anymore.

They enter the heart of downtown a few minutes later, a public square surrounded by office buildings, department stores, and high-end shopping boutiques. In the center of the square, between a small water fountain and an overturned espresso stand, a young man with dreadlocks is throwing bodies onto an ever-increasing pile. As Tak inches past, his progress slowed by a burning Dumpster in the middle of the road, the dreadlocked man looks up from his work. At first he seems surprised to see another living soul, but then he smiles wide and gives Tak the thumbs-up sign. "Christian burial!" screams the man, his voice raw and hoarse and somehow horribly cheerful. "Gotta give 'em a Christian burial!"

As Tak drives on, he glances in the rearview and sees the man grab a dead woman by the hands. Her skirt hikes up past her thighs as he drags her across the cobblestone square, and he takes a moment to adjust it before heading for a fireman hanging from a traffic light.

"How come the birds aren't eating him?" asks Samira without looking up. Her fingers are a bloody mess; Tak briefly considers grabbing her hands but knows it's probably futile.

"I don't know," responds Tak.

"Do you think he's a time traveler?"

"No. They probably just haven't gotten to him yet."

Talking about the birds seems like a bad idea, almost like inviting a vampire inside the house, so they stop. As for the winged creatures, they seem to be ignoring the van altogether. Tak can hear them swooping and cawing overhead, and occasionally spies one huddling on the sidewalk with a chunk of something red and meaty in its beak, but they either can't see the van or don't care.

Two blocks from the police station, their luck runs out. The street is filled with a particularly large pile of rubble, and Tak has no choice but to go up and over a set of newspaper boxes on the sidewalk. He manages to clear two of them, but the third hangs up in the undercarriage. He taps on the accelerator a few times and feels the van rock back and forth, but can't get enough traction to clear the obstacle. After a minute of revving, he throws the van into reverse and tries to back up, but this only serves to get them stuck further.

"Dammit. Come on. Come on, we're so close!"

"T-Tak?" says Samira in a trembling voice.

"What?"

"Tak, look. . . . *Look!*"

He glances up and sees a bird watching them. This one is smaller than the others, making Tak wonder if it's some kind of juvenile. The little bird tilts its head one way, then the other, its black eyes expanding and contracting like a camera lens searching for focus. The top of its head is translucent white, and Tak can see what appear to be little red worms writhing under the surface of the skin.

"Tak?"

"I know."

"It sees us."

"I KNOW!"

A pair of birds come soaring out of the sky and land next to the little one. They shift back and forth on their feet, then cough up something red and wet on the ground before taking off again. This seems to distract the younger bird for a moment; it turns its attention to the snack, giving it a couple of cautious pecks.

"We have to hoof it, Sam," says Tak, his eyes locked onto the small creature some thirty yards away. "The station is only a couple of blocks."

"We're not gonna make it," she says flatly.

"Let's get out and move slow and easy. I don't think the other birds have seen us, so if we can stay away from that little one, we should be fine."

He expects her to argue, but instead Samira unbuckles her seat belt and slides out of the van. Tak's door is wedged up against a light pole, so instead of trying to force it open, he scrambles across the seat and out the passenger-side door, dropping to his feet next to Samira. She has the pistol in her hand and is pointing it at the little bird, index finger shaking against the trigger. Tak places a hand on her shoulder, and the two of them back away from the bird and toward the station.

They move cautiously into the rubble-filled intersection. The little bird is half pecking, half slurping at the meal that was left for it and seems to have lost all interest in the newcomers. Tak and Samira keep their eyes on the bird, moving around the rubble by feeling behind them with their hands. Despite their senses working at full capacity, it seems as if the entire city has suddenly gone quiet—the crunching of their shoes as they scuffle across the broken bits of civilization is louder than bombs.

They clear the intersection and press against the glass doors of an office building. They're now kitty-corner from the bird, maybe a hundred feet away, and it still seems completely focused on the diminishing pile of meat. They can see the top of the police station now, and though it's covered in birds, the creatures don't seem to have any interest in the two of them.

"I think we're gonna be okay," whispers Tak.

The moment he speaks, the little bird whips up from its meal and stares at them, eyes narrowing to a pair of black pinpricks. Its beak works up and down a couple of times before twisting almost sideways. Then, without warning, it spreads its tiny wings and comes flying at them from across the intersection. Tak raises his arms and tries to scream, but before the yell can even form in his throat, a loud report rings out and the bird goes flying backward into a heap of feathers and tangled limbs.

At first, Tak can't figure out what happened. But then he smells the familiar whiff of cordite and sees Samira's trembling hands, and he knows she's shot the thing. The little bird is flopping around on the sidewalk, contorting its body into strange, unnatural positions. The bullet has passed right through the eye and out the back of its head, so by all rights the thing should be dead—but of course, that assumes it's actually alive and capable of dying. After a few more spasms, it lifts its head to the sky and produces a scream that sounds more like a wounded child than a creature from another world. It's this noise, this human sound, that finally breaks what remains of Tak and Samira's courage. Without a second thought, they bolt for the police station.

They scramble over fallen building facades and around panes of shattered glass. They pass a dozen naked corpses with freshly shaved heads and smiles on their faces. They hear the sounds of birds racing and soaring and screaming just above them, but they don't focus on any of this. Their attention is on the steel-and-glass building that is now less than a hundred yards away. And while they're aware that dozens of birds are milling around the roof of the station, they don't have the capacity to worry about such things right now. Their entire world is a set of glass doors engraved with the letters S.P.D.

And then, almost before they know what's happened, they find themselves bursting through those doors and into a small lobby. Samira trips across a large black mat in the entrance and goes tumbling across cold grey tiles, her bloody fingers leaving small trails in her wake. Tak skids over to her side and drops to his knees, worried that some unseen force beyond a simple tangled rug has taken her down. But then she closes her eyes against the pain and gives him a wobbly thumbs-up sign, and he allows himself to relax just a little.

Outside, the sounds of the birds have grown louder. Tak can hear them milling about on the roof, their talons making thin *tik tik tik* sounds against the asphalt. As he watches, one of them flutters down and alights on a planter just outside the front door. It taps the glass with its beak a couple of times, as if trying to figure out how the door works, before shaking its wings and flying off.

"Are they coming?" pants Samira. "Do they see us?"

"They know something's up, but . . . yeah. I think we're okay for now."

"We should hurry."

"Yeah, Sam. I think we should."

She clambers to her feet and rubs her shoulder, which took the brunt of the force when she fell. Finding nothing broken, she gives Tak a quick, frozen smile. He waves at her with the tips of his fingers, then motions toward the back of the station. They open the swinging door between the lobby and the duty officer's desk and make their way farther inside the building.

"Where is she?" asks Samira, as they move past a row of battered brown desks. One of them has an old manual typewriter on it, a touch that she finds almost unbelievable in the age of DNA and other modern law-enforcement tools.

"I don't know. I was hoping she'd be in the lobby."

"What if she's not here?"

"Then we're pretty well fucked."

Tak was expecting to find more bodies, but the station seems deserted. He hopes the officers had the good sense to desert their civic duty and run like hell but thinks it likely they went down fighting. *And screaming,* he thinks as they come to a fork in the hallway. *Don't forget the screaming.*

"What do you think?" asks Tak as he scans the hall. "Left?"

"Yeah, sure. Left."

One large steel door later, they encounter the cells. There are a dozen or so in all, and Tak takes a moment to peer inside each one. When he finds them empty, he turns back to find Samira leaning against the wall and scratching ragged lines into her arm.

"Hey, Sam," says Tak. "Come on. Let's rest for a minute." He wanders over to Samira and pulls her hand away, expecting her to protest. Instead, she just gets an expression of weary resignation and drops her arm to her side. *If this gets much worse, I'm going to lose her for good,* thinks Tak. *She'll just check out, and that will be that. . . . I have to get her somewhere safe.*

He shelves this idea for the moment—although in the back of his head he is already working on a plan—and brushes a stray bit of dirt from Samira's forehead. She smiles faintly at his touch, but the gesture stops below her eyes.

"Hey, come on," he says. "Seriously. Let's take five."

She shakes her head vigorously. "No. Let's find this woman and get out of here. I just want this to be over."

He takes her hand and quickly explores the rest of the station. They find empty bathrooms, more cubicles, and the office of the

watch commander, but no Judith. Finally, when despair is beginning to lock its claws around his heart, he notices a door that he
didn't see before. It's constructed of old, solid wood, and contains
the word INTERROGATION in faded gold letters.

"Hey, we haven't checked in there yet," says Tak with forced
hopefulness.

"Yeah, okay," says Samira distantly.

Tak leaves her leaning against a cubicle wall and jogs over to
the door. It doesn't want to open at first, but then he leans his
shoulder into the jamb and shoves, and it pops open. The room is
dark, save for a dim green glow in the corner, and it takes Tak
a few moments to get his eyesight back. When he does, he sees a
limp, bloody figure in the corner of the room.

"Oh, no," he murmurs.

"What is it?" asks Samira from just over his shoulder.

"It's Judith."

"Is she dead?"

"Not yet," says a faint voice. "But you better get over here
now, or this is going to be a pretty short conversation."

# chapter thirty-two

"What happened?" asks Tak as he uses a damp paper towel to clean blood from Judith's face.

"Birds," she responds in a weakened voice. "When I got here, they were everywhere. I fought my way here but got attacked on the way."

"You survived a bird attack?"

"No. People did this."

Judith's main wound is a massive gash that runs across her stomach and around her back. She wrapped it as best she could with the remains of an old police uniform, but it's a temporary solution at best. Whenever Tak raises the cloth to see the extent of the damage, blood gushes onto his outstretched hands. He's shocked that his friend is still alive at all.

"Goddamn people," she says quietly. "I never did like 'em."

A long strand of wires runs from the back of Judith's head and into the briefcase, then again from there to her laptop. The briefcase is acting as a kind of temporary pacemaker, sending a small electrical pulse through Judith's body every few seconds to remind her heart to keep pumping. But this is a tenuous arrangement; the briefcase is using up the last of its charge to keep her alive. The single glowing light on its row of five is barely visible, even in the gathering darkness of the powerless police station.

"I'm sorry," says Tak as he wipes sweat from her forehead. "I tried to hurry."

"It's okay," she responds. "Knew it was a long shot anyway."

Behind him, Samira is spinning a single bullet on the floor. There is a tired, distant look in her eyes, and Tak is growing increasingly concerned that her mind won't be able to take much more of this madness. "Hey, Sam?" he calls out.

"Yeah?" she responds.

"Nothing. Just seeing if you're okay."

"I'm fine. Just get her stable, and let's get out of here."

Tak turns back to Judith and gives her a weak smile. "You ready for a road trip?"

"I won't make it," says Judith flatly. "The briefcase will run out of power before we get there."

"Okay, but maybe we can . . . I don't know, hook it up to a battery or something?"

"Won't work."

"Goddammit, we have to do *something*! We've come too far to lose it now."

Tak expects an argument from Judith, but she just shrugs her shoulders. This movement causes her to cough loudly, which makes the spots of blood on her stomach grow larger.

"So, what's the deal then?" asks Tak. "We're all screwed? Is that it?"

"We only have one copy of the fail-safe. When I die, it dies with me."

Tak leans forward and puts his fingers together. "Yeah, but can't we . . . I don't know, transfer it or something?"

"I'd have to drill holes in your cerebellum," replies Judith with a chuckle. "Don't think I'm up for that."

"Wait, there's gotta be a hospital around here," says Tak. "We could go there, find the tools you need—"

"No time."

"Well, I'm not just going to sit here and whack off until some bird comes in and punches a fucking hole in my eye!"

"I can carry it," says Samira without looking up.

"You should leave, Tak," says Judith. "Find somewhere to hide."

"Why? So I can watch the world end in style? No thanks. I'd rather find a service pistol and eat the barrel."

"I can carry it," says Samira again, louder.

Tak and Judith stop talking and turn to her. Tak blinks slowly a few times as Judith clears her throat. "You can what?" she says.

"I have that thing," Samira says without lifting her eyes from the floor. "The one in the back of my head. So that means I can carry the fail-safe. . . . Right?"

"No," says Tak firmly. "No way. Sam's already holding a timeline; we can't give her another one."

Judith lifts her head and eyes the young woman in the doorway. Then she reaches out, grabs Tak's arm, and slowly pulls herself to a sitting position. Tak can almost feel the force of will this action takes—it burns off of her in waves. "That's not possible," she says, staring at Samira. "Yates killed the conduits. Why would he leave you alive?"

"Because he gave me the Beautiful Land."

Judith crinkles her forehead and raises her eyebrows. She stares at Tak as if he just suggested they all go bungee jumping over hot lava, then slowly shifts her gaze from him to Samira and back again. The only sound in the room is the metallic whirring of Samira's bullet spinning on the cold floor tiles.

"So what's the problem?" asks Samira. "Give me the timeline and let's go."

"Sam, no," replies Tak. "You don't understand. You can't put two timelines in the same person."

Judith's head suddenly rolls forward, but she manages to keep her balance. "Actually, you *can*, but . . ."

"But what?" asks Samira. She snatches the spinning bullet off the floor and looks up at Judith. "What happens?"

"You lose your goddamn mind," says Tak. "Axon tried it a few times when this project was first getting off the ground, and it never ended well."

"But I can do it," says Samira. "The timeline will still work even if I go crazy, right?"

"Sam, no. It's not even an option."

"It's the only option."

Tak leaps up and kicks a nearby wooden chair. It goes flying across the room and smashes into the wall, knocking a chip of wood from the doorframe. "Goddammit, NO! No. Not happening, no way, no. We're not doing this."

Samira clambers to her feet and puts a hand on Tak's arm, then glances down at Judith. "Give us a minute?"

Judith nods slowly and wipes a small trickle of blood from her nose. "I'm not going anywhere."

Samira pulls Tak out of the room and down the hall, then places a hand on his cheek. He shakes her off and turns away, staring out of a bank of tall windows at the ruined city beyond. "It's okay," she says. "I'll be fine."

Tak runs his fingers through his hair and turns in a small, angry circle. "Sam, if we put a second timeline in you, you'll lose your grip on reality. Then if we don't get it out of you in a goddamn hurry, you'll die. And it's a bad death, Sam. I've seen it. It's a bad fucking death."

"What happened to saving the world?"

"Fuck the world!" screams Tak. "I don't care about the world! I care about *you*!"

"We don't have another choice."

"You know what? Yeah. We do. How about you and me get the hell out of here and go to the Beautiful Land? We can stay there, we can make it whatever we want, we can . . ."

He trails off. Samira shakes her head slowly, then holds her hands out to Tak. The skin around the knuckles is ragged and bloody, the nails chewed down past the quick. "See my fingers, Tak? I do things like this because I spent the last years of my life engaged in some really bad business. . . . Just like you."

Tak feels shame creep across his face and finds he can't look at his friend anymore. He releases her and turns around again, this time staring at the darkened interrogation room. *Damn you, Judith Halford,* he thinks in an unfair flash of anger. *Why couldn't you stay alive?*

"Remember the diner?" asks Samira. "How you told me this whole crazy quest was our chance at amends? Well, at the time I thought you were nuts, but I went with you anyway because I was just happy to have company." She giggles slightly and slides her arms around his waist. "But you were right. This is our chance, and we have to take it. We can't let everyone die while we go on existing, Tak. We wouldn't be able to live with ourselves."

Tak feels hot tears forming behind his eyes and quickly forces them back. "Goddammit," he mutters. "It wasn't supposed to be like this."

"It never is," replies Sam, releasing him. "Go tell her to get ready. I want to pee."

Samira scampers off down the hallway in search of a bathroom. Tak watches her go, then moves back to Judith, who seems to be getting worse by the minute. Her breath is coming in short, ragged gasps, and the stain on her blouse seems much wider than before.

"We good?" she asks quietly.

"No, but we're going to do it anyway. Listen, I need to move you; it's too dark in here for detail work."

Tak puts an arm under her shoulder and helps her to her feet, then grabs the briefcase and laptop, stacking them on top of each other. He can feel Judith's legs trembling, but she sets her mouth into a grim line and begins limping forward, leaning on Tak occasionally for support.

"Christ, Judith," he says, as they shuffle into the hallway. "I had no idea you were such a hard-ass."

"Where are we going?" she says by way of response.

"There's a bank of windows in the lobby. Should be enough sunlight left for me to get the wires hooked up."

Judith nods and continues shuffling. The two of them move down the hall and hang a left, ducking around desks and cubicles as they head for the entrance. Twenty feet or so before they reach their destination, Tak notices Samira standing at the end of the hallway with fear in her eyes.

"Sam?" he says. "Sam, what is it?"

She doesn't respond, and rather than ask again, Tak decides to just move forward and see for himself. Seconds later, he and Judith round the corner and stop. Though the sun is threatening to drop below the horizon, enough light remains for them to see what has Samira so concerned.

The birds are amassing, thousands of them, lining up as far as the eye can see. They perch on the edge of buildings and grip the hoods of cars and make telephone lines sag almost to the ground, a swelling sea of black that grows by the second. Save for the occasional fluttering of wings or the heavy sound of a companion coming to rest somewhere nearby, the creatures are completely silent. They just stare at the police station as if waiting for a grim party to start.

"Well, crap," mutters Tak. "That's not good."

"They know we're here," whispers Sam.

"This doesn't make sense," says Judith. "We used the Machine. They shouldn't be paying this much attention to us."

As they watch, the ocean of birds begins to move. Like the Red Sea parting, the birds shuffle to either side of the street, giving the three people inside the station a perfect view of the new terror that's approaching.

"What the hell is that?" asks Judith.

In the distance, perhaps three blocks away, a twisted, terrible creature is slowly shuffling toward them. Clad in the remnants of a dirty white lab coat and a torn argyle sweater, its legs are pale and knobby things, while its arms are longer and more human than those of the other birds. But the face leaves no doubt of what the monster used to be. There are the faint suggestions of a nose, the shriveled remains of ears, a pair of thin, wrinkled lips from which protrude the nub of a beak. But worst of all are the eyes; unlike the dead black pits of the other birds, these are blue and intelligent and terribly *alive*.

"It's Yates," says Tak finally.

"Please tell me that's not true," whispers Judith.

"No, it's true. I saw him in Australia. . . . Christ, he looks terrible."

The three of them stand in front of the windows, transfixed, as Yates slouches up the street. When he is little more than a block away, he tilts his head an impossible distance to the side and looks inside the police station with one shimmering eye.

"Judith . . ." he says in a bubbling, raspy voice that's somehow audible through the panes of glass. "So nice . . . to see you. . . ."

"Jesus," says Judith. "What does he want?"

"He wants me," says Samira, who is busy wrapping strands of hair around her finger and pulling them out of her head. "He wants the Beautiful Land."

Judith stumbles away from the window with a look of terror on her face and ends up crashing to the floor. "We have to run," she says. "We have to run right now."

"No," says Samira, who stops pulling on her hair long enough to lock eyes with Judith. "You have to give me the fail-safe."

For an eternity, no one moves. But then Yates takes another step toward them and lets out a shrieking caw of laughter, and the spell is broken. Samira drops to her knees next to Judith as Tak begins to examine the holes in her head.

"We'll need about a minute to complete the transfer," says Judith. "So, Tak, if Yates gets inside, you'll have to distract him."

"Oh, that's great," mutters Tak as he plugs a new set of wires into the laptop. "Maybe I'll tell him a few stories about my childhood, see if he's interested." He kneels next to Samira, pushes her curly hair out of the way, and rubs one thumb across the four metal ports embedded in her neck. Samira feels his hesitation and grabs his free hand with her own.

"Hey, Tak?" she says.

"Yeah, Sam?" responds Tak, his voice trembling.

"I don't think I'm gonna see you again, so remember me, okay? Remember how I used to be."

"I'm gonna see you again, Sam. I promise."

She smiles at this, a thin, brave thing that causes Tak to lose what little faith he had in this plan. But before he has a chance to change his mind, he picks up the free set of wires, plugs them into Samira's skull, and flips the switch.

Samira opens her mouth and emits a shrill scream that echoes through the empty corridors of the station. To her left, Judith's eyes fly wide. She makes a strange grunting sound, almost like a noise of realization, before arching her back and digging her fingers into the floor. Tak feels hot tears forming in his eyes yet again, but he brushes them aside and reaches for the briefcase, twisting dials as numbers begin to flash across the keyboard screen. Samira produces a sharp intake of breath, then screams again.

*"Fuck!"* screams Tak as he types. *"Fuck, fuck, fuck it all!"*

The wires seem to come alive, moving and pulsing across the floor like snakes. Tak can hear the birds milling around but refuses to look at them. Samira screams again, and this time Judith joins her; their voices mingling together before suddenly falling silent. For a brief moment, there is no sound at all, but then Tak hears something large and angry throw itself at the lobby windows. Rather than look, he focuses his attention on the numbers flashing across the laptop screen. Moments later, the computer emits a cheery ding, and the numbers stop.

"We good?" asks Judith quietly.

"Yeah, we're good," says Tak as she reaches over and yanks the wires from Samira's head. He expects her to scream again at this, but she just slumps into a little pile on the floor.

"Sam?" says Tak. "Sam, come on, talk to me." When she doesn't respond, Tak leans over and takes her in his arms. A tiny sliver of drool spills across the front of her dress, and Tak gently wipes her off before turning back to Judith.

"How long do we have? How long until this thing destroys her for good?"

"Maybe a day," she replies. She is staring outside in a distant kind of way, watching as Yates prepares to throw himself against the window. "Maybe less."

"Goddammit," mutters Tak.

"There's a garage in the basement," continues Judith. "I looked in there earlier. Take her and get out of here." She pauses for a moment, then reaches into her pocket and withdraws a piece of paper. "Here. I wrote down directions to the Machine."

"What?" says Tak. "Wait, hold on—"

"I'm not leaving," says Judith.

"You'll die here."

"Just get to Montana and activate the fail-safe. Then none of this will matter. Once you reset reality, it will be like none of it ever happened."

"You sure?" he says.

"Yes," she replies. "Yes, I'm sure. Go ahead. Maybe I can buy you some time."

"I'm sorry, Judith."

"Don't be," she whispers. "World ends for everybody, right? At least I'm done helping it along."

Tak removes the gun from his waistband and hands it to Judith, stuffs the directions into his pocket, then slings Samira over his shoulders. *God, she's so damn light,* he thinks as he begins moving down the hall. *It's like she could blow away at any second.* When he reaches a bend in the hallway, he pauses to take a final glance back. He's hoping to catch Judith's eye one last time, but she won't even look his way; her entire focus is on the creatures lurking just beyond the lobby window.

Two minutes later, the powerful engine of a police cruiser roars to life. As Tak crashes through the parking garage gate and out into the dim Seattle dusk, he can hear the sounds of the birds growing fainter. The last thing he sees in his rearview is a massive black cloud descending on the police station. Then he locates the highway, smashes through a wrecked ocean of abandoned cars, and heads east as fast as the cruiser can carry him.

# chapter thirty-three

"I wanted to be an astronaut."

Judith is sitting in front of the windows with a pistol in her hand, watching Yates batter himself against the station's bulletproof glass. Each time the creature slams against it, the pane shakes in its frame. One small crack has appeared at the top of the window, and she figures it won't be long before that crack moves all the way down and causes the entire works to shatter.

"My parents used to make fun of me for that. My parents, my brother, my friends. Everyone, really. They thought I should be something sensible. . . . Like a trophy wife."

She coughs once, spraying flecks of blood across the tile. At the same moment, Yates launch himself at the glass with renewed force, causing the crack at the top to expand another few inches.

"Why aren't your feathered friends helping you, Charles?" she says weakly. "Are they making you earn your revenge? That's deep thinking for something that isn't even alive."

Judith notices a stray cigarette on the ground and picks it up. She produces a book of matches from the pocket of her skirt and lights it with trembling hands. "Got these matches from a restaurant once. It was the night Tak first arrived. He took me out to dinner and told me I was hot. I told him he was an idiot. . . . That was the last date I ever had. Maybe that's why I still carry them around."

Yates seems frustrated; he pulls his head back on its long neck and slams his forehead into the window with a loud caw. One eye is twitching open and shut with rapid speed, as if his blinking mechanism has suddenly gone haywire. "Kill . . . you," he says in a voice that sounds less human with each passing minute. "Kill . . . you . . . Kill . . . Judith . . . Kill . . ."

"Can you believe that?" continues Judith in a calm, almost serene voice. "Half my life spent building the machine that's going to destroy the world, and I went on one date. What a goddamn waste. If I get a chance to do this over again, things are going to be different."

The other birds watch Yates as he spins in an angry circle. They are motionless, save for the occasional tilting of the head or a thin fluttering of wings. Once in a while, a smaller bird will stare inside the station as if trying to figure out what the big deal is, but otherwise, their attention is completely focused on the twisted thing that used to be a man.

"Maybe I could have been a chef," she says, as the cigarette burns in the dark. "That's even better than an astronaut. At least then I'd be making people happy instead of . . . Well, instead of whatever it is that I do now."

Yates walks backward until he's almost at the end of the block, then runs and leaps into the window with full force. The frame gives way with a sickening crack, sending shards of metal and wood raining down to the white tile below. Seeing this, Judith takes a final drag on her cigarette before letting it fall to the ground.

"I don't know how many bullets are in this gun, but I intend to use them all on you. I know I should probably save one for myself, but that wouldn't be nearly as satisfying."

The birds begin to shuffle together, closing in on the station like children smelling pie on a windowsill. Yates rears back and kicks the window once more; as soon as the talon makes contact, the weakened glass shatters inward into uncountable shining shards.

"You want to hear a secret, Charles?" asks Judith, as a thousand pairs of wings suddenly leap into view. "I never did like you."

She smiles to herself, then raises the pistol and begins to fire.

control/alt/delete

# chapter thirty-four

The police cruiser pulls into the gas station with a rattling wheeze. It's been traveling at top speed for nearly seven hours, and despite its powerful engine and finely tuned mechanics, it simply wasn't designed for such abuse. The smoke coming out of the exhaust has a vaguely burned smell, and the hood is hot enough to cook a full lumberjack breakfast on in a matter of minutes.

"Easy there, girl," says Tak as he guides the cruiser next to a set of pumps and shuts off the engine. "Just stay with me. Only two hundred miles to go."

He's talking to the car, but he could just as easily be speaking to the young woman strapped in the passenger seat. Samira hasn't moved since they left Seattle, save to occasionally tilt her head from one side to the other as she mutters something nonsensical. Tak tried to keep the drool to a minimum, but once they passed through Spokane and into Idaho, he decided it was a losing battle. As a result, the front of her sundress is stained with saliva and blood—the latter resulting from a near-constant nosebleed that Tak is unable to staunch.

Before he gets out of the car, he tears off a small piece of shirt and uses it to dab at Samira's face. Once she's reasonably clean, he balls up the cotton and places it inside her left nostril, which has started to spout blood once again. As the flow begins to congeal around the shirt, Samira reaches over and gently places her hand on his arm.

"No people are allowed inside," she says in a voice barely above a whisper.

"What, Sam?" asks Tak.

"Are there going to be robots at the wedding? Because the last time I tried that, the crust just fell right off."

"Yeah, Sam, we'll have robots. Don't worry. Just try to rest, all right? I have to go pump some gas."

"Spider, spider, spider, fly. Underneath the starry sky." She looks directly into Tak's eyes and smiles wide. "We're not supposed to be here."

"Just hang on, Sam. Just a little more."

He slips out of the cruiser and over to the pump. Overhead, the moon provides a glimmer of light around the otherwise darkened station. Tak takes the lack of lighting as a sign the place has lost power; if true, it's going to make fueling up a bit of a challenge.

He pulls a nozzle from the pump and clicks the handle up and down a few times. When nothing happens, he drops it and jogs over to the main building, which is little more than a ramshackle hut with a wooden door and a pair of smudged windows. It's hardly the most attractive place, but when you're the only station for fifty miles in any direction, looks probably don't mean a whole lot.

*I wonder if anyone's alive around here,* Tak thinks as he tries the door and finds it unlocked. *Did the birds make it this far north? Or did everyone hear about the end of the world and decide to leave before management threw them out on their asses?*

Tak's route is taking them across the top of Idaho and onto the northernmost highway in Montana—a barren two-lane stretch known simply as the Hi-Line. The road is dotted with small farm towns and whistle-stop train depots, most of which passed their glory days long ago. Between the interstate to the south and the gradual fading of the family farm, what was once a thriving trade route is now little more than a ribbon of pavement connecting one nowhere to another. But for Tak, the Hi-Line is perfect. The birds seem to be attracted to noise and light and energy; if their plan is to destroy the world, this part of the country should be way down on the list.

It's dark inside the building, so he produces a police-issue flashlight and clicks it on. As if drawn by some macabre fascination, the beam immediately lands on the headless corpse of a man. At first, Tak thinks that the birds have come and gone, but then he examines the body and sees an ancient two-barrel shotgun wedged between its knees and a congealed splatter of red on the wall behind. The body is seated next to a long wooden counter upon which rests a cash register, a plastic tub filled with beef jerky, and a small metal bowl. There is a sign taped to the bowl that reads: GOT A PENNY? LEAVE A PENNY. NEED A PENNY? GET THE HELL OUT OF MY STORE. Tak can't decide if this is supposed to be funny or not.

He pans the light around the room and finally finds what he was looking for: a small red switch labeled with the words SHUT-OFF VALVE. He dances gingerly around the station's former proprietor, leans over the counter, and clicks the switch up and down a few times. When nothing happens, he spins and exits the store, but not before taking a piece of jerky from the bucket. *Gotta keep fueled,* he thinks as he downs the jerky in three massive bites. *Besides, that guy won't miss it.*

He strides back to the car and peeks in the side window, where Samira is slowly moving her mouth in little O shapes. Tak doesn't bother listening; he knows it will be more gibberish, and that will only serve to further upset him. Instead, he opens the trunk and roots around until he finds a roadside emergency kit. He removes a small piece of tubing from the kit and heads off in search of a plug vent that will let him access the underground storage tank.

He jogs around the side of the station and plays the beam around. Someone has dumped a small army of beer bottles in the weeds, and from the looks of the cobwebs, they've been doing so for some time. Tak has a brief vision of the man inside the station stealing a beer from the cooler and ducking back here during the slow days. *Hope you went out with a cold one in your hand, buddy.*

The flashlight moves past the bottles, over an ancient milk crate, around a rusted tank that used to contain propane, and to another thigh-high cluster of weeds. Tak is starting to wonder if the station is too old to have a proper plug vent; if so, he'll have to find the access hatch for the underground tank and pry it up. This is not a promising plan: opening the hatch is a two-man job, and Tak's scrawny arms probably couldn't budge the thing.

He feels an instant of panic at this thought and tamps it down, focusing on his search as he circles the station and pops out on the other side. Taking a moment to collect himself, he begins sweeping the flashlight beam across the ground near the pumps. After a bit, he finally spies a small round knob at the edge of the concrete pump island. Soon he's unscrewing the cap and dipping his hose inside. The smell of gas is strong, and when he shines the light inside, he's pleased to see that the tanks are nearly full. This discovery sets off a round of lively conversation with himself.

"Okay. Gas can. Need a gas can. . . . Actually, I should get a couple and put the extra in the trunk. Then we don't have to stop again. Soooo, yeah. Back in the store? Fuck, I don't want to go back in there. That dead guy's there."

In the end, the dead guy gets one more visit. Tak enters the store at a jog and emerges a minute later with two large cans.

Dropping the hose as far into the tank as it will go, he sucks on the other end until he feels gasoline well into his mouth, then quickly places his end of the hose inside the can. He spits a few times to clear the fuel, but even after he's sure it's gone, the smell and flavor are overpowering. He briefly considers going inside the store a third time for more jerky or a warm soda, but rejects the option. He's seen all the headless dead people he can handle for one day.

When the first can is almost full, Tak hears a shuffling noise behind him. He whirls around with the flashlight raised over his head, ready to smash the intruder across the face. But it's only Samira, who somehow managed to unbuckle herself from the car and is walking toward him with ragged, drunken steps.

"Ah, hell," says Tak. He scrambles to his feet and scampers to her side, placing his arms under her shoulders to prevent her from falling. She looks up at him and grins.

"Oh, hey," she warbles. "I needed to leave. We had a vacation day back in March that I never took."

"You should sit, Sam. You're gonna fall over."

"I once read a book about a haunted cemetery. That's what the man in the video store said. But it's not like he would know or anything." She sways on her feet again and slumps into Tak. He can feel her heart jackhammering in her chest, and curses himself silently for ever agreeing to such a mad plan.

"Dammit, Sam," he whispers in her ear, "I never should have brought you here. I should have tried to do it all myself, but I was just so goddamn lonely. I . . . I missed you. I wanted you with me."

"They're coming," says Samira suddenly. Her mouth is buried against Tak's shoulder, but the words come out clearly enough. "They're coming to eat the world."

"What? Who's coming?"

"Caw," she says in a ghostly whisper. "Caw, caw, caw, caw, caw."

She turns her head until she's looking over her shoulder, then giggles. Hesitantly, Tak follows her gaze and notices a large, pale shape in the dark. He closes his eyes and tries to convince himself that it's not really there, but when he opens them again, a new pair of shapes have joined the original.

"Fuck a duck," he says quietly.

The fluttering of wings grows louder as more birds begin to land around the station. Tak sprints back to the gas can, which has overflowed and is now spilling fuel across the concrete and toward the pumps. Tak snatches the can in one hand and races to the car, then begins pouring gas into the cruiser with abandon. Fuel sloshes over his hands and down his pants, but he doesn't care. Right now, his only thought is to get as much gas in the car as possible before the birds decide to make them a snack.

"Sam!" he screams. "Sam, come on! We have to go now!"

Whatever sense of urgency he feels is completely lost on her; she just stands in place and wobbles back and forth. Glancing at the building where the owner took his life, Tak sees dozens of birds beginning to mill about on the roof. Their talons click and scrape across the tar paper like the warm-up strokes of a washboard player in a jug band.

"Shit, shit, shit," mutters Tak angrily. "I am so tired of you ass bandits!" He can hear them talking now, a kind of click and chatter that simultaneously sounds like nonsense and a language. *Hungry*, they seem to say. *Hungry. So hungry. Caw caw caw.*

The cruiser's tank is maybe half-full when Tak decides they've run out of time. He throws the can to the ground and runs back to claim Samira. Picking her up in his arms, he races back to the car and dumps her unceremoniously in the back before leaping into the front seat and slamming the door behind him.

The moment the car starts, the birds scream to life. They begin flying overhead in large, swooping circles, cawing and shrieking until their cries become a massive wall of sound. As Tak slams the car into reverse and turns on the high beams, Samira starts to laugh. The tires spin against the gas-slicked surface of the road for a moment before finally catching. Tak backs up about fifteen feet and stops, watching in horror as a shaggy black cloud suddenly descends on the station. *It's like ants,* he thinks wildly. *Like watching ants come to a piece of candy.*

The birds are landing all around the car now. He can hear at least one on the roof, while another begins to peck gently at the rear window with a long, pale beak. He's about to slam the accelerator down and try to just plow through them, but then he pauses. Though every fiber of his being is screaming at him to just put the pedal to the floor and book, he can't stop looking at the gas-soaked concrete and the fuel that continues to pour from his makeshift siphon. With unsteady hands, Tak clicks the cigarette lighter under the dashboard and waits. More and more birds are arriving by the second, and somewhere in the writhing black cloud, he catches a glimpse of a white lab coat and a torn argyle sweater.

"Oh, hell," he says. "Is that Yates?"

"Grandpa?" asks Samira from the backseat.

As they watch, the cloud parts and Yates emerges. His transformation from man to bird has progressed at horrifying speed, and there's almost nothing recognizably human about him anymore. He raises one gnarled, shriveled arm and points it at the cruiser as if he's about to make a divine pronouncement—but all that comes out of his mouth is a thin, watery scream.

At Yates's signal, the other birds refocus their attention on the car. Tak sees a few leaning on their claws as if preparing to pounce, but before they can move, the lighter clicks into the ready position.

"Shit on me," mutters Tak as he grabs the lighter and cranks the window. "This is the dumbest thing I've ever done."

Before the birds even realize that his window is down, Tak tosses the lighter toward the spilled gasoline. It spirals in the air, around and around, a tiny circle of red against the blackness of the station, before landing directly in the middle of the siphon's stream. The moment it touches down, a blue flame whooshes to life and begins racing back along the concrete and toward the plug vent.

"Hang on, Sam!" cries Tak. He slams the pedal down and backs up, running over a couple of birds with a satisfying crunch. Then he grabs the emergency brake and pulls, whipping the car around until it's facing the road. He can hear the birds shrieking and cawing behind him, but at the moment he's much more concerned about the flickering fire he sees in the rearview. He throws the cruiser into gear and peels out of the station and back onto the Hi-Line, hoping that whatever gods are listening will grant him time to get the hell out of there. *Twenty seconds,* he thinks as he speeds down the road and watches a small stream of fire expand behind him. *Just gimme twenty seconds, and we're all good. I'd even settle for fifteen. I'm not picky.*

Six seconds later, the station goes up in a massive fireball. Tak sees an enormous cloud of orange death lift into the air behind him as night turns to noon. Samira screams and claps her hands over her ears at the sound of the explosion, a teeth-rattling boom that leaves Tak deaf in one ear. Hot, sticky air suddenly floods through the car, thick with the stench of gasoline and burning feathers. For a horrible moment the cruiser threatens to stall, but then it somehow manages to find enough oxygen to keep the engine firing.

Tak pushes the car as fast as it can go as twisted pieces of metal begin to rain across the highway. Something large flashes in the corner of his eye, and when he turns his head, he sees a huge chunk of shrapnel spiraling toward the cruiser. He cranks the wheel hard to the left; the car skids into the oncoming lane and kicks up dirt from the side of the road as the bottom half of a gas pump crashes to earth where they had been half a second before.

"Oh yeah, this was a *REALLY* bad idea!" screams Tak as he yanks the wheel back to the other side and avoids what looks to be the crumpled bed of an old Ford pickup. It hits the ground and goes bouncing off into a field, where it explodes in a miniature version of the gas station inferno behind them. All along the sides of the highway, wheat fields spring to hellish life as falling debris lands amidst their neatly groomed rows and sparks them to flame.

Tak can feel his eyebrows beginning to singe. He takes one hand off the wheel for a moment and shuts the vents, but he might as well hold back the ocean with a sandbag. The air inside the car gets hotter and hotter until every breath is fire and Tak's vision is a swimming, teary smudge of orange and red. Pieces of the station clatter all around them. Debris patters off the roof like heavy rain. One particularly large piece of wood smashes through the back window of the cruiser, missing Samira's head by inches. The world becomes a terrifying mass of screaming and heat and thunder as Tak races along the Hi-Line like he's trying to outrun the devil himself.

And then, slowly, the sounds begin to diminish. The falling debris slows. The air becomes slightly cooler. The metallic tang in their mouths and noses fades. Tak eases his foot off the gas and allows the car to slow. He tries to pull his shaking hands off the wheel and finds that they won't obey. For a moment he thinks he's gripped the wheel so tightly that it's become part of him, but then he realizes the plastic has melted slightly, trapping his fingers in a rapidly cooling web of goo. He rips his hands away and leaves behind the first layer of skin, but considering that he's still breathing, this strikes him as a very fair trade.

He pulls the car to the side of the road and lets the engine idle as he turns around to check on Samira. Some of her hair is singed at the end, and the skin of her face and hands is cracked and peeling, but otherwise, she seems unharmed. Her eyes, wide as saucers, are locked on the chunk of wood embedded in the seat next to her.

"You okay, Sam?" asks Tak.

"Eggs," she replies without taking her eyes from the missile that nearly ended her life. "We have to remember the eggs."

Tak takes this as a yes. Moments later, they're speeding off into the dark Montana night, leaving a quickly growing pillar of fire and smoke behind them.

# chapter thirty-five

Hundreds of windmills line the small country road, towering over the nearby trees and power lines. Samira stares at them from the broken rear window with an expression of pure joy. Her mental condition has faded badly over the last two hours, and Tak isn't sure she's aware of what she's seeing. But something about the huge structures has grabbed her attention, and for that, he's grateful; it's proof that at least a tiny spark of her mind is still in working order.

"We keep running into windmills, eh, Sam?" says Tak as he drives slowly down the road. The gas station explosion blew out both of his headlights, and the moon isn't providing much in the way of illumination; as much as he wants to reach the Machine, he's more concerned about running into a cow.

"Nothing ever goes that way anymore," says Samira from the backseat.

"Yeah, I know," replies Tak, who has decided to respond to all of her rambling with a show of good cheer. "It's a bitch, right?"

"When he measured the table, it all came out fine. But those people were just liars. I can't eat hamburgers anymore, you know?"

"No kidding."

"Optimal capacity is fading."

"Wow, Sam. That's . . . That's really something right there."

The car makes a slow turn around a bend in the road and glides to a stop. In front of them, perhaps five hundred yards away, stands a long building topped by a round glass dome. The entire structure is ringed by a metal gate and barbed wire, a "keep out" sign if there ever was one. Mounted spotlights move back and forth across the ground in front of the entrance, causing the entire building to glow with an eerie white light. Tak stares with growing excitement until the lights burn his eyes and force him to turn away. For the next minute or so, he continues to see a ghostly afterimage of the building, almost like it's taunting him.

"We made it, Sam," he says, reaching one hand into the backseat. "We did it. It's actually here."

She takes his hand in her own and rubs the fingers slowly before uttering two simple words: "Almost home."

The response is so expected, so *normal*, that for a moment, Tak thinks she's somehow broken free of the two timelines floating inside her. But then he looks back into her eyes and sees nothing but hollow emptiness and knows it was just a lucky response. "Yeah, Sam," he replies as he puts the car into gear. "Almost home."

Tak wipes a smudge of soot from the top of the windshield and drives forward. When he moves within range of the spotlights, he fully expects them to lock onto his car while alarms ring out in the still Montana night. But this doesn't happen. Instead, the lights keep sweeping in their aimless back-and-forth as the car rolls up to the gate. Leaving the engine idling, Tak grabs a shotgun from its mounting bracket between the seats and steps out of the car.

The building seems remarkably undamaged. In addition to the building having power, Tak can see small tufts of grass sprouting up in neatly landscaped patches. Here and there he spies small groups of yellow wildflowers with gnats buzzing lazily around them. He secretly feared arriving at a place that was utterly destroyed, and instead it just appears to be closed for the night. The experience is so odd, he's not exactly sure what his next move should be.

Tak is eyeballing the gate's locking mechanism when he hears a door open in the distance. He tightens his grip on the shotgun and looks for a place to hide, but the spotlights make disappearing impossible. He briefly considers running back to the car but then rejects that option as well—whoever is coming, it's probably best just to have it out and see where things go from there. Approaching footsteps crunch on gravel, and moments later a young man rounds the corner and screeches to a halt.

*Christ,* thinks Tak. *He's just a kid.*

The kid, who Tak would bet good money isn't even of legal drinking age, holds a rifle in a pair of trembling hands. He's wearing a dark black uniform and matching baseball cap emblazoned with the word AXON. Pimples dot his upper lip, where a few rogue hairs are trying and failing to form a mustache.

"Halt!" screams the kid. "Drop your weapon now!" His voice is high-pitched and squeaky, as if puberty isn't done with him yet. He raises the rifle and points it at the area around Tak's head although his shaking hands make it impossible to tell quite where he's aiming.

"Hey, hold on—" begins Tak.

"I said drop it!" screams the kid. His hands are sweating, and one of them slips off the muzzle of the rifle, causing the entire thing to dip toward the ground. Tak raises his left hand in the air and extends it out in a gesture of peace but keeps the other one firmly gripped around the trigger guard of the shotgun.

"Listen, man," says Tak. "You need to listen to me. I'm not going to hurt you, but I have to get inside."

"This is private property!"

"Yeah, have you seen what's going on out here? I don't think your employer gives a fuck who comes into the building anymore."

"I've got orders not to let anyone in."

"Christ, dude. You're kidding me, right? The world's about to end! You should be off smoking a joint and getting laid, not guarding a building in the middle of fucking nowhere!"

The kid's mouth twists back and forth as he considers this point. Tak takes the opportunity to approach the gate, but gets only a step closer before the kid raises the rifle again.

"I said don't move!"

"Actually, you said halt. And then you said drop the weapon. But yeah, I get you." Tak forces a smile onto his face and shrugs. "Look, man, you got a name?"

"Percy," replies the kid.

"Okay, Percy. I'm Tak. The girl in the car is Samira, and she's really sick. I need to get her inside."

"Why? There's nothing in here but offices. Most of the staff left last week, and the rest cut and ran once all that crazy shit started going down."

"I need to use the Machine. I can fix this, I can—"

"What machine? What are you talking about?"

Tak blinks a few times. "Fuck. You don't even know what you're guarding, do you?"

Percy shakes his head angrily. "Look, just . . . turn around. Turn around and leave. When all this gets settled, the people will come back, and you can do whatever you need to do."

"She's going to die, Percy. Everyone is going to die unless you let me inside."

"No. Now get out of here before I put a bullet in you."

Tak feels fear clench his stomach. He looks over his shoulder at Samira, who is now lying against the seat with her head lolling back. He can see her chest rising and falling, rising and falling, as her breaths become shorter and more intense.

"Percy?" says Tak without turning around.

"Yeah?"

"I'm coming in. The two of us are coming in." He turns his head back to the young man with the rifle and the cheap uniform and tries to project a confidence that he doesn't really feel. "If you try to stop me, I'm going to have to kill you."

The kid jerks the rifle up and fires a single wild shot about three feet over the top of Tak's spiky hair. He moves the barrel back down and tries to steady it, but his hands are positively earthquaking now, and the gun looks like it's doing a chaotic dance to music only it can hear. "I'll shoot you!" he screams. "I'll fucking do it!"

"We don't have to do this," replies Tak quietly. He runs his thumb over the cold metal of the trigger and briefly wonders if shotguns have safeties or not.

"This is your last warning!" screams Percy again. "Turn around and leave now!"

"I can't do that, man."

"Turn around!"

"Can't do it."

"Drop the weapon and turn—"

Tak raises the shotgun and fires. It roars in his hand like a wounded animal as the top of Percy's head suddenly vanishes. The kid blinks a couple of times and makes a croaking sound in his throat before taking two steps forward and falling face-down into the dirt. Tak grips his weapon tightly enough to leaves an indentation of the manufacture's name in his palm. A small wisp of steam rises from the missing forehead of Percy's body, and for a wild moment, Tak thinks he's seeing the young man's soul rising up and escaping the world.

"It's not happening," whispers Tak. His shoulder begins to scream in pain from where the gun kicked back when he fired it. Red and white spots dance in front of his eyes, and he feels like he might be sick on the spot. But the mechanics of sickness would come as a relief, and his mind has decided that Tak is unworthy of such a thing. Instead, he simply stands in place and stares as the body of a stupid young kid who is now dead because of him.

"It's not happening," he says again, taking a step forward. He slides one skinny arm through the wires of the gate and hooks a finger around Percy's shirt collar, dragging the body over to him. Something warm and wet clings to the hand, and he has to wipe it on his pants before reaching into the pockets and searching for the gate key he hopes is there. "It's not happening," he repeats desperately. "It's not happening. None of this is happening."

His hand settles around a small plastic object and pulls it free—it looks like a garage-door opener with a single red button. The moment Tak puts his thumb on the button and pushes, the gate rumbles to life and begins to retract. Something along the bottom catches the sleeve of Percy's black uniform and pulls him a few feet across the road before the material finally tears free. The body rolls once and ends up on its side, where Tak can see a pair of surprised, open eyes.

"Doesn't matter," he says as he drops the shotgun to the ground and stumbles backward. "None of it matters. Gonna reset every-thing. He'll be alive. He'll be fine. You didn't kill him. None of it matters."

He bumps the hood of the cruiser with the back of his knee and barely feels it. He moves around the side of the car and slowly climbs into the driver's seat, unable to tear his eyes away from the cooling sack of flesh and bone that not a minute before housed a scared young kid named Percy. "We'll fix it," he tells himself as he releases the emergency brake. "We'll fix it. Amends. We'll make everything better. We'll make amends, then everything will be all right."

Tak creeps the car forward and through the gate, taking special care to stay as far away from Percy as possible. Another thirty feet or so find them gliding up to the front entrance of the building—a plain steel door with the words AXON CORPORATION stenciled in small blue letters. The door is slightly ajar, as if the last person to go through didn't have time to shut it behind him.

"This is going to be okay," says Tak as he climbs out of the car and opens the rear passenger door. "We're going to make everything better."

"I got fruit from the little store," says Samira, as Tak reaches inside the car and wraps his arms around her frail, thin body. "That's what Mom would have wanted."

Tak throws his friend over his shoulders in a fireman's carry. Shock has turned his mind into a blank slate capable of holding only one thought at a time. For a moment, that thought is Samira, but then it fades and is replaced by a skinny young kid with pimples on his lip. *You killed him,* thinks Tak in a moment of near-perfect clarity. *You shot him in the face, and he died. Now you owe amends for that, too.*

He feels bile welling up inside him and forces it back down. Turning to the door, he reaches around it with a single foot and pulls it wide. Bright yellow light spills into the yard beyond, illuminating the courtyard in a cheery glow. "Gonna fix it," mutters Tak. "Gonna set this all to rights."

He passes through the doorway and down the hall toward the Machine. As the door shuts behind him, a single bird begins to caw from somewhere in the nearby dark.

# chapter thirty-six

*My legs are cold.*

This is the first coherent thought that passes through Samira's mind since Tak inserted the fail-safe nearly twenty hours before. It doesn't appear the way most of her thoughts do: one instant flash of idea leading to another before flying off on a tangent that sprouts new life of its own. This thought simply pops into her head and stays there like a lazy houseguest, refusing to lead to anything other than itself. Her legs are cold, the cold is unpleasant, and for a long time, this is as far as rational thought will take her.

*I'm cold.*

Eventually, with painstaking slowness, other parts of her mind click back to life. Thoughts begin to stream through her head: random images, jumbles of sound, names without meaning. And as the neurons slowly spark from their recent slumber, a new, coherent thought finally makes its way into her mind:

*What happened to me?*

Memory begins to work its magic, but the mental slide show is random and chaotic. She sees a dark police station with a woman lying on the floor. This is followed by the smell of gasoline, the crunching sound of wood crashing through glass, and an image of Tak holding a long gun in trembling hands.

*. . . Tak? Tak, wait. Where are you?*

The thought of Tak releases the floodgates, and suddenly her mind is filled with a million thoughts, all vying for attention. The stimulation is immediate and overwhelming, and she hears herself whimper as she moves her head back and forth.

"Easy, Sam," says a voice somewhere near her left ear. "You'll pull the wires out."

*. . . Wait. I know that voice.*

She lassos her mad thoughts together long enough to gain some kind of control, then focuses all of her energy on getting her eyes open. It's a tough slog, far harder than she would have thought, because both body and mind are in weakened states. But eventually, one eyelid slowly flutters wide, followed quickly by the other.

At first, all she can see are dark blurs and light blurs, but soon the blurs merge together and form something recognizable. She slides her eyes to the left and sees an IV stand with a saline drip leading into her upper arm. Moving her eyes to the right, she spots a familiar bundle of wires stretching out across a black tile floor. Brilliant sparks of light are dancing on the surface of everything, reds and blues and greens and other, stranger colors that she remembers seeing for the first time not all that long ago.

"M-Machine," she says finally.

Her voice is raspy and confused, but it gets Tak's attention. He leans down next to her mouth and holds his ear close. "What, Sam? What did you say?"

"Machine," she repeats. "The lights." She pauses for a moment, frustrated at her inability to string a sentence together, then gathers her thoughts and tries again. "Are we at the Machine?"

"Yeah, Sam. We're at the Machine. We did it. We actually did it."

He moves away, and soon the sound of clicking computer keys

fills the room. Samira lifts her head and looks around, then decides that's not enough and slowly pulls herself to a sitting position. The sundress has bunched up around her thighs, leaving her exposed legs to lie on a bare steel table. *That explains the cold,* she thinks as she struggles to adjust the hem. She tilts her head to the side and sees the Machine looming out of the darkness like a giant silver sculpture. Once again, she's amazed at how truly beautiful it is.

"You should lie down," says Tak from somewhere across the room. His voice sounds strange, choked almost, and Samira has a difficult time understanding him.

"What?" she asks quietly. The Machine is making a loud, humming sound, and she knows that her voice can't possibly carry over to where Tak is seated. Sure enough, a few seconds later she sees him hurrying over to her side.

"Sorry, Sam, I can't hear you. What did you say?"

"I said 'what,'" she replies. "I couldn't hear you either."

"I said to lie down."

"Oh." She thinks about this for a moment, then giggles. "This is a stupid conversation."

Instead of responding, Tak leans over and kisses her. Her mind, which was just in the process of getting organized, immediately flies off in a thousand new directions, but this time she doesn't mind. It's a long kiss, a perfect one, and when he finally moves away, she finds that everything is clear again.

"I missed you," he says.

"I missed you," she replies. "What happened?"

"I pulled the fail-safe out of your head." He picks up one of her hands and looks at it with a strange, almost sad expression, then moves back across the room to the Machine's control panel. "I was worried you'd be permanently messed up, but I think you're okay. We should probably run some tests to make sure, but there isn't time."

"Why not?"

"Yates is coming. I can hear him scratching around on the roof. Him and all his little birdie friends."

Samira shudders at that thought. She very much wants to walk over to Tak, but her legs are jelly and would most likely betray her. Plus, there's the little matter of the wire bundle attached to the back of her head. "So I'm free? I don't have a timeline in me anymore?"

"Um . . ." says Tak. She waits for him to say more, but he just puts his head down and returns to typing. A few seconds later, soft green light begins to pour out of the control panel and onto his face.

". . . Um?" asks Samira.

"Yeah, no. I only pulled the fail-safe out. I've got to . . . I'm going to try and . . . Goddammit."

He turns away from her, but not before she sees tears reflected in the green glow of the Machine. This realization leads to another: his face is red and puffy, as if he's been crying for some time. "Tak?" she whispers. "Tak, what's wrong?"

When he finally responds, he speaks to the far wall, as if he can't make himself turn around. "I'm afraid, Sam," he says, his voice trembling. "I'm afraid. I thought I had the guts to do this, but now everything's on the table, and I'm just so goddamn afraid."

Samira is stunned. This is *Tak* for God's sake, her friend who slept in jungles and wrestled bears and always had a plan that worked, no matter how crazy it seemed at the time. The face of fear had always been a stranger to him.

"I'm going to die, Sam," he continues. "Soon. Real soon. Probably before the world resets, I'm going to die. And once it does, I'm going to die again, and I'm going to be alone, and I'm scared."

"You're not alone, Tak. I'm here. I'm with you. We'll do this thing together, we can—"

"No," he says, turning around to face her. "You're not going to be here. You're leaving."

"I'm what?"

"You're leaving."

Samira puts her hands on the edge of the table and slides off. She wobbles in place for a while but manages to keep her balance. She expects Tak to come over and try to stop her, but instead he just puts his head down and begins typing furiously.

"Tak, I don't understand," she says as she takes a step forward. Emotions of every stripe begin to bounce around inside her. She feels like crying and screaming at the same time.

"I have to activate the fail-safe," he says without looking up. The green light on his face shifts to blue as he types. "If I don't, those birds are going to destroy every timeline that has ever existed or will ever exist. They're going to turn reality into a giant, smoking crater, and I can't let that happen."

Samira takes another step and loses her balance. She falls to one knee and waits for a moment until her head gets a little less swimmy. Behind her, the Machine's growl slowly turns into a single, haunting chord.

"The fail-safe will reset everything to the way it was four years ago," he continues. "Before Axon called me, before Yates perfected the Machine, before any of this. But in the new timeline, Judith won't know me, which means they won't get their explorer, which means they'll never be able to make the thing work."

"But that's good. . . . Right?"

"Not for everyone. It's not good for me, and it's really gonna suck for you."

Samira tries and fails to stand, then decides to just pull herself across the ground. "Tak, I don't understand. I don't—"

"If you go back, you'll have to live the last four years all over again. You'll go back to Iraq. You'll watch people explode. You'll see that kid in the chair. You'll see all of it." Tak stops typing and looks up at her, his tears replaced by a look of fierce determination. "I decided a while ago I wouldn't let that happen. So before I reset everything, I'm going to send you to the Beautiful Land."

"By *myself*?" cries Samira. "Tak, no! I don't want to go there if it means that you're going to die!"

"I have to stay here, Sam. I have to make sure this works."

"No! Tak, no! I don't care if I have to see all those things again! I'm not letting you do this alone!"

She struggles to her feet and shuffles over to Tak, collapsing on top of him. One leg snakes out and wraps around him, while the other wedges itself between the chair leg and the console. "I'm not leaving you. Do you hear me? I'm not leaving."

Tak pulls her close and wraps his arms around her waist. "Goddammit, Sam, don't do this."

"You're my everything," she replies, as tears begin to come. "I think you always have been, even when I didn't realize it."

Tak smiles and brushes his hand across her cheek. "I can't, Sam. I'm sorry. I'm so fucking sorry, but I can't."

"Tak, wait! Wait, wait, wait!"

Before Samira can do anything, Tak reaches out and presses the ENTER key. As soon as he does, a massive electrical jolt courses through the wires and into her head. Her legs and arms attempt to spasm, but Tak holds them in place.

"I'm sorry," he whispers again, his voice suddenly a million miles away. "But this is how it needs to be."

He pulls the wires from her head, causing another jolt of pain to flood her body. She wants to scream at him, to beat against his chest and tell him what a terrible mistake this is, but her body is no longer her own. She can only watch, helpless, as Tak disentangles himself from the chair and gently picks her up.

"I just downloaded the Beautiful Land," he says as he adjusts his grip around her waist. "That's why you can't move. Don't worry, you'll be better in a couple of ticks."

"N-no," whispers Samira.

"I actually activated the fail-safe a few minutes ago, but it takes a while for the Machine to build up power. Which means we have just enough time to get you the hell out of here."

He carries her across the room and sets her down inside the Machine. She can see a million lights dancing around the interior of the device, but they are just minor distractions. All of her attention is focused on Tak, on trying and failing to say all the things she wants to tell him.

There's a sudden cracking noise from somewhere above them; Tak looks up and smiles. "I think Yates just figured out what I'm doing," he says. "Wow. He looks really pissed."

"T-Tak," says Samira. She holds up one hand and waves it blindly in the air until he takes it in his own. "Tak, wait. . . ."

"You know how everybody dies, Sam? Well, you're not going to. You're going to go to the Beautiful Land, and you're going to be strong, and you're going to endure. You're going to turn it into something amazing. I know you will."

The lights in the Machine grow brighter and merge into a beautiful pale glow. Samira feels her senses start to overload and shut down, but just before they go, she feels Tak reach out and touch her. He says something then, something she's been waiting to hear for a very long time, but she's unable to make out what it is over the hum of the Machine. And then, just as he's about to repeat it, the world fades away.

# chapter thirty-seven

The girl with the curly black hair sits in front of a computer screen and sobs. The monitor floats on a sea of white light, and for a while it seems to be the only thing that exists in this world. But then time slips by, and a few more details emerge: the hum of a generator; the canvas flaps of a military-issue tent; the unpleasant sensation of relentless, overpowering heat.

The monitor contains a short e-mail. Samira has read it again and again until the words have burned themselves in her brain, and now she's crying too hard to continue. She wants more than anything to read the message one more time, but she can't get any further than the intro before her tears transform the letters into a shimmering smudge.

Someone comes into view behind her—an anonymous young man with short-cropped hair and a dusty camo uniform—and stares. She feels him there and knows that he finds her emotional outpouring to be a disgusting display of weakness, but she doesn't care. She has seven minutes of computer time left, and if she wants to spend it crying, she's damn well going to do that.

Eventually, the man shakes his head and leaves. Alone again, she decides to read the note a final time, no matter how hard such a thing will be. She balls her hands into fists, takes a few shallow breaths, and focuses all of her attention on the screen.

> My dearest Samira,
>
> I understand that you could not make it, so please do not worry. Your mother is with God now, and we have celebrated her life as she would have wanted. When you return to me, I will take you to see her. She is buried under a large oak tree that blooms in the spring. I think she would have liked this.
>
> PS—Your friend Takahiro came to see me. I was very moved by this kindness.

More sobs come, huge, wracking things that threaten to tear her small frame apart. She lowers her head to the surface of the cheap folding table and lets herself cry with abandon. In a secret part of her heart, she hopes that something terrible will happen on her next patrol so she doesn't have to feel this pain anymore. Then she raises her head to the sky and unleashes a heartbreaking wail that continues until the memory slowly fades out like static on a dying radio signal.

samira sits on the lip of the bathtub and tries to get her giggling under control. The source of the laughter is the bathroom itself; she's never seen something so authentically rustic in her life, and it's striking her funny bone in just the right way. The walls are covered in pinewood paneling. There are a couple of black-and-white photographs of a father and son standing around dead deer, and a color snapshot hanging to the left of the towel rack that shows an old man with his sleeves rolled up and a large axe in his hand. But the truly hilarious thing, the one that has her doubled over in laughter and clutching her stomach, is the light fixture hanging above the mirror: a large rack of moose antlers with a small lightbulb fixed on each one. She imagines someone walking into a home-furnishing store, glancing around the Tiffany lamps, and declaring "Actually, I'm really looking for an animal skull with some lights drilled in the top. Do you have anything like that?" Each time she thinks this, she has a vision of a snotty salesman's face scrunching up with horror, and the laughter starts all over again.

Finally, after nearly five frantic minutes, she manages to suppress the laughter by putting her hands over her mouth and closing her eyes. *Okay,* she thinks. *Okay, okay. Get up and wash your hands, but DON'T LOOK AT THE LIGHT. If you take any longer, Tak's going to think you died in here.*

She manages to wash her hands while staring at the floor, then quickly exits the bathroom while drying them on the legs of her jeans. She can hear the booming voice of Tak's father from the other room and wonders how a man so slight can be so intense and scary. She's about to turn the corner and go back into the living room when she realizes that he's talking about her. Curiosity sinks its claws deep, and so instead of heading back, she huddles against the hallway wall and listens.

"She's cute," says Tak's father.

"Dad," replies Tak in the kind of exasperated voice that only teenage males can master.

"Well, she is. If you're gonna make your hay, you could do a lot worse."

"*DAD!* Seriously!"

*Make your hay?* thinks Samira. *What does that even mean?* She runs a few options through her mind and finds them all awkward, so she quickly banishes the thought before she starts laughing again.

"We're just friends, okay?" continues Tak.

"Well, it's a damn shame is all I'm saying. A boy your age should be—"

"Hey!" interrupts Samira loudly as she turns the corner. "Something smells really good!"

Tak spins around in his chair with an expression of mortified shame on his face, while his father just nods. "That's supper," he says. "I think we're almost ready, if you want to stay and—"

Tak leaps out of his seat and throws his hands up. "Yeah, you know what? We really need to go. We got, you know . . . stuff, so we'll just—"

"I'd love to have dinner with you," says Samira. She glances at Tak out of the corner of her eye, sees him glare at her, and has to suppress another laugh. "I mean, if that's okay."

"Sure, it's okay!" booms Tak's father. "We'd love the company. We never seem to meet any of Takahiro's friends."

"Great!" says Samira, throwing herself into a large leather couch. She's about to put her feet on the coffee table when she notices that a stuffed raccoon is in her way. Instead, she folds her feet underneath her, trying desperately not to look at Tak in case his expression causes her to lose it.

"So I have to ask," says Tak's father, leaning in close. "And this is a serious question, so be honest with me."

"All right," replies Samira.

"What do you think of our new bathroom light?"

She manages to hold herself together for nearly five seconds before exploding into laughter as Tak sinks even farther into the couch.

. . .

**the plane soars** along at thirty-five thousand feet. Samira can hear someone impatiently stomping around the lavatory door, but she's past the point of caring. The spot on the mirror is much more important because it won't come off no matter what she does. She's tried paper towels and toilet paper and even the sleeve of her own shirt, but all she's succeeded in doing is smudging it around the glass.

"Soap," she murmurs to herself. "More soap is good. Yeah. That's good."

She pumps a huge glob of liquid hand soap into her palm and smears it on the mirror, then begins to clean furiously. Outside, someone bangs twice on the door, but she either doesn't hear or doesn't care as she continues to scrub and scrub and scrub.

**a young samira** sits on the edge of the water with her father. He holds a long pole in his hands, the end of which slowly bobs up and down in a calm, rhythmic fashion. The ripples created by this action disturbs the otherwise perfect stillness of the lake, sending an eternity of circles wider and wider until entropy finally claims them.

"In my youth, Samira, I used to fish every weekend," says the older man. "My brothers and I would walk to the river and cast out lines, waiting for something to come along and take our bait. Often we would return with nothing, but sometimes God was good, and we would go home with many fish on our strings."

She puts her head under the crook of his arm and snuggles close, enjoying the way he smells of tobacco and sweat and aftershave. He takes one hand off the pole long enough to nuzzle her hair, then returns his attention to the water. Up and down bobs the line; up and down and up and down as the sun begins its descent across the horizon and a fiery trail of orange slowly moves over the face the water.

**samira pops her** head up through the Humvee's gunner position and lets the cool desert air blow through her hair. Behind her, the convoy stretches on for miles, the only visible sign that anything is still alive in this harsh corner of the world. She takes a sip from her canteen and watches trucks of every size and shape slowly wind their way down the blasted highway, headlights twinkling in the darkness like a little row of Christmas lights.

**the boy in** the suit coat and the girl in the yellow sundress encounter each other in the airport terminal. The noise of the crowd rings loud as people move gently around the pair. Occasionally, a traveler will glance at the couple out of the corner of their eye, see them exchange frantic words, and smile at the power of young love. Finally, a uniformed woman announces the final boarding call and the couple parts. The boy with the suit coat raises one hand, waves the tips of his fingers, and moves down the jetway. The girl continues to stand in place, tears rolling down her face, as if she might simply wait there for the rest of her life.

**samira opens her** eyes and sees a cloudless sky of blue. As her ears begin to function again, she hears the distant throb of large metal blades cutting through the air. Grass stalks, long and green, press close like a comforting blanket. She contents herself to lie there and wait, allowing her senses to return in their own time. Finally, she pulls herself to a sitting position and gazes out to the ocean beyond. The rumble of the surf pounding against rocks is a good sound—old and strong and regular—and like everything else in this place, it makes her indescribably happy. She looks down at her ragged, bitten fingertips and knows they will heal. She stares at her swollen knuckles and knows they will never be cracked again. Such things simply cannot survive in this beautiful land.

As she stands, Samira feels the final remnants of her past life drain away, replaced instead by a calm, pure joy. But it's not quite complete; there is a small hole that comes from knowing Tak will never find his way into this world. And while she understands the rest of her pain will eventually fade, she wonders if she will ever overcome his loss.

But she intends to try.

# chapter thirty-eight

The birds are gathering atop the large glass dome over the Machine. Tak isn't sure what genius thought to protect the most amazing scientific discovery in history with a roof made of glass, but he's sure there's a reason for it. *Maybe it collects solar power,* he thinks as he watches more and more creatures land on the dome. *Or maybe it focuses the Machine somehow. Like, cosmic rays or whatever? . . . Hell, maybe they were just tired of everything being underground all the time.*

Tak is leaning against the side of the Machine with a contented smile on his face. The device is nearly cycled to full power, and the angelic chord it's emitting is loud enough to shake his bones. There's something almost relaxing about being this close to the thing; it's like sidling up next to God during the creation of the world.

His mind wanders to Samira as he reaches inside his pocket and pops a single butterscotch into his mouth. *I hope she made it. I hope she made it and she's happy. That's really all I ever wanted.*

His musings are interrupted by a shadowy figure in the corner of his eye. Tak raises his gaze to examine the newcomer and has to suppress a chuckle when he sees who it is. "Well, hi there!" he says, waving his hand back and forth over his head. "I thought you'd never come!"

The thing that Yates has become opens its mouth and screams. The transformation, which was hardly going well the last time they met, has taken a turn for the worse. The pale white skin seems to be losing cohesion and now drips off the muscle in goopy wet chunks. The arms are even tinier than before, little more than nubs poking from the chest. And the face, which had recently looked almost completely birdlike, has now transformed into something twisted and horrible.

"Shit, buddy," says Tak. "You look like ten pounds of crap in a five-pound sack."

Yates takes a step forward and dislodges a claw from his foot. The curved black bit goes spinning across the room and lands, point-side up, against one of the wires snaking across the floor. Tak laughs at this, actually points and laughs, which only causes Yates to quicken his pace. Just before the creature reaches him, Tak feels a giddy joy flood through his system. Then he finds himself flying through the air like a rag doll before crashing into the side of the Machine's control panel.

"You're too late, man," groans Tak. Blood begins to seep from somewhere in the lower regions, and he's pretty sure his leg just snapped. "Waaaay too fucking late. Shit's rollin' now, Yates, and I don't think you're gonna stop it."

Yates screams again as a pair of shabby wings burst from his back and send feathers flying in all directions; the light from the Machine bounces off them as they slowly settle to the ground. As Yates flaps the wings and begins hobbling toward him, Tak only grins wider.

"Yeah, you remember the fail-safe? Remember that? Well, we found it, and we plugged it in, and we turned it all the way on.

We're gonna Control-Alt-Delete this bitch, only when we go back, you're not gonna have me. I'll be swinging free and easy from a rope while you fuck around with a machine you never learn how to turn on. How's that for irony, huh? All your smarts, and you get screwed by a stupid son of a bitch like me."

Yates reaches the spot where Tak is lying and kicks at him angrily. The sharpened claws tear into his stomach, and he suddenly feels the lower half of his body grow cold. Staring down, Tak is amazed to see a large, ragged hole where his belly button should be.

"Aw, come on, man," mumbles Tak. "At least you coulda kissed me first."

The Machine makes an incredible sound as bright light suddenly pours out of it. Yates screams once more, then shuffles away from Tak and over to the control panel. Despite Tak's fading vision, he can see Yates trying and failing to input commands with the stubby remains of his arms. "Oh, yeah, no." He chuckles. "I think you're gonna need more manual dexterity to shut this thing down."

Tak slumps farther down the side of the control panel, leaving a red smear behind him. He suddenly finds it very hard to hold his head up, so he lets it roll off to the side. Soon, his entire body loses strength and slides to the floor, where he ends up on his back, staring at the dome. His eyes move in and out of focus a few times, but when he finally gets them under control, he can see that the birds have begun slamming themselves against the glass.

"Hey, Chuck," he whispers. "Your friends do *not* look happy."

Small cracks begin to spill out across the glass as the birds batter themselves against it. The entire thing has become a mass of crawling feathers and wormy, translucent skin. At one point, a bird smashes its face into the glass with such force that one eye explodes in a burst of black goo; another bird simply pushes the corpse out of the way and resumes hammering.

"Yeah, real pissed," says Tak. The room is cold now, and his mind is beginning to stretch. He can see the lights from the Machine, he can see the birds, but he's not really sure what's real and what's not anymore. Behind him, Yates pounds on the control panel, frantically trying to input something that will stop the timeline from resetting. But his arms are too far gone—he can't even type on the keyboard without mashing half the keys at once. Finally, he utters a high-pitched scream and begins ripping at the wires. Sparks fly from the control panel as the lights flicker, and for a horrible moment, Tak thinks that Yates has somehow done it. But then the Machine springs back to life with a triumphant roar, and even through the writing mass of birds, Tak sees a purple hole begin to tear open the sky.

"There we go," says Tak. "There we fucking go."

Small chunks of glass begin to fall from the dome and shatter. These are followed by larger chunks, then small pieces of steel, then a veritable hailstorm of fuzzy black feathers. Behind him, flames start to lick out from the side of the control panel, but Tak knows this doesn't matter. The Machine has done its job; it can't be stopped now.

Yates seems to sense that the turning point has been reached, and he turns his attention back to Tak. "S-s-suffer . . ." he manages to say. "You . . ."

He moves back toward Tak, clearly intent on making his final moments terribly unpleasant ones, but before he can get close, the overhead dome finally gives way. Uncountable birds pour into the room, their screams and caws melding into the sound of a single, terrible beast. Tak is sure that they are coming for him, but they soar through the opening and head straight for Yates instead.

"N-no . . ." croaks Yates. "No. *NO!*"

The birds descend on Yates like a cloud, tearing and thrashing at him with abandon. Tak hears him scream—a real, human scream—before the cloud slowly moves up and out toward the giant hole in the sky. Somewhere in the center of the mass, Tak can just make out the face of an old man in a tattered white lab coat. His expression is one of pure terror as he finally realizes there will be no reset button for him; the birds exist as an eternal, unrelenting force, and he will be with them for all time. And then the cloud enters the hole and vanishes as if it was never there.

"So long, asshat," says Tak with a cough. "When you get to hell, tell 'em Tak sent you."

A smile creeps across his face as his vision begins to go. He can't feel his legs anymore. He can't feel his body. And as the final darkness descends, his mind settles on Samira one last time. *We did it, Sam. We did it. We made amends. . . . I think everything's gonna be all right.*

Seconds later, a purple hole roars out and swallows the sky.

# chapter thirty-nine

Across the shattered remains of the world, what few people remain climb out of their holes, stare at the giant purple wound above, and wonder what fresh hell has come for them now. Those who have banded with other survivors find comfort in one another's arms; those who are going it alone simply sit down in the dirt and wait for this new terror to arrive. *At least it's not the birds,* they all muse in a shared moment of common thought. *Whatever this is, it's got to be better than the birds.*

When the hole explodes into a dazzling ball of white, they throw their hands over their eyes and turn away, unable to face whatever terrible fate is befalling them. But then they look around and notice something completely unexpected: the world is beginning to change. Smoking wrecks of buildings warble out of existence only to be replaced by structures standing proud and tall. Ghosts of people, billions of them, slowly fade back to life, their chatter spreading out across the planet like a wave. The few survivors wonder if this is the afterlife—if they have somehow made it to heaven to see their friends and relatives once again—only to discover that their own memories are becoming unstable. The events of the past week begin to fade, turning from something real to something that feels like the thread of a nightmare.

One by one, all across the world, survivors begin to forget. They forget the birds. They forget the hole in the sky. They forget the pain and the death and the heartache and instead begin to worry about small things. *Will I be able to pay the mortgage? Where did I leave my car keys? Why won't that guy from the bar ever call me back?*

People who died horrible deaths in the other timeline find themselves walking down streets without a care in the world. Women who threw themselves screaming from the tops of buildings put pencils behind their ears and gossip by the watercooler. Men who attacked each other with chain saws and railroad spikes and a thousand other instruments of death drink beers and watch baseball teams struggle for victory. The world repairs itself. The world rebuilds. A timeline that never should have been is gradually replaced by one where all is as it should be. And as the final piece of the fail-safe clicks into place, the world moves on—with no one imagining that all of existence had just been saved in the most unlikely of ways.

But there are exceptions. There always are.

deep in the heart of Australia, a crew of forty begins to disassemble a massive silver machine. The parts that can be salvaged will be sold for scrap, while the rest will be trucked out of the desert and hauled to landfills. As the crew buzzes around, a man named Hsu stands nearby with his arms folded and his mind deep in thought. *I have a memory of this working. I know it did. But now I can't even recall who came up with the idea in the first place. . . . A time machine? Dear God. What an absurd waste of money this proved to be.*

• • •

**in a penthouse** apartment somewhere on the East Coast, a man named Dennis opens the front door and embraces his daughters in a massive hug. They squeal and squirm as he reaches around their sides and tickles them with glee. As he notices his wife standing in the doorway with a smile on her face, he has a sudden thought that things are out of place. *I was in Nebraska. I was driving a truck and there was a kid who told me . . . No, that's not possible. I'm an accountant, for God's sakes. I don't even know how to drive a truck.*

He puts the thought out of his mind, rises to his feet, and goes to greet the woman he loves.

**in butte, montana,** a young man named Percy Davenport wakes from a dream where he had been protecting the entirety of creation before a young man with spiky hair shot and killed him. He rolls this thought around in his mind for a long moment before turning to look at the beautiful young woman sleeping beside him. *Dude, that was weird. I gotta quit smoking weed before I go to bed.*

**in seattle, a** young scientist named Judith Halford walks out of a conference and into the grey drizzle of a miserable Northwest afternoon. Engaged in thought, with uncountable equations floating around her head, she doesn't notice the man walking toward her with a basket of fresh tomatoes until they collide, fruit spilling in one direction, notebooks flying in the other.

"Aw, crap," says the man. "I'm sorry. I didn't see you."

"No, it's my fault," replies Judith as she drops down to gather her books. "I was . . . I just wasn't paying attention."

She goes to grab the last book and finds he has already picked it up for her. Reaching for it, she notices for the first time that the man is wearing a white chef's coat and a pair of wire-rim glasses. *He's kinda cute,* she thinks to herself in a surprising moment of honesty. *Actually, he's really cute.*

"You a chef?" she asks, taking the notebook from his hand.

"Sous chef," he says. "Working on the real thing though. You a scientist?"

"Theoretical physicist," she says. "How did you know?"

He points down at her name tag, which reads JUDITH HALFORD, MIT. She chuckles and pulls it off before stuffing it into her pocket. "Guess that's obvious, huh?"

"Well, you know. The name tag, plus the glasses, plus all the notebooks. I mean, I didn't go to MIT, but I can put two and two together."

"Oh. Well, thanks. Sorry about your tomatoes."

She stands, dusts off her skirt, and turns to leave. Half a dozen steps later, she hears the man call out her name and turns around.

"What is it?" she asks.

"Hey, look. This may sound weird, but I've got a lot of tomatoes here and it's actually my night off, so, um . . . You wanna have dinner?"

She feels the word "no" on the tip of her tongue as her mind clicks into gear. *Judith, tomorrow morning you have to make a presentation on string theory. Plus, you haven't been on a date in years. You wouldn't even know what to do.*

"Yeah, but I'd learn," she whispers. "I've always been a real fast learner."

"Look, I'm sorry," begins the man. "I mean, you're clearly busy, so—"

"Yes," she says, as a rare smile begins to emerge on her face. "Yes. I would love to have dinner with you."

. . .

**and in new** York City, in the middle of a squalid hotel room where the carpet smells of piss and the sheets smell worse, a young man named Takahiro O'Leary can't answer the phone because the noose is too tight. His plan, ill conceived though it might have been, was to spend the last few seconds of his life dangling from a two-foot length of rope while *Kind of Blue* played in the background. He figured that—

The phone stops.

At first, Tak is sure he can still hear it braying. But then the clock moves again, and the mournful sounds of a trumpet emerge from the battered boom box at the foot of the dresser.

". . . Oh," says Tak. "Guess it was a wrong number."

He stares at the phone in a drunken haze as the chair wobbles beneath him. For a moment he's sure he knew the person on the other end, but then the feeling fades out and is lost.

"Yeah, wrong number. Just a . . . Just a wrong number, is all. Now are you gonna do this thing or what?"

Suddenly he remembers a girl with long curly hair. He's not sure how he knows her, but he does. And he also knows she is supposed to be dead, but has instead made a new world for herself in a place beyond imagining. *I saved her life,* he thinks to himself, the thought clear in his otherwise addled brain. *I saved her life because I sent her somewhere outside of time.*

The image of the girl fills him with peace. For a moment, he considers abandoning his plan, but something in his mind stops him. *I have to go through with this. If I don't, something terrible will happen. A company will come looking for me, and before I know it, I'll be doing things I can't imagine. This is a different world now. It's a different world, and a better one, and I'm not supposed to be here.*

Tak smiles. He thinks about the girl with the curly black hair and smiles again.

Then he jumps.

# the things i want
## to tell you

# chapter forty

"You remember our last night here? Remember how I said that people you know are really just memories? I wanted to explain it better, but then you said something funny and I started giggling and that was kind of the end of it. But I didn't forget that conversation. I mean, not really. We moved on, and a lot of crazy stuff happened, but I still think about it. . . . I think about it all the time."

Samira sits on a small hill overlooking the ocean. Behind her, a campfire burns next to a wooden hut. A thin brown dog lies in the flickering glow of the flames, happily chewing on a bone.

"So I've been practicing," she continues, her voice carrying out into the orange light of dusk. "Little stuff, but I've been working on it. I finally got Bones here, but it's not really him. It's just a dog. He's a nice dog, don't get me wrong, but he's not the same. I just . . . I didn't know Bones well enough, you know? And I think with living things, you have to remember them. I don't know why I think that, but I do. It just feels right."

She stops talking for a moment and stares out at the ocean. Behind her, a set of massive windmills slowly rotate, casting long, twisting shadows on the shoreline. She turns her attention to a spot on the beach, perhaps a hundred yards away, where she has cleared a small patch of sand and surrounded it with rocks.

"It's funny here. Everything is so perfect, and yet it's not like you never feel things. I still get sad. I still get scared. I still . . . I still get lonely. It's just not as intense as it used to be. I can handle it. It doesn't control me."

She looks at the spot on the beach and lets the sounds of the surf and the windmill blades roll over and through her. "So this is kind of it, you know? This is my one shot. And if it doesn't work, if I'm wrong, and my memories aren't enough, then I'm just going to turn away and wait for the tide to come in and never try again. . . . I hope you're okay with that."

Samira closes her eyes and thinks about her friend. She remembers the way his hand hovered above her head one anonymous night years ago. She remembers exchanging a kiss in the backseat of a car the day before her life was put to ruin. She remembers his smell, and his taste, and the stupid things he used to say, and a million other details both large and inconsequential. *I remember you. I remember everything about you, because I know you better than anyone or anything in my entire life. You are Tak and you are real and I miss you terribly. . . . I want you to come back to me.*

She hears a sound, a crunching of footsteps on sand, and suddenly finds herself afraid. The footsteps grow louder before she hears Bones begin to bark happily. Finally, at this, she decides to take the greatest risk of her life.

She opens her eyes.

A young man with spiky black hair is standing on the thin grass in front of her. He has a dazed expression in his eyes, as if he can't quite figure out what's going on.

". . . Sam?" he says finally.

"I need to know it's you," she says, standing up. She finds that her entire body is shaking, and her voice is barely controlled. "I need to know it's you. That it's really you, and not just a bunch of memories I wished into existence because I was lonely. I need to know."

Tak stares at her for a long while. Then he looks to the windmills and back to the ocean, and it's as if something finally clicks inside his mind. He shakes his head in amazement before walking to Samira and placing his hands on her face.

"Holy crap, Sam," he says. "You did it. You actually did it."

"Oh God, Tak. Is this really you? Please tell me it's you."

"Banzai."

## acknowledgments

Thanks to Amazon, CreateSpace, and Penguin for sponsoring the Amazon Breakthrough Novel Award. Hat-tip to my kick-ass editor, Ginjer Buchanan, for helping a noob through the process, and to Kat Sherbo for answering many annoying questions.

Thanks to the other ABNA finalists—Regina, Brian, Charles, Casey, and Rebecca—for continuing to be my support group. I hope you all get published and make fat stacks of cash. . . . Er, I mean, find artistic happiness.

Thanks to everyone who supported the book throughout the contest—specifically Mark, John, Justin, and Hiroko at 8-4, Ltd.; all the cats in the Treehouse; and the unstoppable force of the NeoGAF army.

Thanks to my friends Tim and Shahin for loaning me bits of your lives even if you didn't know it at the time, Steve and Marty for providing years of support, and Tara for designing the original cover. Also, a special thanks to Jayron Finan of the Seattle-based Persian Preschool and to Dr. Ali Parsa of Cal State Fullerton.

Thanks to The Tragically Hip, The National, and Tom Waits for being the soundtrack as I wrote. Oh, and props to Columbia City Ale House for providing the beer.

Thanks to Mom and Dad for putting up with a really weird kid for all these years, and to my sister, Kate, for generally being awesome.

Thanks to Sue for being the best thing in my life. The goat farm is coming, I promise.

And finally, thanks to you for reading, because a writer without readers is just some crazy dude shouting in the dark.